The Angry Angel

Strange, strange was that summer night,
An angry angel beat her drum in heaven . . .

A translation from the Hungarian
by Thomas L. Harsner

The
Angry Angel

Lajos Zilahy

Prentice-Hall, Inc.

New York

To the memory of a
little nation

Mihály Ursi's chalk inscription
on the pedestal of a great winged
statue in Budapest.

Other books by Lajos Zilahy
Two Prisoners
The Deserter
The Dukays

The Angry Angel

Chapter 1

The Great Funeral. The New Lord of the Estate.

On the first of September, 1939, one Budapest paper whose banner headline proclaimed: THIS DAWN GERMAN CANNON THUNDERED ON THE POLISH BORDER, ran this article on an inside page:

Count István Dukay of Duka and Hemlice, scion of the nation-founding line of Ordony, knight of the Order of the Golden Fleece, this noon unexpectedly expired at the age of 71. His death on this fatefully historic day conveys the impression that István Dukay was the first victim of German cannon, as if atop some ancient bastion, he received the barrage of howitzers in the breast, his top hat, white carnation, and goldheaded walking-stick scattering in the flames. All this is not pure fantasy. The aged Count's heart attack came last night while listening to war news over the radio. His death seems not only the death of a single individual, but the death of a whole era, because sometimes long eras also die of such sudden heart attacks in the first seconds of a cannonade, but History's thick-skulled coroners usually recognize such an analogy only decades later.

István Dukay's death raises the question of the future fate of one of the largest landed estates in Hungary: the one-hundred-and-ten-thousand-acre holdings with its huge Castle of Ararat, the ancestral Dukay palace on Septemvir Utca, countless apartment houses, mines, mills, sugar factories, and innumerable art treasures. The lawful heir, Count Ostie, in recent years has resided in New York. Will he relinquish the presidency of his great American corporation, Republican Agricultural Chemical, for the lordship of

Ararat Castle? This question understandably excites Hungarian public opinion, not merely from a social but also from a political point of view. If Count Ostie should choose America, the enormous patrician fortune in Count Johy's hands would become a tool of Nazi politics. We firmly hope that Count Ostie Dukay in days such as these is aware of the obligation to his homeland and ancestral name. It does not seem doubtful for one second that instead of New York, he will choose Ararat.

Ostie's letter to his wife in New York

Ararat, September 5, 1939

DEAR, DEAR GWENNIE:

I am afraid that the tempest of the new war does the telephone lines no good—yesterday I barely heard your voice. Now that my final decision is taken, only the formalities of transfer remain, and at the end of the month I start back. My further plan is to add another wing to our house in Connecticut; I'll call it Little Ararat and shall settle the whole family there if they are willing to come. I won't insist on Johy, being unwilling to cause Hitler so irreparable a loss.

But I must tell you everything in order, and report first on Papa's funeral. When in the afternoon I went back to the sanatorium, the efficiency of the nurses had already removed not only the bedding but the bed itself— Papa lay on the floor on the bare bedsprings. You can imagine what I felt. He was like an abandoned parcel no longer of any value. The dead who lie on the ground mercilessly reveal the crushing force of death. Poor Papa! Now he seemed decidedly smaller than in life. I believe this happens to all who die, as if in our lives it were possible to delude our fellow men, but at such a time everything comes to light. His chin was already bound with a white kerchief, as if now, after death, he were suffering from an excruciating toothache, which he was enduring with his characteristically distinguished calm. For a long while I gazed at his handsome oriental face, in whose pale contours only the Dukay "saber

4

nose" seemed larger. If I remember rightly, Flaubert wrote that the noses of the dead always grow larger. I should have liked to sit down next to him on the floor in the empty room, but feared someone might unexpectedly open the door on us. I couldn't move from his side. In his clasped hands, Mama had placed a gold crucifix, on his breast lay a few roses from Zia, his forehead showed a faint mark of rouge where Kristina had kissed him for the last time.

An hour later, in Septemvir Utca, the family conference was already assembled to discuss details of the funeral. Kristina, who can only think in terms of Hapsburgs, and who witnessed the exceedingly simple Madeiran funeral of King Charles, argued that we should have an ostentatiously simple funeral for Papa. But Uncle Peti, who on the basis of ancient traditions—remember?—nine years ago staged Zia's and Filippo's colossal wedding feast, this time, too, brought with him in his briefcase detailed blueprints for the "grand obsequies," as though this were some Hollywood scenario. Consulting the family archives he took Benedek Dukay's sixteenth-century funeral as his model. It was the first time I presided over such a family conference, which you can well imagine did not exactly proceed like a board of directors meeting in New York. Between Kristina's and Uncle Peti's extremes, I decided on a compromise.

By eight in the evening the catafalque stood ready in the hall of the palace, where all night long, liveried Dukay footmen successively stood watch. Innumerable wreaths covered even the walls. On a velvet cushion lay Papa's decorations: the Order of the Golden Fleece, the Iron Crown first class, the Great Cross of the Papal Order, the French Légion d'honneur—some sixteen in all. Next day in the early morning hours, the public began to flood in. They gazed at Papa's face as though it were that of some Hungarian Tutankhamen in a gold mask, the deceased Pharaoh of exotic manly beauty, wealth, rank, mirth and frivolity. I suppose they looked on his life, too, as upon some costly bejeweled sedan chair, eight-horse tally-ho, or museum cannon, a considerably outmoded product no longer to be manufactured in the workshops of the twentieth century.

5

We shipped the coffin by night to Ararat, where the castle already had arrayed itself in full funeral pomp. On the third, Sunday morning, a funeral mass was held in the chapel of the castle with Uncle Zsigmond officiating. In the great U-shaped courtyard more than a thousand persons waited in perfect silence. It was as if the fountains also wanted to surpass themselves on this occasion. Their rays shot up unusually high, and fell like rainbow-hued dust in the sunlight.

We family members waited in the big red salon which was lit by the curious green-gold light that glitters on the back of the Spanish beetle. The branches of the venerable wild chestnut trees sifted this light through the broad windows, dappling not only the frames of the pictures, but Kristina's shoes and the tip of Uncle Zsigmond's bishopal nose. I go into such detail so you may understand how improbable all this around me seemed. The house where I was born and raised, after my few years in New York had become indescribably alien. From the enormous depth of the room and the antiquity of the furnishings and painting emanated the atmosphere rather of a princely court in Florence, the great castles of the Loire Valley in days before the French Revolution, or even more the air of the post-Napoleonic *Tiers État*—a thing which while I lived here I never noticed.

Mama stood in the center of the room, still regal in bearing. To her right stood Kristina and Zia, thick mourning veils completely enveloping them. Only from their white faces were the veils drawn aside. It created general scandal when Johy appeared in the green shirt of the Arrow Cross Party at his father's funeral. Uncle Peti called him to account; he answered that his dress was a "military uniform." I said not a word to him. Your favorite, Rere, with his half-witted modesty, stood a bit out of place in the family picture, but, judging by his blissful and touching grin, he apparently felt that the whole company had gathered in his honor. He held his top hat in front of his chest like some huge chalice from which he was about to toast the Prime Minister who was present.

6

Only occasionally he would crinkle his nose, because Johy's green shirt reeked of strong perfume. In the group among distant relations whom you still may recall, there stood Uncle Dmitri with his bald skull, long thin yellow mustache, threadbare trousers and self-shined shoes, resembling a puppet who during Lenin's revolution had been yanked from his half-million-acre estate in the Urals to pop up as Russian announcer on the Hungarian radio. And there beside him stood two of my cousins: the short-necked little Marquis de Ferreyolles, descendant of the Sun King's one-time marshal, and Baron Ubul Lerche-Friis of Danish descent, the genial and slightly stammering Ubi, your table companion at Zia's bridal banquet. Now you were present in the room, too, but only in the form of your life-sized portrait which still hangs above the piano. While waiting I looked up at you several times: your painted glance gazed from far, far away at this group dressed in black, as if in the next hour the grave were awaiting not only the head of the family but all of us. Your glance from the great frame kept saying: "Come back, don't stay with them!" We all seemed like tragic shadows on a lost continent. Mama, in mourning from tip to toe, appeared to portray Europe in the center of the group. Kristina, in her black veils, the dispersing smoke of Hapsburg dreams. Johy's tall fragile figure with his "striking Niebelung beauty" of profile, his unsuccessfully masked arrogance, his hand held stiffly on hip, represented that German spirit which since the Carolingian emperors has confronted all European peoples with an unslakable thirst for power. Hitler now wants mastery of the globe, Johy is far more modest: he will be satisfied with the Ararat estate. Zia seemed aristocracy's Cinderella in the group, while Rere's affectingly silly grin represented the dimwitted human millions who now again without protest will allow themselves to be led to the slaughter.

Do you remember my bat-eared uncle, Prince Fini? When we composed the death notice, he wanted to omit Mihály Ursi's name from the ornate family roster, because *dieser bauerische Name* had the effect of a foul grease-spot

7

on the crested, expensive paper. You know how much I love and respect Mihály. Also he is an Ostyak. He stood quite apart from the group, holding the hand of his little three-year-old daughter, the sole Dukay grandchild. With his high, overcast brow, he stood beneath the portrait of Papa in his red riding-coat, as though he were the living conscience of Europe—in fact, of the whole globe. Whenever I glanced at him, I was reminded of the latest article by the president of Harvard University, in which Mr. Conant wrote: "There are men whom Communists consider Fascists, and Fascists, Communists. Sad to say, this invaluable and progressive species of mankind is growing extinct in the United States." Little Zizi looked up at her father and unexpectedly broke the deep silence, her tongue stabbing at the words:

"P-p-Papa, are they g-going to b-bury you, too . . . now?"

Only Zia broke into a smile through her tears. The grave silence sent admonishing looks toward Zizi. Mihály leaned down and whispered to the child, reassuring her I suppose, that he was disinclined as yet to lay himself away in the Dukay mausoleum.

Finally we got under way. Behind the hearse, I led Mama by the arm. After us came the four brothers and sisters: Kristina, Zia, Johy, and Rere. At the start there was some confusion, the servants could hardly twist from Rere's hands a pink parasol of Mama's. Rere was right— the sun blazed so that even Uncle Zsigmond kept mopping the perspiration from his neck.

The first group in the cortege, immediately after the casket, consisted of the family and relatives, members of the aristocracy, the government, the Parliament, the military, and representatives of foreign legations. A few yards farther back came the head bailiffs of the four Dukay domains. Behind them Mr. Johnson, the English stablemaster, led Papa's favorite mount, with an empty saddle.

Then followed the castle staff of fifty-two persons, led by Mr. Gruber, the "Grubi" you like so well, who for forty years was Papa's most private secretary. The grief on

8

the faces of the numerous staff betokened not merely reverence for Papa's memory, but anxiety for their jobs, where for decades they had stolen to their heart's content.

In accordance with Uncle Peti's scenario, the staff was followed by a chorus of school-children from Ararat, then twelve beggars dressed in mourning, bearing lighted candles and wooden crosses. After the beggars came the young men of the village on horseback, their round hats trimmed with feathergrass, wearing Magyar cloaks and wide pantaloons, holding the bridle in their left hand, and from their right trailing ancient halberds rummaged from the attic of the castle. Then—to my surprise—came the Dominican and Franciscan friars in their hair cowls. I had blue-penciled this scene from the scenario, but Uncle Peti smuggled it back. Finally, on a caparisoned horse in silver harness, carrying a red and blue standard edged with gold—the silken ancestral banner torn by the bullets of ancient battles—came a visored knight in armor, whose identity was unknown to me. Only later did I discover that the turkey-breasted plate armor concealed my valet, Tobias. But I shouldn't want you to regard this procession as comical. On the contrary, there was in it a certain tragic, antique dignity. Uncle Peti exhibits a refined taste in resurrecting such traditions. As the procession left the courtyard, from the top of a table a motion picture camera began to whir, just as at Zia's wedding, if you remember. No doubt you, too, will see Papa's funeral at some newsreel theater on Broadway: "HUNGARIAN FEUDAL LORD BURIED IN POMP."

The mysterious knight in armor was followed by sundry delegations, among them the Loyal Legitimist Subjects of the Magyar Holy Crown, the Magnates' Casino, General Artificial Fertilizers, Ltd., the Riding Club, the Federation of the Descendants of Árpád, the Hog Breeders Association, and Lord knows what others. Unofficially, of course, marched among them the little old hunchbacked Baron Hici, whom I knew to be executive chairman of the International Federation of the Collectors of Piquant Photographs, whose honorary president Papa had been.

9

Poor Papa, these last years no longer able to attend even the estate business conferences, last season boarded a plane —for the first time in his life!—so he could preside at the federation's annual meeting in Amsterdam.

Following the general public, a twenty-member gypsy band closed the procession, but tunes did not resound as at Zia's wedding. The smoky-faced "swallows," as Papa called them, now mutely carried under their arms fiddles veiled in mourning. The whole black procession moved silently, like some gigantic dark shadow projecting the new World War upon the emerald-green lawns. During these moments the British ambassador was delivering England's declaration of war to Germany. In the great silence, only the church bells of the village down in the valley sounded, barely audible, as if the immense foliage tents of the trees in the park had banned from the vicinity of the castle this little ringing of church bells, along with all exterior sounds. You will understand how all these thoughts kept surging up. One wheel of the weighty hearse was badly greased —only its plaintive little whine could be heard. A tiny, weeping sound—as though the racked, naked body of some legendary nymph in Papa's life were twisted onto the spokes of the wheel. Luckily, the children's chorus welled up in a touching funeral hymn. Then the silence became even greater. The occasional swift, rapturous scream of some bird of prey sounded high in the air, or from beneath the leaves the solitary little cello of a hidden turtle-dove, breaking off in alarm at our approach. On Klementina Meadow a roebuck sprang from the hawthorn. He stopped short in confusion before the funeral coach, and in this brief moment it seemed as though he had appeared at the instance of the wild beasts of the forest to view the dead hunter's last journey. Then he bounded away in the direction of the game preserve, tossing high the white patch on his rump.

At last we arrived at the vault. Instead of funeral speeches, the gypsies surrounded the casket, placed their crepe-covered fiddles under their chins and very softly began to play. This was so touchingly beautiful that my tears too began to stream. They played Papa's favorite tune, the famous Dankó song: "Let the fiddle be mute and no bird sing . . ." to whose accompaniment in Papa's youth Hussar sabers broke the mirrors of cafés, large banknotes fluttered down upon the cymbalons, and pistol shots of disappointed love crashed into cello and bull fiddle held high. Everyone was shaken, everyone felt in the marvelously soft music that now truly "the fiddle would be mute" and "no bird would sing" for a very long time, in the history of man. Behind the dreamy soft cadence of the fiddles everyone clearly heard the ghostly rumble of German cannon—in their thoughts, I mean.

My bat-eared uncle, Prince Fini, at the family conference had objected to this gypsy music: he found it a distastefully barbaric Magyar affair. Now, patting back a yawn with his hand, he turned to Uncle Cini who was standing next to him—you may remember him, the one-time foreign minister of the monarchy, who even now is looked up to as the greatest expert in world politics.

"*Sag' mir, Cini,*" whispered Fini softly in German. "What do you think? Will we get into this mess too?"

Uncle Cini, who was staring at the door of the vault with his bloodshot eyes, inferred that the mess referred to the vault, but Fini in time added: "I mean into the war, we Hungarians." It always strikes my ear when two German aristocrats, who don't even know Hungarian, say: we Hungarians.

Uncle Cini shook his head so decidedly that his aged parchment face almost rustled:

"*Ungarn? In diesen Kriege?!* Nonsense!!"

His pronouncement did not, however, sway my decision, which I announced the following evening at the family conference. I let Mama act as chairman, you know how passionately she likes to preside at Catholic women's societies. Briefly, this is what I said: "Since my marriage and business interests tie me to America, I find it essential to appoint a permanent deputy to manage the affairs of the estate." It seemed natural, that as the heir next in line, I would appoint Johy. Johy sought to appear elegantly at ease, but was so nervous that he stuck two fingers in his neck, as if the green shirt were choking him. Mr. Gruber had mentioned that Johy had recently lost another tremendous sum at rummy in the Vienna Jockey Club.

"My first thought," I continued, "was naturally Uncle Peti, but I fear, not so much because of his advanced age as because of the effects on his valuable linguistic research, that such a tiring task . . ."

Uncle Peti, whose features by now were a cross between those of an Asian falconer and a university professor with heart trouble, quietly stroked his beard and nodded assent. You must know that his heart trouble stems from the unrelenting battle he has been waging over the years with his rude adversaries in the columns of *Our Tongue*, yielding not a hair's breadth from his stand that the word *Hun* derives from the word *Hiung-yang*.

"Unfortunately," I spoke up again, "for this task the female members of the family may not come into consideration."

Johy was pale and green from excitement, because after this introduction only his name could follow. My words sounded almost ceremoniously:

"I have therefore resolved to entrust with absolute authority over the affairs of the estate my brother-in-law, Mihály Ursi."

My announcement was followed by deathly silence. Mama's face remained immobile, Kristina gazed into the smoke of her cigarette, but Zia impulsively turned her face toward me and fixed upon me a gaze filled with terror, protest and reproach. Out of propriety I did not look at Johy's face. I only saw him get up and disappear. Mother's face, as she followed his exit, seemed to reflect fear that in the next moment a great detonation would be heard, because Johy had blown out his brains. I had no such anxiety. In seconds he returned, in his hand a copy of *The Great Fallow*. He resumed his place, leafed through the book, then, stressing every word, in a voice screeching with excitement began to read the following lines:

"Hungarians sit here above a treasure-trove of natural resources, with four million landless peasants condemned to death, when this fallow could give prosperity to thirty millions. The key to this treasure has been pocketed by the Dukays and their fellows. In the feudal and church estates I seek the assassins of a whole nation."

Johy shut the book with the gesture of a great magician who has just charmed a rabbit out of an empty top hat. My poor little Zia swept her glance from one face to the other as though she had been the accused. I am extremely sorry you weren't present: you might have been witness to a truly aristocratic Magyar mode of thought. Uncle Peti! He spoke up first in the painful silence, in the same tone as at a session of the Academy. As he turned to Johy there was something paternal in his voice, but nonetheless a severe and dignified reprimand. Again my heart ached that we have no children, because it struck me that this Dukay line is not the least of breeds. This is what Uncle Peti said:

"With this portion of the book I myself am not in agreement either. But we are here not in Berlin or Moscow. We respect the complete freedom of thought and criticism. This question does not come within the sphere of a family conference. When Mihály wrote this book he was not yet a member of our family, he did not even know Zia. If he overstepped the rightful bounds of criticism, he has atoned for it, because the independent Hungarian courts sentenced him to a year in prison."

Then his falcon's head turned to me:

"I thoroughly approve your choice!"

Zia, who can never experience the rendering of justice without tears, hid her face in both hands. I too was deeply affected by Uncle Peti's words. I do not want to use high-sounding phrases, but I think you also will feel that in these moments the remnant of the better spirit of Hungarians joined battle with all German thought. Mama with chairmanlike gravity shook the little silver bell, which was quite pointless, because after Uncle Peti's words deep silence descended upon the table. When I was alone with Zia, she turned on me:

13

"What do you want with Mihály? After I finally succeeded in creating a quiet little nest, why do you want to
drag us out of it? Did you see Johy's face? He'll kill him!"

I could hardly reassure her. I reminded her of the old
Hungarian saying: *A disznótor nem eröszak*, which means
something like . . . An invitation to a turkey dinner is no
armed robbery. I told her she should discuss the matter at
leisure with Mihály, not forgetting, though, that if Mihály
declined, Johy would be in the saddle.

Next day I was at their home. Before Mihály spoke,
he caught Zia's eye, they exchanged a little smile, then he
said:

"I accept the commission, but fear you won't be able
to meet my conditions."

"Let's have them."

"First the castle. Forty guest rooms have stood empty
for years. In those parts there is a great need for hospitals.
So the castle—"

"Agreed!" I cut in. Once you, too, had such thoughts
when we planned to reside in Hungary.

"My other condition is far weightier," continued
Mihály, meanwhile again trying to catch Zia's glance, in
which he was unsuccessful. Zia looked straight down at
the rug and seemed unhappy.

"God be thanked, your American enterprises render
you economically independent. I shall only accept your
commission if I may use all superfluous revenue from the
estate for an anti-German campaign. Starting a newspaper,
pamphlets, organizations . . ."

Without hesitation I answered:

"For my part, I accept this condition too, but I must
discuss the matter with my wife. I feel certain that Gwen
will also accept it."

That was when I called you on the phone. I think
now I have written you everything which didn't fit in the
phone call. Just a few lines more to tell you how the family situation will size up after I depart: The castle will be
converted to a hospital, but in the south wing we shall reserve a few rooms where family members can spend week-

ends. Here will be Mihály's office too; he will spend at least three days a week at Ararat. Zia was unwilling to give up their little flat in Buda, or Zia Photos. The only permanent resident of the castle will be Rere, for whom, at Dr. Freyberger's advice, we shall set up a carpentry workshop in an empty storeroom, so he can occupy himself—with completely blunt tools, naturally. While I was writing this letter, Rere appeared on tiptoe, leaned over me and said: "A kk-kiss for Gwen." His letter K sent a tiny spray of spittle onto the letter paper. You can see its traces on the first page.

By yesterday Mama had already withdrawn to her own little country manor, where, as you know, she carries on her charitable activity in a day nursery called the Glass House. There, according to Kristina, quite amazing things occur: it is not grown-up women who give birth to infants, but infants to grown-ups, because Mama appoints every impoverished aristocrat as diaper-overseer, bird-feeder, inspector of rattles and such like.

Johy is maintaining his quarters in Septemvir Utca, where he will sell out Hungary cheaply to the German ambassador. According to Mr. Gruber, he dreams of shortly becoming Gauleiter in Hungary. Last night at supper, Kristina between soup and meat announced that in the morning she had become engaged to the Hungarian diplomat, Borsitzky. Doubtless as I write these lines she has already divorced Borsitzky. But more probably, this Borsitzky does not even actually exist. No other news for now. I long for you so! Many, many kisses.

OSTIE

A few days after the funeral Ostie's car was proceeding on the hilly roads where there weren't even villages. His sole passenger was Mihály.

"The Cave I am going to show you," said Ostie, "I discovered at the age of eleven with a friend of mine named Helmut. Helmut, while swimming, had found an underwater passage leading to a cavern; then, with a rope round my waist, he dragged me after him. Inside the hill we emerged in a subterranean lake.

15

We climbed out onto the rocky shore. Helmut's flashlight at once took possession of the tremendous cavern. He announced that we call the cavern Helmut Cave, and lest there be any dispute about ownership rights, before I could say a word he punched me so hard that I fell back into the lake."

"What became of Helmut? Is he a Gauleiter now?"

"No, the following year he stole his brother's motorcycle and smashed himself to bits. Consequently I named the cavern the Dukay Cave, but to this day I have never betrayed the secret to anyone, except Zia, and I haven't shown it even to her. I suppose everyone has a Cave, at least in imagination, where he can retreat from civilization, the family circle, and the other torments of life. My father had a tiny little room in the tower of the castle which he called the Grumbler and where he would retire for days after a bad tiff with Mama. In 1933, when Hitler came to power, I was already a member of Parliament and then I still thought I would play an important role in Hungarian politics. Since the underwater passage was a rather disagreeable means of entry, with laborers brought from Italy I quite secretly arranged to have a huge stone gateway made for my cave above the level of the river in such fashion that even a car on a raft might enter. You'll soon see that from outside, even from quite close, it is impossible to detect the gateway—so perfectly does it imitate the natural cliff wall that a kingfisher even built a nest in the cracks."

"What did you intend to make of the Cave? A Party center?"

"Not exactly, though Helmut and I originally planned to move permanently into the Cave and only sometimes foray for women, food and gold. This would resemble a Party center, though not entirely. I did not participate in the next election—taking final leave of Hungarian politics, I went to America, got married, and the rest you know."

On deserted roads, during a car ride of several hours, talk turns to many things.

"Father always said," continued Ostie, "that I was no longer a count, but only some banker-like fellow. Maybe so. I was always full of ideas for making money. I thought of a Cavern Restaurant too. Did I ever tell you the story of the hermit? He was a Hussar officer who served with me—we called him Topi. A

16

likable, hair-brained chap who drank his champagne every night next to the gypsy band and 'set to music,' as he described it, some five thousand acres; that was the amount he squandered on gypsies. Such an upright Hussar officer sooner or later puts a bullet through his head. Topi chose another solution. He went deep into the woods as a hermit. He garbed himself in a hairshirt and cowl, a rope round his waist, from the rope dangled a wooden cross. He ate roots and berries, his hair and beard grew until even nightingales nested there. His uneventful days passed in fervent prayer; he asked God's forgiveness for his many debaucheries. He caught a bear cub, raised it, tamed it, slept with it in a cave. Years later a hunting party accidentally came upon Topi just as he was roasting trout and fieldfare over the embers. They tasted it— 'Divine!' they exclaimed in chorus. I won't prolong the story. By the following year an auto caravan daily surrounded Topi's cave. All that changed in his hermit's garb was that at his side, dangling from the end of the rope, was a corkscrew, instead of the cross, and he charged five times the price for French champagne. Not a penny did he pay on his establishment; the guests were enchanted by the idea of sitting on mossy trunks and eating with their hands. The only illumination by night was an open fire, but two gypsy bands played, and in Hermit Inn lovely girls, undressed to resemble forest nymphs, waited on the customers. Topi became a very wealthy man. I rail at this country and I couldn't even live here any more, but when I think of such things my heart aches. Where will I find a hermit like that in America?"

The car turned off the road and, cautiously rocking along over the peaty meadow, came to a stop at the river bank. On the flat shore, roots of old black birches and willows with smooth-laved muscles resembled human arms or legs bent at the elbow or knee. At times giant lizards seemed to assume the form of weird unearthly monsters as with matted manes they fled, boring themselves into the ground at the approach of the two men from the city. The wild terrain was quite deserted, as though not only human but even animal life had died out over a wide radius. In the honeyed light of the September afternoon the leaves of the cornelian cherry and boxthorn waved an orange and carmine farewell. The silence was only broken by the rush of the river as it hurried toward the Danube, as though the latter were the

17

Orient Express which only slowed down a bit at the mouths of tributaries—and the Ipoly hurried on not to miss it, fluttering its waves and bundles of foam, sometimes falling to its knees in the rocky channel and at the turns crashing into the high steep cliff wall of the far shore.

Ostie for a long time stood silent on the river bank. Mihály Ursi said nothing either. He sensed that Ostie was not merely enjoying the beauties of the landscape, but taking leave of Hungary.

Then they got into a boat and rowed to the opposite shore, where, a bit lower down, Ostie moored the boat to the steep cliff wall. First he looked around to see that no one was near, then he stuck a great key into a crack in the wall. The stone gateway opened in well-oiled silence, like the door of a huge safe, with the difference that it swung inward. Their boat was swallowed by the mountain; inside, the yellow beams of their flashlights danced over the black mirror of the lake and the high stalactite ceiling of the great Cave.

"On top of this hill once stood the ancient Zoskay fortress, demolished back in Tartar and Turkish times," Ostie began to explain. "Did you ever see the Pállfy Fortress at Vöröskö? All the old fortresses were built this way. Their cellars above have secret steps leading into the depths, partly to assure a water supply, and partly so fortress-dwellers could escape if the walls of the fortress were breached."

Beneath the ceiling of the Cave a fractured waterfall limped down the zigzagging cliff wall. Now, too, it was as Ostie and Helmut first glimpsed it: hobbling as if on a stick and moaning plaintively like some bewitched old crone in her black dress edged with white foam lace. And it impressed one's fancy like Eternity sentenced to geologic life imprisonment.

"Be careful, don't stumble," said Ostie, as they climbed the uneven cliff steps. "Look at these hollows carved from the rock. Our ancestors kept Tartar and Turkish prisoners chained to the walls of such narrow cubicles, where the unfortunates couldn't even stand up. Those larger cavities were probably secret store-rooms for arms and food."

Proceeding upward they shortly glimpsed a palm's breadth of sky, then emerged into the great crater-like cup of the hilltop,

18

where crumbling black stone walls spoke of ancient cellars, but over the centuries the populace had carried off the loose bricks of the ruins.

"Our fathers had a wonder weapon," said Ostie as they climbed to the top of the walls and looked down. "During a siege, they would roll great boulders, which like huge grasshoppers would skip down the steep hillside to the Mongol camps, where they did more damage than a modern TNT bomb. I guess you understand why I brought you here and why I told you, and you alone, the secret of the Cave. It affords perfect shelter not only against bombs, but against the Gestapo. I hope you and your friends may never need it, but the good Lord only knows what coming years will bring. In any case, here is the key to the Cave. Take it but say nothing to Zia. She would laugh at both of us."

Saturday noon Ostie summoned all the employees of the estate to the great terrace of the castle and in a brief speech invested Mihály Ursi with complete authority. They listened in glum silence. Among them stood the most perfect butlers, trained by Herr Jordan, the major-domo, who—not accidentally—was the very image of Emperor Ferdinand V, because his mother once served as a housekeeper in the palace of Archduke Charles Leopold. Trained by Herr Jordan, these perfect butlers never stole three or four Havanas from the rainbow-colored large boxes, never secretly drank a few gulps from the French cognac, as the playwrights imagine it in every comedy. No, these perfect butlers made whole bottles of Hennessey and Tokay disappear by the dozens because they knew how to manipulate delivery bills. These perfect butlers always found and returned the lost, semiprecious jewels of Countess Menti or Kristina; in most cases they stole them themselves in order to find them without pain. They well knew that a butler's honesty is like the large silver buttons on livery which from time to time need shining. These perfect butlers always gave back the wrinkled banknotes forgotten in the trouser pockets of the guests, they dry-cleaned and ironed them and presented them on silver platters, showing them off like the ribbons of their own Légion d'honneur, but in the county bank they always enjoyed large loans, taken for the appendix operations of their aunts or for the dowry of their nieces though their aunts had died decades ago and they did not have any nieces.

19

Needless to say, in the end these loans were always paid back to the bank by the angelic Countess Menti. The muscles of their features were entirely degenerated, but behind these wooden masks they concealed very definite opinions about all the intimate secrets of the castle's inner life; in the toilets they very diligently read all the liberal papers which were most strictly banned from the castle by Count Dupi.

Now none of them knew what their fate would be in the hands of the new master. Count Dupi loathed figures. He hadn't even known how many apartment houses he owned. This professional astronomer seemed to be formidably learned in algebra, he knew much more about addition and multiplication than Countess Menti did. The same thoughts went through the minds of the gamekeepers, the forest engineers, Monsieur Cavaignac, the French chef, and all the way up to the estate agent, who was a King's Councilor, and who, instead of a few dozens of cognac, during thirty years stole more than eighteen hundred acres. Now all of them anticipated the worst.

Ostie journeyed away in the evening hours, leaving behind him in the hands of Mihály Ursi not only the huge Ararat estate, but another entail: the responsibility for the fate of Hungary.

It would be an exaggeration to say that Mihály Ursi's personality and actions mirrored the history of mankind in this fatal decade, or even the history of his little nation. His name will not be mentioned in any schoolbook, and though later his name appeared in the world press and radio, it bobbed and glittered only for a few seconds like an empty tin can in the thundering Niagara of world events. He was only a small but deep line and a bitter smile on the face of the unknown man who during and after World War II took over the role of the unknown soldier.

He lived through four different regimes: his childhood in the time of Franz Joseph; his youth between two world wars; his manhood under Nazism and Russian Communism. The records of all the courts in which he was tried, all the carefully prepared speeches of the prosecutors, all the objectively motivated verdicts of the judges, strictly following the dictates of the reigning laws of these four regimes, indicate that Mihály Ursi was a restless, ever resisting and conspiring revolutionist, a stupidly obdurate and cruel subversive element, who deserved his final fate. When four regimes, ideologically so different, unanimously state with the very same words that he was a "real danger to society," this general judgment could not be mistaken.

Still, without the slightest intention of doubting the Zarathustran bulls of all the parties which are, after all, destined for the ages, nor the apostolic heights of all the controversial ideas in our days, we cannot help remembering Li-Pu-Ten, the ancient Chinese poet of the Cha-ong Dynasty, who said that there were times not certain men were dangerous to society, but certain societies were mortally dangerous to every honest man, and it was the prosecutors and judges of all the different regimes, dressed in beautiful scarlet speeches and in dignified black palls of their moral declarations, who were the unbelievably reckless, conspiring, amazingly stupid and bestially cruel subversive elements, and not the unknown man on trial.

Looking at Mihály Ursi at the very threshold of World War II, on his shoulders the burden of a great responsibility, entrusted with absolute authority over the affairs of the Ararat estate, entrusted with the conscience not only of a Hungarian, but we might say of a world citizen, having in our possession some data of his biography, we think we should pause to say something about where he came from, and how he traveled in his childhood and youth before arriving at the black gate of September 1939.

Chapter 2

The Childhood and Youth of Mihály Ursi.

We have no means of ascertaining the day, month or year of Mihály Ursi's birth. Incredible though it may seem, even the exact century is in doubt.

At the moment of his birth in a poverty-stricken miner's hovel, his father held a kerosene lantern so that the doctor might be able to see better. Atop the chimney of the lamp he had placed bread crust, which, as is well known, draws up the flame and makes the light brighter. A woman from next door, who came to help, followed an ancient superstition in biting off the umbilical cord of the newborn infant. At the moment of the child's birth the silver watch of the side-whiskered mine doctor, who was redolent of mustachio pomade, showed three minutes before midnight in the nineteenth century. At the same time, the cheap cuckoo-clock on the wall, seemingly changing its very tone, had ticked gaily into the twentieth century some two minutes before. For Mihály Ursi was born on the night of December 31, 1899, in Hungary.

Which timepiece was right? The old-fashioned doctor from the mining company argued for the nineteenth century, while the socialist miner who fathered the infant vehemently took the part of the cuckoo-clock on the wall, which had never once let him down when he left for work in the pre-dawn darkness. A violent winter storm served to increase the uncertainty. The mining hamlet being far from the nearest town, the wind blew the midnight chimes in the opposite direction; so when the doctor at the height of the debate opened the window, only the cry of the wind could be heard.

The wind wailed, and by now the newborn infant wailed too. If we put our trust in the old doctor's watch, the wind was the voice of the departing nineteenth century weeping myriads of snowflakes from the black firmament at the moment of its passing, doubtless with the thought that though certain struggles for freedom weighed on its conscience, it might merit grace before the Creator by having in its final months successfully summoned forth the first Hague Peace Conference. If we accept the testimony of the cuckoo-clock, then the wind moaning in the forest of Holod was the cry of the newborn twentieth century. But why waste time on a few minutes? In the recorder's office the father entered January 1 as the birthdate of his son, not only defending the cuckoo-clock against the assaults of a rust-cogged silver watch, but also giving expression to his socialist hope: that, since he had succeeded at the last moment, as though fleeing some black danger, in tossing his child across the barrier of Time, his son, when he grew up, would repudiate all ties with the ruling ideas of the nineteenth century.

These miners' dwellings all under one long roof—each unit consisting of one room, kitchen, and tiny yard—clung to each other like swallows' nests on rafters above the ox-stalls. Poultry scampered in and out of the earthen-floored rooms, but the miners could not afford to fatten pigs.

Of Mihály Ursi's childhood we know only that till the age of six he went barefoot summer and winter. He received his first pair of shoes when he was enrolled in elementary school. The shoes were several sizes too large, and his father with his own hands nailed strips of copper on the toes to make them last a few years. The school was about two miles from the mining hamlet. In winter the children would set out in the dark of dawn and return home only after nightfall. They brought their own lunch —miners' children could always be recognized by the slice of pumpkin their mothers would tie around their necks with string each morning. The meager diet of the poor miners' children need not, however, bring tears to a sensitive reader's eyes. Only of late have Western kitchens generally adopted the pumpkin upon ascertaining its rich vitamin content and excellent regulative effects. The Hungarian peasant in Asia had already been aware of this for some twenty thousand years.

In other regards, too, the umbilical cord of the Holod region was not yet quite severed from nature. At ultraexclusive restaurants in Paris and London the greenish, transparently jelly-like

23

and almost spherical, cooked eggs of the lapwing are accounted the rarest of delicacies. Children brought these from the fens of Holod by the basketful. In springtime, nesting crows would blot out the sky in croaking clouds above the forests by the Danube. The unfledged nestlings made a wonderfully delicious soup. So, at hatching time, the tips of the trees blackened not only with crows but birds of a larger variety; these last, naturally, the children of the miners. One Sunday afternoon, the obese and nearsighted mine superintendent of Holod went eagle-hunting, with the result that the aforementioned side-whiskered mine doctor redolent of mustachio pomade plucked seventeen pellets from the seven-year-old Mihály Ursi's rear.

Not only tree-climbing, but tower-climbing seems to have figured among his hobbies. It would entail detailed psychiatric analysis to determine what bearing this childhood passion may have had on his later astronomical career and, in general, on his political thinking, which always ardently sought the heights.

In the yard of the Korona Tavern in Holod stood a four-hundred-year-old stone pile which, in Turkish days, had served as a watch-tower. Children were most strictly enjoined not to climb it. One afternoon the tavern-keeper glimpsed a child perched on the tower, whistling away, hands in his pockets. With a hoarse bellow of rage he shook his fist and his *chibouk*. A stone slipped from beneath the foot of the startled Mihály, who lost his balance and fell sixty feet. The child's plummeting body pierced like a bullet the decaying thatched roof of the ancient ice-house adjoining the tower. Reaching the ground, Mihály darted through the open door of the ice-house and might still have been running had he not been caught by villagers on their way to church.

In his eighth year he caught a double case of diphtheria and scarlet fever. His convalescence left him with a temporary squint, and walnut-shell glasses were the remedy prescribed by the mine doctor. The boy's mother with the point of a pair of scissors bored minute holes in the center of two empty walnut shells, and for months Mihály Ursi wore this outlandish contraption held together with string. Since the tiny openings did not show objects to one side, his eyeballs were forced always to look straight ahead. If we knew more about the formative aspects of

24

the human soul, we might conjecture that these walnut-shell glasses may have influenced his character development.

Those were years when epidemics of children's diseases summoned many miners' offspring to the presence of the Lord, but this sort of "birth control" as practiced by Nature, was not too efficacious, for in the bleak little yards of the miners' hovels, children teemed like sparrows in the threshing fields after the harvest. Mihály Ursi, as a single child, was accounted a rarity.

The approach of winter always brought grievous cares to the poor miners. One ugly November morning the neighbors made a horrible discovery. A miner had exterminated his whole family and then killed himself. Little seven-year-old Mihály Ursi watched through the paling as they carried the corpses of the two parents and their eleven children from the tiny house. Later, when we quote from his article on the threatening growth of population, we shall see to what degree his outlook was affected by this childhood memory.

But his childhood abounded in gay hours too. Palm Lake, just outside Holod—so-called because it was scarcely bigger "than your palm"—afforded a wealth of pleasures. On its shore stood a solitary bathing-cabin—for the use of the obese mine superintendent and his family, naturally. The miners' children did not insist on cabins or even bathing suits, and used only sunlight for a towel. The mine superintendent must have weighed well over three hundred pounds. The children always giggled to see him trying to squeeze his flabby bulk into the cabin. When he stepped out, he would lift a roll of fat on either side of his waist and there secrete cigarettes and matches before submerging in the water. After bathing, he would reach into these naturally watertight pockets of fat and light a cigarette. The children could never laugh enough at this.

A bathing-cabin, even after ten years, does not alter its dimensions. The mine superintendent, on the other hand, grew fatter by the summer. And so one fine day the miracle happened: the cabin—yes, the cabin—headed for the lake! Till the urgently summoned carpenter could liberate the mine superintendent from his walking prison, the children rolled in the sand, screaming with glee.

The mine superintendent kept a single-horse carriage in

which he drove to town from Holod. Once, halfway there, the bottom of the carriage fell out. In vain did he yell at the coachman—the iron-rimmed wheels clattered dreadfully on the cobbled road. On that occasion the mine superintendent was forced to run, locked in his speeding prison; and by the time the carriage finally halted in town, he allegedly had lost over twenty pounds.

The small fry of the mining hamlet were divided into two factions. The "Turkeys" wore turkey feathers on their hats, the "Crows," crow feathers. Those who had no hats wore the insignia on their jackets, and those who had no jackets, wore it on their shirts.

In the camp of the Crows we meet for the first time with the name Kurdi. Sandor Kurdi, who was the same age as Mihály Ursi, was the captain of the Crows; his brother, Joska Kurdi, a year younger, served as a Crow without rank.

Our data is not sufficient to clarify the different ideological lines of the Turkeys and Crows. We only know that a steady war had been raging between the two gangs, usually for the sovereignty of the southern shore of little Palm Lake. It was waged in winter with snowballs—the officers had the right to wear icicles as swords—in rainy springs and autumns with mudballs; and in summer occasionally with well-dried horse-buns. They used to take prisoners, and for the sake of simplicity, they killed them. For the executions they used firecrackers instead of rifles, but after the shot the condemned prisoners were obliged to collapse and not to move for half an hour. Because nobody had a watch, sometimes the dead had to lie on the ground for an hour or more. To make it real, the grandson of the doctor spread red dye from a bottle on the faces of the executed prisoners, who after the half-hour had the right to jump up and run away.

In one of the battles seven-year-old Joska Kurdi was captured with another Crow warrior. When he was led to execution, his fellow Crow was already lying on the ground, immobile, his face covered with "blood." Little Joska became so frightened he started to scream desperately. Mihály Ursi, eight years old then, but already the Major of the Turkeys, granted him mercy. On that day Joska Kurdi joined the Turkeys, and he was always at the heels of the "Major," whom he regarded as his big brother.

Joska was a bony, thin, undernourished boy, and, especially

26

in wintertime, his red-black hands—red from the cold and black from the dirt—contrasted with his pale green face in which his frightened small eyes were framed in the pinkish rings of his chronically inflamed eyelids. His low forehead seemed even lower than it was because of the thick hair which had never known a barber, and when once a year he received a hasty haircut, his head became ridiculously laddered with white stairs, the traces of his mother's busy scissors. His skull was stone-hard, especially to the benign and patient explanations of the old schoolmaster. Joska always sat on the last bench. He preferred the traditional gatherings of corn-peeling and feather-plucking, the monotony of which was eased by the sweet thrumming of zithers and the choir of folk-songs; and Joska breathlessly listened to the toothless old women's tales about the *Táltos*, the stallion with a human brain, the *Garabonciás* whose ragged cloud-coat could make him invisible. From his earliest childhood Joska was possessed by the dreadful, commanding power and authority of these superhuman forces.

His father was a shepherd. His mother was known as Lovely Juli, and lovely she was, with a willowy waist, laughing cherry-red lips always on the verge of song, radiant hazel eyes, and hair which she rubbed with porcupine fat to make it soft and lustrous, tied back daintily in a chignon. The shepherd adored his wife.

In the first months of their marriage the landowner ordered the young shepherd and his flock to a distant pasture. The shepherd took leave of his seventeen-year-old wife and at daybreak commenced the long trek, plodding after his sheep. But that midnight he appeared again at his house with four comrades, and their husky shoulders smashed open the locked door with a single heave.

Needless to say, the landowner leapt from the bed in a state of undress, and Lovely Juli buried her head deep in the pillows —her scream frozen in her throat. Very often, at such moments, the roused husband seizes an ax or a gun—and the jury, particularly in France, always absolves him.

Shepherd Kurdi acted otherwise. "Good evening, your honor," he said in a comparatively unruffled and friendly tone. "Be so good as to get up on this table." The four other shepherds seized the landowner and laid him on the table. The presence of

27

these fellow shepherds in the affair came close to constituting an example of mob law.

Meanwhile the deceived husband took from their white linen wrappings the tools he used for castrating rams. Having administered the anesthesia with traditional herbs, he began the operation with a practiced hand. The human testicles he threw to his dog, stopped the bleeding, sewed up the wound, and then said:

"Thank you, your honor."

The four shepherds politely helped the landowner to his carriage waiting at the edge of the dark garden. After the husband had carefully cleaned and put away his tools, he undressed and lay down in bed next to his wife. Laying his heavy, hamlike hand on Lovely Juli's head he said to her: "Don't cry." Till the day of his death they lived happily together.

The landowner made no official complaint, because, as he well suspected, he would have been laughed at rather than pitied. Instead, he sold his estate, and moved to another part of the country. Nor did the tale end unhappily for him either. Forced to abandon the reckless and costly amours which were ruining his life, he became an enterprising and successful farmer.

Mihály Ursi might have been ten years old when, in the autumn twilight, two "candles" appeared in the tiny yard. That was the colloquial term for the rooster-plumed gendarmes, whose fixed bayonets gleamed candle-like at dusk, and who were always engaged in lighting up dark corners. The "candles" took with them Mihály Ursi's father, along with seven other miners. Grouping in frightened clusters, the miners' wives whispered that the men were in trouble for distributing socialist leaflets.

At this point we should know that the world movement called Socialism had veered so sharply toward class hatred that at the turn of the century the Fabian Socialists of London, and the so-called revisionist group of German Socialism, were striving desperately to set Marxism back on the right track, as if it were some locomotive run berserk, now threatening to demolish the walls of castles and factories.

Two days later, three of the eight miners came back, among them Mihály Ursi's father. He had no word to say of the interrogation at the *gendarmerie,* but his lips were swollen and blue

28

and the bridge of his nose was broken. To the day of his death the bone stood awry, and this was particularly apparent when he laughed.

We have mentioned that the mine superintendent was very obese. Fat men often have soft hearts. When he learned that Mihály Ursi's parents intended to apprentice him to a locksmith after four years of grade school, he called for his carriage, since furnished with a double bottom, and drove to the high-school principal. He knew the boy not only through the adventure in the course of which the side-whiskered mine doctor had extracted seventeen pellets from his rear; but the Ursi boy, in return for cast-off clothes and left-over food, had frequently swept his yard, shoveled snow, and ingeniously cleaned his hunting rifles and pipes with the aid of a crow's feather dipped in kerosene. He could also be entrusted with the silver and was strong enough to bring a whole bushel basket of plums from the garden. His replies verged on the insolent, but always reflected intelligence. The mine superintendent, for the time being, took upon himself the expenses of Mihály's schooling.

No particulars are at hand relating to the first years spent at the *Gymnasium*, save a letter attesting to his intellectual development and which, incidentally, pays tribute to the U.S. Post Office, having arrived despite a somewhat ambiguous address.

Missriss Szanto Borbala Amerika Bruklin Lafayet utca 435.

DEAREST AUNT BORI! For your birthday I enclose four pressed violets, which I picked in the woods at Holod, because mother said you like things reminding you of your childhood and native land. My birthday will be on January first. For Uncle János' birthday in August I'll also send something nice. My birthday falls exactly on New Year's Day. There's lots of time till then. Since my birthday is on January first it will be a double holiday, I might almost say triple holiday, because then I will be twelve years old and twelve is a round dozen. If you want to send me something, Aunt Bori, for this big triple holiday, please send me a bicycle. I kiss your hands and the hands of Uncle János.

MIHÁLY

29

We possess no evidence relating to the arrival of an American bicycle.

In his fifth year at the gymnasium he was threatened with expulsion. One morning, Herr Beck, at the start of the German lesson, opened his desk drawer. A bullfinch flew out, knocking off Herr Beck's pince-nez. Though the whole class had sworn not to betray the miscreant, a weak character, the son of the apothecary, disclosed that Mihály Ursi had brought the bullfinch to school and secreted it in the desk drawer.

At the faculty conference Herr Beck demanded a *consilium abeundi* for the culprit, plus parental compensation for his broken pince-nez. The first to oppose the motion was the physics teacher, who, from beneath his impenetrable walrus mustache, rumbled that never during thirty-five years of teaching had he chanced on a student able to grasp the law of Gay-Lussac at first hearing, and that by and large Mihály Ursi had shown unique brilliance in the subject of physics.

The conference, by a vote of four to three, decided against the *consilium abeundi*.

His first Budapest sojourn was memorable not only for the marvels of the capital, but because his aunt, with whom he spent his summer vacation, served in the household of Mr. Ady as a cook. Endre Ady, "the poet of fate" was only thirty-seven years old then, but already a shadow of himself, his death only a few years away. His trembling fingers were yellow from countless cigarettes, his huge brown eyes swollen by sleepless nights, by pints of black coffee and brandy, his face greenish gray from mercury, the only cure in his youth for syphilis. His revolutionary, obscure style, a thundering music of words, his demoniac attacks against the Old Order, his desperate Cassandra cries sounded like a sharp trumpet in the sleepy marshes of Hungarian life. He came back from Montmartre's cafés with Rimbaud's clairvoyant drunkenness and Verlaine's powerful decadence, but mixed with deep oriental mysticism. He was the target of the bearded academicians, and the idol of the younger generation: Ady, ADY—but his name was taboo in the schools.

The fourteen-and-a-half-year-old Mihály Ursi eagerly ran out many times a day for cigarettes, but more often for brandy.

On August first, the world war broke out. In the early

morning hours of that fatal night in 1914 the dark, staggering figure of the poet of fate appeared at the door of his smoke-filled study.

"To the printer. Quick!"

A sheet of paper, pencil-scribbled lines on it. A poem. A poem which a few days later was memorized by thousands, then declaimed by famous actors, then set to music by a composer. Mihály Ursi on the way to the printer stopped on the street, and was the first reader of the poem, which since has become immortal; its visions and morbid predictions have wondrously come true.

> Strange, strange was that summer night,
> An angry angel beat her drum in heaven . . .

While he was reading the first two lines, a tremendous stampede of a thousand horses on the wood-paved Andrássy Út filled the air. A Hussar regiment on its way to the battlefield.

> Our old servant secretly fled,
> And our best colt broke a leg.

Vague and dark words. He could not understand them, but when he closed his eyes he sensed them. "Our old servant secretly fled"—the Old Order ended. "Our best colt"—the youth of Hungary. And if a colt breaks a leg it is doomed to death.

From that day he often heard the Angry Angel beating her drum in heaven. But life is much stronger than any vision of death.

It was spring of the following year when he first encountered love.

He became tutor to the children of the wealthy local liquor manufacturer, who were being raised by their parents on a genteel plane. The French governess was called Madot.

Everything happened very simply. One evening when the parents were away and the children already in bed, Madot led to her bedroom the lank, chestnut-haired tutor, who was swallowing hard, hands dripping with perspiration in his excitement.

The warm, heavy smell of the room, the mixture of cheap

31

French perfume and the heated female body; the pinkish light of the small silk-shaded night-lamp; the almost inaudible but melodious *tick-tock* of an old porcelain clock in the frightening depth of silence; the fiery taste of the curaçao liqueur; all these sank more vividly into his nerves than anything he had or was ever to experience. He saw and touched the naked body of a girl in the burning heat of sexual mystery. He left the room sad and disgusted, with a strange and cold emptiness which was quite natural for a sixteen-year-old boy whose high idealism first met the smelly reality of sexual love.

This affair lasted more than a year and provided Mihály with a facile command of French.

In the fall of the following year, November, 1916, right in the midst of the war, the Austro-Hungarian Monarchy fell apart. To be more precise, first only the head fell off, but this head was most large and ponderous.

Franz Joseph passed away in his eighty-seventh year, having reigned four years longer than Queen Victoria—sixty-eight years in all. His death terminated an era in European history which today is more distant in our recollection than the wondrously happy age of King Asoka of Belhar who enjoyed the tutelage of the Seven Paths in the third century before Christ.

Only massively great personalities can reign for so long. Franz Joseph's accomplishment was the more astounding because he held together a monarchy which, two years after his death, disintegrated into its components—a shrunken Austria, a truncated Hungary, an augmented Italy, a new Poland, Czechoslovakia, Yugoslavia and Rumania—all later falling an easy prey first to German, then Russian occupation.

The secret of Franz Joseph's long reign, and of the cohesive force he represented, lay in an absolutely uncompromising consistency. Many an anecdote circulated about the Emperor. The last, which we located among later notes of Mihály Ursi, stemmed from a highly connected distiller who heard it at the great funeral in Vienna. The event occurred a few days before the death of the Emperor and was in connection with the proposed ennobling of Professor M. In his eighty-fifth year the Emperor fell so gravely ill that the "modern" Professor M. was also summoned to the imperial sickbed. The professor thoroughly examined the octogenarian, prostatically too, with a vaselined glove drawn over his index finger. So successful was his cure that the Emperor even participated in an ibex hunt some months later. It being customary for the Monarchy to bestow the rank of baron on outstanding medical men, the Austrian prime minister proposed Professor M., who had saved the Emperor's life. Franz Joseph turned irately on his prime minister: "Are you joking? Would you have me make a baron of the man who stuck his finger up my ass?"

Such was the force which held the Monarchy together. Men whispered the news of his passing. "Franz Joseph is dead, but no one has dared to tell him yet."

Before Christmas the boys were abruptly given final examinations so lenient that even the apothecary's son was passed after replying that Shakespeare was the incumbent president of the United States. The inalterably stringent laws of pedagogy relented the moment it became a question of throwing young men into battle.

Mihály Ursi, who on January 1, 1918, completed his eighteenth year, was called to the colors. After three months of emergency training, during which he had ample opportunity to acquaint himself with the incredible obtuseness and sadism of training officers, he was assigned to a company which was ordered to the Italian battlefield where, amid the giant barren peaks of the Dolomites, the collapsing Monarchy launched its last and bloodiest assault. According to military historians, the Battle of Montello outdid even the hell of Verdun. On June 14, an eerie night regarding which we find ample and precise details in subsequent notes of Mihály Ursi, the steel-helmeted troops were already lying in dense brush by the river bank. Even whispering was forbidden.

"What time is it?" asked someone. "Ten minutes to three," voicelessly replied a phosphorescent wristwatch. Three A.M. was the zero hour set for the river crossing. At three, precisely, the throats of cannon and mortars simultaneously lit up the darkness with streaks of angry yellow flame and filled it with a sound of crashing firmaments. The mad din seemed one colossal blanket of thunder in which the human ear could hardly distinguish the deep roar of heavy mortars from the sharp crack of lesser calibers.

Simultaneously, for a whole hour, came yellowish bursts of deadly mustard gas. Then the first pontoons were launched. Italian artillery, numbly silent in the first hours of the surprise assault, now suddenly blazed into action. Above the river, war-planes appeared, flying low and laboriously on their double can-vas wings, through smoke and flame proceeding almost as slowly as pelicans, their motors and machine-guns emitting a sort of benign whir as of sewing machines appearing amid the hellish clamor to sew up the rents in the sky and in the waters of the Piave. The river spouted great white water-towers where heavy Italian shells struck near the pontoons. At such times the river, with a foaming bellow of rage, would rise from its bed like some wounded antediluvian monster. Temporary bridges splintered like matchsticks when a shell found its mark; horses and men swept by with the current, and a wild crush developed round the ladders and pontoons. Everyone wanted to be first to climb down and rush across, first to storm the Italian positions—not in a delirium of heroism but driven rather by the torturingly unen-durable desire to get it over with, to get everything over with since there was no way out anyway. Fire and water boomed in the air. The last rung of a ladder broke under Mihály Ursi, sending him sprawling on the ground with his heavy gear. The others stormed past him, trampling his hands with their hob-nailed boots, thinking he too had been hit by machine-gun fire, for at the bottom of the ladder lay the moaning wounded and the silent dead. He would have had strength enough to crawl to some more sheltered place, but remained motionless there under fire, letting the others trample over him. In the clashing tornado of raging artillery, he gazed with narrowed eyes at two small blades of grass before him on the ground, as though in final sur-render to something.

For two whole hours he lay motionless. Murky clouds swirled with urgency across the sky, as if silently mirroring the battle below in the valley.

There was no crush around him now, for at this point the crossing had been completed. He raised himself on one elbow to look around. The Italian machine-guns in the caves of Mon-tello had already silenced the steel-helmeted troops reaching the farther shore, and above Montello, enveloped in smoke and

34

flame, pigeons soared, first winging their way upward then all darting arrowlike in the same direction, carrier pigeons above the thunder and clouds of yellowish gas, taking the place of telephones, speeding to tell headquarters how far the attacking infantry had reached on the slopes of Montello. As he watched the pigeons flying through smoke and bursting flame, the splintering crash of mortars shook the sky like shrill maniacal laughter.

We find ample and precise details in his diary about these hours, and the following days, which deal with the struggle of his own conscience, and his encounter with Sandor Kurdi, the former captain of the Crows, and Joska Kurdi, who at this time had already reached the age of seventeen, been drafted, and served in the same company.

> . . . then I got up, threw from myself all my weapons, retaining only the emergency kit with two days' rations, and set forth toward Conegliano, the terminal of supply and troop trains, about twenty miles from the battlefield.
>
> The night was dark and rainy. The thunder of gunfire slowly faded behind me, but I could still differentiate the sharp rapping of infantry rifles, and the rattle of machine guns. Sometimes big trucks came on the road in the darkness, without headlights, carrying ammunition and reserves, supplying the hell around Montello with dynamite and with the blood of young soldiers. Later, batteries drove past, but I heard only the snorts of horses, the rattle of bridles, the crack of whips, commands lost in curses, the clatter of gun carriages. It was ghastly.
>
> Then I walked on again in the dark rain. Before dawn I sat beneath a tree. I was deadly tired but my thoughts were buzzing terribly. A raindrop, fat and lazy, dripping from a leaf, and falling on my aluminum canteen, gave a more solid noise than the faint and faraway gunfire. I was already far from the battlefield, but I was not happy. I felt a piercing pain in my heart: I doubted again the justice of my desertion.
>
> Then my thoughts turned in another direction. I felt it not only my right to desert, but my duty. If everybody

35

surrenders to this futile death, who will stand up for the soldiers still alive? Who will stop this awful massacre? We are fighting here not for our country, not for our liberty, but for Hohenzollern and Hapsburg imperialism—against the Italians, against the nation of Dante, Leonardo and especially of Garibaldi whose legion fought together with Kossuth.

In the monotonous music of the rain and in the sounds of the distant gunfire I started to make a speech aloud. "Hungarian compatriots! The moment has come to shake from our necks the German yoke. They have for centuries been driving us to slaughter so they might save their creaking throne! Each crack in that throne is cemented with Hungarian blood! If we now unite, if we now arise, we will succeed where Kossuth failed! Our blood and the blood of our sons . . ."

In the following days as he journeyed toward Budapest, wherever he looked there were the vineyards and orchards, the black- and red-roofed villages, the calm and beautiful Italian landscape.

One day he sighted a detachment of military police coming toward him. He left the road and advanced through a swamp, among the tall reed stalks, as far as he could. He found a dry spot and lay down, feeling himself secure. Then suddenly the reeds rustled. His heart stopped beating. A moment later he saw the intruder's hand, then his cap, among the spikes of the reeds. It was another deserter from his company. All together twenty-seven boys were hiding in the reeds, among them the two Kurdi brothers: Sandor and Joska.

Now they headed for Budapest with false travel orders, even using the military trains. During July and August Mihály Ursi hid in Budapest, wearing civilian clothes. In the final months of World War I deserters so multiplied that the firing squads could hardly keep pace with their work. Night after night the "candles" of the military police would go looking for deserters, their lines combing the city precinct by precinct, as a great net combs the bottom of the sea.

In September Sandor Kurdi was caught in this net, and on

the night of October 17, Mihály Ursi too. A few days later he was sentenced to death by a court martial. By that time behind the bars of the vaulted and pillared corridors in the huge Maria Terézia Barracks there were thousands of unkempt soldiers in nondescript gray rags, crowded like wild beasts in some fantastic human zoo. To the left, in a special doubly-barred cell, were the prisoners awaiting execution. However, until their own turn came, they were led out each time to witness the fate of a deserter. Mihály Ursi's diary describes the execution of Sandor Kurdi.

. . . but officers too, of various ranks and companies also flocked there in great number, attracted only by curiosity. And newspaper men arrived in breathless haste. Apart from the latter, no civilians were allowed to be present.

The onlookers watched in stifled silence when at a captain's command half a battalion formed an "execution square." In the great heat the newsmen pushed their hats to the back of their heads, made industrious notes and whispered excitedly.

A few seconds later they brought in Sandor Kurdi. He entered at the gate, between two warders of the military tribunal, his hands tightly manacled. It was obvious that he still didn't know what was happening to him. Nevertheless, he seemed disquieted by all these preparations. From time to time he would glance to the left or right, only moving his eyeballs, so that at such times the whites of his eyes showed.

One wing of the "execution square" opened before him silently and ceremoniously, as it were, like some great portal made up of live and precisely coordinated bodies of soldiers, a portal concealing things horrible and incomprehensible. This live wing of the portal closed behind him just as silently. Now he stood in the center of the square. A tall military chaplain with sunken temples stepped up to him, holding a crucifix, and said loudly, so the newsmen could hear too: "Be calm, my son. Your counsel telegraphed His Majesty for a pardon an hour ago . . ."

Sandor Kurdi acknowledged these words with a very determined nod and with the expression of one who knew

37

in advance that everything would turn out all right. Young Charles IV, the last Hapsburg, during the short two years of his reign lived in the thoughts of every soldier as one who in secret was doing his utmost to break from the deadly German embrace and contract a separate peace.

The warders, who till now had accompanied Sandor Kurdi, stepped out of the square. The next instant, the military prosecutor had the bugle sounded. The sharp blast of the bugle came unexpectedly to everyone, and resounded in the quiet courtyard like a giant, blood-curdling scream. Yet it only consisted of a few high notes signaling "Attention." The prosecutor hurriedly mumbled the sentence . . . "in violation of paragraph 183 of the Military Code, which according to paragraph 198 entails . . ." Then he turned to the captain standing next to him: "Captain, I deliver the prisoner into your hands."

The front end of the square opened at the barked command of the captain, and four tall Bosnian soldiers wearing red fezzes stepped into it. These were the executioners. The captain turned and said in an official tone to the deathly pale prisoner: "Have you any request?" Sandor Kurdi, whom they had unshackled in the meantime, brushed the back of his hand over the drops of cold sweat pearling on his forehead. The realization of his fate must have dawned on him at that moment. He clasped his hands and in a pleading, tearful tone whispered to the captain, as though he had some confidential message for him:

"Captain . . . I'll behave!"

"What is your last request?" asked the captain once more in the same tone.

"Please, Captain, don't have me shot!"

"What is your last request?" asked the captain now for the third time, in a raised tone.

"Captain . . . I'll serve faithfully from now on—"

"Whom do you wish to blindfold you?"

"Captain—"

"I asked: do you wish anyone to blindfold you?"

Sandor Kurdi looked down to the ground as though

he himself at this moment considered the question of crucial importance. Then quietly, but resolutely, he said:

"Joska. Josef Kurdi, my brother."

The captain turned toward the soldiers.

"Is Josef Kurdi here?"

But Joska was nowhere to be found. He had been more cautious than to walk with girls in the dangerous Budapest nights; after his arrival he had immediately gone underground.

Another soldier, a friend of Sandor, a bowlegged private, jumped obsequiously before the captain. The man meanwhile shouted and moaned incoherently. His friend stepped up to him and, with a kerchief the warrant officer gave him, blindfolded Sandor Kurdi's eyes; it was evident by his motions that he wanted to appear very proficient before the captain. Then he saluted with a smart click of his heels.

Beneath the blindfold the prisoner suddenly grew silent —as if not only his eyes, but his soul too, had become aware of the darkness and silence. The chaplain pressed the crucifix to his mouth, and the captain shouted:

"To your knees!" The prisoner kneeled obediently. The four Bosnians approached to within a step of the prisoner, and aimed their rifles. Then a drum sounded, but I did not see the drummer. It made me feel, as the horrible barrage in the battle of Montello had, that the Angry Angel was beating again her drum in heaven. The raised sword of the captain gleamed flamelike in the sun. As he slashed downward, the four rifles discharged simultaneously. The kneeling deserter fell on his face to the ground.

"Doctor!" shouted the captain. And his cry sounded as though only some untoward accident had occurred, something greatly surprising him too.

At the end of October, 1918, Emperor Wilhelm's Germany and the Austro-Hungarian Monarchy looked like factory chimneys exploding in a slow motion picture: still standing but already slowly leaning with broken backbones, being only split seconds

39

away in their hideous movement from the huge dust-clouds of their final collapse.

The Hungarian Revolution broke out on the night of October 30. Seventeen-year-old Joska Kurdi, who had been unable to save his brother's life, led the revolutionary Holod miners to the Maria Terézia Barracks to free the prisoners.

It may have been six o'clock in the morning when an enormous throng forced its way through the gates of the barracks. There were women too, of proletarian appearance, their lank hair streaming from beneath shawls and battered hats. Some bore a brace of rifles, the heavy gunstraps tugging at both their weak shoulders. The crowd had already broken into the armories, but did not shoot, only shouted as they flooded through the gate, sweeping the guards before them. And then an astonishing thing happened: the crowd rushed to the cells and in a twinkling the heavy iron bars were bent down as though a single giant hand of colossal strength had wrenched them loose, ripping chunks of wall with them. Through the torn openings, they hauled out the prisoners one by one. Shouts, wails, and screams filled the air, but they were cries of joy and wild rapture. A well-dressed young woman ran up and down before the bars, wringing her hands: "Paul! Are you there? Paul!" Joska Kurdi made a funnel of his hands and tried to outshout the hubbub: "Mihály Ursi! Is Mihály Ursi here? His father is looking for him!"

Mihály glimpsed his father's face, which was wet with streaming tears, and at the same time he was laughing; and the asymmetry of his nose became clearly marked. Joska Kurdi and the old socialist miners of Holod cautiously plucked Mihály from among the jutting bars as from the throat of a mammoth tiger. They carried him and the other condemned prisoners on their shoulders to the street, where by now hundreds of thousands surged, crying and singing. The open windows, too, filled with heads, and flowers were being strewn from on high.

A hundred mounted policemen approached, who a few days previously had routed demonstrating throngs with the flat of their swords. Now they pranced their beautiful horses under a rain of flowers, floating high above the surge and clamor, sometimes leaning down to shake, with their white-gloved hands, an unknown hand stretched toward them.

These were the first hours of the bloodless revolution. This was how and when the institution of the Magyar Kingdom expired after nine hundred and eighteen years, for Saint Stephen, the first Hungarian king, was crowned exactly in the thousandth year of our Lord.

Chapter 3

The Brief Months of the Republic and the Even Briefer Span of the First Commune. Alma Mater's Sweet and Fervent Years.

Who has seen the wonder of a calf's birth? First, moist with glistening rainbow-tinted membranes appears the empty hard-blown sac which opens a path in the cow's uterus for the calf about to be born, and, its work done, bursts. Such was the sac they called Menshevism in Russia which opened a path in the uterus of revolution for Bolshevism. Later, this empty sac was called by other names; nationalist, democratic or coalition government, but in each case it performed an identical function.

So, too, the democratic Republic of Hungary, conceived in a rain of flowers, having accomplished its preparatory work, burst five months later.

The consolidation of Lenin's Bolshevist revolution in Russia—if we include clergy and peasants—demanded the lives of two million men. In Hungary the toll was far less, though for this we must not reproach the *Lenin Fiúk*—"The Lenin Boys." The paltry result came not from their lack of industry, but from the shortness of time. In August, the Commune collapsed. Béla Kun and his general staff fled to Moscow, but in their feverish haste they absent-mindedly left behind in Hungary not only most of their comrades, but innocent tens of thousands, to stew in the flames of reactionary vengeance.

That year a similar calf was born in Bavaria, but it lived an even shorter time than the four-and-a-half-month-old Hungarian communist regime, for Lenin's Russia in 1919 could hardly help itself, much less others.

Once fallen, an idea has always been doomed to suffer a hysterical revenge. After the fall of the Paris Commune in 1871 well-dressed French ladies dug out the eyes of the Communards with the points of their beautiful and fashionable parasols. After the Commune's demise in Hungary, power was assumed by the handful of men constituting the eagle-plumed White Army, even the rank and file of which consisted of former officers of the Monarchy, who differed in various ways from the Lenin Boys, among other things in the fact that they wore white gloves when hanging occasional Communists and very many innocents deemed Communists in the hurry of the moment; and though the white gloves scarcely affected the fate of their victims, this in itself was enough to show that Hungary had returned to the "gentry" era, aptly designated by one historian as the neo-baroque.

Young Mihály Ursi spent the months of the Commune and the White counterrevolution, when gallows in Hungary outnumbered clothesracks, far from the scene of events, some thirty-five million light years away, in the celestial regions of the constellation Andromeda, for after the war he enrolled in the astrophysical department of the University of Budapest, where, surrounded by his bolometers, actinometers, pyrheliometers, and prismed spectroscopes, he grew so absorbed in the dimensions of space that he could not spare attention for the insignificant events in Moscow and Hungary. We might say the stars barred his way, guarding his youthful revolutionary ardor from the clutches of Communism, an imminent danger, if solely for the reason that his father not only joined the Party, but played a prominent role in the directorate of Holod.

When the new regime jailed him, a few of his comrades from the mines undertook to liberate him in the ensuing battle. Two gendarmes as well as Mihály's father fell victims to the bullets and ax blades.

In Paris in June, 1920, at the palace called the Great Trianon, they signed the peace which lopped off two-thirds of Hungary's ancient territories.

On the day the Peace of Trianon was signed, all the church-bells of mutilated Hungary tolled; the peasant women, too, were dressed in mourning, and the seven million remaining Hungarians cried desperately for revision.

Since the white-gloved army and the new Christian government, for various reasons, were in no position to declare war either on the Little Entente, or on England, France, or the United States, they decided to declare war on the Jews of Hungary. Thus, Hungary once more could claim pioneer laurels. On her soil appeared Communism for the first time in Europe, and now, far in advance of the Germans, bloody anti-Semitism.

Nationalist propaganda identified Communism with the Jewish race, naturally maintaining silence on the Communist persecution of Jews, both bourgeois and intellectual, who had shown no enthusiasm for their doctrines of redemption.

One night something happened to Mihály Ursi which crystallized his opinion on this issue for the rest of his life. University students wearing the insignia and pie-plate caps of the Turul Society, and armed with crowbars, each night would stop passers-by and if they found a Jew beat him to a pulp. In accordance with confidential orders from higher up, the police discreetly kept their distance.

That night Mihály Ursi was detained by three Turulists. At such times it was no identification card they asked to see, but the male organ, which was examined by the light of a match to see if it were circumcised. At their challenge Mihály Ursi with lightning swiftness showed them his fist. A savage struggle ensued, which a policeman watched from his doorway vantage, coming forward only "at the end" in keeping with the aforementioned orders from above. The young combatants, blood streaming from mouths and noses, were taken to headquarters where it was ascertained that the three Turulists bore German names. From this period dates Mihály Ursi's first "political" article, which was published by a liberal journal as a letter to the editor.

. . . in the ancient Magyar tongue, the word, *turul*, signified a large species of hawk, which Magyar tribes used as their battle insignia while still in Asia. These flat-capped terrorists armed with iron bars seek through their Turul insignia and the title of their association to stress that they are of old Magyar stock. Never has Hungarian history witnessed a more reckless and insolent fraud. Just examine the names on the official membership records of the Turul Society, Mr. Editor, and you would immediately assume you were in Germany.

Respectfully, URSA MAJOR

44

It was the first time he used Ursa Major as his pen name.

The imagination of the young astronomy student was captured by the Latin name of the Big Dipper not only because it curiously resembled his family name, Ursi, but also because Ursa Major—for those who did not know its true meaning—sounded like a mysterious military title. Perhaps he remembered his rank of major in the Turkeys, when he was a child. But by now the fights were waged not with horse-buns, and not for the shores of tiny Palm Lake, but for the invisible shores of human rights.

During the struggle with the Turulists, one of the crowbars had knocked out Mihály's right eyetooth. The narrow silver band at the base of the new tooth, revealed that it was artificial, the masterpiece of some inexpensive or institutional dentist. The day after the encounter, as he left for the dentist's, a circus clown wearing a hat five sizes too small, regarded him from the mirror, for on his head beneath his hair the crowbars had left lumps the size of his fist. These swellings vanished after two weeks, but never the contusions in his soul. It was then that he first actively entered the arena of politics.

At the university were a number of liberally minded "true Magyar" students studying astronomy. With them Mihály Ursi founded a secret society, called the "Stargazers," whose membership was soon swelled by like-minded students in architecture, chemistry, engineering, geology and other departments.

The Stargazers were joined in a short time by the young workers, who called themselves Social Democrats, though there were many secret Communists among them. This ally was recruited by Joska Kurdi.

These young workers brought to the camp of the Stargazers not so much their deep devotion for human rights, but rather their mighty muscles, and the brass knuckles sunk deep in their pockets. And now the Stargazers, too, stalked Indian-file in Budapest by night. Though far outnumbered by the Turulists, they wreaked havoc among them whenever cries for help issued from the dark side streets.

In the circle of Jewish university students the Stargazers reaped legendary fame. Everyone knew that the leader was Ursa Major, the tall, spare student of astrophysics in the threadbare

45

suit, with the lofty forehead and ever-enigmatic smile who already had left a tooth on the battlefield of Human Rights.

It happened on one of these nights that a bespectacled, light-weight Jewish student, absent-mindedly gesticulating to himself, was walking home on the street, coming from an endless argument with his friends over whether or not Boltzmann's entropy theory was greater than Einstein's theory of relativity. It was well past midnight; the streets were hardly lighted because of the coal shortage. But in Ernst Tronfeld's brain, the formula of entropy burnt with such terrific light that he did not observe the huge snake. Yes, like a huge snake, the Turulists sneaked out of a side street in Indian file. "Hello, boys," said Tronfeld, still absent-mindedly, when he was surrounded. "Show your document!" said a hoarse flashlight behind which the face was invisible.

Tronfeld was not a member of the University Sports Club. He was neither a broad-jumper nor a sprinter, but reliable medical sources inform us that there are moments and situations when even the most fragile human body achieves miracles. Tronfeld jumped away like a giant kangaroo, and with Olympic speed dashed toward a faraway street-lamp, yelling for help. The Turulists went after him, and the distance between hunters and hunted narrowed dangerously. Tronfeld had not yet reached the lamp when from another side street appeared the Stargazers, led by Ursa Major and Joska Kurdi. They threw themselves like a dark wall between Tronfeld and the Turulists. In the light of certain recent experiences, the Turulists did not start a fight. After a few seconds of tense silence, they slowly retreated. The Stargazers escorted Tronfeld home. "Thank you, Major!" he said in a trembling voice.

For the sake of brevity the Stargazers called their leader Major. Joska Kurdi always snapped to attention whenever he reported to the Major.

A twenty-year-old man has already received the shape of manhood. As Ursa Major's photographs show him in the early twenties, he was slender and tall for a Magyar, about five feet ten. Whenever he smiled, his brown eyes grew narrower. It was a tiny sign of far-off Asiatic origin, although his straight nose could easily have been part of a fine Anglo-Saxon face. The set

mouth rarely showed the longish, even teeth—where at the base
of the right eyetooth gleamed the narrow silver band. Two deep
lines ran down his inquisitive face, giving a certain hard man-
liness to the otherwise youthful countenance.

His chin was strong; he seemed to have an idea of poise,
of keeping himself under control in any circumstance. He rarely
laughed aloud, his hidden warm smile shone only on the large,
soft and sensitive lips. The muscular neck and broad-boned
shoulders were reminders of his peasant origin, but his hands
were those of an intellectual, long and slender, the fingertips
tapering delicately.

He was a passionate cyclist, and on special occasions a
mighty drinker. During the stormy night of his twentieth birthday, having filled and refilled his own glass until late morning,
it was he who finally put his closest friend, Jani Hamor, the
"champion drinker," to bed. He was not quick of wit, but had a
slow oriental sense of humor. While he was helping the very
drunk Hamor home, Hamor suddenly stopped, looked down at
his feet, and with a mortal sadness observed: "I've lost one of my
shoes." This observation was the more curious because both
shoes were still on his feet, but with Hamor alcohol operated in
reverse, and he saw only one shoe instead of four. "You can't
have any use for just one shoe," said Mihály. "Throw it away!"
Hamor took the wise advice, threw away one of his shoes, and
limped home in the other.

The Major, in whose quiet voice there had always been a
quality of command, had only a few close friends. Most of the
Stargazers found him very difficult to know. He had a mildly
absent-minded air, which had a great appeal, especially for
women. He contracted no venereal disease, though at that time
it was almost obligatory among students. He had had many affairs, and was famous for his sexual potency.

He had fallen in love with a young actress from the small
Buda Theater who sometimes appeared at the Stargazers' table
in the Café Gugger. His love was not in vain, and after the first
stormy night, Ilon pleaded with him: "Please, swear, that you
won't tell your friends!" Ursi was hurt, but before he left he had
to repeat his vow on bended knee.

The next evening when he appeared in the café and Ilon

47

was sitting once again at the crowded table of the Stargazers, Hamor turned to him: "Ilon just told us what you did to her and how many times. Aren't you ashamed to do such things to an innocent girl?"

Ursa Major was the great impressionable. He was always deeply moved by great pictures, sculptures, buildings and natural beauties. He seldom went to the theater, except to see the classical plays and the new prima donna in the suburban Buda Theater. He did not like fiction, he read only those novelists and playwrights for whom the story was nothing but a seductive cloak for talks about mankind's problems. His idols were Leo Tolstoy, Romain Rolland, and Bernard Shaw.

To be an ardent revolutionist, one needs haunting memories, deep wounds in the soul. Mihály Ursi was ten years old when his father came back after the interrogation at the gendarmerie with swollen blue lips and a broken nose. And, as a deserter, he had waited long days for his execution.

The same applies to Joska Kurdi, for his brother's execution left a searing wound in his memory. We do not know what would have been the course of life for the prematurely balding, guitar-playing "Papushka," if his brother Sasha had not been hanged by the Czarist government. Lenin was sixteen years old then.

But there was a great difference between the two Holod boys: Mihály Ursi and Joska Kurdi. The astrophysics student had already become a member of the middle class, and Joska, who had received his higher education in the Young Communists' School, remained a Jacobin.

The final aim of a democratic revolutionist and a Jacobin is the same: the salvation of mankind. The difference is that a Mihály Ursi followed in the path of human rights, rebuilding but saving the foundations of society, and a Joska Kurdi wanted to raze to earth-level all human institutions and kill anyone standing in the way of the unique idea. During the months of the short-lived communist terror, eighteen-year-old Joska was a plain-clothes night policeman armed with an old rifle. Every light had to be extinguished at nine P.M. If Joska saw a lighted window after nine, he shot into it without hesitation. We don't know whether or not there were any victims of his shootings. We only know that, among others in those days, a medical student pre-

48

paring for his examinations forgot the curfew and was killed by a bullet fired through his window.

A democratic revolutionist fights first for liberty and second for justice. A Jacobin fights to establish "total justice" without delay, and liberty may limp behind a poor second, or not at all. But for the time being there was no break within the Stargazers between the Young Workers and the university students.

In the fall of 1921, the throneless Charles IV again appeared on the Hungarian horizon, like some comet from the firmament of the Hapsburg Era finally completing its spectral, parabolic course. Now he sought to regain the Hungarian throne by force of arms, and his Royalist troops clashed with the Regent's forces, consisting mainly of university students in civilian clothes, most of whom held a gun in their hands for the first time. The great Battle of Budaörs, which finally put a period to the destiny of the Hapsburgs, consisted of scarcely more than an hour and a half of lackadaisical firing, but Mihály Ursi received a bullet in his upper left thigh—and the wound, the size of his palm, healed badly.

In the year 1923, the Stargazers decided to overthrow by revolutionary means the pseudo-democratic reactionary Horthy regime whose chief pillars were feigned Magyars of German blood, and to establish a really democratic Hungarian republic led by "true Magyars." Sitting in the Café Gugger, Mihály Ursi composed the proclamation which he read in a whisper to his friends, lest it be overheard by card-playing pork dealers at the neighboring tables. We quote a few lines of the proclamation:

> . . . and thrusting aside stupid and hopeless irredentist policies, we seek to live in peace, but in an established economic and military union with our neighbors—Austria, Yugoslavia, Czechoslovakia, Rumania, Bulgaria and Poland—so as to comprise a firm and powerful block in the Danube basin, one hundred and fifty million strong. This we deem the sole defensive bastion for little nations against the constantly recurring attacks of German and Russian imperialism.

We cannot maintain that these wise and farseeing words reflected thoughts original to Mihály Ursi. These were the Cassandra-like prophecies of the aged exile Kossuth at the end of the last century. But in the twenties too the idea of a Danubian federation lived in the manifestoes of a few political writers greatly ridiculed by patriotic parliamentarians and editors who, to use the words of the proclamation, "battened like maggots in the open wounds of the mutilated nation."

Among the Stargazers Jani Hamor was the most ardent. The boys called him "White Top," in part because his glowing optimism painted everything gleaming white, and in part because his skinny six-foot frame resembled a whitewashed pole. Also he never wore a hat, for mixed reasons of health and economy, so that his tumbling pale blond hair always lay lankly on top of his head like a brush freshly dipped in white paint. The hatless brush of hair was always seen bobbing high above the other patrons when he appeared at the revolving door of the Café Gugger. Striding impetuously, he seemed at every step about to fling away his long arms and legs as superfluous appurtenances.

We mentioned that the Stargazers were very poor, but the poorest of all was their own leader, the Major, who slept on a sofa in Hamor's tiny furnished room. This circumstance disturbed White Top's romantic affairs. Hardly had the Major laid his head on the sofa when he began to snore. It was even worse when he stopped, for after a brief and deceptive lull he would begin grinding his teeth and emitting horrible groans and cries, doubtless plagued by wild dreams about the Danube Valley. One night the sofa disappeared from the room. "The landlady took it. She needs it," apologized Hamor. "That's quite all right," said Mihály Ursi. He folded up a carpet, lay down on the floor and in a few moments was snoring.

In those days it happened that the astrophysics professor in whose laboratory Mihály already served as assistant, naturally at the incredibly low salary commensurate with a high post in research, said to him: "Why don't you look up Madame X?" Mihály Ursi's reminiscences refer to the lady in question only as Madame X—out of manly discretion.

In the background of this visit, apart from Mihály's personal housing shortage, was the general housing shortage. The government had ordered that apartments of more than five rooms be requisitioned. Madame X, a widow, living alone in a sumptuous eight-room apartment, had asked her professor friend to recommend a young scholar without a family to whom she could nominally lease three rooms, so as to avoid having to share her apartment with a family composed of many children. The professor's choice fell on Mihály Ursi.

It was plain to Ursi that he was conspiring to nullify a regulation in the interest of social welfare by depriving a refugee family of a roof. But after so much shivering and sleeping on the floor, the rich warm comfort of these lodgings appealed to his lower nature.

Madame X took him by the hand:

"Come, let me show you the bathroom."

Not even in American films had Mihály Ursi seen such wonders. A sunken marble bath, hand towels and Turkish towels, enormous pieces of soap, a scented treasure of silver and gold toilet articles.

"Unfortunately," explained Madame X, "there is only one bathroom in the house so you will have to share it with me."

Had Mihály Ursi possessed an ear for such nuances, he at once might have gathered from the soft lilt of the phrase "share it with me," that Madame X already regarded him as first-rate sexual material. But in those days he had had no contact with such elite circles and imagined that women's romantic proclivities decreased in inverse ratio to their affluence.

The next day, the footman reported certain confidential matters to Madame X regarding the new tenant. In the morning, while brushing Mihály Ursi's suit, he had found half a stale roll in the left-hand pocket of the jacket, and in one of his shoes the eight of spades! At first he conjectured that the young professor might be passionately addicted to cards and carried the eight of spades as a charm, but then he noticed a hole in the sole of the shoe, so undoubtedly the card served as defense against the autumn slush. All this deeply affected Madame X, because she found that the young scientist had a noble brow, smoldering deep brown eyes, and undeniably graceful hands. She was pleased with her tenant's modest yet dignified reserve. By the

51

second week they were having tête-à-tête suppers, heightened by a small convivial bottle of French champagne. After the first such repast, Madame X proposed a game of mah-jongg, then quite the rage, because recently she had read in a novel that the empress Catherine II, while playing taroque with her handsome body-guards, had cheated constantly so they might win. The plump and short-necked empress in this unobtrusive way paid with her gold pieces for certain services not strictly pertaining to the pages of history. Mihály Ursi, however, regarded all games of chance as an idiotic waste of time. So Madame X, when she grew avid for the company of her new tenant, solicited his aid in solving cross-word puzzles. To her amazement, she found that when it came to tantalizingly enigmatic phrases such as: "crossed the Alps with elephants," "the seventh planet," "the Czech exponent of the Danubian Confederation," and like questions of hor-rendous difficulty, the young scholar effortlessly reeled off the answers, displaying proof of the dazzling breadth of his culture.

It was winter again, but Mihály Ursi still wore his light gray summer suit. The only change in his dress was that in his shoe the ace of clubs replaced the eight of spades, and this card in turn gave place to the jack of diamonds. One Sunday all the Budapest papers carried a full-page advertisement blazoning only three words: "Watch for Neumann!" When the imagination of the capital had been strained to the utmost, the great secret was revealed: it was the premiere of the Neumann Department Store, the first American-style fashion shop for men and women.

"Let's get into the Neumann contest," proposed Madame X one evening. The contest promised a complete wardrobe to the author of a winning slogan of less than ten words. Mihály Ursi, then writing his first essay on the duration of the Super Nova, shied at this sort of intellectual competition, but Madame X in-sisted, "just for the fun of it." Making her mouth tiny, she set the tip of her pencil to her pursed lips, arraying her faultlessly cosmeticized features in an expression of profound thought. Mihály Ursi, after a few seconds' reflection, scrawled: "Clothes make the man, but *Neumann* the *new man.*"

Then, stifling a slight yawn, he excused himself and went to bed.

Next week, in choking excitement, Madame X called the laboratory: "Have you heard the news? No? Didn't you read the morning papers? You won the Neumann contest!"

Mihály Ursi's room filled with the marvels of fashion. Six suits of clothes, tuxedos and swallowtails, jackets, a winter coat, a topcoat, a raincoat, hats, caps, silk shirts, pajamas, a wrist watch, an alarm clock, toilet articles, golf sticks, a fishing kit, and objects galore, impossible to enumerate. The Neumann Department Store seemed almost suspiciously generous.

At this time Mihály Ursi did not know that Madame X owned the majority of stock in the Neumann Department Store, that the contest was her idea, and that she had chosen the winner, doubtless in emulation of Catherine II. According to Honoré Balzac, women reach the peak of their physical and spiritual incandescence in their fortieth year. Madame X was approximately that age.

In those Freudian years a Vienna professor wrote that a new kind of poverty was appearing in the modern world—sexual poverty—and that its starving victims sometimes came close to madness.

Mihály Ursi usually returned home late in the night, but the door of Madame X's bedroom was always left half open, and her voice would sound as softly as a Lydian flute: "Good night, Miki!" Mihály, his brain filled with the Magellanic Clouds and the problems of the Danube Valley, after endless arguments in the Café Gugger, would answer only with an absent-minded "Good night, Madame."

One afternoon he was reading in his room when Madame X abruptly entered, then in great embarrassment began running around the room with shy, apologetic little shrieks, desperately seeking for a door. She was stark naked. It hardly seems possible that she could have confused the two doors of the connecting bathroom, one of which led to her bedroom and the other to "Miki's."

She belonged to that category of women who though forty, become sixteen immediately they undress, the explanation for this being that neither on the streets nor in society can they display their shapely little breasts, the white velvet of their thighs

53

or the virginal mold of their loins; on the other hand the most expensive clothes and finest cosmetics cannot hide their wilted lips, bluish teeth or mauve rings under the eyes.

Her sparkling eyes were as black as her dyed hair and her other hairs, which also were dyed a deep black to make an enchanting contrast with her snow-white skin. One must understand that after so many widowed years and unsuccessful "Good night, Mikis" she had to show the secret beauties of her body to the young, shy and innocent scientist.

Their affair began that day. In judging Madame X, we must not think that it was only a matter of famished widowhood on a rampage when she so eagerly pounced upon the young scientist. No, it was far more. She had fallen irretrievably in love with him and determined to become his wife.

A few weeks later she apprised her "fiancé" of hidden intricacies of her finances. Fantastic vistas opened before Ursa Major. It was then he learned about her majority share in the Neumann Store and also about certain Swiss and London accounts indicating that Madame X's fortune exceeded half a million dollars. Her first husband had been an international *faiseur*.

One morning the Major summoned Hamor, and in his old tone of commander-in-chief bade him alert the Stargazers' long-dormant Military and Economic committees. That night he issued the following brief order:

"Establish what can be done with half a million dollars on the basis of the old plans." The boys were astounded by these words, if only because the Major's face showed a four days' growth of beard. They could not know that shortly he planned to marry Madame X and that the beard was to serve as a means of bridging the not-inconsiderable age gap between the prospective spouses.

The Stargazers' Military and Economic committees withdrew to another table, whence, an hour or so later, they returned with detailed calculations showing that half a million dollars was more than sufficient to overthrow the regime. True, the Regent's army during the past three years had grown in strength, but the purchasing power of the dollar had similarly increased, for Hungarian inflation still raged.

The data in our hands is silent on what occurred between

him and Madame X in the few weeks before their scheduled marriage. We know only that when his roommate came home one night, to his numb horror he glimpsed Ursa Major lying on the sofa, deep in the sleep which comes from a serene conscience and also snoring in a fashion reminiscent of the most dreadful nights.

The fact that by the sofa stood the Major's old battered shoes, in one of them the last-used jack of diamonds, indicated that the pilgrim of dreams had brought with him none of the lavish Neumann prizes. He was then twenty-three years old.

Chapter 4

Mature Manhood. Nobel Prize and Bicycle Pump. First European Trip. Encounter with Human Stars.

Snow fell in flakes the size of visiting cards as the train approached Stockholm in a strange blue twilight. Never yet had he been in Stockholm, which in his fantasy occupied the place of the Alexandria of Ptolemy and Callimachus in pre-Christian centuries: high, dizzyingly high above the barbaric world of those days.

At the station he was met by the dwarf Hungarian Minister and by the Swedish Secretary of Education, who headed the Nobel Committee and who was nine feet tall. They escorted him to his hotel in whose countless windows Hungarian flags were draped in his honor, and on the balcony of which was a huge banner: "Welcome Prof. Ursa Major." Photographers' flash-bulbs and the whir of movie cameras followed him to his room, accompanied by mounted policemen in gala uniform to keep back the throng.

At noon, in the seven-hundred-year-old City Hall, there was a banquet of a thousand covers in the splendid Gold Room, where even the tablecloths were of gold-cloth. He sat next to Princess Ingrid, a speaking likeness of the new young prima donna of the Buda Theater. The king wasn't present at this first banquet, because the speeches of Nobel Prize winners were uncensored, everyone saying what he pleased; whereas royal ears are not accommodated to the reception of all sorts of talk. When his turn came, he said:

"Mankind's improved lot will be conceived in the laboratories of research scientists. From this womb composed of glass, nickel, physical and chemical elements, higher mathematical equations and philosophic thoughts, science will present the future with the giant and resplendent children of the Hindu

56

Gilgames legend. The reason our modern world ranks lower, particularly in a moral sense, than the age of Pericles or Saint Thomas Aquinas, is that we have awaited the birth of a nobler future from sterile wombs, degenerate dynasties, ambitious and empty-headed statesmen with their Councils of Five, white-gloved military officers, Turulists, and so-called constitutional parliaments with their motley cohorts of venal representatives. For the past six thousand years these sterile wombs have spawned only blood and filth: hermaphrodite Pharaohs, Machiavellian diplomats and atrociously asinine peace treaties. We have made immense sacrifices in all sorts of wars, meanwhile dragging Galileo to court. If at the end of the past century those six Russian peasants bitten by a rabid wolf had not accidentally been brought to Paris, to this day no one would know the name of 'crazy' Pasteur. The research scientist, by comparison with a country bank director or a suspender-salesman, even today is only a proletarian, the most neglected stepchild of modern society. Only a few men like Nobel are endeavoring to save the honor of our society."

When he resumed his seat in a storm of applause, Princess Ingrid, the king's niece, fervently pressed his hand under the gold tablecloth in a way that seemed more than mere congratulation.

The king made up for his absence at the banquet by giving an intimate supper that evening in his palace. Here, however, there were no speeches.

The etiquette at the Swedish royal court is extremely strict. At receptions the king is always the last to step into the room, and then everyone rises. The reception of Nobel Prize winners is the sole exception. The king, already waiting in the hall, arises as they enter. Through this formality a special respect is expressed for the world of the intellect. The king, when he stood up, seemed tower-tall. From pictorial supplements everybody was very familiar with this nearly seven-foot, gaunt, pince-nezed figure, generally portrayed tennis racket in hand at some bathing resort in Southern France. They were all in formal attire; the king as well, with a ribbon-forest of decorations on his dresscoat. After the playing of the Hungarian anthem, the king approached him, presented him with a great diploma, a weighty gold medal

57

and a check equivalent to thirty-five thousand dollars. Then, confidentially inclining to his ear, His Majesty asked whether he would be willing to marry Princess Ingrid, who had fallen desperately in love with him at the banquet.

Mihály Ursi sat alone in the Café Gugger as he reviewed this dream he had dreamt the previous night on Hamor's sofa. Certain details of the vision approached reality, because in connection with the Nobel Prize conferred on the Danish scientist Johannes Fibiger for his discoveries relative to the origins of cancer, yesterday's papers had described in detail the pomp of the Stockholm festivities.

He sat by the large window of the café, and through the glass and the threads of brown rain looked toward the door of the butcher shop on the other side of the street. He looked in that direction, because it was already three in the afternoon and he still hadn't eaten a thing.

We usually dream about things we have lost. He dreamt about the Nobel Prize because he realized that he would never be a great scientist. His interest in politics was not benefiting his astrophysical studies, and his astrophysical cast of mind certainly did not advance his political career. Though he was an excellent orator, his tenor voice sounding deep and warm, his speeches in the "True Hungarians' Society" were on a too highly philosophical level.

He had become entirely disillusioned with politics, which he felt was based only on the passion and especially on the stupidity of the masses. He felt very bitterly that something was wrong, very wrong, with human society. He felt it as deeply as if it were his own private trouble.

It was. He had already passed his twenty-sixth year, he spoke good German and French, poor English, and he could easily read Italian and Spanish. In the public libraries, which he frequented, he had read everything from Plutarch and Suetonius to Gibbon, Marx and Lenin. He had read H. G. Wells' *Outline of History* three times; he knew more about social science than all the Hungarian congressmen put together. He already had his diploma as an astronomer; but he had no job.

Those were the years of the great unemployment crisis for university graduates in Europe, especially in Hungary. The wise Hungarian government solved the problem. The winter was extremely long and cold, the streets were blocked by deep snow, so the government gave preference at snow-shoveling jobs to those who held diplomas—in the night hours, so as not to shame them. That winter Ursa Major made his living in this way.

The waiters—politely—did not come to his table to take his order. In the waiters of the Café Gugger resided a vast reservoir of psychological insight. The majority of their guests were unemployed young graduates.

It was March, and the snow had already melted away. For three weeks he had not paid his check. He felt his credit had struck rock-bottom. He noted with alarm that the headwaiter was approaching his table without being summoned, pencil and huge leather purse in hand. The headwaiter came close, his face severe.

"I'm sorry, but I can't wait any longer for your unpaid bill. Allow me, Professor, to propose a cash loan to you," he said, opening his large leather purse.

This was the relationship between waiters and intellectuals in Budapest. It is amazing how, under such circumstances, the Café Gugger managed to flourish. We are forced to assume the existence, among the ice-locked arctic regions of modern economy, of hitherto mysteriously uncharted points where the hot springs of humor and warmheartedness operate in the fashion of gold washing. Such loans, sometimes years later, were always paid back with generous tips

Oh yes, the Café Gugger was the abode of youth, high spirits, shining poverty, daring dreams and inexhaustible humor. Ursi had just come back from the lavatory, where ancient custom decreed that squeezed half-lemons be placed in urinals in accordance with certain hygienic considerations. A sign was placed above the urinals, and he recognized Hamor's handwriting: "Please, don't take the lemons home. Thank you." The guests left the lavatory screaming with laughter, Ursi smiled, too, but on this afternoon, looking into the monotonous spring rain, he nonetheless felt that it was a quagmire of slow but certain rot. Not only the Café Gugger, but the whole of Hungary.

The political situation had become consolidated. The new liberal government had established a so-called land reform, rooted out the anti-Semite terrorist elements, and allowed a free press to write violently for or against the rising Hitler. What could the Stargazers fight for? The wind had been taken out of their sails. They rarely appeared in the Café Gugger, and most of them were already married, Joska Kurdi, too. He had settled down in Holod as a carpenter.

Everybody had forgotten the name Ursa Major. He was again nothing but Mihály. Sitting alone in the Café Gugger he thought: I must tear myself away. The words of Horace came to his mind: *"Non mihi rebus conjugere conor!"*—I won't let things get the better of me.

There were still lights in Europe—great lights, but he had never yet been outside of Hungary. He felt he ought to go to Oxford to hear lectures on the astounding new theory explaining why the great Milky Ways were retreating from the earth with almost the speed of light. It would be good to spend a semester or two at the Sorbonne in Paris, and at the Friedrich Wilhelm University in Berlin. And there was that other great question: the fate of Hungary and all Europe. He ought to travel to Prague, to talk with Havlicek, the great Czech spirit fighting against the German danger, who wrote: "If Prussia were a free and constitutional land, we western Slavs might long for union with her. But Russia is a despotism: and alas, we other Slavs must shun our own brother as our greatest foe . . ."

The time had come to transfer the great concept of the Danubian Federation from the table of the Café Gugger to a larger table. In Vienna he ought to look up Count Coudenhove-Kalergi, standard bearer for the concept of a United States of Europe. In Zurich he should look up Romain Rolland, author of *Clerambault, Histoire d'une conscience pendant la guerre,* who had made such remarkable efforts to reconcile the French, German and Belgian viewpoints. In Geneva he ought to take a look at what the League of Nations was doing. He should speak with jovial Litvinov, who looked like an old Russian babushka and was fighting for a peaceful understanding between the Soviet Union and the Western Powers. And in Geneva perhaps he could get to speak with Aristide Briand, whose thin mustache was yellow like that of all true elderly Frenchmen, and who wore his great mane as country barbers arrange their display wigs into which they stick their combs while at work. In vain did revisionist Hungarian papers tear Briand to pieces; in his grumpy heart the concept of European collaboration nestled deep. And he should get to London with certain questions for writers named H. G. Wells and George Bernard Shaw; but that was already so enticing a project that, sitting there in the Café Gugger, it seemed too lovely even for a dream.

Money, a great deal of money, would be needed for such a European tour. Where could it come from?

One, only one way offered itself: prostitution. He had to sell himself. The word *prostitution* exactly expressed the picture which appeared in his misery-laden soul, but in this case we are not to think of it in a physical significance.

For a genuine statesman, for a genuine artist or scientist there can be no compromise—such thoughts were written on his grim face when on that afternoon in the Café Gugger he finally took pencil and paper, and began to sketch the preliminary design for a bicycle pump, because he knew much about the kinetic nature of gases and the behavior of compressed air. He sometimes rented a dilapidated bicycle for a whole Sunday —he adored these solitary soundless flights, surrendering his forehead and thoughts to the swirling breeze—and he would cycle even to Holod, where he would look up Joska Kurdi and his father's old friends and pass the time of day with the aging miners. As he pedaled along, now the front, and now the rear bicycle tire would feebly expire.

In April of 1926, under the trademark U-Pump, he patented his invention, which a bicycle factory immediately bought. The U-Pump functioned splendidly, pumping fresh energy and new possibilities into his life too.

We have no data on his Vienna, Prague and Zurich journeys. We do not know whether he talked with Havlicek, or met Count Coudenhove-Kalergi and Romain Rolland; nor have notes survived to show whether in Geneva at the League of Nations he interviewed French Prime Minister Aristide Briand and Soviet Foreign Minister Litvinov.

61

Of his Geneva impressions only a few lines remain in his diary.

A few well-intentioned French, Dutch and Swedish delegates had already labored long to introduce the Hungarian and Rumanian delegates to each other and, in the atmosphere of a friendly supper, allay the tense hatred between the two nations, which was primarily caused by the fate of the Hungarian minority in Transylvania, now annexed to Rumania. The Dutch delegate accosted the great Hungarian statesman in the corridor of the League of Nations: "Your Excellency, Titulescu is standing there by the pillar. Let me bring him over to shake hands." The Hungarian statesman appraised the situation through the smoke of his cigarette holder, and said: "Not now. Next time." It went on that way for months; meanwhile poor little Hungarian school mistresses were being expelled in droves by Rumanian authorities in Transylvania.

One afternoon the Hungarian statesman was descending the grand staircase of the League of Nations, just as the tall Rumanian was coming up. The Hungarian statesman with the tip of his elbow nudged his Dutch friend: "Now!" The introduction took place, the first handclasp, the first conversation between the two nations. The reason for the long delay proved simple. The Rumanian was nearly seven feet tall—had the introduction taken place in the corridor, Hungary would have had to look *up* at Rumania. On the staircase, however, it transpired that the lanky Rumanian stood two steps lower, and Hungary could look *down* at Rumania. In the corridors of the League of Nations this meeting was discussed for weeks, and everybody lauded the Hungarian delegate's conceit as the most ingenious of diplomatic moves. "What future can such a League of Nations have?" asked Mihály Ursi's diary.

From Geneva he journeyed to Paris. From this period dates a letter to Hamor which, after dealing at length with his Sorbonne professors and their lectures, reads:

I am writing this letter in a café near the Avenue de l'Opéra, perhaps at the same table where sat our poet of fate, Ady, at the turn of the century. Our old professor S. highly recommended this café to me. Paris still preserves

62

something from the Belle Epoque: in this café all the wait-resses are entirely naked except for their colored sandals. When you pay your bill, you put the coins on the very corner of the table and the girls—with gracious belly move-ment—remove the coins without touching them with their hands, feet or mouths. Try the same trick with Ilon, and tell Mr. Gugger that if he introduces the same system, his café will be a tremendous hit in Budapest.

The end of the letter turns to French politics:

The thought has formed in my mind that democracy is the best tailored, finest looking, most comfortable garment. But only for vacations, in the summer and when the sun is shining. If a storm arises, we get drenched to the skin in this lightly woven luxury garment, perhaps even catch pneu-monia. When it begins to thunder and lighten, we must don storm coats and heavy, ungainly black rubber boots. Hun-gary allows the spread of the Hitlerist movement among the German minorities on grounds that everyone may say what he pleases. It is suicidal stupidity to fight with the paper scroll of a democratic constitution against the swords, dag-gers, bombs and propaganda snares of an alien doctrine seek-ing to engulf us.

He transferred his headquarters from France to England. His notes for these months mostly deal with astrophysical studies, and sometimes with his impressions. "Whenever I look at the English way of life and politics, I see myself, as a Hungarian, as though in the curved mirrors in an amusement park, once very tall with mosquito-head, then compressed to a dwarf broader than high." He described his meeting with "the greatest writer of our day" at 10 Adelphi Terrace.

George Bernard Shaw's face was an almost comical cinnabar red, not apparent in his photos, but his very first words were typi-cal of him.

"I am very fond of Hungary. A great nation! She was the first on the continent to produce my earliest plays."

63

Listening to his guest complain of being often embarrassed in London by his poor English, Shaw said solemnly: "Don't let that bother you. In England, no one speaks English correctly, except me."

At the end of their talk, Ursi quoted H. G. Wells, saying: "Christianity is mankind's greatest and finest thought; the only trouble is that it has never been tried."

"I believe," remarked Bernard Shaw, "that Chesterton wrote the sentence. But the aphorism is so ingenious that posterity will attribute it to me."

And from under his great brows, his eyes peered slyly at his young Hungarian guest.

In the spring of 1927 Mihály Ursi took leave of England, and directed his star-seeking pilgrimage toward Germany.

In Calais, he accidentally missed the Paris express. In the town's rectangular main square, every third shop sold champagne. One woman, her eyes shaded dark lilac to the size of small saucers, seized his arm, and holding a black-necked bottle of champagne in her other hand, jabbered and gesticulated. Calais was the center of cheap champagne manufacture. It seemed that the effervescent wine bubbled from the very wells, and they even watered their bullocks with unsalable champagne. The ox-eyed lady demanded seven francs for the bottle and when he said *five!*—she impulsively kissed his ear. The cork popped like a pistol shot. Toward the tiny tables in the deserted little store floated, one after another, the loitering figures in the square, as if sprung to life from the writings of Balzac or Pagnol. There were among them husky-shouldered dock workers and truck drivers, but also others who had the appearance of civil servants, their pointed beards skewered by extremely high, soiled collars; they wore black-ribboned pince-nez, and in the button-hole of one threadbare redingote blushed the ribbon of the Legion of Honor. As many figures, so many splashes of color—pimpled winy noses, sailors' arms with obscene tattooed de-signs. A rumpled old man, with the look of a hobo, seated him-self at the table with an amazingly courtly apology: he described himself as a pomologist, but smelled very badly, and Ursi feared that lice might drop from his beard onto the table. Naturally, he was offered a glass of champagne. Wealthier guests ordered

64

thimble-glasses of brandy, probably on credit, because only after considerable argument, backed by oaths and words of honor, did the ox-eyed lady deign to serve them. During the voluminous discourse, not one was incommoded by the hand-rolled, burned-out cigarette stub dangling from his lips. After reserved and laconic London, after the bearskin-helmeted, sparkling neat guards at St. James Palace, this enchanting, Legion-of-Honor French dirt, enchanted him: the lilting and feverish hum of the French language, where bearded cello tones rumbled and the daggers of sharp words flashed . . . *Dis donc, mais dis donc, tu entres dans mon cul!* . . . and when two men, choking lilac-red, shook fists under each other's noses and one felt that knives or revolvers would be jerked from their pockets, an unexpected word would set off an explosion of laughter. Spirits soared. Someone sat down at the decrepit piano and with smoldering fire began chanting: *"Je ne veux qu'une nuit, une nuit toute entière . . ."* A few voices chimed into the *"Je ne veux,"* then everyone, the terrace, the couples walking on the square. Two minutes later the whole Place d'Armes was singing along with them, and countless heads in open windows joined the chorus; it was as if the Tour de Guet had taken the bass and the bronze tenor of the one-eyed Léon Gambetta's statue had rung out, too. Even the lighthouse sang, while its bright shafts sought to whiten the black sky above the town, though as the brush of light moved on, the sky became even blacker than before.

On the square, the windows of some houses were already mirroring the red-gold light of dawn, when, from the pedestal of the Gambetta statue, Ursi addressed the crowd. Everyone had champagne bottles and glasses in his hands, the two ruddy-cheeked, black-mustached policemen as well, who from beneath their flat gold-braided caps watched over the peace. He commenced his speech by saying that in Germany a maniac named Adolf Hitler was shouting louder and louder, his party was growing, a great danger threatened the free democracies, particularly France. His words provoked such laughter that he could not continue. It was as if the whole Place d'Armes and the very Tour de Guet were rocking with mirth. Only Gambetta's one-eyed bronze face remained grim and distant, as though he were still reflecting on the happenings at Sedan. The crowd began to sing the Marseillaise. They took Ursi to his hotel on their shoulders, but dropped him at least three times along the way, doubtless on purpose, for the French basically detest a foreigner, even if he pays for the champagne. It was a glorious night.

It happened that on that day he was not the sole passenger to miss the Paris express. Two ladies, who had stayed a second and a half too long in the Calais station's rest-room, touching up the rouge on their lovely lips, had to spend the night in the same hotel as Mihály Ursi. But they couldn't sleep for the loud singing and carousing. One was thirty, the other only sixteen, but they were sisters: the Countesses Kristina and Zia Dukay, who were returning home from Scotland. Young Countess Zia climbed out of bed, drew back the curtains a little, and witnessed the inflamed oratory indulged in, on the pedestal of the Gambetta statue, by a young man with lank hair hanging down his forehead, and obviously far from sober: *"Les réactionnaires!* . . . *Les cléricaux!* . . ." and then: *"La liberté!* . . . *L'égalité!"* And it sounded as if he had also shouted: "Kossuth!" But at that instant he tottered and nearly fell from the pedestal.

Mihály Ursi, in May of 1927, arrived in Berlin. In those years giants appeared on the cathedras of modern science in Weimar Germany: Einstein, von Laue, Nermst, Schroedinger, von Johnen, Planck; between classes, along the corridors of Friedrich Wilhelm University sometimes two or three Nobel Prize winners could be seen smoking their cigarettes. Not only German, but Latin, Anglo-Saxon and Far Eastern faces were to be seen at lectures, the scientific Mecca of the globe being represented by Kaiser Wilhelm Institute and Friedrich Wilhelm University. German science held out tremendous prospects for a suffering world. In every laboratory world-transforming projects were in the making, new dietetic vistas, the revolution of plants. The Jewish professor Haber told the Scheideman government: Never fear, with the waters of the sea I shall pay the billions of German reparations.

He spent several years working out in his laboratory an industrial process for separating minute amounts of gold from sea water. Having achieved this, he chartered a boat equipped as a pilot plant and sailed to Brazil, where the ocean was particularly rich in gold.

Nothing seemed unattainable, the Promised Land was within reach, $E = mc^2$, $S = k \log W$, the natural sciences were proclaiming a new gospel.

During the lectures of the professors the students sometimes began energetically scuffing the soles of their shoes on the floor; this was the custom at German universities if students failed to understand the lecture. The professor at once repeated his explanation. It was always the Japanese who most often and most vehemently scuffed with their little shoes. There was a strange and mystic atmosphere of devotion in the classrooms, but sometimes the irrepressible imp of student mischief would pop up his disheveled grinning head. Professor von Johnen announced one of his lectures as "The Instability of Matter"—and when he stepped into the lecture hall and hung his hat on the rack, the iron rack fell with a great clatter from the wall, because deft hands had loosened it so that even the weight of a hat made it fall. All this was a comic demonstration of the instability of matter, but it was likewise youth's eternal revolt against the unendurable weight of authority.

A Hohenzollern sat in an armchair, his great boots crossed, when Mihály Ursi one evening appeared at a musicale in the home of Professor von Johnen. The daughter of the house clamped the violin under her chin, gave it a last tuning, making herself a funny little double chin. Her white-blond hair gleamed in the candlelight, and the candles conspired to evoke a Mozartean atmosphere; some famous name sat at the piano, though you couldn't tell who; melodies fluttered as softly from the violin as the flames from the candle-wicks themselves. *"Ah, wunderbar!"* whispered someone, but still the whole thing seemed a reflection of the *Fräulein's* desire to get married, the sooner the better, if possible as brilliantly and romantically as the candlelight gleaming in her hair. Later Professor von Johnen stepped up to Mihály Ursi: "One of my assistants is a compatriot of yours. Tronfeld. Ernst Tronfeld. *Er hat eine sehr, sehr grosse Zukunft!* Von Johnen raised his great white hands in the air. "Oh, *ein Phaenomen!*" Schroedinger joined them, then Professor Nermst, and now, as they talked among themselves words like these could be heard: *"Ordnungsprinzip . . . Entropia . . . oh, ja Tronfeld . . . Tronfeld ist der einzige . . ."* All this affected Mihály

67

Ursi as though they had already awarded the Nobel Prize to Tronfeld, about whom he had completely forgotten.

The next day he visited von Johnen's laboratory, which bore greater resemblance to a bicycle-repair shop than to the Olympus of modern physics. Before him, in a soiled white work-apron, stood the twenty-six-year-old Ernst Tronfeld. Mihály Ursi long and smilingly shook Ernst's hand, mottled and sticky with oily acids . . . *oh, ja Tronfeld . . . Tronfeld ist der einzige . . .* he perceived a giant in Tronfeld, a giant of the future, and Ernst Tronfeld saw the same sort of giant in Mihály Ursi. So this was Ursa Major, who saved him from the Turulists' hands that dark night in 1920. This was the Ursa Major whose very appearance was impressive—how warmly his voice resounded from somewhere deep in his chest, how frank and spontaneous the glow of friendship in his great brown eyes; behind his smile could be seen the little silver band on his right eyetooth.

After they had briefly but ardently concluded their exaggerated expressions of mutual esteem, they agreed to have supper that evening at Holzer's. In the little restaurant with its white tablecloths a few fancy liqueur and cognac bottles placed at the center of the table continually tempted middle-class guests, but usually in vain. "We'll try this!"—Mihály Ursi lifted a flask toward the waiter—"Let's see what the Hungarian aristocracy is worth." It was the famous Dukay Peach Brandy, the vignette flaunting the Dukay crest, a black millstone on a cordiform escutcheon with double bars dexter and cerulean with argent, topped by the eleven-branched coronet.

The conversation was in the tone of two men of seventy, although they were still only twenty-six and twenty-seven. Their observations winged from the heights of wisdom and experience, for the strength of young generations knows no hesitation or mercy in the pronouncement of judgment.

From the Hungarian aristocracy talk shifted to the European situation, then to the world at large, then to Kant, Nietzsche, Humboldt, Fichte, Hegel, who brought renown to the University of Berlin. Then there were phrases like: "Einstein once said to me . . ." or: "When I discussed this with Bernard Shaw . . ." —and they uttered the names of Shaw or Einstein as though they were deserving of a certain degree of respect, undeniably gifted young beginners, whom one must not, however, take too seriously. From the fate of mankind, to the universe was but a step: they had arrived in their particular realm. ". . . Oh, entropy is greater, far greater, than the energy equation," said Tronfeld; "to my mind Boltzmann is far more than Einstein. Entropy! *Progress* toward something! The ultimate goal of the motions of the universe and concurrently of all living creatures!" Ernst's pencil at first automatically sought to write the entropy formula on the tablecloth, but then he seized the menu and on its margin inscribed: "$S = k \operatorname{Log} W$." It was already two hours after midnight, and the waiter in an apologetic whisper reminded them that closing time was long past. Ernst tried to snatch the check from Ursi's hand—"Please, at least half of it"—but in his words was almost a shiver of fright because, glancing at the check, he saw that his wallet could not manage even half the bill. Fortunately, Ursi insisted.

They were the last guests to leave. The waiter, of Slovak origin, who had only two years of elementary school and had never seen a mathematical equation in his life, noted on the margin of the menu the cryptic symbols: $S = k \operatorname{Log} W$. He cried toward the kitchen: "Say Fritz, was that *Leberwurst* quite fresh?" But no, nothing wrong, next day the two gentlemen came again, in fact ordered *Bayerische Leberwurst* again; once more they were the last to leave, and this time the back of the menu, too, was all scribbled with numbers, diagrams and unfamiliar words. The waiter now kept his eye on them constantly: currency smugglers, spies, Spartacus Communists—that's what they must be.

After closing-time at Holzer's, their stroll took them to distant side streets; they didn't even know where they were as they stopped occasionally in the pouring rain, loudly debating with sweeping gestures, as though their business were urgent and importunate. With their twenty-six- and twenty-seven-year-old youth they were seeking to save the world.

One dawn months later Ernst said: "If once I succeed in finding this substance, would you let me name it *Urstron?*" Urstron? Splendid. A happy and modest fusion of two names: Ursi-Tronfeld. Urstron. Very good word. Excellent. Concise. Anatole France once said that at first nothing occurred to him but the enchanting title, *Révolte des Anges* . . . in that title was as much latent energy as in dynamite; with elementary force the rest of the novel welled up around the title. Urstron! Magnificent. Congratulations! Mihály Ursi still didn't know what Urstron was, but he felt something tremendous behind the word . . . *Oh, Tronfeld ist der einzige* . . .

At the neighboring table a Hanoverian family was celebrating some anniversary; now and again coarse German guffaws would burst above the foaming beer steins. At such times Ernst in the midst of an exposition nervously jerked his agitated face toward them, then to the right, the waiter would drop a platter. . . . "What an accursed racket here! . . . so, in a word, let us proceed from the fact that all explosive materials are unstable by nature and I need only minimal exterior force to upset their equilibrium. If I strike dynamite with a hammer, it explodes. So if I assign myself the task, here in the Café Hamburg, of blowing up a munitions tower say in Vladivostok or San Francisco, the handle of the hammer must be very long, invisible and noiseless, now this substance which I have been working on . . ."

"Leave us alone now," said Mihály Ursi irascibly to the waiter who was wiping the table. Waiters the world over wipe tables when they want to eavesdrop on the conversation of suspicious guests.

"This long handle of the hammer," continued Ernst, "would already be within our reach via electronic waves, the theoretical side gives no trouble—but, and here comes the big But . . ."

Mihály Ursi at the moment was unconcerned with this BUT. Urstron had exploded not a munitions tower in Vladivostok, but his fantasy . . . a country without an army, only a few engineers, and Urstron . . . a weapon which cannot attack, only defend and command . . . what an amazing tool of world peace! War has erupted in Manchuria? Put down your arms! No? And munitions dumps blow sky high, the cartridges in cannon and small arms go off—each soldier's munitions pack begins to crackle; everything explodes, the gasoline tanks of all cars and planes . . . Ernst Tronfeld was taken aback by this explosion of fancy; as a serious scientist he already regretted his mention of the whole Urstron theme. Politics and natural science cannot find room in one brain simultaneously. Ernst with great efforts tried to beg

70

back Urstron from his friend. Long and despairingly he explained the negatives, his arguments playing like fire hoses on Ursa Major's blazing fancy . . . "You must understand that this is only theory, the practical solution is further away than liberating energy from uranium or taking a trip to the moon."

"What about cosmic rays?" asked Ursa Major in a tone implying that cosmic rays might possibly be ordered from the waiter idling by the wall.

"Cosmic rays are too hard, we don't know how to handle them, and know next to nothing about them."

The last night before Mihály Ursi traveled back to Budapest at the end of his great European tour, during a long walk, dawn was breaking and at the far end of Unter den Linden the bronze horse beneath Frederick The Great was already emerging with graceful prancing steps from the morning fog; and still they stood there under the statue, though hoarfrost whitened the November dawn, and who can tell how they got from birth control to the duration of materials—"because, if you consider that quantum curves, after all . . ." In the middle of the sentence Mihály Ursi glanced at his watch: "Forgive me. My train leaves at seven and I'm not packed yet." They clasped hands, looked deep into each other's eyes and embraced.

Tronfeld, though trembling with cold, kept standing beneath the statue of Frederick The Great—till his friend, neck deep in his rolled-up collar, disappeared in the fog. I'll bite off my head if, ten years from now, he isn't president of the new Hungarian Republic, thought Ernst to himself, if for no other reason than that a man would always rather see his own friend as head of state than some stranger.

71

Chapter 5

The Big World and the Little World, Which Proved Greater than the Big World.

The Big World was of course America. In the spring of 1930 Mihály Ursi crossed the Atlantic Ocean on a bicycle, just as he had bicycled through Europe during the past few years. Although the bicycle factory had shifted to a much better T-Pump, he was being sped over the ocean billows by the last labored breath of the U-Pump. Alas, modern inventions wreak frightful carnage among each other just as the Tyrannosaurs and Trachodons millions of years ago in the primeval slime.

He arrived in New York on the sixth of May. In the shivery and nauseating dawn those travelers who now glimpsed America's shores for the first time dragged themselves on deck so as not to miss the moment when, at the blast of insistent boat whistles, somewhat sleepily and grimily, the first rays of dawn finally appeared from the upper bay and, like skillful mechanics in the employ of the universe, set to work with their delicate ultra-violet tools to unwrap the Statue of Liberty from its foggy mists, as though it were a colossal diadem wrapped in some sort of white tissue paper and cotton. Though he detested obligatory thrills, it was a tremulous moment for him when the great statue, with an almost visible movement of greeting, raised its great bronze torch already lit by the rays of morning.

In the blue-gold radiance of May, New York was suddenly revealed to them and obligingly began to rotate its amazing and colossal backdrops before the incoming ship. So this was New York! The expressions on the faces of his traveling companions were transformed as though they were now listening to the crescendo of architecture's greatest symphony in stone, or rather as if they were gazing at some mammoth conflagration: at the height of the clouds, millions of windows glittered with the red rays of early morning. A voice, coming from the sort of man who likes to glorify himself by disparaging everything, said: "What's so wonderful about these skyscrapers? How do they differ from magnified graphs of stock market quotations? Dollar-millions began to boast and outbid each other with the tips of skyscrapers. That's all."

On the pier Ursi was greeted by his American relatives, the Szantos. János Szanto, once a miner in Holod, married the sister of Ursi's father, Borbala Ursi, and a year later, in 1911, they emigrated to the U.S.A. Before descending to the depths of a Pennsylvania mine, János Szanto was advised by a friend of his that for an immigrant the most important thing was to learn the language of the country. Szanto took the friendly advice, caught every word from his fellow miners, and in three years spoke perfect Croatian. Those days his wage was very low, but after ten years of hard labor he succeeded in saving six thousand dollars. He hitchhiked to New York to search for fellow Hungarians on the East Side, and have a good time. He encountered two well-dressed and very sympathetic Hungarian gentlemen, who generously paid for dinner and wine, and then proposed a game of cards. By midnight Szanto had already lost three thousand dollars. When, at five in the morning, the last pennies of his six thousand had disappeared into the pockets of the two well-dressed and sympathetic gentlemen, the miner stood up, tightened his belt, and like a true Hungarian, said: "Well, easy come, easy go." Since then he had been working in a New York hospital as a handyman. Mrs. Szanto worked too, baking and selling very good doughnuts. Their only child Andrew was twelve years old.

After a vociferous meeting with kisses and embraces, they escorted their "famous" relative to a modest hotel, and left him alone to recover.

An hour later the newcomer set out on an exploratory promenade on Fifth Avenue.

At the site of the future Rockefeller Center, he watched for long minutes as huge bulldozers—it was the first time he had seen such machines—plowed their rhinoceros foreheads into little

73

old one- and two-story houses, their frightful jaws biting out bedrooms and kitchens. He saw with his own eyes how the Machine Age was swallowing up the forms of life of the last century.

After lunch he went to a movie, and saw technology's newest wonder, one of the first American "talkies." In his diary he prophesied no future for this invention. Its tinny tones affected him like a very beautiful but very stupid lady who, unfortunately, has opened her pretty mouth. . . . "I still maintain my view: the aim of art is not painstakingly to imitate reality, but to transport us as far as possible from this quagmire. Down with the naturalists!" he wrote in his journal.

Before supper at the Szantos', he asked Andrew to take him to Kossuth Square, which was less than five minutes from Lafayette Street where the Szantos lived in Brooklyn. He told Andrew how the exiled Lajos Kossuth arrived in December 1851 at New York harbor after the failure of the Hungarian war for liberty. Kossuth had been met by a tremendous cheering crowd. People jammed Broadway and all New York's church bells were ringing.

As they started home, the astronomer stopped a passer-by:

"Excuse me, I'm a stranger here. Could you tell me, sir, why they call this Kossuth Square?"

The man looked down at the sidewalk.

"Ko-suth . . . I think it's some Indian word."

"Thank you so much."

By the time they got home, the goulash was ready, which Mrs. Szanto cooked in the yard by an open fire, the kettle hanging from a trestle, to remind them of the Magyar *puszta*. They had only one other guest, old Uncle Imre, whom Mr. Szanto introduced this way:

"Here you see the wisest fellow from the Austro-Hungarian Monarchy, because in 1897, when they called him to the colors, he chose New York instead of the Budapest barracks. Tell Mihály how you became a head chef."

"Well, son," began Uncle Imre, who looked like a rich man, "back home I was a traveling salesman—men's fashions, shirts, ties, and fine rubber suspenders, quite a novelty in those days. When I got off the boat here in New York with the big crowd

74

of other immigrants, some agent yells: 'Any cooks?' I raised my hand quick, though I never was in a kitchen except if the cook was female, young and pretty. So I got work right away. They kicked me out of the first joint in an hour. From the second, only next day, from the third, only five days later. And now, my son, I am the owner of one of New York's biggest restaurants."

Mrs. Szanto lovingly put her hand on Uncle Imre's shoulder and said in her high-pitched voice:

"This good man is even more famous for giving the American language its only Magyar word: *goulash*. Americans can thank him that instead of goulash they are fed old chopped-up suspenders. Right, Imre dear?"

"That's right," nodded Uncle Imre modestly.

"Now have a taste of *my* goulash!" cried Mrs. Szanto, beaming proudly as she served the steaming plates.

"For immigrants," Ursi wrote in his diary "the United States is like a strange magnetic field in which people change their original specific gravity. They become stone-men who sink immediately to the depths, and bubble-men who bubble up to the tops of the skyscrapers. Uncle János is a stone-man, and Uncle Imre is a bubble-man."

His trip to Washington in the following days embraced very far-reaching political plans.

The Anglo-Saxon word *hobby* is difficult to translate into any language. There are those who collect only seashells of the *Xenophora pallidula* variety and take round-the-world trips in the hope that on some tropic coast they may locate the fingernail-sized shell still missing from their collection. And there are politicians who become specialists in the tax system prevailing in Afghanistan or among the Kapingamarangi Islanders. In those years two American senators were profoundly concerned with the questions of Hungarian revisionism.

The meeting took place in a suite of the Hotel Willard. Ursi elucidated his old dream of the Danubian Confederation to the two senators. He explained that the still feudal Hungarian regime, through a bloodless *coup d'état*, had to be transformed into a democratic republic before the country, with its festering revisionist wounds, became a tool of the Germans. Hitler was

75

shouting louder and louder, his party expanding. England and America had to make order in the Danube Basin before it was too late.

"American capital," he said, "could make excellent investments by buying up all the natural treasures of the Danube Valley; oil, bauxite, warm springs and much else. It could build hotels for the growing tourist trade, and create a power and irrigation system whereby the Danube and its tributaries would clasp in a natural and powerful embrace the economic entity of Austria, Czechoslovakia, Hungary, Yugoslavia, Bulgaria, Rumania and Poland. The diligent millions inhabiting these lands would greet such economic 'servitude' with boundless joy. In the days of modern press and radio a clever propaganda can lead the masses to hell or heaven. These millions of workers and peasants care nothing for power politics; believe me, gentlemen, they want only water for their fields, better tools and slightly higher wages in the factories. They only want to live, work and perhaps bowl a little Sunday afternoons. And they would like to raise their children in peace."

The two senators patiently listened to the arguments of the young Hungarian scholar who had been recommended to them by Sir Thomas Harcourt, the great Oxford professor of astronomy. "Dr. Ursi" spoke English quite well—only the words *weapon, nevertheless* and *theater* betrayed his Kapingamarangian origin.

"England and America," continued Dr. Ursi, "behind the economic scenes must build the Danube Valley into a powerful bastion between German and Russian imperialism, much like Metternich's monarchy, but naturally within a modern democratic framework. Numerous and well-staffed 'police' cadres must be organized. It is essential at once to manufacture heavy artillery. Planes and tanks are needed by the army of the Danubian United States. In this federation each little nation would be represented in a joint parliament, but in all political, military and economic questions its 'advisors'—the three great powers, France, England and the United States—would have the final say. To such a solution, believe me gentlemen—I am a man of the people—all the little nations in the Danube Valley would

76

willingly subscribe. The Nazi hawk hovers more and more threateningly above us. We chicken nations always had to flee under the wings of the hens."

Sometimes he jumped up from his chair, the swing of his sentences throwing him now toward the wall, then the window. At such moments the mute spectacles of the senators followed the quickly moving figure whose necktie, suit and shoes were rather shabby, whose hair, especially around the ears, was ripe for a little chat with the barber's scissors. He seemed to be flying in clouds but undoubtedly there was a cold logic in his talk, and at the same time the heat of a visionary faith.

"Senators! Conceive of this bloc of one hundred and fifty million people in the Danube Valley as a tremendous tank. This tank of colossal strength now sprawls rusting in some twelve pieces being fought over raucously by junk dealers calling themselves statesmen. Trust us, trust the people, and we will rout these crooked politicians—*les marchands de la gloire!* You will have no more to do than assemble the parts and oil them a little."

"How much would that oiling cost?" asked the younger senator, a furtive smile in the corner of his mouth.

Mihály Ursi consulted the memorandum in his hands, which had been diligently prepared by the Stargazers' financial experts.

"Twelve billion dollars. Do not be surprised, gentlemen, at the lowness of the amount. You must remember that in these countries the purchasing power of the dollar is still phenomenal."

The two senators exchanged glances. With cordial handshakes they thanked him for the "interesting, but really very interesting" exposition. The minute and a half during which Mihály Ursi gathered up his maps and during which only the rustling of paper sounded, seemed strikingly long, almost distressing.

"Nice fellow," said one senator after closing the door behind their guest.

"Ye-es," mumbled the other, then adding in a tone that might equally have been praise or disparagement: "He is an astronomer!"

While still in America Ursi received news of his appointment as assistant director of the National Institute of Astronomy in Budapest. This modest but secure position could not have come at a better time.

We have hardly any biographical data relating to the next few years. From the fact that in 1932 he discovered a new star near the constellation Andromeda we must conclude that in those years he was again completely immersed in his scientific studies. It seems probable that the Washington failure banished from his soul, once and for all, the fine dreams of the Danubian Confederation. But in 1933, reading Franklin D. Roosevelt's book, *Looking Forward,* he planned that some day he would write the Hungarian "New Deal."

That summer he was able to save enough from his salary to spend his vacation at a little Italian bathing resort. His choice fell on Mandria, whose modest prices and isolation seemed to favor work on his book entitled *The Great Fallow.*

Mandria, not far from the Dalmatian shores, was the single and extremely dirty fishing village on the tiny island of the same name. This did not prevent the Hotel Varcaponti's and the Pension Zanzottera's advertisements from referring to Mandria as an international watering place. Nowhere is the human community warmer, more colorful and intriguing than at such an "international watering place" where bathrooms have not even been heard of. From the hills at dusk floats the fragrance of olive groves, and the Adriatic turns into a single giant opal. In the cool shade of the wild-grape arbor in the courtyard of the Hotel Varcaponti one works undisturbed even in the daytime.

Mandria was the little world which in Mihály Ursi's life proved greater than the Big World. In Mandria the recollection of the two American senators faded away, and dwarfed to insignificance was the radio's great sensation that Dollfuss, the Austrian chancellor, had been murdered in his office by Nazi putschists. In Mandria even the constellation Andromeda dwindled to nothingness when on the Corso Mussolini appeared a young lady in a daringly scant bathing dress, her body still bedecked with saline pearls left by the blue waves from which she had emerged.

It all started when early one morning he went rowing on the mirror-smooth sea. His coat lay before him on the front seat

78

graphic artistry in Paris had been lavishly paid to teach her the principles of lighting, the laws of composition, the relation of background to predominant figures and forms, the subtle accent of poetic and musical statement of a glorious sunset or a pair of old shoes. Even a snapshot could be as high art as a canvas of Rembrandt or a poem of Baudelaire, and the flight of a gull could resound like an octave by Chopin.

But all this was an unreal world in Mandria. Only a real human being is able to give us the perfect illusion of final security, only a human being's voice, look, the touch of his hand affects us like a clear and consoling message of the universe in which we are so small. This man could be a friend, a doctor, rarely a parent, more rarely a sibling, but without exception anybody who has fallen in love with us. Passionate love, gleaming toward us, is like a magnifying glass which enlarges our ever-aching sense of smallness, and makes visible values in us we did not sense before. If this magnifying glass happens to break, we weep at the loss of the optical illusion about ourselves.

So Zia, in her exile in Mandria, had been weeping not so much for Filippo, but for herself.

Then came the astronomer. Another magnifying glass? More, much more than that—the huge lens of Mount Wilson's telescope. From his brown eyes poured such light that sometimes Zia closed her eyes and shivered. The deep tone of his voice, too, was full of this strange warmth. His tenderness, his considerateness, was different from that of Filippo and the other playboy aristocrats. More primitive but more intuitive, more colorful and more pliant, though in his behavior there was a definite toughness. When the question arose whether to go fishing or rowing, whether Zia should wear her blue sweater or her brown sport jacket, whether she should or shouldn't send a wire on Otto Hapsburg's birthday, it was always his will which triumphed. At such moments Zia felt the sweetness of obedience, though she considered herself, not without reason, very strong and independent. When once, with a little laugh, she confessed it to Mihály, a philosophical explanation followed. The thirst for obedience is eternal in every human soul. We have denied it since the Reformation and the great French Revolution, but the truth is that we are weak and cowardly in all things which are concerned with our

81

inscrutable fate, and we are always thankful for a seemingly reliable hand which pushes us toward a decision. He added that, unfortunately, dictators build their power on this thirst for obedience in the human soul.

Zia had already decided in Mandria to marry Mihály. Now, at this first meeting in the Septemvir Utca palace she told him.

But Ursi shook his head in refusal. Teréz Hemli, yes, but the Countess Terézia Dukay, no! The manuscript of *The Great Fallow* was already at the printers. What would the Stargazers, and the millions of landless peasants in whose interest the book was written, say if the author, their apostle, were to marry into that very hundred-thousand-acre feudal estate which the book attacked most violently? Treason, treason, treason! Again someone had betrayed the Magyar people.

The Great Fallow appeared and had such huge success that the courts of the Horthy regime sentenced the acclaimed author to a year in prison.

After his release he took to wife Countess Terézia. The marriage was received with mixed sentiments by the members of the Dukay family.

Chapter 6

In the Eagle-Nest. Journey to Moscow. The Angry Angel
Beats Her Drum Again.

To know something more about the Dukay family, we
must go back to Asia. Thousands and thousands of years ago,
north of the Ural Mountains the Ostyaks were peace-loving
fishermen and reindeer breeders, who were oppressed by a nomad
Turkish race. These horse-riding ancient Turks, the eagles of
the steppes, always attacked the weaker races in the immense
theater of Asia's plains from Korea to the Black Sea for gold,
for women, for food, but especially for slaves. The Hungarian
nation originates in great part from the oppressed Ostyaks and
the restless, imperialistic ancient Turks. The Ostyaks became the
Hungarian peasantry, and the Turks, the nobility and aristocracy.

The Hungarians appeared in Europe in the ninth century
when, after Attila's unsuccessful attempt to dominate the world,
the infinite plains of Asia still poured into the West the polyglot
nomadic races whose numbers dangerously increased as their
pastures in Asia decreased. The terrific pressure of Asia's swollen
population had already crushed the Roman Empire and Charlemagne's great Frank kingdom—in these chaotic centuries the
westward migrating oriental tribes were both pursuers and pursued.

"Here we will stay!" said Árpád, who headed the seven
Hungarian tribes, riding his snow-white horse and surveying
the middle of the Danube Valley with his sharp eyes under his
eagle-feathered iron helmet. Infinite green pastures, ancient oak
forests, hordes of bison, moose and boars, clouds of wild fowl,
the rivers full of huge sturgeon, hot springs on the shores, rich
golden, silver and copper veins in the rocks, and this earthly
paradise was surrounded by the wonderful and inaccessible natural fortress of the high Carpathians.

But all these treasures did not reveal their dark secret—Árpád could not see into the future, he did not know that he stopped on the very threshold of West and East, and in the coming millennium his small nation would have to fight with two swords in hand for its life and liberty, westward against the Germans, and eastward against the Tartars, Turks, and Russians.

In these days of the Hungarian incursion, Chieftain Ordony, the first ancestor of the Dukays, established the family fortune by the right of *primo tenure* on land. During long centuries the Ostyak slaves and the Turkish lords frequently intermarried, still later the Dukays married into German, Italian, French, English, Russian and other aristocratic families of Europe, but Zia's father, István Dukay, preserved the dominant characteristics of some ancient khans and sultans.

The aging but still handsome lord of Ararat, the popular Count Dupi, whose flamboyant gestures, whose affairs with peasant virgins, stage stars, and queens had grown into exaggerated legends at the Café Gugger's and country casinos' tables, to everybody's surprise, gave his blessing to Zia's marriage with Mihály Ursi, "the communist peasant," "the crazy astronomer." Count Dupi liked Zia, "the cricket," best of his five children, but when Zia, on the day of the wedding, fulfilled the condition of her marriage contract, and distributed her dowry, the three-thousand-acre domain, Terézia Manor, among the landless peasants of the region, Count Dupi shut his door in her face. This manor was the most ancient part of the Dukay lands, coming down from the time of Chieftain Ordony.

Zia's mother, *née* Princess Klementina Schäyenheim-Elkburg, called by everybody *die gute Menti*, was a living encyclopedia of saints' biographies; she knew who the sisters of St. Zozimus were; why, when and how the bearded St. Teophanus was beheaded by the heathen. She could talk ingeniously for hours about the economic and spiritual problems of world Catholicism, but when somebody turned the conversation to the theater, she remained silent, since she was not altogether sure whether Molière was still living or not.

Countess Menti used to stand on Buda street corners distributing Bishop Zsigmond's leaflets entitled "Why Has the Bible Endured?" to the well-dressed, dignified criminals enjoying

84

a walk in the sun. *Die gute Menti* was exactly like those Florentine virgins of Fra Angelico dwelling forever at heaven's gate.

From the icy heights of the Schäyenheim-Elkburg princedom she regarded Zia's marriage as an accident or an incurable disease by God's will, and cooled down toward Zia with genteel forgiveness. Confusing always the word *astronomer* for *gastronomer*, she treated her "great scientist" son-in-law with the same exaggerated tenderness and love as she did Herr Jordan, the chief butler, because she lived in a constant but perfectly controlled fright that Jordan, who was indispensable in the household and had the air of some strange dignity, one day with a big kitchen knife would kill the whole family and set the castle on fire.

The eldest son in the family, Count Rere, was born an idiot in 1895. Now, over forty, he still had the brain of a four-year-old child, and he strayed around the huge park of Ararat like a perfectly trained, harmless animal, not quite housebroken. He had a benevolent, ever grinning horse-face. He insisted summer and winter on wearing jackets, striped trousers and a derby, but no shoes. Over his shoulder was slung a large leather case for binoculars, in which he used to keep blackberries, sometimes a dead magpie, and sometimes live young rats. Rere loved everything and everybody on earth, and he was loved by everybody. Unintentionally, he made everybody laugh at even the most tense and bitter moments. In his trouser pockets there were always several pounds of large, rusty storeroom or small fine Wertheim keys, which had disappeared mysteriously from the castle.

Rere was in his upmost happiness when he learned that "Ziza" would again have a "hubsband." On the occasion of Zia's first wedding with Prince Filippo, he sent to Zia a huge bouquet of wildflowers which also contained molted pheasant and crow plumes, toadstools and an old brush sodden with dried paint. Now he wrote a very long letter which began: "my Beloved ziza and Mlhiaylhy! On this blessed Ocassion I Wish you the best occasion . . ." His letter was accompanied by his carefully selected gifts: for Zia two large rusty keys and one of Kristina's old hats, and for Mihály the family doctor's walking stick.

Kristina was born in 1896. At the age of sixteen, during

an elaborate reception on Bösendorferstrasse in the Vienna Dukay palace, attended by the elite of the Monarchy, Kristina's first poem "The Goose-Girl," recited by a great tragedienne of the Burgtheater, was greeted by stormy applause. She was much, much more beautiful than the poem. Later in a parlor game she had to retrieve her forfeit with a kiss from a twenty-four-year-old captain of the Brandeis Dragoons who happened to be the Archduke Charles, the heir presumptive. A few weeks later a fortune-teller told her: "Someday you will hold the king's heart in your hand." In 1922 this prophecy came true when, in Madeira, the Portuguese doctors, Leito Monteiro and Nuno Porto, in accordance with ancient Hapsburg traditions, removed the heart of the last Hapsburg emperor, Charles IV—the Countess Kristina, who had followed her eternal and hopeless love, the king, to exile, held the silver platter on which the dead king's heart was placed. Since then Kristina had been aimlessly wandering around the world. She won a contest in Biarritz for "the world's most beautiful chin." One could see her frequently in the company of Alfonso, the abdicated king of Spain, who stole her heart, and then with a Balkan tobacco king, who stole her jewels. In family circles she was always mentioned with an *Ach, Kristina!* Two years later she settled down in a remote wing of the huge Ararat Castle, and started to write her long-dreamed-of novel, *The Ordony Chieftain*, which she planned in ten large volumes. She never liked things on a small scale. Now, at the age of forty, she was still beautiful, though her graying hair was untinted, her fine profile resembling a withering water lily in the park's fish-pool.

She regarded Zia's marriage as a romantic revolt, ". . . ach, a rhapsody of depth and height, science and aristocracy." Among other things she liked her new astronomer brother-in-law because she was an ardent astrologer.

The next Dukay child, born in 1898 was—finally!—a boy. "Finally," because Count Dupi was already anxious over who would be the heir apparent to the whole entailed wealth and estate. The boy inherited the physical and spiritual characteristics of his grandmother, the last member of the extinct Zoskay family. His nickname became Ostie, because whenever Count

Dupi looked at the short-necked, thick-set boy, he would say: "He doesn't look like a Dukay. He is an Ostyak."

Ostie was a rebel against the way of life of his feudal "Turkish" father. He did not drink, he did not gamble; instead of ladies' locks, he collected diplomas. He was a liberal, an anti-Hapsburg, and an anti-German. He married the American Miss Gwen Steele. During his wedding banquet in Ararat, Countess Menti turned to her new American relative Julian K. Steele, the bride's father, manager of a Chicago packing house, and, with the air of a Princess Schäyenheim-Elkburg, graciously inquired about the current price of snake and dog meat in the Chicago markets. Before Julian could collect himself to reply, Ostie tenderly informed his mother that she had mistaken Chicago for Peking.

Before Ostie knew Mihály Ursi, he was very anxious because he adored Zia. But at his first meeting with Mihály, Ostie immediately recognized in him the three most important qualities of a man: strength, honesty and talent.

Ostie's younger brother was quite a different type: tall and thin, he inherited the Schäyenheim-Elkburg features. On the photographs from his childhood he is a perfect blond cherub out of a Königsberg fairy-story book. At seven he already hated Ostie for the simple reason that not he but Ostie was the heir apparent. Countess Menti was pleased to get a wonderful tutor for him, a soft-spoken, highly educated young scholar from Vienna, who from the first moment adored Johy so much that one night, still lecturing about Metternich's policy and Grillparzer's poetry, he climbed into Johy's bed. He was a homosexual.

In the letters patent when the Dukay entailment was founded in 1826, it was stipulated that the heir to the entail must marry a lady with at least sixteen paternal and maternal ancestors from the highest degree of aristocracy. When Ostie married Gwen Steele, Johy armed himself with lawyers, but lost his case. Knowing this, we can imagine what was Johy's reaction to Zia's marriage to Ursi, who had even fewer aristocratic ancestors than Miss Steele.

Zia was the youngest of the family.

After the marriage the new couple moved to a modest flat

in Buda. Zia opened Zia Photos, and became a professional photographer. The prison sentence had deprived Mihály Ursi of his position with the National Institute of Astronomy. He lived on the uncertain honorariums derived from his scientific and political articles.

But their marriage was very happy. It was a great diamond, fine-cut and glowing with inner fire, atop the huge rubbish heap of rotting sexual, religious, and ideological conflicts of modern marriages. So exceptionally perfect was it that we find it necessary to study thoroughly the vast library of books devoted to the world literature on problems of marriage with a view to ascertaining what might have been the secret of Mihály Ursi's and Zia Dukay's beautiful, passionately ardent yet wondrously harmonious union. Unfortunately, books such as *The Secret of a Good Marriage, Philemon and Baucis, The Rosary of Marriage*, are mainly written by sacrosanct bishops or the old-maid presidents of women's societies who in unctuous words distribute advice, and graciously exhort apoplectically raging spouses to show each other kindness. While these authors never had a sexual life, and hold the double bed no more important an article of furniture than the kitchen table, another group of authors falls into the opposite extreme. Proliferating dangerously in Freud's wake are the "psychoanalysts," who in unfamiliar "private universities" secure fancy diplomas at bargain rates within a few weeks and after bidding adieu to their honest civil vocations as watchmakers, bird dealers and corn surgeons, in more profitable and distinguished psychoanalytic offices destroy human souls. *Psychosomatic Prophylaxis, Secrets of the Rhythm of Coitus*—the publication of such books in millions of copies can be explained by the fact that they look at the problem of marriage purely from the sexual side.

The perusal of this extensive world literature yields but a single instructive sentence, one written by Karinthy, the Hungarian Mark Twain, in the album of a distinguished lady: "Man and woman can never understand one another, because each wants something different: the man the woman and the woman the man." The lady in question found this apothegm highly imbecilic, being unaware for one thing that even the wittiest sayings of Montaigne or Goethe are separated only by a hair from the grossest idiocy, and for another, that this deep ironic wisdom expresses the most that can be said regarding the insanely complicated problem of marriage.

We shall nevertheless endeavor, in possession of the facts of Mihály Ursi's and Zia Dukay's exceptionally happy marriage, to delineate the importance of three crucial factors.

1. *The attraction of opposites.* In the world literature of marriage we find theories that blond attracts brunette, the short the tall, the fat the thin, the passionate the phlegmatic, the young the old, the poor the rich, the Mohammedan the Greek Orthodox, the Jewish the Christian, the Slav the Latin—all of which to our mind is nonsense. In Mihály Ursi's and Zia Dukay's happy marriage the attraction of other opposites functioned. Mihály Ursi saw in Zia the cut flower of highest aristocratic breeding and refinement, the fragrance of which was amazingly pervasive even in a house apron amid the palate-tickling odors of the little kitchen in the Buda flat. Carlyle wrote that the dandified one-time country lawyer Robespierre deep in his soul felt such unendurable respect toward French aristocrats that he preferred to guillotine them all. Whatever we may say, there are mysterious lineaments of aristocracy from which no one can withhold his awe. At the same time, Zia, completely disillusioned with the aristocracy's empty and decadent way of life, saw in her husband the resplendent and giant child of the Hindu Gilgames legend. He was an emissary from proletarian depths, fresh in strength, noble of spirit if only because she herself comprehended neither relativity nor the entropy theory, nor the difference between the American Republican and Democratic parties, nor the background of Moscow's immense and bloody purge. They constantly looked up to each other.

2. *Religion and ideology.* The two most dangerous diseases of marriage, religious and ideological conflict, were not present in their lives. Both were Roman Catholics. Zia cherished the faith of her childhood nurtured in the exquisite little chapel of Ararat Castle like some extremely fragile crystal goblet, a most venerable and priceless family heirloom which by outward and inner commandment she must always carry with her carefully and tenderly wrapped. It was something not of great use in

everyday life, but there were hours when the soul stepped from the aching body as from a soiled nightdress, and at such times the little crystal goblet filled to the brim and one could drain to the last drop its miraculous balm. Zia never missed the first Mass Sunday mornings at the Chapel of St. Rita in Buda, but during Bishop Zsigmond's very lengthy sermons—she herself did not understand this strange association—her thoughts inevitably strayed to the recipes in the French cookbook *L'art de bien manger*.

Mihály Ursi, like the majority of natural scientists, did not believe in God. More exactly, his concept of God was different from that of most religions.

He imagined the Ultimate Secret as a blank tablet on which everyone can write what he pleases. Whatever he may write— Immaculate Conception, The Eight Paths of Buddhism in the chalked inscription of Gautama Siddhartha, $E = mc^2$, or the theory of quantum curves, all were no whit nearer the solution. Dull are the natural scientists who look down upon little peasant women hurrying to church, hearts joyous with the miracle of the wedding feast at Cana, and dull the clerical souls who in every Galileo see an atheist, because he reacts to their dogmas with a mild forgiving shake of the head. Once at a poker party Zia witnessed her uncle Bishop Zsigmond examine with a trembling hand his last card, which was just what he had hoped for. He looked up at the ceiling and said: "There *is* a God!"

"Let's not laugh at His Eminence's innocent slip of the tongue," remarked Mihály. "When I reflect that at the Beginning of the Beginning, when in the dark and frigid Void only shimmering gases swirled, through the accidental effect of some enormous heat or pressure two hydrogen atoms turned into an atom of helium and through a like accident amid the uncontrollable turmoil of energies the quantum curves of all the elements came into being, when in the primeval slime from the single and accidental meeting—one chance in quintillions—of elements thus far unknown to us the first minute spark of life flamed up; when I reflect that in our lottery tickets, virus infections, auto accidents or even our meetings with our future mates *chance* is continually at work, then I am inclined to call God, Chance, the great wondrous Chance whose omnipotent power to create or destroy, give or withhold, alike determines the fate of galaxies and bacilli. I believe in my own God."

Their ideology was identical. Mention of Hitler's name gave them both the ague. Generally speaking, both believed in Western democracy, Mihály with some reservations and an occasional sharp criticism, Zia, in her casual acquaintance with politics, rather on the basis that among her brothers she best liked Ostie.

No financial questions could arise between them, for both worked for a living and now Zia, too, was without a fortune.

3. *Physical health and sexual harmony.* In the world literature of marriage counsel we agree with a Paraguayan author who writes that a physical defect in one spouse, an amputated hand or foot, tuberculosis or cancer are far lesser obstacles to true tenderness than perspiration of the hands, halitosis, picking the nose, chewing nails or other bad habits easily overcome by a little will power before we drive our beloved mate to the madhouse or suicide.

A Lithuanian author writes as follows: "Wedded couples should beware of straying into perversities the natural outcome of which is that after gratification they not only detest each other's bodies but themselves too. The foundation of lasting happiness is not merely normal and moderate sex life but ever-present modesty. A pretty little slipper is far more enticing than a naked foot, which is perfect in only the rarest instances. The same holds true for diaphanous nightgowns."

Under the pseudonym "Anada" a distinguished Spanish lady gives the following advice to women: "We should show gentle resistance even if fainting with desire. Just as the highest culinary art knows the refined use of special and rare spices, so in minuscule amounts and with the same high art must we apportion the necessary sexual spices to marriage, in most cases we may only hint at them. Do not at once sit in your husband's lap and begin to bite at his earlobes when he returns home tired from work. Only put your spices in the soup when it nears the boiling point. During a long and happy marriage it was always my time-tested artifice before going to sleep, when leaning over my husband in putting out the light, to let the nipple of my breast just graze his forehead or the tip of his nose ever so slightly and ticklingly, and always as if it were but an accident."

We have quoted these excerpts because only in negative fashion can we deduce the inner secrets of Mihály's and Zia's exceptionally happy marriage—of which naturally we can know nothing.

They lived quietly in their little home on a steep and picturesquely beautiful street in Buda. In the evenings Zia would come home tired from her studio, Zia Photos, which began to yield better returns than her husband's astronomical and other articles published by Hungarian and foreign journals. Zia broke contact with her old aristocratic circle. Only Kristina visited them frequently.

In September 1936, with great radiance a new and amazing Super Nova appeared in the firmament of their marriage: Zizi was born.

In the summer of 1937, Kristina, whose resolves were always swift and extraordinary, turned up at their home one afternoon with the words: "Let's go to Moscow." In those years the Intourist Bureau, with headquarters in Warsaw, shipped trainloads of inquisitive visitors to the Soviet Union.

We find it particularly important to learn with what feelings Ursa Major looked upon the Soviet Union in 1937. There are many notes about their Moscow journey in his diary.

We have named Kristina *Propuska* after the Russian word meaning a small official slip of paper before which all doors open. Without Kristina we couldn't even move. She is an enchanting Propuska on two legs—and what attractive legs—knowing everyone, beguiling everyone. To her the American ambassador was just Joe, Voroshilov only "Hello, Marshal." We hardly spend anything. Kristina acts like the ambassador of the universe, carrying us to diplomats' luncheons and suppers, to the summer places—*dashas*—of commissars, as if we were her gloves. Naturally she obtained excellent tickets for the great Sports Parade at which we got a close look at Stalin, who was reported in Budapest to be ill of cancer and dying. A wish-dream of certain circles! Stalin seems a strong and healthy man. Sometimes he turned to whisper to his entourage, who would laugh at his evidently jocose remarks. Strange, seeing him in the flesh I had the feeling that he very much resembled my father, particularly his forehead and mustache.

On this day Moscow was arrayed in red flags, in portraits of Lenin and Stalin the size of house walls. From the façade of a government building a 35-foot plaster statue of Lenin hung high above the street. I have witnessed such hero worship only in the advertising of film stars on Broadway.

Even more astounding was the parade of some fifty thousand soldiers and civilian athletes. Group colors were borne by girls in their hair, by young men in their hands— they gave the impression of a giant live flower garden rolling on in a wondrous unending flood of youth, beauty, health and strength. God in heaven, what an uninhibited wellspring for the increase of population! Then came four thousand athletes from Asia's farthest reaches—what Mongol, Turkish, Tartar, Uzbek and Ostyak faces!—a hundred and twelve varieties of mankind dwell in this gigantic realm. And their music. Huge ox-horn trumpets, soft reedpipes, primitive drums: millennia of the East resounded on these instruments as they tossed into the air their sharp curved swords in ancient religious dances. Already at the ballet performances in the Opera we had observed that Russians have the gift of blending mass motion and color with breathtaking artistry. Never had I thought to see the Soviet people in such a mammoth revelation of flower and song.

His visit to the Soviet Academy convinced him that the Kremlin was far more liberal to science, particularly to basic research, than Western states generally. Professor P. enjoyed a monthly salary of 20 thousand rubles. For his finely tailored suit of choice material he paid but 1,200 rubles. He had a villa on the shores of the Black Sea. All this exceeded von Johnen's pay in Berlin, Harcourt's at Oxford, or Professor Klimm's at Mount Wilson. The Hungarian government supported all research at the University of Szeged with exactly the same sum as was needed to outfit a single Hungarian recruit.

93

On the streets and in the general outward aspects of life there is no trace of the theme of feverish conversations at diplomatic soirées: the fearful and ruthless momentum of the purges within the Party and the Army. On June 12 they shot Marshal Tukhatchevsky and seven of his generals, all so-called "Soviet heroes." In distant parts of the Soviet Union, too, trials are being speeded, whispered rumors set the number of executions at many thousands, including people's commissars, ambassadors and persons in the very highest posts. More than a hundred thousand prisoners await their uncertain lot in jail.

All this is in defense against Hitler's fifth column. It has already penetrated deep into the Soviet Union. Stalin is right. These accused were aiding Hitler. It is also time for our government to strike at Nazis back home.

At the lovely little theater built for the foreign diplomatic corps, in comfortable roomy armchairs, from alongside tea tables they viewed the Soviet film *Peter The Great*. Needless to say, their invitations were obtained by Propuska. Kristina and Zia saw only the artistic side of the film. They were enchanted—rightly so—by the direction, the *décor*, and especially the splendid actors.

"The film awakened curious thoughts in me," Ursi wrote. "Why pick Peter The Great? This film is the heroic epos of Russian imperialism. Could this be the true face of the Kremlin?"

After a two-week sojourn in Moscow they returned to Budapest.

The events of 1938 and 1939—the Nazi occupation of Austria, the Munich Pact with its dazzling hope of world peace, then the seizure of Prague, followed by the Ribbentrop-Molotov Pact, are so well known that in our biography it would be superfluous to enlarge upon them. In August 1939 Mihály and Zia attended the Cracow festivities.

Below Cracow a throng of a hundred thousand filled the plain whence a quarter of a century previously, in the summer of 1914, the Polish legions of the big-mustached Pilsudski set forth. The Marshal's heart they buried at Vilna; his body rests at Cracow Cathedral, but his spirit came amazingly alive on this anniversary.

From Cracow the bells were tolling. In the thirteenth century the sentinel in the belfry had also tolled the bells when the Mongols astride their small shaggy horses appeared in ghastly hordes on the plain below the city. And he tolled, and tolled, desperately tolled the bells until in the shower of bearded Tartar arrows the bell rope fell from his hands. Now too, the bell sounded the same warning of historic dangers. Its lament now tolled this single word: *Dan-zig . . . Dan-zig . . . Dan-zig . . .*

Around a great hill gathered the crowd. From the most distant villages, setting out on foot toward the Mecca of resurrection, aged little peasant women had brought in their handkerchiefs the soil that made this hill on which now a tremendous funeral pyre burned. The bells were still tolling when words of command sounded and the crowd silently opened a path for someone as if Kosciusko or Pilsudski were approaching, vision-like, riding a snow-white stallion. The program read: "The first relay racer is Kazimir Kilinski, great-grandson of Piotr Kilinski, the cobbler of Cracow who brought five thousand bootmakers and tanners to the standards of Kosciusko." The grandson of the eternal fighter for freedom wearily kept lifting his hairy legs glistening with sweat, and his dusty track shoes; his striped track shirt was also soaking with perspiration and his chest heaved in uttermost exhaustion, but in his right hand he held high the burning torch. Kazimir Kilinski stopped before the great pyre and with a last effort of his gasping lungs cried:

"Vilna!"

And he threw his torch on the pyre. Pilsudski's heart greeted the pyre: flame to flame. The moment was overwhelming. One could hear the Polish women sobbing aloud. In Kilinski's tracks came the second, then the third and the fourth relay racer, the flames came from every region of Poland and as the torches flew to the pyre, tired lungs hoarsely shouted: "Lemberg!". . . "Varso!". . . "Grabovno!". . .

And from Cracow the bells still tolled: *Dan-zig . . . Dan-zig . . . Dan-zig . . .*

95

A week later, August 31, 1939, Thursday night, when news buzzing and swirling in the ether no longer left any doubt as to what would transpire within a few hours in the Danzig affair, everybody kept watch at the radio till midnight. A somewhat chaotic fragment from Zia's diary speaks of these hours.

. . . and my nerves hum and my head hums too. . . . Against my custom I drank two glasses of brandy. . . . I am completely intoxicated . . . not so much from the brandy as from that black alcohol flowing toward us from radio bulletins. Inside me Danzig and everything gets mixed up with the ancient and horrible Eastern legends I must read as an assignment for Kristina who now is writing a novel about Chieftain Ordony, the thousandth page of which is still only part of the introduction. Naturally it is my task to make extracts from the sources. She only writes and writes—I don't blame her for burying herself centuries deep, so as to escape from reality. But where can Mihály and I and Zizi take refuge? Merciful God, what are they preparing in the world? Oh, how my head splits.

Berlin, Warsaw, London . . . already they are tuning, tuning their instruments: Elephant-bodied bass viols, violins, xylophones of bayonets and sterilizing knives, prodigious flutes carved of arm-bones, which they hide temporarily under their music sheets. The audience gathers, gathers, but in the box tiers the emperors, kings, shahs, tenno, presidents, führers, duces, caudillos, neguses, people's commissars and generalissimos, gauleiters and other skull-faced notabilities have not all taken their places. Well, it seems all of them are here now—a roar of applause greets Toscanini. No, no, no, no it isn't he! From a dark vent beneath the stage slithers forth a bloody bearded great brown snake, with wide-sweeping bows hissing patriotic smiles toward the crowd, with forked tongue strewing black lightnings into the air, then tapping the music stand with the tip of his tail as with some conductor's baton. The heart-rending scream of an infant sounds as one musician blows tentatively into his mouth organ, drops blood. The cellist, an adherent

96

of the cult of arm twisters and leg breakers, stops tuning and places in his vest pocket the mauve human kidney on which he was resining his bow. Already the wattled, motley-bellied toads of the concentration and PW camps have put trumpets to their hideous lips, their scaly fingers poised over the keys, and the cult of intestine-gulpers raises black oboes. The silence and tension is unendurable . . . now! The snake's tail lifts high in the air and strikes downward like a conductor's baton . . . it has begun.

It has begun. It has begun, again it has begun. Merciful God, have pity on us.

Again it has begun.

Chapter 7

Taking Over. The New Journal Is Launched.
Mr. Gruber's Strange Role.

The day after the funeral of Count Dupi and Ostie's departure to New York, Monday morning, Mihály Ursi, a sheet of paper in his hand, strode hurriedly through the long corridor of the castle, whose walls were covered with the antlers of stag, mouflon, ibex and red deer, with stuffed eagles, boar tusks and engravings of English hunting scenes. Two steps behind him came "Grubi," the old secretary of the late Count, his full name being Marton Gruber, who, whenever he fell behind his new chief, quickly caught up with light dancing steps that belied his two hundred pounds.

Reaching the study, he remained standing before the desk in the pose of a humble secretary. His heart was beating hard—these moments would decide whether the new chief would retain him or not. He was practically deaf in his left ear, but thus far he had successfully kept this a secret from the world. He did not know much about this "peasant." Strange world! There he sat now in the leather armchair of Count Dupi.

Ursi attentively scanned the draft of the official-sounding document drawn up by Mr. Gruber determining the allowances due the widowed Countess Menti, Kristina and Johy in accordance with Ostie's decision. Zia had refused an allowance. Ursi for himself established the very modest salary he had last received from the National Institute of Astronomy.

While reading, Ursi snapped the metal guard off his pencil and the little click sounded to Grubi as if the new chief had cocked a pistol. He leaned forward a little, with his one green and one brown eye watching for the word at which the point of the pencil would go off. Ursi's little worn metal pencil, which under ordinary circumstances grubbed among the secrets of the

98

universe, to Grubi's eye possessed a curt, determined and even ruthless character. Reproachfully it tossed onto the word *Schayenheim* the two dots of the German *Umlaut* over the letter *a*: *Schäyenheim*. In changing the second *l* in *Ellburg* to the letter *k*, he glanced sidelong at Grubi.

"Hm!" remarked Grubi, scandalized, as though the culprit had been absent somewhere. In his first secretarial assignment he could scarcely have introduced himself in a worse light. After forty-two years' service, he had made two errors in the maiden name of Countess Menti. This astronomer would never forgive him. In vain to plead that when an Austrian princess married a Dukay, her maiden name dwindled to less importance than the little silken rectangle which below the neck of a sable cape almost furtively bears the firm's name.

The astronomer's pencil again assailed a word, but Grubi no longer bothered to look, because he felt it was already a foregone conclusion that he would be dismissed. The chair creaked dismally as he let himself down into it—by now it was all the same, why stand there at attention? Would he get a pension, and if so, how much? No more luxurious private quarters in the castle and at Septemvir Utca. An end to trips, to Havana cigars, extravagant tips, French cognac, Paris theaters, African safaris, scarcely worn, beautiful overcoats, in fact even scarcely worn, beautiful women whom he had received in the way of crumbs from the table of Count Dupi.

"Grubi speaks nine languages," Count Dupi used to boast of his secretary. Of the nine languages only two were *bona fide*: Hungarian and German. The other languages were only represented by an old folk-song apiece, of the off-color variety, because Grubi in his youth had been a *chanson* singer in a Vienna café of ill-repute where, during an all-night carouse, Count Dupi had discovered in him the world's most matchless secretary; but later he himself came to believe that Grubi had renounced a diplomatic career to serve him. Once on a trip to Spain, when a customs officer on the frontier became annoying, Count Dupi rumbled to Grubi: "Tell this donkey who I am. Tell him I'll phone the King of Spain at once!" Grubi turned to the customs officer and with stern-knit brows addressed him: *"Yo te quiero, amada niña mía, igual que ama la flor la luz del día!"* He couldn't

99

have said anything else, because that was all the Spanish he knew. The opening words of the old folk-song meant: "I love you, my darling, like flowers the sun!" The Spanish customs officer began to grin and replaced in the valise the big box of Havanas. No wonder then, that Count Dupi became convinced that Grubi spoke better Spanish than Don Quixote.

Such thoughts occurred to the sixty-year-old Marton Gruber, who was already deaf in the left ear. He stared at the rug with an expression envisaging the bleak furnished room awaiting his remaining years as gloomier than a coffin.

"You may type it now," said Mihály Ursi, handing back the corrected draft.

"How many copies, Professor?" asked Grubi, rising from the chair and resuming the secretarial tone.

"Five . . . say six."

Mr. Gruber, with a formal nod, prepared to leave. But then, to his great surprise, the new chief reached after him and took hold of his arm. He faced him, looking silently for a few instants into his eyes, then quietly said:

"Zia thinks the world of you."

This warm human tone struck so unexpectedly to Grubi's heart, that his eyes filled with tears. The "peasant astronomer" warmly shook his hand.

"I hope we can work together to the end of our lives."

Old Grubi did not answer, nor could he have, because his lips began twitching violently. Almost by force he tore away his hand, and, instead of the door, swung toward the fireplace, on his way to the corridor. Out there too, he bit his lips to hold back his tears. Not once during forty-two years had he heard such warm human words from Count Dupi. Never, never. Nor from anyone in the family. Even if the words were kind, they always came from somewhere on the heights. Mihály's were the words of a friend to a friend.

Zia's Letter to Ostie in New York

Ararat, October 30, 1939

My dear Ostyak,

I know that Mihály industriously sends you official reports, but I think sometimes a little female chatter may be welcome. Well, first of all, the family. Mihály's spectroscope and bolometer have also examined Mama's day nursery, the Glass House, and have discovered dreadful sunspots in the running of affairs. Kristina is right: there are more employees than infants. They have taken very mean advantage of Mama's naïveté. We shall tactfully dismiss the aristocratic diaper overseers who do nothing but play croquet and bridge all day long. Mama appears only seldom at Ararat, and at such times seeks a bit of ribbon or a little image or an old letter from her closed room. In her appearance there is something apologetic, and at the same time a queenly offense, not directed at persons, but at the sunset, the clouds, the whole world—you know Mama.

You were wrong in assuming that Kristina's husband Borsitzky does not actually exist. Nor was your guess correct that if there were such a man, Kristina would divorce him in a matter of days, for the divorce only took place last Thursday, after two long weeks of marriage. We were all sorry to hear of it, because we thought Kristina's rhapsodic career would settle down at the side of the extremely likable and even-tempered Borsitzky, who spent three weekends with us. Kristina says there were two reasons for the divorce: Borsitzky invariably wore an undershirt, and once had quipped about Otto, "that everlasting king." The divorce proceedings were initiated on grounds of mental cruelty.

We haven't seen Johy since the funeral. Some days ago, I met the old gatekeeper of the Septemvir Utca palace, who said that Hitler himself often visited Johy at his quarters. Our old Paul's mistake may be due to the fact that these Hungarian Nazi leaders wear Hitler mustaches and in general ape the Führer.

Speaking of the old gateman reminds me that Mihály now has settled the personnel question all along the line. I was terribly afraid that everyone would hate Mihály: the opposite happened. He only dismissed a few persons, many of the elderly ones retired voluntarily, and most of them embarked enthusiastically on the nursing course, which carries a "diploma," as Feri the footman remarked. Apparently the instinct of getting ahead is in every man's heart.

They're crazy about Mihály, his chief devotee being Grubi, who, a few days after you left, said to me: "Countess, you know how much I loved your father. I don't know of another at whose side one could *live* better. But for your husband I would be willing to *die* at any moment." That means a lot, coming from him. Grubi seldom wastes his breath.

Six oxen couldn't drag Rere from his workshop. All day long he saws and hammers. Now, having built a boat for the fishpond, he is engaged in great preparations for the launching ceremony. Already he has written Uncle Zsigmond, because he cannot conceive of his boat without a bishop's blessing. You should see Rere, plane in one hand, turkey drumstick in the other; according to Kristina, he sometimes bites into the plane by mistake—he just beams happily, and we naturally keep praising the masterpiece which is more like a piano crate than a boat. It's hard to keep from laughing, because, apart from Rere, everybody knows that the launching will come to nothing, because the boat won't fit through the door, so either the workshop or the boat would have to be taken apart.

Gaston de Ferreyolles got back recently from Paris; he thinks that in the era of bombing planes neither the Anglo-French nor the German side dares to launch too big a war. The French and German soldiers only shout derisive songs at each other: "We'll hang our linen on the Siegfried line!" to which coarse German humor replies: "You'll have reason to launder your pants!" Gaston even sang the German song at the piano, but I don't remember the exact words. The music to both songs was catchy.

Speaking of more distant relatives, poor Uncle Dmitri lost his position at the radio station, because his new set of false teeth gave his voice such a hiss during the Russian newscast that the Soviet Union protested in a diplomatic note. That, of course, is not true—only Kristina says so. Since the Ribbentrop-Molotov Pact Uncle Dmitri has been playing with the idea of returning to his one-time estate in the Urals as *kolkhoz* manager, and claims that at heart he was already a Communist in the Winter Palace, as royal steward for Czar Nicholas. I imagine Uncle Dmitri would be more aghast than anyone, were they to shove a Soviet passport into his hands. In him, all this is pure nostalgia. Mihály offered to aid him with a modest monthly sum, which he declined with an apologetic smile. What he lives on we cannot imagine; but though his clothing is threadbare he is always neat and cleanshaven. Never does he neglect to bring Zizi some trifle. With wondrous art he succeeds in preserving the air of the Russian grandee—unfortunately his new teeth do hiss a little.

The outfitting of the hospital proceeds at such a pace that we plan a New Year's Day opening. The great dining hall [for three hundred years the scene of resplendent Dukay weddings] is now transformed into a ward. The castle doffs its ornaments as our great grandmothers discarded their jewels, crinolines and trains after a royal ball. The silken tapestries have vanished from the walls, everything gleams in white antiseptic oil paint, and the portraits of forebears in silver breastplates and leopard skin *kacagäny* have yielded place to stark medical diagrams depicting human brains, the circulation of the lungs, the convolutions of stomach and intestines. I think Mihály already wrote you that Kristina's physician, Dr. István Freyberger, will head the hospital. For a long time he wouldn't accept the post. Mihály whispered behind closed doors with him for days. I imagine these whisperings were connected with some sort of anti-German politics, because Freyberger is of Jewish descent, and has adopted that mode of conversation, whereby he objectively dissects the faults of his race. He is a most genial fellow, highly cultured, a first-rate doctor, professor at the university, past sixty I should judge, with dense bushy silver-white hair, tall, his shoulders somewhat stooped. Don't be surprised if in my next letter I announce Kristina's marriage to Freyberger. They are constantly together, quite inseparable. In poor Kristina there is a sort of flight, she herself does not know whence or whither.

I think that for the present I have said all that needs to be said. Except that Mihály's launching of the journal makes me not at all happy. I don't like to see him plunging into politics again. Tomorrow the first issue will appear: on the twenty-first anniversary of the Hungarian October Revolution. God in heaven, how these two decades between the wars have flown!

I should like you, along with my kisses, to pass on to Gwen a request of mine. American papers reach me regularly and I find it difficult to resist one or two ads. I want Gwen to please send me some *base coat* for nail polish, then *hair lacquer* and *curlers*, which are unobtainable here. A Fifth Avenue shop advertises lovely nightgowns; sleeveless, cut deep in back, shirred under the breast with a girdle decorated with tiny flowers and slit to the knees from the hem. Gwen knows my measurements. I embrace you both.

ZIA

P.S. Send some recent American literature: Hemingway, Steinbeck, Faulkner. If you think of Mihály, send him some Upton Sinclair.

With regard to the new anti-German weekly there were already great consultations in the middle of September in the Café Gugger, where veteran one-time Stargazers again began to gather, by now with bushier mustaches and paunches of assorted sizes. After the titles *Trumpet, Rise Magyari, Little Nations of the Danube Valley* and *Silver Deer*, in fact even *Ursa Major*, were rejected, in discussions lasting till midnight, they unanimously accepted Hamor's suggestion and the new journal's name became *Kolomp*. Only one Stargazer thought the title idiotic, taking offense because they had voted down his *White Stag*. The others found *Kolomp* not only a beautiful-sounding ancient Hungarian word, but one possessing symbolic significance. It not only meant the melancholy-toned metal bell which, at the bellwether's neck, fills the Hungarian *puszta* with marvelous music, but it also meant the collecting and uniting of the Magyar flock. In fact, according to Hamor, in *Kolomp* the voice of distant centuries could be heard, when the tolling bells in the watch-towers of Cracow or Buda signaled danger approaching now from the west, now from the east. "The title is beautiful and

104

ingenious!" remarked Ursi. They silently pressed Hamor's hand. They couldn't congratulate him enough.

This great enthusiasm cooled considerably when, after the appearance of *Kolomp,* a pro-German humorous journal, *The Pin,* feted the appearance of the paper with a full-page sketch. In the bellwether one could clearly recognize Mihály Ursi; Hamor, to whom twins had been born, was portrayed as a great ram with recurved horns, and other Stargazers were similarly portrayed as rams and wethers, while a flock of sheep represented the Magyar people being led astray. Behind the flock, in bustard-feathered hat, delineated as a Hungarian shepherd, came Churchill with a great cigar in his mouth, while the herding dog was tagged "Wall Street."

Kolomp's following issue answered *The Pin's* attack with a full-page sketch of its own. The ingenious artist in this sketch truly distinguished himself. By way of a footnote to the Ribbentrop-Molotov Pact, Hitler and Stalin were shown locked in close embrace. They both stood with their huge boots planted on the prostrate body of Poland. The picture was movingly dramatic: Stalin stood on the stomach of vanquished Poland, one of Hitler's boots was gouging out an eye of the corpse. But the two dictators were portrayed as composites: Hitler had the countenance and garb of Frederick The Great, while Stalin continued upward into a short-necked high-corseted ample-bosomed female figure with the lineaments of Empress Catherine II, implying that German and Russian imperialism through the course of history were always the same—one hundred and fifty years ago, Frederick The Great and Catherine II had divided Poland between them just as now. In the background of the sketch were the little nations of the Danube Valley, their faces distorted by fear, as they beheld the fervid embrace of Hitler and Stalin.

We reproduce a few excerpts from the first issue of *Kolomp:*

> Jefferson was right in saying of the small nations: *an aristocracy of virtue and talent!* The ancient constitutions of small nations are patents of nobility sealed not by Emperor Leopold or Louis XV, but bearing God's own hand. The great nations in their abundant wealth to a certain

extent grow colorless, but small nations must constantly give tidings of themselves through exceptional achievement. Record-breaking milch cows, runners of amazing endurance, cheeses of rare aroma. Their folk-costumes, traditions, painters and stalactite caves they bear as Cleopatra or Queen Victoria the badges of empire. Small nations are sometimes laughably arrogant on the score of their freedom and independence, at times they make quite a superfluous racket, but still they throw off sparks of inspiration to mankind. Fashion designers of the Place Vendôme or Fifth Avenue gladly purloin the design and coloring of a Magyar or Rumanian peasant woman's bodice.

What awaits you, little nations? While we write these lines, in the Polish people's deep bereavement a gigantic Missing Person from Nowhere roams. What happened to those ten thousand Polish officers, who last were seen nearing the forests of Smolensk and Katyn? And as we write these lines, from the snowed-in forest slopes of Viipuri white-garbed Finnish partisans on skis swoop like lightning. The shores of Lake Ladoga teem with Russian corpses frozen black; these white apparitions have already destroyed three Soviet divisions, sleds against tanks, sharp hunting knives against machine guns—little Finland in these hours is writing the new Kalevala, world history's most heroic epos of freedom.

Lenin, in one of his speeches, with fiery words denounced Czarist Russia for having occupied Finland in 1805. But Lenin is already dead, Trotsky lives in exile and now Litvinov is not Foreign Minister, but the man whose name means hammer: *molot*, Molotov, a worthy companion for Ribbentrop.

Little nations, prepare for the worst. You too, Hungary, prepare for your life and death struggle.

Around the middle of November, Count Johy spent Sunday afternoon at Ararat Castle. He yielded to the persuasion of Countess Menti, whose maternal heart strove to preserve the family peace. Kristina and Zia exchanged only the briefest courtesies with Johy, while Mihály, pleading work, withdrew.

That afternoon precipitated a painful scene; painful and violent. From the corridor sounded Mihály's angry shouting. The heads of Kristina and Zia appeared inquisitively in the doorway. They only saw Mr. Gruber hurrying out, but stopping for an agitated backward glance. This glance roused Mihály to new fury.

"Get out of here! Quick!"

Mr. Gruber for still another moment exchanged a glance of foaming rage with his chief, then disappeared at the turn in the corridor. Johy also witnessed the scene.

Stepping into the room, Mihály threw himself into a chair and it seemed as though he couldn't even talk from agitation. Then he muttered, as though to himself, and still panting:

"Scoundrel."

"What happened?" asked Zia and Kristina together. Countess Menti and Johy stepped nearer, awaiting the answer. Ursi heatedly explained.

"Once last week he came into my room and in a 'fatherly tone' warned me that I was politically quite on the wrong track— the new Germany must not be defied. Two days later he gave me the friendly counsel that I should forswear all contact with my Jewish friends."

After an instant's pause, Count Johy's cloyingly soft voice spoke up.

"Everyone has a right to his own con-vic-tions, wouldn't you say, my dear Mi-hály?"

"He said we mustn't allow Freyberger in the castle."

"Ah!" said Kristina, this *ah!* speeding from her lips like an arrow. Countess Menti listened as though no aspect of the conversation had anything to do with her.

"But that wasn't why I threw him out," continued Ursi. "A few moments ago I was phoning Ostie in New York. My friend Hamor arrived, stepped into the next room and saw *Herr* Gruber, his ear pressed to the keyhole, eavesdropping on our conversation."

Hamor's tall figure and disheveled white brush-head had already appeared in the room and now with mute nods confirmed the fact.

Wrath flamed on in Ursi. "My own secretary! That's the man I embraced!"

A long silence followed. Zia's face, especially, reflected deepest consternation—as though learning of the death of some family member they all loved. Mr. Gruber, Herr Gruber, Monsieur Gruber, Grubi, Uncle Grubi . . . for forty-two years he had been more a part of the castle than the venerable oak by the main entrance.

Kristina spoke up, directing her pensive words at the ceiling.

"Of course, Herr Gruber! His German blood, too, broke out in a rash. Victory blasts of Teutonic trumpets awaken everyone's dormant German consciousness."

No one listened to her neatly turned phrases that might have graced a novel. Johy, though the shot went home, smiled superciliously, the tip of his elbow resting against the fireplace —as if the whole scene had only served to justify him.

Zia, standing by the window, saw old Grubi lugging a small and a large suitcase down the steps to his own little Topolino car, which he had received two years before from Count Dupi in commemoration of his fortieth anniversary as secretary. Now there was no footman to help him with the heavy luggage. He could hardly squeeze his huge paunch into the tiny car. Zia's eyes grew moist. Grubi, Uncle Grubi. . . . How much fun you could always have over him. One of his eyes was green, the other brown. Despite his heavy body there was always a dancing lilt to his steps. With what feeling he could whisper *"Au clair de la lune"* and *"Yo quiero mía amada"* in his cigarette-ravaged voice while accompanying himself at the piano. When he was explaining something to someone, during his cascading sentences he would poke his unsuspecting listener so vigorously with his index finger, that he almost lost his balance—Grubi at such times would run back a few steps, stop suddenly and over his shoulder look back silently but triumphantly with his motley eyes at whomever he had vanquished. He did this several times with Countess Menti too. Grubi was the family's real brains, the final counselor, the wonder-man who understood everything, solved everything, attended to everything. His head and two hands were constantly packed with notes, and for the most part he drove his car without hands, and negotiated even the turns skillfully, while he jotted down in his notebook the family's myriad commissions, for the Topolino was so tiny that the steering wheel pressed deep into his belly, so that he drove the car with his stomach muscles and that, too, was such fun.

Grubi, Uncle Grubi. . . . Now he took the wheel in his hands—no more commissions, no more use for the little note-books. Kristina also stood there by the window, silently watching Herr Gruber's departure, which looked as if someone still alive were participating in his own funeral.

"Prodigious and sinister things must be happening in the world for men to change like that," whispered Kristina.

When the little Topolino disappeared beneath the trees of the park, Zia rested her arm on the window jamb and began weeping quietly.

Chapter 8

Herr Gruber Dons a Green Shirt. Ernst Tronfeld Appears on the Horizon. Great Plans in the Cave.

An article appearing two weeks later in *The Pin*, commencing as a dissertation on heraldry, continued thus:

. . . generally throughout all Europe, the ordinary nobility have five, knights six, barons seven, while counts flaunt nine and princes eleven branches on the coronets above their crests, on their letter paper, signet rings, silver, handkerchiefs and underdrawers. Let us not forget about luggage, harness and brands on the rumps of cattle. Mediatized princes wear closed coronets edged with ermine. In Hungary only one family of counts wears an eleven- instead of a nine-branched coronet: the Karolyis of the Kaplony line. The tenth branch of the Dukay coronet is a mistake of the emblazoner, while the eleventh was the grant not of Leopold II, but of an expectant fly. The writer of these lines had occasion to peruse the archives of the Dukay family, and with the finest of Zeiss lenses in hand, ascertained that on the original document the proud eleventh branch of the coronet was an ordinary flyspeck. Of the Dukay counts now living, the one most certain of a great political future, the deeply cultured and gifted, humane and social-minded Graf Johann von Dukay alone uses only a nine-branched coronet above his crest. Sovereign taste and a comprehensive grasp of history saved him from falling victim to such vain pretense. Unfortunately we cannot say the same for other members of the family. But let us not rummage too much among the private affairs of the Dukays, which hide an even greater flyspeck: Ostie Dukay, who took his ancient rank, his London-tailored suits, and a virility doubtless without peer in degenerate America, and invested them in a rich American marriage just as nowadays wealthy Jews change their ill-gotten depreciating currencies to dollars. The unjust caprice of fate and of an antiquated law of entail have made this fathead Ostyak heir to the tremendous Ararat estates, and while himself squandering the hard-earned fruits of Magyar labor in New York night clubs, he has entrusted the pernicious-minded Mihály Ursi, to whom the Hungarian courts a few years ago meted out a severe prison sentence, with full control of the affairs of the estate.

The article was signed "Marton Gruber."

"Lucky for him," said Kristina, "that Papa isn't alive. He'd splinter his thickest walking stick on him."

Ursi, standing near the wall, his hands clasped behind him, made no comment. Kristina arose, walked over to him and whispered from behind her hand, though only the two of them were in the room:

"The magnifying glass was not in his hands but in mine. On that one point he is right. It was a flyspeck!"

And Kristina sailed out of the room with the mien of the family archives' goddess.

Herr Gruber was already wearing the Arrow Cross Party's green shirt, black breeches and black boots, a becoming uniform for tall slender men—less so for potbellies. When Count Johy proposed Grubi for membership, Party leaders regarded Marton Gruber with his nine languages and his diplomatic background as a pre-eminent asset if only because the most valuable members of the Party were dismissed secretaries, fired footmen, deceived and divorced women, the pure flame of whose ideals was also fed by personal malice. His linguistic abilities and diplomatic gifts raised Herr Gruber within a few weeks to the supreme general staff of the Party. He knew innumerable compromising tidbits about Ostie Dukay, Kristina, Zia, to say nothing of the affairs of the half-witted Count Rere. These family secrets he could present so comically, that one of the hyena-faced Party leaders, later a prominent mass murderer, nearly split his ribs laughing. When Mihály Ursi fired Herr Gruber from Ararat, he projected him not downward but upward. Grubi naturally became adviser to Count Johy, and in the Septemvir Utca palace the footman once more brought him breakfast on a silver tray.

Early in January, an elderly gentlewoman appeared at Ararat. She was Ernst Tronfeld's mother.

"What news of Ernst?" was Ursi's first question.

The widowed Mrs. Tronfeld settled herself slowly in the chair, pressed her handkerchief to her mouth—only seconds later could she speak.

"Ernst has been taken to a concentration camp."

These brief words struck Ursi like a death notice.

"Ernst? Why the last time he wrote me was from Rome."

"Yes, but when war broke out he returned to Berlin. Professor von Johnen assured him that Jewish scientists would be exempted. Forgive my troubling you in this. I know how dear a friend you are to Ernst. I've succeeded in discovering that Count Johy is on very intimate terms with the German General von Klapper, commandant of the concentration camp. If you would be so good . . ."

Her tears prevented her from finishing the sentence. In Ursi's memory rose the misty dawn when in Berlin beneath the statue of Frederick The Great he bade his friend farewell with the feeling that within the next ten years in Ernst Tronfeld's life the Nobel Prize was inevitable.

"Alas," said Ursi, "I fear my appeal to Graf Johann von Dukay would have quite the opposite effect."

"Perhaps your dear wife, Countess Zia. . . ."

The widowed Mrs. Tronfeld's glance now reflected persecuted Jewry's hidden, distraught, alarmed little suspicion of everything Christian, as if this tortured maternal glance now said: You are compassionate and anti-German, but somewhere there is always a family or other connection leading to the German executioners.

Ursi slowly shook his gloomy brow.

"Neither my wife, nor Kristina. That road I find impossible. Please don't lose hope. You can imagine that I'll do everything within my power."

It was already dark, a black winter night. Herr Gruber had just returned to the Septemvir Utca palace from an important Party conference. In his room, above the broad French bed, was a framed engraving in color, a portrait of Hitler which shows him in a Caesarean pose, wearing a long military cloak, at his boots a beautiful German police dog displaying luxuriant tints of black and yellow. Reaching his room, Herr Gruber lowered himself into an armchair, but so weary was he that he didn't even put aside the open copy of *Mein Kampf*. His expansive posterior settled on the chapter in which Hitler was expounding that Germany would not repeat the first world war's insanity of fighting on two fronts. In the presence of others Herr Gruber would in no case have seated himself on *Mein Kampf*, which at this time on the part of a loyal Nazi would have seemed some such irreverence as if Bishop Zsigmond were to sit upon an open Bible. But now Herr Gruber was alone. Wearily closing his one green, one brown eye, he clasped his fingers over his belly, intending to snooze a bit. Always at such moments the telephone rings. Grubi with a sleepy motion of his hand reached for the receiver.

"Hello. Henrik? Yes, just got back from the Party meeting. . . . Right, the usual place in half an hour."

Into the black night, with upturned collar, stepped from a street phone-booth the mysterious Henrik who, naturally, was Mihály Ursi. Grubi's dramatic expulsion from the castle, with Hamor acting as false witness, had been a scene devised in advance. The Stargazers needed a reliable agent to infiltrate the camp of the enemy. No one seemed better suited for this role than the "dismissed" old secretary, who was of German extraction to boot. Hamor on several occasions voiced his surmise that Mr. Gruber was Jewish, but our data fails to support this assumption. According to one personal document, Grubi was born an Austrian Catholic, son of a baker in Vienna; but in his case such documents are hardly conclusive, because Grubi all his life had a penchant for false papers. Once—that was before the first world war—Count Dupi could only shake off a conquest by arranging to have the redheaded lady seduced by his friend Prince Klopecky, a Latvian landowner. Needless to say, the prince was Grubi, against whom the lady subsequently filed a paternity suit, but all the private detectives in Europe were unable to pick up the trail of the motley-eyed prince.

Ursi at first would not approve Grubi's dangerous undertaking, but Grubi cut him short: "I've already lived my best years. And one other thing, boys. Such a role is tough. Reinhardt, my childhood friend, used to say to me: 'Grubi, Grubi, I'll always regret that you didn't become an actor. You'd have outshone Pallenberg!'"

Certain it is that Grubi played his present role splendidly. He was the one who staged the expulsion scene too, for which two rehearsals were held in secret. Women could not be initiated into the dangerous game—the war, which already blazed along the fronts, had become a hushed game of life and death in countries still neutral for the time being. Though it was Grubi who for forty years composed and signed Count Dupi's numerous and most beautiful love letters, he was not a writer. *The Pin* article was written by Ursi. And for approval, they had sent it to Ostie in New York. The original manuscript in our hands shows that the qualification "fathead Ostyak" was written in Ostie's own hand.

On this evening, Ursi arrived first at the "usual" place. In a northern precinct of Budapest, at the end of the last century a street was named after the father of Count Dupi, Count Peter Dukay, who for a short time was personal minister to Franz Joseph. The street was called by the footmen of Ararat Castle: "His Excellency Count Peter Dukay's Street."

Count Dupi never knew the location of his many apartment houses. The address of this one, however, he knew exactly, and chose its tenants too. In fact he himself planned one of the ground-floor bachelor apartments with its secret rear entrance. This apartment Mihály Ursi found listed in the inventory of the estate. The apartment was under the name of István Basha, house superintendent, in which pseudonym we can easily discover the reference to a Turkish pasha, this play on words was the sole poetic effort of Count Dupi. The luxuriant rugs of the three-room apartment, its broad divans, sumptuous bathroom, the beautiful nudes of Degas, Rodin and Renoir on the walls, framed sketches from *La Vie Parisienne*, all served not only art and luxury but primarily Count Dupi's secret love life. On the table lay a huge silver-clasped photo album bound in pink silk, a de luxe edition of the International Federation of the Collectors of Piquant Photographs. Countless fingerprints on the pages of

114

the album gave testimony that for half a century, innumerable shapely feminine hands had leafed through this album. Why go to the trouble of lengthy and arduous courtship? Just leave the reputable widow or the obstinate little lady alone with this album for a quarter of an hour. The dazzlingly reckless and beautiful photographs did their work mutely. Like furtive warm hands they tenderly but surely loosened even the tightest of whalebone corsets, or the most hidden clasps of modern silken underthings. In one secret drawer Ursi found an appurtenance available in all the more elegant and well-equipped Paris *maisons d'amour,* an artificial male organ of rubber, which indicated that the old Count to the day of his death had not given up his passionate quests. These compromising objects, including two wardrobes full of women's letters bound with varicolored ribbons and separately grouped, the collection of hair, both from the head and elsewhere, Mihály Ursi personally burned, and of these matters naturally made no mention to Zia. After getting rid of the apartment's harem-like furnishings, his first thought was to let the apartment, but on Grubi's advice he retained it. They too might need such a secret establishment, though for a different purpose. From the apartment on Peter Dukay Street, by the rear door, the Goddess of Love departed and ceded place to the Shadow of Death. Within these walls the members of the anti-German underground met.

When, in answer to three short rings, Ursi opened the door this evening, Grubi at once launched into a long account of what had happened at the secret meeting of the Arrow Cross Party. But Mihály Ursi interrupted him. "My dear Grubi, there is something far more important. You must contact Johy immediately. One of my best friends has been taken to a German concentration camp. You must go with Johy to Berlin and bring Professor Ernst Tronfeld back to this apartment at the earliest possible moment."

"How much . . . ?" asked Grubi, at once broaching the practical aspect of the question.

"Tronfeld was a professor at Heidelberg University. Jewish and left-wing. What would be your estimate?"

Grubi's eyes for a few instants remained fixed in space. Then, in the tones of an expert, he replied:

"We settled the Schlesinger case for fifty thousand pengös. A professor, I'd say, would be definitely more expensive."

Two weeks had not yet elapsed when, late one night, Ursi waited at the secret apartment until the three short rings sounded. On opening the door, however, he met with a disagreeable surprise. From behind Grubi, a little man stepped into the hall, introducing himself with a deep bow.

"Doctor Tronfeld."

Good God, this is some mistake!—it may even be that the Germans deliberately tricked Grubi—was Mihály Ursi's first thought.

"Stay here a few minutes," said Grubi to the frightened little man, before he disappeared with Ursi behind the closed door of the room.

He swiftly related the story of the two Tronfelds. After the German general von Klapper, via Johy, had set Professor Tronfeld's price at a hundred thousand German marks, half of which was destined for Johy's pockets, Grubi, escorted by a German orderly and bearing in his hand the discharge order signed by the General, had appeared at one of the barracks. When the German orderly shouted Doctor Tronfeld's name in the ill-lit putrid-smelling barracks, this little Tronfeld leapt like a cat from one of the piled-up box crates serving as beds. When Professor Ernst Tronfeld staggered forth from deep in the barracks, this little Isidor Tronfeld stammered his apologies with a smile that froze into a death mask. He hadn't known there were two Tronfelds in the barracks.

"I was already in the Eden Hotel with the Professor," continued Grubi, "but couldn't forget this little man's deathly smile of apology. To play safe, I had been discussing the 'sale of a steam mill' with Johy and von Klapper. To Johy I said that von Klapper's goods did not meet specifications, the boiler of the mill was badly rusted—just look at the Professor, he would scarcely live another week. So the sum would be paid only if I got the Professor's brother, Isidor, in the bargain. These two Tronfelds aren't related, but Isidor is a lawyer and I thought we could use a lawyer, even a rusty one. N'est-ce pas? Next day, Johy brought Isidor's discharge order and then—"

116

"Where is the Professor?" cried Ursi, who had been listening impatiently to the long discourse.

"He'll be along. He just stopped off at the post office to phone his mother."

A few minutes later, Mihály and Ernst fervently embraced. And while Ernst sobbed wordlessly on Mihály's shoulder, Grubi and Isidor, the rusty little lawyer, tactfully left them to themselves.

Ostie did not know Tronfeld, but in a brief New York telephone conversation was only too happy to approve the payment of a hundred thousand marks "receipted in due form," because that incidentally gave them a powerful weapon against Johy, whom they all rightly feared. The receipt read:

Received this day 100,000 (one hundred thousand) marks, from the widowed Mrs. Samuel Tronfeld, in full payment for the steam mill on my estate at Gere, Hungary.
Berlin, December 18, 1939

Inasmuch as Johy had long since gambled away the last farthing of his paternal and maternal inheritance at the Jockey Club in Vienna, official investigation would find it most difficult to locate a nonexistent steam mill on a nonexistent estate. That steam mill might greatly impede Johy's gauleiter dreams, to say nothing of General von Klapper's military career. The Führer never jested in such matters. Only recently he had executed the commandant of a concentration camp for a similar "steam-mill" transaction.

When they were alone, and already deep in talk, Mihály asked Ernst: "How is German uranium research progressing?"

Ernst, whose face had grown appallingly thin, answered in a whisper.

"A few days before my arrest I spoke with Professor von Johnen. When war broke out, he, too, was a member of the delegation which reminded Hitler how important this matter was. Hitler's first question was how long it would take to make the first uranium bomb. Four to five years, said the scientists. Hitler waved them off. Let them propose something they could produce in four or five months. The German professors founded the Uranium Club, but received scarcely any government support."

For a few moments, both fell silent, then Mihály spoke. "When the Germans provoked French and English declarations of war, to many this seemed lunacy. But we Stargazers knew that last December in Professor Hahn's laboratory the uranium atom already had been split. More than eight months went by before war was declared. I can only explain this German lunacy by assuming that in those eight months there was secret progress in uranium research, about which even von Johnen knows nothing."

"Perhaps. I don't know," whispered Ernst.

Ursi again noticed that men who came from Germany, Italy, Spain, or the Soviet Union talked in whispers, even when already in neutral free countries, and among their most trusted friends.

Ursi rose and began pacing to and fro. Then he stopped by the wall, hands clasped behind him, and in the corner of his mouth appeared that bantering little smile which sometimes unexpectedly imbued his stern, care-lined face with childlike wistfulness.

"What about Urstron?"

Ernst did not look up, but his bloodless lips took over Mihály's smile like a gleam of reflected light. Gazing straight ahead, he nodded almost imperceptibly, his thoughts visibly bathing Urstron in this moving and embarrassed little smile. Urstron, their youthful dream, appeared above the table as when two men, after long decades, find themselves seated side by side at a frock-coated, bemedaled banquet, both of them now prominent figures, discussing matters of high political or social import, cautiously and awkwardly avoiding the names of onetime playmates and their little native town, because above their decorations and graying hair continually hovers a joint and horrible childhood memory.

"Did you give it up? Did you give it up for good?"

"Of course," said Ernst briefly. And with his accustomed gesture, his outspread fingers sought to comb back his hair. But the absent-minded fingers combed only air, because from his head and the rest of his body all the hair had been shaven in the

118

concentration camp at the first delousing bath. That was what happened with every prisoner in the first half-hour, with the women, too.

After a long pause, Mihály again spoke up, still standing by the wall:

"Suppose I were to set up a special physics laboratory for you?"

Ernst's smile again soured his sunken face. Mihály's words alarmed him. It struck him that deep down in this man's soul the dream of Urstron still glowed like the eerie light of some mysterious radioactive metal. Maybe that was why he had dug him out of the concentration camp. After a few instants, he said in a dry distant tone:

"There would be no point to it. First of all, such a laboratory is enormously expensive. And you know better than anyone that no practical results can be expected of research."

"What would a modern physics laboratory cost?"

"Good Lord! First we'd need a cascade generator capable of at least a million volts. And all the other machinery and equipment! Seventy or eighty thousand dollars. Plus at least one assistant and two mechanics."

"The Stargazers can provide you as many as ten assistants. I swear they are as gifted as the Germans. The expense . . . let's say, roughly a hundred thousand dollars. Listen. Immense funds of the Dukay estate lie rotting in bank accounts. From Ostie Dukay I have orders to buy and buy: shoelaces by the ton, soap, cement, aspirin—everything, because he thinks the Germans sooner or later will drag Hungary into the war; in a few years all goods will be worth many times more than Hungarian paper money. If I buy equipment for a physics laboratory, I'm not tossing the family fortune out the window, but saving it."

Ernst's tone was still defensive:

"You must consider that what we once discussed in Berlin with youthful heads—"

Mihály cut short his words:

"In those days, you said the splitting of uranium was unimaginable within a hundred years. You needn't blush now, Lord Rutherford said much the same thing. You said that *Urstron*, the electron, the meson, even today are less than real. I say to you: there is one chance in a thousand—all right, don't shake your head, one chance in a million—or even less. But that chance *exists!"*

Ernst, propping his elbows far over the table, listened to his friend, as he once had in the Holzer Restaurant. Now too he enjoyed the flight of Ursa Major's fancy. He enjoyed that warm baritone, the distinct Magyar flavor of his intonation. He regarded this man of the stars, this deliberately pacing figure, no whit taller than he, yet whose compact muscle and bone weighed at least twice as much, and thought: if only some electromagnetic balance could weigh the force of will and the glow of fantasy! . . . oh, yes, again he remarked as once in Berlin, that their friendship was deep and sincere because what was lacking in one existed in the other—in a Freudian sense, both were *super-egos* of each other on different levels. He reflected that the human soul, the human will, sometimes needs quite minuscule amounts—one part in a million—of illusion, just as living organisms need infinitely minute amounts of vitamins. In Mihály's line of reasoning was something which to Ernst now seemed to say: Dire times await us, especially me. Leave me your Urstron, or even the faintest hope of some such miracle. I beg you not to take it from me, I need it. Leave me this speck of vitamin to fire will and action.

It was some such thing that Ernst heard from the figure standing silently by the wall, the man in whom he always saw Ursa Major. Now Ernst, too, gazed into space. He had lost his glasses when, in the camp, a *Kapo* had struck him in the face with his fist. His near-sighted eyes stared somewhat blindly into the air.

His voice still protested apologetically: "I don't want to disparage the Dukay estate, but . . ."

"Say it. You mean I shouldn't mistake Ararat for America. There you are right. Your talents would find far greater scope in America. Well, then you must go there. After all, that is where all modern physics is by now."

Ernst wearily closed his eyes, as if all light painfully afflicted his rigid near-sighted eyeballs. His fingers nervously began to rub his forehead, his face, all the way down to his mouth, then his chin, just as if he were trying to wash away something quickly and thoroughly from his tortured, sallow face. Memories of the camp assailed him. Unexpectedly and with brutal force these horrible memories would pounce upon him even after he was free. A man realizes the magnitude of danger only after it is past. A prisoner most feels the pressure of his handcuffs just after they are removed. As at the Hotel Eden and on the train, here too the air around him filled with the oppressive stench of the barracks, the unwashed sick human bodies, the filthy shreds of clothing, all mingling with the odor of urine and of sour bread. Four, sometimes five men would lie, in cratelike beds, these open crowded coffins stacked one atop the other almost to the ceiling. Ersatz coffee for breakfast, thin soup at noon—this watery diet made the blood serum seep through the walls of the veins, the tissues fill with water, legs grew swollen. Exhausted bodies fell prey to dropsy. Dostoevsky wrote that in Siberia the worst punishment was to have prisoners dig great ditches which they were then ordered to fill up again. Nothing is more horrible than the knowledge of work done in vain. In the camp they had to carry heavy rocks to the top of a hill and lug back those same rocks. At night when they lay down, the blood serum accumulated through the watery diet slowly filtered back from swollen limbs into the bladder. Some hid empty tin cans under their shirts and made water into them, because urination in the vicinity of the barracks was forbidden—who would have had the strength to stagger every half hour to distant latrines through black icy rain? To sleep, to sleep, to gather strength; sleep became even more important than nourishment—the filled cans would overturn in the hands of the sleepers, urine trickling onto those below . . . curses, fist fights . . . raw-nerved prisoners . . . . a Brunn textile dealer and he, the professor from Heidelberg, had torn and bit at each other like wild beasts and at such times the clubs of the *Kapos* would make order as if the barracks were the stinking cages of wild beasts. No, no, no . . . try not to remember anything . . . General von Klapper was a fine man, dispensing friendly words and smiles among the prisoners who at his approach snatched from their shaved heads their *Mütze*, the peaked little striped caps—oh yes, a fine man indeed was General von Klapper. His eight-year-old little girl sometimes gave prisoners lumps of sugar—sweet little blond angel—but one

Sunday afternoon, at the other end of the camp General von Klapper amused himself by having a German soldier throw Jewish infants high in the air for the Herr General's target practice. His little girl stood there beside him, clapped her hands at each shot, stamping with her little patent-leather shoe: *"Noch einmal, Papa!"* "Once more, Papa!" Was it true, or only a nightmare?

Ernst's tortured face suddenly turned toward the wall, as if he wanted to convince himself that Ursa Major was really standing there. Yes, there he stood, hands clasped behind him, mute, lost in thought. There in truth stood his friend.

America? Should he go to America? He didn't know English. He felt so deathly tired. And something else! Perhaps a weakness of nerves or character: he bowed too deeply before authority and tended to lose himself, a thing immediately noticed by authority—which then not only looked down on him, but began treating its devotee roughly. Be it the Prussian von Johnen or the Jewish Professor Haber: that is the psychology of authority. The only man who really looked up to him and his talents stood there by the wall, hands clasped behind him, still mute, and as if sad and baffled by his refusal. Ursa Major exaggerated, of course he exaggerated through his enthusiasm, he thought more of him than he really was, but perhaps this was exactly the vitamin lacking in him, Ernst Tronfeld. And in Berlin, too, it had been the height of his desire eventually to be master in his own laboratory. This hadn't worked out in Heidelberg and in America the weight of authority would be even more crushing.

In the long tense silence Ernst spoke:

"Maybe you are right."

His nervous fingers again began rubbing his forehead, then his face, down to his mouth and chin, now as if wanting to rub his drawn face with some magic ointment. His thoughts flamed like those great greenish electric sparks in cathode tubes. *Urstron* was impossible of course . . . but *that* of which von Johnen also spoke . . . that something lurking in cosmic rays . . . great God, if some miracle happened and something were to spring from the mesons, then all Germany might be held in check, the whole bloodthirsty crew . . . but careful, in the vicinity of Ursa

Major his imagination was already hurtling toward the mesons. But why all this caution? Where does serious science end and wild fantasy begin? Who can tell?

Ernst slowly shook his head.

"I won't go to America. I'm staying."

"Have you reflected carefully?"

"Yes."

Instead of a handclasp Mihály Ursi gave Ernst a great clap on the shoulder. He sat down beside him, drew his chair closer, and now his voice likewise fell to a whisper:

"Before leaving, Ostie Dukay showed me a cave . . ."

He related everything about the Cave. The boys, the electro-physicists, the architects and the engineers, who in times long past had sketched the little printing press for forging five-dollar bills and pound notes, today they were all full-fledged scientists, but they possessed the same unquenchable determination . . . in the mountain was a hidden stream and waterfall . . . electricity directly at hand . . . for such a secret laboratory you couldn't dream of a better place than the Cave.

Midnight had long passed, yet they talked on, debating in whispers, figuring and drawing on slips of paper—"I think the generator might be here . . . over there we could have . . ." Again it was 1927 and they were at the Holzer Restaurant in Berlin, but now the waiter did not eye them suspiciously, and at the neighboring table coarse German guffaws did not explode over foaming beer steins. Consulting now in the secret apartment on Peter Dukay Street, they were no longer the happy and bold but rather the despairing heartbeats of modern science and human rights.

The cigarette smoke in the room was thick enough to bite.

"Those hollows can easily be transformed into living quarters," said Mihály, explaining his rough sketch of the Cave.

Their thoughts had already carried the big cascade generator into the Cave, in whose inner recesses could still be found the gnawed bones of primeval moose, the cave whither man in Tertiary times had fled from the mammoth monster called Brachydiastematherium or from the Machairodus, the bloodthirsty saber-toothed tiger.

123

Chapter 9

The Opening of the Hospital. Strange Patients. An Attempt on the Life of Mihály Ursi.

In January of 1940 the hospital was ready to open, but still they could not decide on a name. Ostie's wife in a long cable from Florida expressed appreciation of the honor, but instead of "Gwendolyn Hospital" proposed the name "Zia Hospital." This on the other hand was unacceptable to Zia. After Ostie, in his turn, had protested naming the hospital after him, Countess Menti at the family conference in her gentle, unprepossessing voice mentioned that in the seventh century after Christ there lived in Anatolia a saintly monk, later canonized by Pope Gregory, who with herbs and the hearts of doves miraculously cured all kinds of disease, even total blindness. She proposed the name "Saint Petrakoghiorgos Hospital." Kristina spoke up against the suggestion, saying that from their attempts to pronounce the name of the hospital the local peasantry would develop cancer of the tongue. Zia's proposal to name the newly renovated castle "István Dukay Hospital" was likewise opposed by Kristina.

"Let's not offend Papa's memory. If Papa should see that his study has become a storeroom for bedpans and rubber sheets he would immediately have an apoplectic fit. You remember how we had to keep the thermometer from him, because he would always smash it against the wall."

Before suitable names for institutions and societies can be born, or excellent titles for novels, plays or journals, the one and only simple word must first slay a host of mad ideas. *Ararat Hospital* finally opened at the end of January, informally and without the presence of newspaper photographers.

The maintenance of a sixty-bed charity hospital runs extremely high. But Ararat Hospital cost hardly anything. Nurses and other hospital employees were recruited from the servants of the castle—even Monsieur Cavaignac, the French chef, remained at his post with his cherry-red nose and cinnamon-hued mustache. Countess Menti was persuaded to disband her nursery, the Glass House, that hotbed of idleness and theft. The sum thus saved covered most of the expenses of Ararat Hospital. Food came straight from the estate's immense truck gardens, orchards, poultry farms and ranches, even from the game preserve. Dr. Freyberger refused to accept any honorarium as hospital director, for he still retained his prospering Budapest practice and spent only three days a week at Ararat.

We have mentioned that the Stargazers, as originally constituted, was not made up exclusively of astronomers, but of "true Magyars" who kept their eyes on the stars. To be a true Magyar in this symbolically named circle was synonymous with utter detestation of Hitler and his cohorts. Among the members were some of German descent as well as Jews, among them doctors and hospital experts who took a hand in equipping Ararat Hospital, setting up its budget and running the whole establishment, therein exhibiting an almost suspicious altruism.

"Dear Mihály," wrote Ostie from New York, "I couldn't believe my eyes when I received the budget of the hospital. You have really accomplished wonders in showing how fallow wealth can be turned to social profit. I congratulate the author of *The Great Fallow*. I hereby appoint you president of the new Hungarian Democratic Republic."

We at once comprehend the selfless zeal of the Stargazers' experts on learning the secret aim of the hospital. From its very inception there were at least twenty patients among whom Freyberger distributed nervous disorders, weakness of the heart, Quincke's edema and other diseases difficult to check on, much like false passports in the land of death. These men from Poland, Czechoslovakia, Yugoslavia and Austria had fled the clutches of the Gestapo. Aside from the Stargazers' innermost general staff, and Freyberger, no one knew about them, neither Zia nor Kristina, not even the two assistant doctors.

The personalities and pasts of these "gravely ill" patients, their individually rich and heroic lives, will descend without trace into the graveyard of time. Nor have we here space and time to dwell on the underground movement's fantastic store of reckless ingenuity. We cannot, for example, follow the further career of Dr. Isidor Tronfeld, from whose abdomen Freyberger cut a bit of soft skin to compensate for what circumcision had so rashly deprived him of. After the operation, possessing indubitable proof of his Aryan origin, Isidor Tronfeld under the name of Heinrich von Gruppenberg, and on the recommendation of Mr. Gruber, became a zealous member of the green-shirted Arrow Cross Party.

On the headboard in private room number three Freyberger wrote the medical term: *Dacryocistitis*. In the bed lay a rather tall and meager man, a German railway engineer, called Hermann Stolz. He had never been an engineer, he had never been a Hermann or a Stolz, but his documents were authentic. The real Hermann Stolz had been killed during the bombardment of Warsaw.

The Dacryocistitis-stricken patient's real name was Kazimir Kilinski. We first came across the name Kilinski at the Cracow festivities. A few days before the outbreak of the war, the program on Pilsudski Day noted that Kazimir Kilinski was the great-grandson of Piotr Kilinski, cobbler of Cracow, who had brought five thousand Polish bootmakers and tanners to the standards of Kosciusko. Kazimir, first of the relay racers, threw Vilna's torch on the great pyre.

According to Mr. Gruber's reports, behind the closed doors of Count Johy's quarters in Septemvir Utca, military experts of the Arrow Cross Party predicted an indubitable German victory from the fact that Hitler had eight hundred and fifty thousand men under arms, plus ten million reserves. He began the war with twelve thousand military planes, and under Goering's guidance German factories were turning out an additional twelve hundred each month. Meanwhile France and England combined had only eight thousand planes and their monthly production barely exceeded seven hundred. All this undoubtedly indicated that Germany would win the war within a few months.

The military experts of the Arrow Cross Party were wrong. Among other things, they neglected to take into account Kazimir Kilinski's dog named Rapczyk, whose racial purity, to be sure, failed to meet the specification of the Nürnberg Law: He was a mixture of police dog and Saint Bernard. Rapczyk alone kept a whole German division at bay. This, stated baldly, sounds like an exaggeration, but we shall immediately understand on recalling that Soviet raw material of prime importance to Germany flowed along Polish railway lines, and the bridges and tracks along this one-thousand-mile stretch kept exploding mysteriously. German military guards by now watched every foot of the line and no living man was allowed near the tracks. Birds, foxes, rabbits and dogs were naturally exempt from this prohibition. So Rapczyk—and many similarly trained Rapczyks—would take a time bomb in his mouth and place it expertly by the tracks. Within minutes, the approaching freight train would become a tangle of wreckage. Kazimir organized and headed underground groups charged with blowing up trains. But the day came when he and a few companions had to flee.

While in subjugated Czechoslovakia and Poland the horrible atrocities of Gestapo retaliation raged, newsreels showed the world the festive inauguration of German-Czechoslovak and German-Polish cultural and sport associations with the usual enthusiastic toasts and broadly grinning faces. From these grins the hapless Poles were already fleeing in such multitudes that the Germans were using electrified barbed wire to seal off the Carpathian passes on the Polish-Hungarian frontier.

One Sunday afternoon toward the end of October, the commanding German officer of a German frontier booth was notified by telephone from Warsaw that racing motorcyclists of DPS, the Deutsches Polisches Sportsklub, would make a turn round the booth. Around three o'clock, as eight roaring machines approached, the German frontier guards, arms flung high and shouting a spirited *"Haidl!"*—Heil Hitler!—proudly noted that the swastika-decked machines were ahead. The only surprise was that the racers failed to slow down for the turn, and by the time the German guards hastily reached for their weapons, the last of the machines had whirled past the bend in the valley, which was Hungarian territory. No need to mention that the racers were Poles of the underground, or that on the swastika-decked leading machine the windbreaker helmet hid the face of Kazimir Kilinski. Knowing this, it is easy to understand how Kazimir, through the Stargazers, got to Ararat Hospital, but just how Rapczyk happened to show up two weeks later is a mystery not clarified by any data in our possession. The Polish word *Rapczyk* means "spotted," and Rapczyk inherited this spottiness from his erring Saint Bernard mama. The enormous Bismarck-faced animal lay in the sun all day long at the main gateway to the hospital and kept his past in darkest secrecy, just like his master, on whose headboard the medical term: Dacryocistitis—inflamation of the tear glands—chanced to be appropriate, for Kazimir Kilinski, champion runner, dog trainer, railway "engineer" and successful motorcycle racer, in truth symbolized the inflammation of the tear glands of the whole Polish people. His condition was rendered graver by the fact that regarding his brother Piotr, a young major on the Polish General Staff, so far no news, no news at all, had come from the war prisoner camp at Smolensk and the forests of Katyn.

In private room number five, there was a certain Italian art dealer named Scipio di Caruccio, who had fallen ill on a Budapest business trip and, according to Dr. Freyberger, might have cancer of the stomach.

"How do you feel?" inquired Zia, on a regular hospital visit.

"Thank you, a little better," whispered Scipio di Caruccio, who affected a sparse, shiny black beard, as zealous Fascists had lately.

Zia of course could not have surmised that a more thorough examination would have revealed Signor Scipio di Caruccio suspect of quite other things than cancer of the stomach. His real name was Slobodan Tuykovich, but we need attach no special symbolic significance to this, since the name Slobodan, particularly among mountain-dwelling Yugoslavs, is extremely common. *Slobodan,* in the Serbian language, means "freedom." Slobodan Tuykovich finished his schooling in Trieste, where he acquired a faultless knowledge of Italian and German. By the early thirties, under the name Scipio di Caruccio, he was already playing much the same role in the Italian Fascist Party as Herr Gruber did in the Hungarian Arrow Cross Party. Slobodan, like his hard-bitten type of Yugoslav in general, liked to express his political convictions unequivocally, lucidly, briefly, preferably with pistol shots. We cannot tell how much of an art expert he was, but we do know he was an expert marksman, and in the late twenties earned his living on music hall stages by shooting earrings from his "wife's" ear with an arrow and bow at a distance of ten paces. His later career led him in quest of other targets, but we don't possess information as to how many human deaths burdened his conscience. His underground associates knew him as Slobo. There are men, slaves to some curious fixed idea, who stake their lives on climbing Mount Everest, or on reaching points in the jungles of Brazil, where no white man has set foot. Slobo, these last years, had staked his life on killing Hitler.

We know Count Johy to have been passionately addicted to cards and constantly struggling with financial crises. So it came most opportunely for Johy, when Grubi introduced to him Signor Scipio di Caruccio, the great Italian art dealer. Johy had no right to sell the painting hanging in his room, Pieter Breughel's *The Census of Bethlehem,* which with other *objets d'art* was the property of the entail, but Grubi reassured Johy that as Cicero wisely phrased it: *Inter arma silent leges*—in wartime not only the Muses, but the laws are silent, too. Besides, in the course of strictly confidential talks behind locked doors, Signor di Caruccio guaranteed so perfect a copy for the empty frame that even the greatest Budapest experts would not detect it. Actually there was no need for this forgery, because Slobo at a glance ascertained that the Breughel hanging in Johy's room was only a mediocre copy. This Grubi knew too, having been present when Count Dupi ordered the copy thirty years before at the Brussels Museum. Signor Scipio di Caruccio promised Johy thirty thousand dollars for the "wonderful" Breughel. This was all the easier for Slobo, because his total fortune barely exceeded the thirty lire in his left trouser pocket. He merely flaunted the thirty thousand dollars before Johy, who he knew had easy access to the highest Nazi leaders, even Hitler himself. Of this Johy himself liked to boast. The talk being of pictures, he just incidentally mentioned that the Führer was deeply attracted to painting.

"And what a great painter he would have been!" said Johy, *"Ach, grösser, viel grösser als Tintoretto* . . . he could even have been a . . . a Tintorissimo!"

Then he added that the Führer once told him it had been his lifelong ambition to be able to spend but two minutes daily before Tintoretto's *Annunciation,* which he had seen in Venice at the Scuola di San Rocco when he first met the Duce.

An exciting remark, particularly for the ear of a Slobodan Tuykovich, Slobo at once hatched his plan. He would inform Johy that he could only pay the thirty thousand dollars if Johy obtained an audience for him at Berchtesgaden to present the Führer with Tintoretto's *Annunciation* in token of the Italian Art Dealers Association's homage.

The hospital's head nurse was Schwester Hilda, her true name being Marja Drda, a rather ascetic-looking spinster, but in our hands are a number of photographs showing her between the ages of twenty and thirty-three, when her career and fame soared highest. These photos reveal that she possessed a type of beauty rooted in reckless and provocative good humor, which was astoundingly apparent not only in her face, in her hands, and in the movements of her whole body, but in her very dress, flowing from the crown of her hat even to the heels of her shoes. A piquant and somewhat Slavic nose perched good-humoredly on her face, like the hat slightly askew on the head of a tippler. Her full and finely arched mouth appears to laugh at these photos even when she is trying her best to be serious. Her large, almost too large, light gray eyes were plum-shaped and gave the impression that their owner used them not so much to see with as to laugh by their light. Women in perpetual good humor, whose eyes are ever laughing, within minutes become most boring. This was not the sort of laughter reflected in Marja Drda's face and eyes. Here was something deeper, almost philosophic—a laughter disdaining everything, but in a well-intentioned forgiving way, with a touch of sadness. She tended toward medium height, with the slight boyish build which always exudes an air of virginity, though nothing was further from Marja than virginity.

She was born in 1904, in western Czechoslovakia, the daughter of a master smith at Kladno. She was not only shockingly uninhibited in speech, but had a rather exhibitionist nature, making no secret of the minute particulars of her love-life. This we might call style, a style quite extraordinarily effective with a certain type of man. Marja herself related that when not yet quite fourteen, wandering alone one night on the streets of Prague, heavily painted, she was accosted by a constable who took her to the station house on suspicion of prostitution. During her interrogation she obstinately maintained she was a virgin,

130

which happened to be true, but the officer of the law wouldn't believe it. "How can I prove it? See for yourself!" insisted the innocent girl. The constable was an older man, but his days as a recruit had taught him the police axiom of conscientiously examining all possible evidence, and he therefore accepted this proffered mode of proof, the more so since at that late hour he was on duty alone. Having convinced himself that the suspect had told the truth, he reproved the straying maid with fatherly words, provided her with moral admonitions, and, loyal to the spirit of the state's Department of Public Morals, escorted her home in the dark night, incidentally mentioning at parting that the following Wednesday at one hour after midnight he again would be on duty alone at the station house. This was how Marja's love-life began—but not where it ended.

In 1920, at the age of sixteen, when Entente missions and grandiose *faiseurs* swarmed in Vienna, Marja Drda for a short time appeared on the stage of the Apollo as a Hawaiian hula dancer. Her thorny Czech name, Marja Drda—which after the first bottle of champagne no member of the Entente mission could pronounce or write in his secret notebook—spread its dry air-thirsty wings toward international fame as Maria Darida. Her first admirer observed that the name Maria Darida echoed the loveliest tones of the Hawaiian guitar.

In 1923, she had her own villa at Semmeringen. In the center of her spacious reception room—in accordance with her own plans—was a mosaic-tiled sunken pool. Submerged in its perfumed waters, quite naked, she received her visitors, including reporters from the Vienna journals. The name Maria Darida was continually cropping up in gossip columns, linked to prominent figures of highest rank.

In contrast to the mosaic pool and the naked beauty in it, a Madonna hung on the wall above a vigil light. Marja's parents had been very devoted Catholics, she had grown up in a religious atmosphere. It is not a rarity that God and free love meet in their purest form in the lives of courtesans.

The picture was a copy of Raphael's *Madonna*, the most popular model for commercial painters. The huge original fresco in the Vatican has four other figures: Mary Magdalene, the Apostle, and two little angels leaning their elbows on powder-puff clouds; Marja's picture was only 25 by 20 inches, showing the Madonna with her flying veil, and the Christ-child in her arms. Only a half-portrait, but it was smoky, its frame worm-eaten: certain proof of great value for those who do not know anything about art. Marja bought it in a small antique shop in Prague, with the first money she made with her body. She was fifteen years old then, and she was especially enchanted by the inscription on the greenish brass plate of the frame: *"L'ung me fait paour, l'autre joye et liesse."* Neither the art dealer nor she understood the words, but they were beautiful and mystic. Later a scholar admirer of hers explained the archaic French words: they were from a prayer, written by Villon, the great balladeer of the fifteenth century, the greatest lyric poet in the world, who had nothing but a knife, trousers and a beard—his knife killed a priest when he burglarized a sacristy, his worn trousers hung from every bedpost in the most exclusive boudoirs—he finished his life on the gallows, but there was never a beard on any human face more soaked by tears than when Villon sobbed in his songs about the struggles between his soul and body.

It happened many times that Marja, emerging from the mosaic-tiled pool, and still naked, knelt and prayed before the Madonna. Villon's line inscribed on the picture meant: "The one makes me afraid, the other joyful and lusty."

Maria Darida became acquainted with a member of the Dukay family, Ostie Dukay, then a young man of twenty-five, who spent most of the year at the Dukay palace on Bösendorfer-strasse. Vienna—at least so far as high spirits and night life are concerned—recovered faster after the war than Budapest. It was family tradition that a twenty-five-year-old Dukay always needed more money than he had. The private banker, in making the loan, intimated that he would be most grateful if the Count would introduce him to Vienna high society. The money-lender's wish was tantamount to a stipulation. Ostie Dukay held a great banquet at which he seated the banker next to the Archduchess Arabella, who graciously inquired about the general economic situation. The banker, conversing for the first time with a live archduchess, was so overcome that he bounded from his place and in a short but very fine and touching speech emptied his

132

glass to the Archduchess and the great future of the House of Hapsburg.

The Archduchess Arabella listened to the speaker with tears in her eyes, but at the conclusion of the toast an astounding thing happened. The Archduchess arose. "Now let's get down to business!" said she, simply, and within seconds divested herself of every stitch of attire. Her example was followed by other princesses and countesses present. It is superfluous for us to note that Archduchess Arabella was Maria Darida, and that the other ladies, too, were nymphs from the Graben, the West End of Vienna.

News of the banquet naturally spread quickly in Viennese circles, reaching the ear of a renowned professor at the University of Vienna in the version that Maria Darida had founded a nudist club. He telephoned, therefore, to the artiste, expressing his keen desire to attend a meeting of the club, *selbstverständlich nur aus reinem wissenschaftlichen Gesichtspunkt*—from a purely scientific angle, of course. Some days later, a liveried footman ushered the renowned professor into the hall and informed him that the rules of the club obliged everyone to disrobe before entering the salon. The scholar of numismatics and the art of the Isaurian period tried to protest, even offered a small bribe to the footman, who, in view of strict orders, would not relent. *Schaun Sie, Herr Professor* . . . and he showed him the cloakroom filled with discarded articles of men's and women's apparel. Shoes, stockings, women's lace panties, men's underdrawers, in fact even a truss hung from a hook. At the sight of the cloakroom, the renowned professor gave in and, with the footman's zealous aid, disrobed. When he entered the salon, sixty persons awaited him, the flower of Vienna society, completely dressed, gentlemen in white ties, ladies in evening gowns. The footman's role was played by Count Ostie Dukay.

Maria Darida's youth abounded in such adventures. In the late twenties she could be seen on the French Riviera, where in 1929, after winning second prize at the Cannes tennis matches, she was introduced to the Prime Minister of Monaco, at which occasion Maria Darida, with a lightning-swift motion, placed her right breast in the hand extended by the seventy-six-year-old and

133

somewhat nearsighted statesman. According to the reputed testimony of eyewitnesses, she had an exquisite little breast, but data in our possession does not confirm the authenticity of this story.

Completely authentic, on the other hand, was her marriage, contracted in 1932, with Count Dmitri Shornikov. Throughout her courtesan career, Maria Darida maintained the principle that there was no need for her ever to marry anyone. Consequently, in those years she married only six times in all. But her marriages were extremely short-lived, and always served some practical purpose. When she decided to transfer headquarters to South America, she considered it essential to appear as a countess in the great hotels of Brazil and Argentina, so she instructed Europe's marriage brokers to find her a count as a husband, urgently, within two weeks, because she already had her steamship ticket. The first offer came from Budapest, naturally, and then, for the second time, she came in contact with the Dukays, though without the knowledge of the family members. From one of Zia's letters we may recall the name of Uncle Dmitri, who was the Russian news announcer with Radio Hungary. His father, at the close of the last century had married a Dukay countess, and Dmitri inherited half a million acres on the slopes of the Urals, but nowadays was poorer than a churchmouse. The matrimonial contract was bound by the strict proviso that after the civil ceremony Uncle Dmitri would receive from the broker the stipulated five thousand dollars, but was not so much as to address the lady, who would depart immediately after the formalities. Meticulously shaven, his shoes brightly polished, waiting in the anteroom of the registry office, he reflected that the lady whose name they hadn't mentioned, was undoubtedly some old hunchback, Lord knows what sort of monster. He gaped in astonishment when, on the trimmest of ankles, without so much as noticing anyone, a gorgeous young creature swept through the anteroom. Upon rattling off the formalities, the bewitching fairy hurried back to her car, not having tossed her husband a single glance. In the anteroom, Uncle Dmitri, without even counting his money, snatched the five-thousand-dollar envelope from the hands of the broker and, leaping several steps at a time, rushed after his wife, whose hand was already at the door of the car. Uncle Dmitri clasped his hands prayerfully:

"Dearest lady . . . I implore you . . . Consider that I am your lawful husband . . . one . . . only one night is all I ask . . ."

Maria Darida, without relinquishing the handle of the door, surveyed Uncle Dmitri, who then was already sixty-five years old, but whose erect carriage, long thin yellow mustache and whole appearance preserved something of the onetime atmosphere of the Winter Palace. She said to the Czar's former officer-of-the-guards:

"All right . . . if you return the five thousand dollars."

Uncle Dmitri hastily reached into his pocket. Next morning, again without a penny, he appeared at the microphone to continue announcing the Russian-language news. Maria Darida disappeared from his life like an exquisite flashing vision.

In 1933, for a few months, Marja was the wife of an aging Swedish envoy, and she was called Her Excellency Madame Maria Gustave de Paulsen-Tarrasch. We need not remember this long name because Marja herself did not precisely remember the names of her husbands, but during these months at her receptions in the Faubourg St. Germain she behaved in the fashion befitting the glacially elegant wife of a Swedish diplomat. She divorced Gustave de so-and-so because she had fallen desperately in love with another man.

It frequently happens to great courtesans or *grande dames* of blinding beauty that for their sole, real and only desperate love they choose, not a Rudolph Valentino or a virile and exotic prince, but a waiter or a poor bank clerk, who bites his nails and hardly has shoulders.

Almost the same thing happened to Marja. The man's name was Maxim Narokov, a young Soviet diplomat, in whom she perceived those depths of purest love "only the Russian soul is capable of." Maxim was different, oh, so different, from the petty diplomats of the Faubourg St. Germain, whose highest endeavor was to find ways of telling ladies the most piquant stories without risking a slap in the face. The lisping André Foltys, the one-eyed debonair Eliskases, the trap-shooting champion Ollando —all the ones who desperately sought an affair with her.

How different was Maxim's humble silent love—like Vanya's fatal passion for Natasha in Dostoievsky's *The Insulted and the*

Injured, her favorite novel. Maxim was the only man before whom she would not have pronounced a double-entendre, with whom she had never progressed even so far as a kiss—the only man with whom she was mortally in love, as well.

Maxim did not pester her with flowers and phone calls; but if she chanced to enter a shop in the Place Vendôme, Maxim, half a minute later, would be standing at the opposite counter with his back to her as though he hadn't even noticed her presence. They always met by "accident." At the races, too, he seemed to have emerged from the ground as he tipped his hat with an embarrassed smile. And when, at a close-packed cocktail party a hand from behind or beside her would offer the flame of a cigarette lighter, it was sure to be Maxim's. The hand would disappear—at such times they mostly didn't even speak—yet the little click and spurt of flame sank into Marja's heart.

There was something touching in Maxim's apparel, too. Generally speaking, the Soviet diplomats never knew the address of a good tailor. They held knives and forks differently, too, and even in the way two stiff fingers would hold a cigarette, the way they kissed the hands of the ladies at legation receptions—oh, yes, there was something of *The Insulted and the Injured* in them. They were treated by the Ollandos and Andrés like distant, poor, unschooled cousins of the civilized whites. As André related: back home their families slept as many as twenty in a room cluttered with unwashed pots and pans, perhaps they earned a living by gelding horses or cleaning cesspools, they made primitive guns from gaspipe and terrified the world with a new redeeming doctrine masked in a bushy Russian beard— André could go on and on in this vein.

Maxim spoke French as it is spoken by those who learn the language in their twenties at a great distance from Paris, but the two had always conversed in Russian. Strolling with Maxim in the Bois, Marja refurbished her rusty command of the language.

When Maxim was transferred from Paris and unexpectedly vanished from her life, her colorful but exhausting career no longer interested her. The story is told of Tristan Bernard, the great French playwright, that one day he went to withdraw his last hundred francs from the French National Bank. The building was guarded by a soldier with a fixed bayonet. With his bankbook cancelled, Tristan Bernard walked over to the soldier, laid a hand on his shoulder, and tersely said: "You can go home now."

Some such thing happened in Maria Darida's life too—as if high spirits and foolishness, love and youth were present in our lives in the form of a bankbook, and then comes the moment when our cancelled bankbook is returned to us at the cashier's window. One fine day Maria Darida said to her secretary, her maid and her chauffeur: "You may go." Maria Darida vanished from the scene, her melodious name shrank back to the thorny Marja Drda, and in the little Czech town Kladno, where they knew nothing of her past, she put on thick cotton stockings and wiped off her make-up. She had a chapel built in Kladno; she knelt and prayed before her Villon Madonna for a reunion with Maxim, who was more for her than simply a man whom she loved. Maxim Narokov was the Unobtainable, the earthly happiness which we pursue in vain; Maxim was like Maeterlinck's Blue Bird.

Marja took a nursing course, and worked in hospitals. In her case it would not be right to say that she was surfeited with life. At the height of her career, even in her stormiest years, she would often disappear for months at a time. At such times, under the name Marja, she would scrub the steps and lavatories of pest-houses or do the roughest manual work at cloisters. No, no, she did not have to atone for anything. She never felt guilty. But she had a dread of hereditary blindness. In her family there were three such instances. Things were going too well for her. She laughed too much. Fate was too generous. If she went off somewhere to work, this gnawing dread ceased. She felt as though she had somehow propitiated Fate.

Seeking causes for the transformation in her life we must also consider that in 1935, with Hitler already in power two years, Nazism threatened Czechoslovakia with annihilation. And Marja Ddra in ensuing years proved a glowing patriot. Many believe that courtesans are morally quite depraved. This is a mistake. Let no one be deceived by the impetuous license they allow themselves in sexual matters—differing from some of their fellow women only by engaging in this openly and frankly, without hypocrisy. The lives of courtesans teach us that generally a great soul dwells within them, and not unworthily have they received the touching memorial which Dumas *fils* raised to them in his *Dame aux Camélias*.

Over the week end Uncle Dmitri sometimes appeared at Ararat, occasionally even exchanging a few pleasant words with "Schwester Hilda," but he did not recognize his one-night wife.

Though Marja Drda was still only thirty-six years old, her hair above both ears was already graying, she wore horn-rimmed spectacles and in her Red Cross uniform she seemed nearer fifty.

We already know the patient in the hospital's private room number two: Professor Ernst Tronfeld. His diagnosis spoke the truth: general debility. But the effect of the fattening cure, aided by the rich buffalo milk of the estate, already showed, and on his face and head the hair shaved off in the German concentration camp had grown a quarter of an inch.

Once or twice a week, private cars would take these "critical" cases to Budapest, to the famous Rudas Medicinal Baths. The cars naturally did not stop near the baths, but on Peter Dukay Street, where at Count Dupi's onetime secret bachelor quarters meetings of the underground movement were held.

While Freyberger was successfully re-establishing the physical state of his patients, the Stargazers' general staff began work on the Cave to set up Ernst's secret laboratory. But the outfitting of the Cave demanded not only excellent engineers, but workmen, and very dependable ones, too. These were available from the ranks of socialist, more exactly, communist, workers in contact with the Stargazers. Ursi exercised extreme caution in choosing his men, because once before in the course of his life, betrayal had swept him into grave danger, when the apothecary's son "snitched" on him, revealing who had hidden the bullfinch in Herr Beck's drawer. Such a memory makes a man wary the rest of his life. This time the Nazis might stealthily secrete some live bullfinch in the drawer, but times and affairs had progressed, and in the event of betrayal a *consilium abeundi* meant certain death.

The outfitting of the Cave marked the reappearance of Joska Kurdi in Ursa Major's life. Kurdi, now thirty-eight, was not only dependable in his work, but personally knew all the workers—their past, their characters, their mode of thought—and only hired the most trustworthy. It was primarily owing to him that the secret of the Cave, even in the most critical days to come, was never whispered to the Gestapo.

In the New Year issue of *Kolomp*, 1940, on the occasion of his fortieth birthday, Ursi wrote an editorial from which we quote the following passages:

> In seeking to understand the historical background of the birth of our century, we do not need to bury ourselves in bottomless libraries, it is enough to turn our attention to two men in Europe.
>
> The thirty-eight-year-old German emperor, Wilhelm II, wore a silver breastplate between the wings of his snow-white cape. This man, who had the ancient stone gate of Jerusalem razed so as not to have to dismount before entering, concisely and brilliantly personified the overweening Prussian spirit which Nietzsche had lifted to philosophic heights. In all the German schools, geology, the multiplication table, even the Ascension of Christ, became transmuted into a German sword. "A giraffe is an extremely long-necked animal," began the zoology hour, "indigenous to territories in Africa which should have become German colonies long ago; but England, which is only a little island, and France, which . . .
>
> "And to quote our great philosopher Nietzsche: 'The noble rage springing from the passion for destroying the enemy, this is the globe-shattering fury of soul without which life is intolerable for the great German race.' "
>
> The other man, a guitar-playing, small, thirty-year-old lawyer—his friends called him Papushka because of his large, bald head—in the first days of 1900 published a modest book in Zurich: The *Aims of the Russian Social Democrats*. Vladimir Ilich Ulianov for the first time used the pen name "N. Lenin," remembering the giant river Lena, the melting ice of which thundered through the region of his exile in Siberia.
>
> Turning our eyes from Europe to the Far East, we notice a tiny bloodstain on the coverlet of the infant century:

in the summer of 1900 on a Peking street the German ambassador lay murdered, the first victim of the Chinese Boxer Rebellion protesting European imperialism.

To examine the metabolism of the twentieth century, or to put it more exactly, its economic condition, we have only to remember that in 1900 stockbrokers on the New York Exchange were ripping jackets from each other's backs in a frantic buying spree. President McKinley signed the Gold Standard Act, the aureate fanfare of which enticed not only hidden dollars from stockings and mattresses, swelling to many many millions, but even from Europe money began flowing into Wall Street like some new warm Gulf Stream. The U.S.A. till the end of the century had only flaunted its resources without proving anything. At the Chicago World Fair for the first time it flung aside its mantle like a wrestler entering the ring, and astounded the world with its bulging industrial muscles.

In the huge stream of many nationalities more than four million immigrants had already arrived in New York Harbor from the Austro-Hungarian Monarchy alone.

Happy was the whole world when the twentieth century was born. Gypsy music and wine-mellowed laughter rang out. On that New Year's Eve the whole bourgeois world laughed, most irresistibly at Montmartre *réveillons,* because Paris was the capital of the laughing world.

La Belle Époque! In the Bois, magnificent thoroughbreds sped courtesans' carriages, whose wheels seemed almost to play melodies by Offenbach, while the Blonde Wonder disparaged the horses of the Brunette Wonder for being the gift of a mere Russian prince rather than of the King of Portugal, as hers were. There was a stupendous emancipation in this *Belle Époque:* respectable young matrons laughingly tossed aside the girdles of chastity prescribed for all females by the prudery of Louis Philippe and the rigid morals of Queen Victoria. A woman was no woman, if she did not deceive her husband; a man no man if he did not seduce the wife of his best friend. The impetuous rejection of earthly cares made the trivial and unessential all-important and indispensable. *Le superflu, chose si néces-*

saire!—these words were the ones that governed the ways of society.

The Great Revolution of Laughter had been at its peak when the new century was born, and set free the grosset ribaldries in literature and the arts. In a rain-streaked, jumpy, primitive film the ebullient French *esprit* transcended even the obscenities of Aristophanes and Euripides. The brief film opened by showing a peasant working his garden. A sudden grimace contorts his features as he claps his hands to his stomach, indicating with the exaggerated mimicry of the old silent films that he has urgent business to attend to. A neighbor sees him squatting by the fence, approaches from the other side on tiptoe, through the fence extends a shovel beneath his friend, spirits away the result unnoticed and replaces it with something else. When the peasant rises and, yielding to immortal custom, turns for a brief backward glance, he is bewildered to see a duck egg on the ground. The second reel conveys us to the spacious council chamber of the Académie française where forty green-frocked Immortals are seated around a table on the center of which rests a duck egg. Biological, anthropological and ornithological Immortals debate the marvel of the egg with a vehemence that even leads to blows, but they cannot agree. In the third reel we are again in the council chamber of the Académie française. This time the center of the table is occupied not by the duck egg, but by the peasant himself, crouching with rolled-down trousers while the forty Immortals await the result with baited breath.

It was with such hearty raucous laughter that the twentieth century set forth toward its unknown destiny, but during its first minutes one of the ridiculed Immortals was still working in his shabby laboratory. Something peculiar had happened the other day. Henri Becquerel chanced to leave a kind of chemical salt on a photographic plate along with some half-eaten bread and jam; and though the plate was carefully wrapped in black paper, it had behaved in a surprising fashion. This substance was named uranium after the seventh planet Uranus.

141

At the end of January 1940, in the sleepiest month of the "phony war," when neutral Hungary still enjoyed great freedom of press and speech, the Stargazers held a great mass meeting at which Ursi delivered a one-and-a-half-hour speech. The auditorium of the university was jammed. We quote a few sentences, merely to clarify the sequence of events:

. . . German agents occupying high posts in our own country are making every effort to get us into this war.

. . . oh, yes, we've just regained a great part of our truncated country. And whom have we to thank?—ask the German agents. It is not France, England or the United States. It is the new powerful Germany. That is true. But I cannot refrain from reminding you of the old tale of the gentle wolf who had been feeding the frail lamb with fatherly affection, right up to the day he devoured it. Are we blind to the fate of Poland?

. . . for not without reason did Nietzsche write: "So often as the German attains power and might . . . vast and terrible fear rises among the nations of Europe . . . who have all felt the wrath of the blond Teutonic beast."

The following day there was a dinner party at Septemvir Utca: the result of Countess Menti's solicitous diplomacy. She did not know exactly what such words as *Fascism, Nazism* or *Communism* meant. She had never regarded Ostie or Mihály as liberals, Johy as a Nazi, Rere as an idiot; they were quite equal in her heart: they were her sons. The great battle between dictatorship and democracy, represented now in the persons of Johy and Zia's husband, was nothing to her but an uneasy family squabble, and her motherly instinct tried to smooth it over by every possible means.

Unhappily she could not have chosen a day less suitable to her purpose. Mihály's speech had stirred vehement controversy all over town. Police cars were rushing to quell wild battles between Nazis and socialist workers in taverns on the outskirts. When Mihály and Zia entered the sitting room, copies of the leading local Nazi newspapers lay scattered over tables and armchairs. One flaming editorial ended with the words: "The Hungarian fist will mercilessly crush such traitors as Mihály Ursi."

During dinner not a single word was spoken about his speech, thanks to Countess Menti, who tirelessly steered the conversation. She turned to her son-in-law:

"What is your opinion, dear Mihály . . . is there any life on the other planets? On Mars, for example. . . . Oh, how interesting!"

Countess Menti throughout her life had been a master of conversation when the silence grew oppressive at the dinner table.

After dinner Ursi sought to leave unnoticed, but Johy caught him in the doorway.

"I want to talk to you."

"All right," said Ursi, rather coldly. He was fully aware of what Johy wanted to discuss, and he only wondered whether he should give him money, and if so, how much.

Entering the study Johy took the seat behind his desk, and Ursi occupied the armchair facing it. Johy did not roll his *r*'s, rather he uttered them too softly. His tone was distant, firm and unfriendly.

"My dear Mihály, my lawyer definitely states that from the Gere estate some three hundred acres are still due me."

His porcelain-blue eyes sometimes lost their color. Now he fixed this grayish glance on Mihály in a strange way. His words were not only a legal absurdity based on an audacious lie, but his attitude was blackmail on a grand scale, packed with hidden threats.

"After my beloved father's death," Johy added, "when we divided the unentailed family fortune, I suffered a terrible injustice."

Ursi's quiet smile was tinged with irony. After a few seconds of very profound silence, Johy said in a low, but highly supercilious tone:

"My dear Mihály, very soon the day will come when you will badly need my help."

Ursi narrowed his eyes.

"What do you mean by that?"

143

"Well, you read the editorials about you, didn't you?"

Ursi wore that quizzical smile which he always accompanied by scratching his shoulder with his right hand.

"You think the Germans will win this war?"

"I most decidedly do," Johy said, and suddenly dropped his little icy smile. He again fixed his grayish glance on his brother-in-law. "I'm afraid we're straying too far from the point."

Ursi nodded, and said calmly:

"I absolutely reject your claim to the Gere estate."

He nodded curtly, his usual habit in announcing some important and final decision.

Johy's temples grew pink and a swift blue light flashed in his eyes as he came to his feet, sinking his fists deep in his trouser pockets.

"Listen, Mihály—"

Ursi, with a quick glance at his watch, cut him short.

"You will excuse me . . . I must go."

And he strode toward the door, leaving Johy a lank figure suspended in mid-air.

Two days after the dinner, in the early darkening winter afternoon, Ursi and Zia set out on their usual week-end trip to Ararat. They were about halfway there, when a large sedan drew past their car at high speed. There was the blast of two revolver shots and the windows of Ursi's car fell in clattering fragments. Zia screamed loudly and fainted. Ursi, his left hand on the wheel, his right supporting Zia, drove on slowly to Ararat.

Neither was wounded.

Chapter 10

Zia's Audience with His Serenity The Regent.
Flight toward America.

Zia's letter to Ostie

Budapest, Feb. 5, 1940

DEAR OSTIE:

You already know all the details of the attempt and I don't suppose you take Mihály's theory seriously either, that only drunks were firing from the sedan. Not even Mihály himself believes this, he is only trying to reassure me and perhaps himself too. You know how he is: when danger comes, he likes to talk of something else. My opinion remains the same as during our brief telephone call: the assailants in all probability were young Arrow Cross hoodlums. After his speech, in addition to the attacks of Hungarian papers, Mihály also received the honor of being singled out by the *Völkischer Beobachter* in an article entitled *"Der ungarische deutschfresser Flammarion."*

Of course we said nothing to Mama about the assault. When we told Kristina, she looked into space and quite softly said: Johy. To me this again is nothing but Kristina's extravagant and sometimes idiotic fancy. Not for an instant did it occur to me to suspect Johy's hand, even in the background. Of course in Arrow Cross circles he makes no bones about his opinion of Mihály; and it is also true that these times can turn a human soul inside out, just like a stocking or a glove—look at Grubi!—but I find it utterly inconceivable that Johy should sink to the abyss of fratricide. As I see him now, I can only pity him for his abnormal life and political fanaticism, and hold his environment entirely to blame. Mama's angelic naïveté did not recognize the dan-

145

ger in Otto Kliegl, that accursed devil of a tutor she provided him with, and when Kristina warned her, Mama replied that Kliegl, who knows so much and speaks so eloquently of Chancellor Metternich, could not possibly be a homosexual. In Johy I still find traces of high and noble thought—alas, it's all too late.

But now I want to report to you on a matter I have concealed even from Mihály, because he would hardly have approved of it. I had an audience with the Regent.

You will understand why. It came to my ears that His Serenity was also indignant over Mihály's speech. I wouldn't mind if they banned the *Kolomp*—between us, it is doing very poorly and I think the editing is weak—but I feared that sooner or later Mihály would clash with the government, too, and they would lock him up again. So I wanted to smooth things over between the Regent and Mihály, or putting it more modestly, the line represented by Mihály and you and me and many other sober-minded persons.

The morning after the attempt I telephoned Pista Horthy, the dancing partner of my girlhood—I think we were even a little in love with each other—in a word, I asked him to obtain for me an urgent audience with his father. I received an appointment for that same noon through the cabinet office.

The sun was shining as I walked up to the castle in my new little veiled spring hat and navy suit, a masterpiece of the Dux Salon. From this you can already see that I was doing my utmost in the interest of democracy. When I stepped into the courtyard of the castle, the changing of the guard was still going on, to musical accompaniment. Voltaire writes that compared to Frederick The Great's changing of the guard at his palace in Potsdam, the Trojan War was child's play. To my mind, the Potsdam parade must have been child's play compared with the way in which halberded, eagle-feathered, leopard-skinned guards relieve each other at the Royal Palace in Buda. Papa always said that ever since this "sailor on horseback" became head of state, the Royal Palace in every way ridiculously exaggerated the air of the Franz Joseph period. Yet Talleyrand back at the Congress of Vienna reminded the Czar Alexander that the smaller a country is, the higher heels it wears.

I waited a good half-hour in the Regent's anteroom. His aide-de-camp, costumed like a Hungarian Lohengrin, from time to time carried on whispered telephone conversations, but said nothing to me the whole time. I became resigned to the fact that his silence and whispered telephone conversations also belonged to the tremendous *hauteur* of the place. I kept thinking how Papa would have grumbled if he had been sitting next to me during the long wait. Of course, he looked down on the gentried Regent not only out of Dukay pride, but on a legitimist basis too. It also occurred to me that there might be formalities connected with an audience. The Regent is treated like a king, he behaves like a king—he learned this side of his job well, for he was long aide-de-camp to Franz Joseph. Again I recollected Papa's saying: "What would you say if my valet became head of the estate?" For a moment I hesitated: should I ask the mute aide-de-camp whether, in leaving, one must back out of the room here too, as at the court of Franz Joseph? I never liked to stumble backwards, as you know—in the Dux Salon's masterpiece I especially didn't want to risk landing on my rear.

How would he receive me and how would he react to what I had to say? I had never yet spoken with His Serenity. When he was at Ararat some twenty years ago on a boar hunt, I was still only ten years old, but I remember clearly that when he asked Rere what career he would choose, Rere, after some reflection, said modestly and very gravely: "I want to be a lioness." According to Kristina, the Regent's personality is fascinating; foreigners have the same opinion, including John Galsworthy. Uncle Peti adjudges him an excellent horseman, but says there are differences between a bridle for a horse and a bridle for a government, and he would have done better to remain president of the Hunt Club because his capacities range no higher. After which Kristina told us—I don't know whether it was true or only a fantasy—that when he received the Corvin Medal winner, Professor Konrad, the world-famous physicist, the

Regent talked for a whole hour of nothing but horses. The aide-de-camp, who was present, apologized profusely to Professor Konrad after the audience. "His Serenity mistook you for Mr. Pongrac, the noted horse breeder, who also has an audience today."

"I hope," said Professor Konrad, "that I didn't talk any nonsense. I had a mount once, and I know something about horses. The thing that worries me, though, is what Mr. Pongrac will have to say about thermo-dynamics and relativity."

Finally, through the cushioned door pirouetted a red-eared figure in a morning coat who in his confusion bowed deeply once more to the closed door. The aide-de-camp with a significant gesture indicated that I might enter.

My first impression was favorable. Nine years ago, when I saw Mussolini, the reception hall of the Palazzo Venezia was so enormous that the Duce at the other end of the room looked like a mouse, and I thought a pair of roller skates might come in handy to negotiate the distance along the marble floor to his prodigious desk. But this room was rather small and not a bit ostentatious. The seventy-one-year-old Regent hastened toward me with a friendly smile and his first words, in the tone of a gallant old cavalier, praised my little veiled hat. So it began well.

He wore his admiral's uniform, displaying only the red ribbon of the order of Maria Terézia, and on the left hip of his coat there was the three-inch-long golden cord which looked like a yellow worm. It was for the chamberlain's key of office. Don't forget to explain to Gwen that to be a chamberlain, among other things, one had to prove that all one's ancestors through seven generations came from noble families. Every application for this little golden worm had to be accompanied by 127 birth certificates, going back to the eighteenth century. And tell Gwen that when Papa received the Golden Fleece he had to prove his blue blood through nine generations with 511 birth certificates of our ancestors. She will scream with laughter.

The Regent's golden worm reminded me that the Hapsburg Law was much more severe than the Nürnberg

148

Law. I really don't understand, my dear Ostyak, why you don't like Hitler.

The Regent's face was exactly as it is on the silver five-pengö piece: silvery gray hair, and a silvery glint even in his freshly shaven face—the sharp Savonarola profile, the imposingly large nose, the narrow chin jutting sharply forward, which according to Lombroso signifies a lofty and firm will, and according to Papa, pig-headed stupidity. Medium stature, but stately bearing, crisp courtly movements. Here and there a German word slipped into his speech as he ushered me to a chair near his desk. Remember, Papa always said that his voice resembled that of a toothless hag? This isn't true. But in his voice there is a certain soft, almost feminine resonance, as when in our childhood we hummed through combs covered with tissue paper. On his desk everything was neat as a jewel. To the right of the red leather blotter pad lay at least twenty pencils, blue, yellow, red, green, black, ranged with micrometric precision, all with overlong points. I recognized these pencils from Kristina's description, for she has often visited this room with her world-redeeming plans. She once allegedly asked the Regent: was it true that at his court there was a rank with general's pay called Royal Hungarian Pencil Sharpener? I wouldn't put it past her. Our crazy sister also observed that the pencils had such long points because they were attempting to imitate the Regent's nose.

The Regent rested both hands on the leather pad and waited for me to speak. His hands were slender, but well-knit, like those of a good horseman, and on the backs were large, flat, indistinct freckles; his left hand wore a massive emblazoned signet ring. Slowly I drew off my butter-colored gloves and, in the deep stillness, consulted with one of them as to how I should begin. At times like these, when you want to be very wise, you usually blurt out some idiocy. The quiet had grown long, when I began speaking slowly:

"On my husband's upper left thigh . . ."

I swallowed hard, realizing that I had made a false start. The Regent jerked back his head in surprise; knowing the "insane" Dukays, he braced himself, I imagine, for some frightful intimacy and feared that I had mistaken him for a psychoanalyst.

". . . on his upper left thigh," I continued, "is the scar of a deep wound. He received that wound as a young technology student, while fighting in Your Serenity's forces against the returning King Charles. And last night an attempt was made on his life."

In a few words I described the incident. The Regent, leaning slightly forward, listened with narrowing eyes. Sometimes he made a gesture as if to stroke the lobe of his ear with his signet ring finger, but this only served surreptitiously to cup his ear. This was Papa's trick too, when his hearing began to fail. The Regent sometimes pressed his forefinger to his nostril, as though trying to shove his great nose a little farther over on his face; then, pinching his tremendous olfactory organ between two fingers, he would, with a swift motion, replace it. These all seemed habitual gestures.

"Beyond any doubt," I continued, "the attackers were Arrow-Crossists. Just like those who last year tried a bombing attempt against Your Serenity. By this I only mean to say that my husband, even if he differs on social matters and in the German question, can be no enemy of Your Serenity. Though of simple working class origin, he is as pristinely Magyar as Your Serenity—or, let us say, myself."

The Regent with a pensive gesture reached toward the row of pencils, but on the way the hand after all decided not to disrupt their exquisite soldierly array. A bit of irateness crept into his voice and the silvery face reddened too.

"My dear Countess, your husband is a left-wing radical. I shall speak frankly. I, too, was most painfully affected when Count Ostie chose your husband, of all people, to administer the estate. According to my information, in America Ostie maintains close contact with ultra-left-wing Roosevelt circles, and surreptitiously intervenes in Hungarian politics. After the first world war a Count Karolyi led this nation into revolution. Does a Count Dukay now hanker for this accursed role?"

150

The tone was hostile and aroused my hostility too. With a rather nervous motion I adjusted the veil on my hat.

"Would Your Serenity prefer all of us Dukays to follow the lead of Graf Johann von Dukay?"

The Regent dismissed Johy with a deprecating gesture.

"It's true," I continued, "that my brother is close to the highest Washington sources. And it may perchance interest Your Serenity that in his letters he continually writes that the United States, for any number of reasons, cannot allow Nazi Germany to win. So if—"

"That is only what American Jews imagine."

"So if Hungary, on Germany's side . . ."

The Regent touched my arm. His tone and gesture were almost fatherly.

"Dear Countess, put yourself in my position. The Peace of Trianon sliced away two-thirds of this thousand-year-old country. Beyond its frontiers the minority rights of three and a half million Hungarians have been trampled into the dust. For twenty years Paris, London and Washington have turned a deaf ear to our cries. Your dear husband forgot about this in his speech."

"He has not forgotten. I am afraid Your Serenity forgets how Lord Rothermere's great press empire championed the cause of Hungarian revision."

"But not the governments in power! The New Germany had to come to help us recover a great portion of our compatriots. And regarding the other matter . . . American official and public opinion is isolationist through and through. America will not interfere in this war. That is what my diplomats report. I am afraid, my dear Countess, that your sources are not entirely reliable."

I felt a ripple of heat that made my forehead burn.

"Hungarian diplomats speak excellent English and French because they are mostly aristocrats by birth. But their horizon hardly extends beyond the bridge tables. I know them: these gentlemen, almost without exception, are first cousins of mine."

The Regent's hand now reached with a decided ges-

151

ture toward the pencils; with his palm he carefully adjusted them, with the result that the pencils lost much of their originally perfect pipe-organ symmetry. The gesture seemed a sort of admission; he too, I suppose, had his opinion of aristocrat-diplomats. Aware of momentary victory, I quickly shifted to another question:

"My brother Ostie writes that in America the Bundists have called to their banners over a million persons of German descent. How long will America stand for this? Isn't Your Serenity troubled by the constantly increasing number of young Germans in scout uniforms going from village to village, making lists of everyone who shows even the remotest trace of German descent? Even I appear on their lists."

The Regent, his head tilted to one side, gazed at me, smiling.

"Could it be that you are ashamed of your German blood?"

"On the contrary, I am proud that my great-grandfather on my mother's side, Prince Heinrich Schäyenheim, was a good friend of Goethe's."

"My wife is also of German origin. Perhaps she, too, is on the German lists."

"No, Her Serenity is on the Jewish list. Just like Mrs. Eleanor Roosevelt and Cardinal Falkenheim, who figured in the *Sturmer*'s issue of last week, which incidentally asserts that Winston Churchill's original name was Baruch."

The Regent waved his hand in disparagement, with the gesture of a horseman.

"All newspaper men are idiots, didn't you know that? As for our German minorities . . . suppose I were to appear in the United States and begin listing all citizens of Hungarian descent. Wouldn't I have a right to?"

"The question is, with what intent?"

"Everyone has a right to remember his grandparents and the old homeland."

"I consider it improbable that Your Serenity would appear among the Hungarians of Cleveland to incite them

152

against the government of the United States. Nor is it likely that Your Serenity contemplates riding into the White House on a white horse."

"You never can tell," said the Regent with appealing humor. I continued in a serious vein:

"But such are Hitler's dreams. Some days ago, we were at Count Pál Teleki's, who is industriously collecting German press attacks against Hungarians. He showed them to us—he already has a libraryful. And *Mein Kampf* also regards us as a people 'in the way.' "

The Regent's face turned grave.

"Dear Countess, I cannot tell you all I discussed in my last talk with Hitler. But believe me: Germany has no hostile intent toward us. The Führer likes Hungarians. He spoke to me with genuine admiration of the Hungarian soldier's matchless bravery—and it is a historic fact that the Hungarian soldier fought . . . fought *Hals zu Hals* with the Germans in the first world war."

This somehow sounded as if we had won the first world war, but for some sly reason had kept it secret till now. Kristina, too, told me that the Regent was no man to stop talking, once he took the floor. A long explanation and frequent nose-shiftings elaborated the theme of present-day Germany's dazzling military might—and then, German science! More and more German expressions mingled with the Hungarian words . . . the German wonder weapons now being developed! . . . *unglaublich!*

During the extensive lecture I gazed at the pencils, pencils which can sign laws, death sentences, even declarations of war. They seemed instruments of a choleric disposition; at the same time, I reflected that it was the fate of these same pencils that if one pressed a bit harder, their oversharpened tips inevitably broke. In a pause between sentences, I rose from my chair. This you may regard as a victory of self-control, for there was a moment—nowadays my nerves are not of the best—when I wanted to weep and scream. I definitely got the impression that this man would plunge us into war on the side of the Germans. I am afraid you will be right. In getting up, I committed something of

153

a *faux pas;* for etiquette, I know, prescribes that an interview ends only when the head of state rises. But I didn't bother about that now. The Regent rose, too.

"Please tell your husband that neither from the left nor from the right will I tolerate any action against Germany. Thank you for coming, Countess."

As he accompanied me to the door, his tone grew milder:

"I am a friend of England. I particularly admire her Navy. I sent my son, István, to America, to work in the Ford factory. Yes, now I stand by Germany. But I am certain this war won't spread. In a few months it will end in compromise, you'll see: Western capitalists and the German Nazis will fall on each other's necks."

As he spoke these words, I thought of Papa's saying, that after the Regent's grand entry on a white horse, through some mistake they sat the horse in the Regent's chair. Did you ever hear of such a thing! "Compromise within a few months! And that Washington in time will embrace the Nazis!"

You can understand that I didn't say a word to Mihály about the audience, not even afterwards—that would only have been pouring oil on the flames. And Mihály already burns with too high a flame. I feel he is concealing a lot from me; he spends all his time at the Café Gugger conferring with the Stargazers, about whom I cannot exactly tell whether they are glowing patriots or just rhapsodic Bohemians. I feel—though maybe I'm only imagining things —that among the patients of the hospital they are hiding terrorists who have fled here from abroad. For me, two men in particular have an air of mystery: one is a man named Hermann Stolz, who speaks German with the most horrible Polish accent—I can only vouch for his dog. Rapczyk they call him—a creature so huge that he seems a cross between an elephant and a Saint Bernard; he rubs up against everyone so amicably that he is constantly bowling over smaller persons and children. He has already knocked Zizi over twice. The other strange character, a certain Scipio di Caruccio, has a sparse, shiny black beard like the onetime Mantuan princes of Gonzaga and, behind this beard, allegedly conceals a cancer of the stomach. He is an art dealer by occupation. I first grew suspicious on hearing a whinnying guffaw, once when I was passing his room. Opening the door, I saw that he was reading Mark Twain's essay on the German language, in an Italian edition he had found in the library. A man with cancer of the stomach doesn't guffaw like that, particularly when he is alone. And yesterday I slyly asked him whether he perchance knew who painted the *Dives and Lazarus*. He didn't know. An Italian art dealer, ignorant of Bonifazio Pitati's works strikes me as suspect. I could swear, too, that our hospital superintendent's real name is not Schwester Hilda. I find this woman early every morning in the chapel, kneeling in deep prayer; in her room there is a cheap Madonna with an archaic French inscription, which I don't quite understand. This mystical woman in her Red Cross uniform reminds me of Charlotte Corday, who thought she was doing her country a great turn by cutting down Marat with a broad-bladed kitchen knife as he sat in his bath. Or maybe Schwester Hilda is only a morphine addict. At all events, there is something deeply disquieting about her.

You remember how miserable I was over your entrusting the estate to Mihály. After my first unlucky marriage I found in Mihály the man I love, and who I know loves me too, in the highest sense of the word. The Zia Photos, our warm little nest in Buda, Zizi . . . I have discovered the sunshine in life, calmness and equilibrium, and this I want to defend with all my strength.

After the attempt and my conversation with the Regent, I feel certain that if Mihály proceeds farther along this course, "his goose will be cooked," as Gwen would put it. My plan is ready, which is why I have written this letter —I hope you'll back me up.

I very much want you to summon Mihály to New York under the pretext that you must discuss estate matters with him; after all, there was talk of such a trip from the very start. Mihály will find it natural for me and Zizi to go along. Once we are in America, you—as you already once suggested—will find Mihály a chair in some American university, and I will inform him that *under no circumstances* will I return, insisting that he, too, stay in America till the war is over. My further plan is to establish Zia Photos over there. I know that I am setting a trap for him, but this is the only way to save him from certain destruction. If I lose him, then I too must perish. We can find someone to run the estate. I should recommend Endre Makkosh; as you may remember, he was town clerk at Ararat, and it was he who performed my civil marriage with Filippo. He knows every man on the estate and is extremely intelligent; these last years I read some first-rate agricultural articles that he wrote—to me he is the most sympathetic among all the Stargazers. He has an even firmer hand than Mihály, I think. He'll defend the estate against Johy like a lion.

According to my plan, we could leave by early April. Every Thursday night I am alone; call me on the phone. I embrace you all.

ZIA

DEAR GWEN! In an American magazine I saw some very sweet children's dresses. Over here we have little choice in such things. I enclose Zizi's measurements: please send a few, mainly traveling things—I rely on your taste completely. Many kisses and thanks. Z.

P.S. You might send a few cartons of American cigarettes too; we can hardly get them here any more."

Two months later, at the end of March 1940, Mihály, Zia and Zizi left for America. Ursi planned to stay six weeks, but decided on the trip for quite other reasons than Zia supposed.

Apart from the electric lighting, the interior work of the Cave was finished and on the Ides of March, that great day of Hungarian freedom, the Stargazers opened the Cave to "traffic."

Present at the first secret meeting were Ursi, Ernst Tronfeld, Grubi, Kilinski, Tuykovich, Marja, Jani Hamor, and Joska Kurdi. At the great oak table only candles burned, whose light gleamed weirdly on the ceiling's exquisite stalactites and, at the farther end of the "hall," on the black mirror of the underground lake. Not only the surroundings, but the talk too, seemed far distant from reality.

First Joska Kurdi reported briefly and lucidly on the work accomplished and on expenses, which were surprisingly low because he had used workers "impelled only by the Idea," as he said, and none would accept wages. This made Ursi happy, especially because it showed that Hungarian workers regarded the Cave, and everything related to it, as theirs. In a few heartfelt words he thanked Joska Kurdi for his truly splendid and zealous work and asked him to convey his gratitude to the workers. Then he gave a resumé of the world situation. After the Soviets had attacked downtrodden Poland the previous fall, the Stargazers had turned violently against Russia. He read a speech of Lenin's in which, appealing for the rights of small nations, Lenin condemned Czarist Russia for occupying Finland in 1805. A mask had been torn from the face of the present-day imperialist Kremlin. At the same time he had to bridge the matter somehow, lest there be a rift between Stargazers and Communists. Marja, representing Czechoslovakia, and Yugoslavia's "Scipio di Caruccio," Slobo for short, were likewise strongly pro-Soviet, while Kazi Kilinski divided his hate between Hitler and Stalin in the same fashion that German and Russian troops had partitioned Poland between themselves.

Kazi, champion runner, dog trainer, railway "engineer" and successful motorcycle racer, had the bad habit of reclining half across the table on his elbow when listening to somebody's important words. At such moments he twirled the long hairs of his eyebrows between his thumb and forefinger, creating a masterfully spun mustache, which he usually forgot to smooth down, so that, especially during serious and dramatic conferences, this dandified misplaced mustache gave a comical twist to his meager greyhound face. Added to that, when he spoke German, his Polish accent was grotesque.

"*Nyiht ferrrgessen, Brrruders,*" he said, "the Soviets are now helping Germany to wipe Poland off the map, just as Catherina II, Frederick The Great and Marrria Terrrézia, *diese fette Hurrre;* but when Moscow's press explains today's situation by saying they are afraid of Western *kapityilizm,* it is not telling the truth. Against whom did the Red Army secure bases in Latvia? Against whom, whom, whom? Against England? Against America? Nonsense!"

Instead of "nonsense," he said a terrible word, fortunately in Polish. Then he explained that at the frontiers of famished Germany the great Ukrainian wheat fields lie like the huge fat belly of Russia. The Kremlin draws Eastern Europe over this naked belly like some blanket, whose upper edge is Finland, for naturally the huge belly's navel, Leningrad, cannot be left outside the blanket.

His interpretation was accepted without debate. Then, on the basis of letters from Ostie, Ursi reported on the American situation.

"Those who say all America favors isolation," wrote Ostie, "are unaware that in American foreign policy an immense revolution is in progress toward internationalism—this being most vividly expressed by the change in Republican Senator Vandenberg."

Then Ernst Tronfeld spoke; in quiet, matter-of-fact terms, he declared that though material resources were at hand, he found the installation of the cascade generator in the Cave extremely problematical. For the time being he considered this superfluous in any case, because he was still concerned with theory. Again his voice had a defensive tone, which was quite needless, because Ursi had never so much as mentioned the word *Urstron* to the Stargazers. They received Ernst's words without comment.

Then came the great sensation. Marja spoke up:

"I think the time is ripe for Slobo to present his plan."

Marja's voice seemed so freighted with mystery that they all glanced at Slobo's bearded face.

"I think I am not alone in my conviction," said he, "that for everything now going on in the world, one, only one man is responsible: Hitler. The first world war was started by a Serbian named Gavrillo Prinzip, who murdered the Austrian crown prince and his consort. It is fitting that the second world war be ended by a Yugoslav. With the help of Mr. Gruber I have already taken the first step in my plan."

Reaching into his briefcase, he extracted a huge photo showing Goering in his most resplendent air force marshal's uniform. The photo was inscribed: *"Meinem guten Freund, Signor Scipio di Caruccio, mit bestem Dank für den Holbein. Goering."* The photo passed from hand to hand—Grubi's modest expression did not reveal the remotest interest in the matter.

"Holbein's *Lord Cherford*, which I presented to the Marshal," continued Slobo, "gave me a chance to sound out Goering tactfully: what would the Führer say if Italian art dealers were to present him with Tintoretto's *Annunciation?* Goering replied that the Führer would doubtless be overjoyed."

Slobo did not elaborate his plan further, but all of them at once sensed what was brewing. An audience at Berchtesgaden, the ceremonious presentation of the painting, whose frame held the time-bomb that would tear to pieces those present, including the donor. For Slobo Tuykovich it was worth giving his life to enter world history in this fashion.

When Slobo finished, no one looked at him. Nor did they look at each other. But Ursi felt he was able to weigh the unspoken thoughts. Nothing was further from him than racist theory, but at this moment, when he faced three Slavs—Marja, Slobo and Kazi—he felt again the Slav proclivity for assaults and assassinations. Especially in the hands of Russians and Serbs, revolver and bomb are traditional political arguments. That sort of political weapon holds no appeal for the Magyar soul, though that is no boast. It may as easily be a weakness as a virtue.

In the great silence Joska Kurdi spoke up; without understanding Slobo's German words, he may have caught something of their drift. His black eyes in the red rings of his inflamed eyelids shone excitedly, and his words contradicted Ursa Major's thoughts about the noble Magyar soul.

"If you please, gentlemen comrades, I now work as a carpenter in Hunnia's scene-painting workshop. Next Thursday Dr. Goebbels is coming to visit the studio."

"Was sagt er?" asked Slobo, turning to Ursi.

Mihály explained in a few words that German propaganda had already reached a hand toward the Hungarian film studios: At Hunnia they were making German films, and Goebbels wanted to appraise for himself the results of the "cultural exchange."

Slobo shook his beard as if to intimate that Goering already had been at his mercy once, but he wasn't hunting sparrows. At Slobo's shake of the head, Joska Kurdi added, with a gleam in his eye:

"If you please, gentlemen comrades, I have a man on the lighting crew, who for the sake of the Idea, would gladly drop a lamp by accident on the Doctor's head. A big arc-lamp like that would send the Doctor straight to *gajdesz.*"

Joska with his interpolation gave the impression of a child obstructing the work of grownups by his desire to "help." Grubi laughed aloud. Joska's mode of speech, too, had a comic ring: "gentlemen comrades," then the oft-recurring "Idea," but now especially the word *gajdesz,* which in the days of the First Commune was used in the lingo of communist terrorists to mean death. Ursi didn't even translate Joska's words to the Slavs.

"There is something far more important now," he told him curtly.

Joska nodded, his face showing no offense. Compliance, the result of Party education, was among his virtues.

Marja and Kazi as well as Slobo, were impatiently waiting for the "Major's" reply. It was not easy to phrase.

"In the days of the Austrian Anschluss," said Ursi, "the Linz radio announcer called Hitler God. I am afraid that, as things stand, Hitler would be more potent dead than alive."

"Before the Germans realize," interjected Slobo impulsively, "that they are being led by a maniac, many millions of men and much else will perish. We can't wait."

Kazi continued Slobo's words:

"Our movement is not for the manufacture of theories, but for action. *Aktion, meine Brrruders! Aktion!*"

Marja nodded mutely. The stalactite ceiling and the more distant hollows of the Cave echoed at every loud word. But now there was such tension in the air that even Marja's silent nod seemed to awaken an echo. The tall candles on the table, the eerie atmosphere of the Cave, as they composed Hitler's death warrant, the expression on the faces by candlelight, the fantastic nature of the plan, even the title of the painting: *Annunciation*— this was more than the secret parley of a few men, all this seemed like the secret and futile dream of many millions: Kill Hitler!

Hamor spoke up:

"Slobo is right. We must try everything."

Grubi also nodded reflectively. On Ernst's immobile face and high forehead was written something to the effect that he was willing to jot down an equation, the technical result of which might conceivably in a split second destroy ten million men, but the primitive bloody liquidation of a *single* individual was not in his sphere.

Slobo again spoke. "The Tintoretto cannot be counterfeited, if only because it is on permanent exhibit in Venice at the Scuola di San Rocco. But it can be bought, because the Italian government, particularly in view of the great coal shortage, is grabbing up hard currency with both hands. According to my plan, I'll launch a drive among Italian fascist art dealers, who will rush to get their names on the donors' list, but knowing them as I do, that won't bring in a thousand dollars. Assuming that the Italian government asks half a million dollars for this great Tintoretto, I must produce the balance myself, cleverly and unobtrusively. That takes no special skill: men obligingly wink at such things provided the money actually materializes. I'll start the drive with a sweeping press campaign—enthusiastic articles on the Italian art dealers' noble gesture. Where will we get the half-million dollars? A single source occurs to me: world Jewry, to whom it will certainly be worth the price if the world is rid of Hitler."

Slobo turned to Ursi:

"You mentioned that you are planning an American trip at your brother-in-law's invitation. I speak no English and do not know a soul in America, yet that is where the great Jewish organizations have their headquarters."

Resistance to the whole plan was still active in Ursi when he spoke.

"Don't you think that the Jews would make a bad bargain? Maybe Jews in German concentration camps can still be saved. For Hitler the Germans would wreak horrible vengeance on them."

"Why on the Jews?" Slobo raised his bearded aquiline head. "Everyone will know that a Yugoslav did it!"

He spoke as if the matter already had gone off without a hitch, and in that death-defying gesture of his head was already

161

something of the assurance of seeing the name Slobodan Tuy-kovich in the history books.

Grubi spoke up, twiddling the thumbs of his hands clasped over his great paunch:

"I feel no such concern. From what I know of the inner mood of the German people—many of the generals, too, abhor Hitler—they will be more likely to sigh in relief than think of revenge."

After Grubi's words, to which Hamor also nodded assent, the "Major" could not in any wise say no. But he found Ostie unsuitable as an intermediary. He would possess good connec-tions with world Jewry in such an ultra-delicate question, but knowing his mode of thought, Ursi felt certain he would have rejected the plan. He turned to Ernst:

"What is your opinion?"

Ernst pensively nodded.

"I can give you a letter to an important and reliable man in London and New York, too."

Two weeks later, the twelfth of April, Mihály, Zia, and Zizi arrived at Calais, where, on their way to London, they spent the night in the same hotel they had stayed at thirteen years before when Mihály and Zia did not know each other.

Zia clapped her hands in surprise:

"Good God! Were you that drunken swine?"

Then they reflected on the weirdness of Fate. Two persons whose lives had become so interwined, once, somewhere in the past, had rushed by each other like comets in space, without colliding. And to top it off, even their rooms in the little Calais hotel had been adjoining. It was a curious feeling to meet with the past.

Mihály accosted Zia: "Excuse me, Miss, forgive my forward-ness. Allow me to introduce myself . . ."

Zia entered into the game, protesting in mock alarm:

"How can you think of such a thing, sir! I'm not in the habit of being picked up—I'm just an innocent little countess. Promise that you'll behave."

She took Mihály's arm and they set out for the Place d'Armes in search of their youth. Zia then was sixteen, Mihály

162

twenty-seven. Zia stopped in front of the statue of the one-eyed Gambetta:

"Here is where you stood, on the pedestal. You had lost your hat, your hair hung down over your forehead: that was how I first saw you, shaking your fist and shouting: '*Les cléricaux . . . les réactionnaires! . . .*'"

Even after so many years she imitated Mihály's voice to perfection, of course exaggerating his bad French accent.

Zia was gay as a lark all the way. She was happy over the trip to America—she had no inkling of the great mission on which Mihály was bound. After supper they put Zizi to bed in "Kristina's room" while they took possession of their "old" rooms. But they could not sleep. They set out on another stroll, and looked up at the Tour de Guet, on whose walls could still be seen the marks of German cannon from the first world war. The shops were closed, the great bright shafts of the lighthouse did not sweep over city and sea. As though walking through a dead city, now for the first time they experienced a total blackout.

At three in the morning Ursi was startled out of a deep sleep by a phone call from Budapest. Chief physician Dr. Burger spoke, but he at once recognized Grubi's voice:

"Yesterday Princess *Garia* suffered a nervous breakdown and is now in a critical condition. Her condition was brought on by her neighbor, Herr *Braun,* who demanded that he be allowed to drive his herd of cattle *across Princess Garia's estate* so as not to have to go *round the Carpathians.* Herr Braun has his eye on a large estate in *Rumania*—note this: *Rumania.* The Princess cannot decide this difficult question, and one member of the family has already left *for Rome* to consult with Monsieur Noir. I must ask you, Professor, to postpone your American trip and come straight back to Budapest. You, too, are urgently needed at the bedside of Princess Garia."

Grubi put down the receiver before Ursi could answer, thereby further emphasizing the imperative nature of his call. Zia in the next room did not awaken at the ring of the telephone. In his half-sleep Ursi didn't even switch on the light during Grubi's talk, and now he stared into the dark, his eyes rigid. In his head was the confused hum of Grubi's words, whose meaning

163

he could easily decipher. Horrible! If Hungary let the German Army through, she would lose her neutrality. They were late—too late with all their plans. He didn't once close his eyes till it was light.

Zia and Zizi were still asleep, when early in the morning he went down for breakfast. On the square men stood in groups, excitedly discussing something. Did they know already? He stepped to one of the groups and asked a deathly pale old gentleman what had happened.

"Allons, vous ne savez donc pas que Danemark n'existe plus?"

The radio was already crackling: that dawn, at about four, German armored cars had rolled into deeply slumbering *Denmark!* At once Grubi's night call became clear to him. The Germans themselves had planted a "secret" report that they were heading toward the wheat fields of Bessarabia and the Rumanian oil wells—they wanted to distract attention from their surprise attack in the west.

The Place d'Armes was swarming with people. In the wake of the German attack came terrifying rumors, as in a tornado's path swirl torn signboards, open umbrellas and the roofs of houses. The German juggernaut was moving against the world. The Germans had secret wonder-weapons. England was unprepared, France weak, in the United States dwelt forty million Germans, Hitler would occupy South America by telephone, because his fifth columns in Argentina and Brazil had already completed their work. The Calais-Dover steamship run was already suspended. Clipper traffic had stopped too, and owing to the threat of German submarines the *Queen Mary* would not leave Southampton for New York.

Zia was still in bed when Mihály told her all this. Her face grew quite small and turned ashen gray.

That very night they journeyed back to Hungary.

Chapter 11

*Star of Compiègne. The Mysterious Death of the
Hungarian Prime Minister.*

Kristina, who moved in all higher circles without dis-
criminating as to party, sat between the German minister and
Johy, sipping iced tea—the whole atmosphere reminding her of
1937 in Moscow, when, before invited diplomats and a few select
guests, they showed the film *Peter The Great*. But now it was
the turn of German imperialism's blinding might: the original
film made at Compiègne. German history always abounded in
gods, drama, thunderous legends, but the first minutes of the film
surpassed all these.

The identical railway car stopped at the same spot as it
had twenty-two years ago. But now from the car alighted not
the shadow-like wraiths of a vanquished Germany, but the
Führer and his entourage. They set out toward the forest clearing, where stood a pillar commemorating the French victory of
1918, the bronze relief showing the vanquished German eagle
transfixed by the sword of the Allies. This premature boast was
now bedecked with swastika flags. Hitler stopped before the pillar
and looked up. His glance was the mute, and simple, yet powerful and serene manifestation of historic greatness. Then he turned
with his entourage—among them the great-bellied Goering,
marshal's staff in hand. In the light of that June afternoon under
the great plane trees, Hitler's face wore a solitary majesty such
as only Michelangelo had carved on the face of Moses, or as
Carlyle wrote of Dante: "His face prisoned in icy crags, his gaze
as though writing in the void."

Then came something unexpected. Hitler's face suddenly
changed to a shark's face, as always when he smiled. A broad
and vulgar grin now appeared beneath his well-known mustache
and with his ungainly boots he lurched into a clumsy dance.

The German minister, who still apparently retained some remnants of taste, said to Kristina in an embarrassed whisper: "This scene will be cut from the film."

Kristina did not make any remark, she did not even look at the German minister. She just gazed at the screen with frozen face. But, when on the following week end at Ararat she spoke about the Compiègne film, she said:

"I must confess that in the depth of my soul I never denied some mysterious human and historical greatness in Adolf. But now—all right, the scene will be cut from the film and from the eyes of hundreds and hundreds of millions of people—but never from my eyes. I've never seen a mask fall as completely as at that moment! It was horrible to see those boots dancing a jig of joy, I couldn't help thinking that a glove, flung on a table, but still keeping the delicate warm lines of a hand—or a hat, hanging lonesomely on the rack, sometimes reveals much more about a man than anything else. Those boots came to life, terrifyingly—they changed into a human face as in Li-Pu-Ten's poem, the black whale swimming in a purple sea of blood."

Kristina looked around at her audience as if frightened that she had said too much. She turned to the fascist Scipio di Caruccio, with whom she liked to walk in the park, talking about Fra Bartolommeo or the dynamic bodies of Michelangelo.

"*Scuzare mi*, Scipio."

Slobo's face behind the Scipio-beard remained expressionless. They sat in the park around a large, very old oak table which seemed to be deeply rooted in the soil with its barked elephant legs made of natural stumps. On that very large table there was plenty of space for Kazi's elbow as he leaned forward, and while excitedly listening to Kristina's words, twirled his eyebrow into the usual dandified mustache. A few of the more intelligent patients usually joined the week-end parties.

"*In derr Pollischen Schullen,*" Kazi said, "they have already introduced a new German textbook in which a whole chapter is devoted to Genghis Khan, who ordered eighteen million people massacred—*nyiht ferrgessen, achtzehn million!*—only in the city of Herat, two million!"

Nobody ventured a comment. Zia, in a white summer *rekli* with Magyar trimming, mutely trained her apple-green eyes on

166

one face after another, then she crossed to Kazi, whom she knew only under his false name, and whispered:

"Herr Stolz, would you be a dear and take a walk? There are thirteen of us around the table."

"*Ferrtzoyhen Sie, Grrefin,*" Kazi whispered back, "but if I go for a walk, that's when there'll be thirteen."

Zia's troubled green eyes took another rapid census of those present. She snapped her fingers when she observed old Count Dmitri, who, with his bald skull and long sallow mustache, sat half-hidden behind Mihály.

"You're right. I always forget to count Russia," said Zia with a meaningful smile.

"*Nyiht ferrgessen Rrussia,*" grinned Kazi. Whenever he spoke up, the Bismarck-faced Rapczyk who lay next to his master's feet, extended his big flaglike tail from under the table and waved it approvingly.

Ursi toyed with a silver ashtray, scrutinizing its engraving as intently as if the whole conversation did not interest him. And still his forehead strained to express something beyond words. Ernst Tronfeld sat next to him, seemingly in the same mood. Ernst was the only person around the table who, during the whole time, did not say a single word. Sometimes, with five fingers, he combed back his hair which had grown long since the concentration camp.

Countess Menti wore a mustard-hued summer gown with conservative high-buttoned champagne-colored shoes, which under the table reproachfully eyed Kristina's and Zia's frivolous open sandals. *Die gute Menti's* head was tilted slightly to one side and supported by a long, white, Schäyenheim-Elkburg forefinger.

"Schwester Hilda" sat next to old Count Dmitri. Marja looked distinctly unwell. In the frame of the Red Cross cap her face was pale, old and tired—a perfect mask for a former Maria Darida, though there was no danger that her onetime husband, Uncle Dmitri, now well over seventy and already losing his sight and hearing, would ever recognize her.

Whenever Marja happened to glance at the long, sallow mustache of Uncle Dmitri, all her six husbands' faces flashed back into her memory. But her circling thoughts always returned

167

to the deeply set blue eyes of Maxim Narokov, the young Soviet diplomat. Was he still living?

Marja had every reason now to be in a bad mood. Last week from her underground friends in Prague she had received horrible news again. Among others, Papa Dybowski, the old doctor in Kladno, everybody's papa, was taken away and shot by the Gestapo. When would all these horrors end?

István Freyberger, whose corn-colored linen suit was as wrinkled as his face under his silver mane, spoke up with the scalpel of objectivity, as he usually did.

"Very great things can be achieved only by the cruelest means. Civilized people have always been overthrown by barbarians. The early Greeks were far less civilized than the natives of Crete, the early Romans were more barbarian than the Etruscans. Charlemagne's Teuton forces . . ."

"You want to say," Countess Menti interrupted Kristina's personal physician, without moving her cheek from the supporting Schäyenheim-Elkburg forefinger, "that it will all end with a Soviet conquest of the entire world, don't you? I am not willing to subscribe to this theory of yours. Unlike Pelagius, the English theologian of the fifth century, I take St. Augustine's side when he says . . ."

Though the silence above the table was politely attentive, nobody listened to Countess Menti's long explanation of original sin.

A week later, during a dark night, under the guidance of Joska Kurdi, Slobodan Tuykovich disappeared from Ararat Hospital.

His disappearance is no mystery to us at all. Like so many others, Slobo could not know that the Germans would stage a surprise occupation of Holland, an event completely foiling Slobo's *Annunciation* plan, because Goering, who was very partial to art treasures, made a hurried appearance at the Amsterdam Museum "just to have a look around" and on glimpsing Holbein's *Lord Cherford,* he at once telegraphed the Gestapo to apprehend a bearded imposter, one Scipio di Caruccio, even if they had to dig him out of the ground. An identical telegram went to the police of allied Italy and friendly Hungary.

Slobo, tossing aside his Gonzaga beard and his mellifluous pseudonym, moved to the Cave, whose dry and airy upper recesses, simply but comfortably furnished, were already waiting for just such contingencies. Slobo was not disconcerted by solitude. Mihály provided him liberally with reading matter, and at times when he visited him, the hollows would resound with Slobo's sonorous baritone, which he accompanied with his own guitar: "*I ako su odletjeli zdrali* . . ." On the shores of the black underground lake the downward-drifting cadences of this ancient Montenegrin song dating from Turkish days glowed with fire and sorrow. All this sounded as though it weren't even Slobo but the Cave itself, singing.

Kristina, at the end of September, brought the confidential news that Prime Minister Pál Teleki had fallen out violently with Ribbentrop and only the presence of tactful Italian Foreign Minister Ciano, the "handsome movie actor," had saved the situation. It happened at a table in the Belvedere, where Ribbentrop and Ciano, dressmaker's shears in hand were partitioning Transylvania between the Hungarians and the Rumanians. Random strokes established demarcations on the great maps which, in actuality, sliced in half the pews of churches on the frontier, and possibly even the beds of married couples. Ribbentrop hated Teleki, in whom he saw a wily and dangerous traitor to German interests. He hated the Hungarian count's great culture, his horn-rimmed spectacles, and especially that gesture of this fragile little man of Japanese stature, whereby he would raise high his left elbow and, during consultations, scratch his left ear from behind his head.

Kolomp was going from bad to worse. Even its anti-German articles were forced to stutter, because all Hungarian public opinion was sunning itself in the light of German victory. It seemed natural and convenient that German arms should recover the sundered national territories without Hungary herself having to lift a finger. The Regent paraded on a white horse into Transylvania, where with astounding dispatch an enormous plaque was set up to commemorate the great day. Huge gold letters on the plaque awarded the Regent the title of "nation-enhancer." In the Café Gugger the Stargazers sat silently staring into space.

169

They and a very few others in the country still did not know, though they felt, that the time would come when a horrible price would be exacted for this "enhancement."

Count Johy domiciled his friend Erich von Ehrenthal, a tall slender example of faultless Aryan beauty, in his Septemvir Utca quarters, their bedrooms immediately adjoining. Regarding this quiet scandal, the diplomatic bridge table circulated the story of how Johy appeared before the Führer at Berchtesgaden to secure highest sanction for an important private matter. "I have decided to enter into matrimony with Erich."

"Erich?" cried the Führer, dumbfounded. *"Tun Sie das nicht, Herr Graf!"*—Don't do that!

"Warum, mein Führer?"—But why not? "Erich is so sweet, so affectionate, and I'm desperately in love with him. What objection can you have to the marriage, my Führer?"

Adolf kept shaking his head obdurately. "It distresses me to bring up this question," declared the Führer, "but didn't you know, my dear Count, that Erich has Jewish blood?"

The author of the story allegedly was Kristina, who in these weeks made her decision to marry István Freyberger.

Isti is now sixty years old. I am forty-four [she wrote to New York]. I'm tired, Ostie. And I feel like a child who has strayed into the dark: tearfully I seek someone's hand. My life and events in the world have turned somber. At the gateway of the menopause all women meet with the inscription: *Lasciate ogni speranzá*—Abandon all your hopes —I too have arrived at the gateway of this hell: savage headaches, dreadful buzzings in my ear. Just think what it means to start up in your sleep at night, crying for a doctor, and have to wait, wait hours till the doctor awakens, dresses, gets into his car and arrives. From now on, I'll just reach out my hand in the dark and, instead of a bell, shall press the nose of my sleeping spouse, and the best of house-doctors will be right at hand. I love Isti very much: I have found in him a man of high quality, near whom I feel secure and calm.

According to the latest Hungarian laws drawn up along Nürnberg lines, one who marries a Jew counts as a Jew.

170

This does not trouble me in the least. I have no wish to desecrate Grandmamma Jefi's blessed memory, but no one can tell what tender, lavender-scented secrets the past of our ancestors may hide.

I hope I won't be burdening you with my requests: Please, send me a light woman's saddle, because these days they ship all our leather to . . . well, you guess to which country. Though I understand that over there even toothpicks are motor-driven, in Virginia there may still be a few upright gentlefolk who ride horses. Don't forget to include a few cartons of cigarettes in the package.

Many kisses,

K.

In the middle of January 1941 Johy gave a large cocktail party at Septemvir Utca, to which Mihály and Zia were naturally not invited. Among the pro-German guests and diplomats present were members of the Soviet Legation too. Moscow had just restored to Hungary the flags of a hundred years ago captured by the Czar's armies when they helped the Hapsburgs beat down Kossuth's fight for liberty. The week before, the film *Peter The Great* was shown in Budapest, the Soviet and German ministers sitting in the same box and almost embracing. The faces of the guests beamed with joy: the Germans had already occupied Western Europe, France included, and to the East the Soviet Union was their ally—who could have doubts of ultimate German victory?

To the cocktail party Kristina brought with her Marja Drda, whom she knew of course only under the name Schwester Hilda. Kristina had become very found of "Hilda," and walked a great deal with her in the park—here at last was someone who patiently and attentively listened to Kristina's endless themes for plays and novels. "Shake off your trance. Come along with us and mix with people. You'll wither away in this old hospital!" That morning Kristina took Marja to the hairdresser's, with that expansive friendship women show friends who are not dangerous rivals.

Marja was now undeniably radiant. Her ash-blond hair, parted in the middle, caught the light, and the delicate line of the shoulders, set off by a sedge-colored cocktail dress, was Maria

Darida again. The hubbub of German, Italian, Russian and Hungarian conversation, the faces, drinks, cries of greeting . . . nothing had changed since the cocktail parties in Paris and London, and her glance half sought old friends in the crowd. She was standing by herself beneath Corot's *Woman in Purple* when the Italian minister accosted her, neither knowing nor caring about the identity of the owner of the gray, plum-shaped eyes, the intriguing feminine face with the short Slavic nose wedged lion-like into the beautiful forehead. Their conversation could not have been too absorbing because Marja's glance strayed fitfully toward a corner of the room. She had perceived someone regarding her with marked attention. By the Chinese lamp stood a solitary figure with his arms crossed. As often as Marja looked in that direction she felt the steady gaze. The light was such that she could not make out his face, but she felt she had seen him before.

When Kristina took the Italian minister in tow, this man came straight to her. Small light blue eyes sat deep in his lean face. With two fingers he brushed back a pencil-thick lock of ginger-colored hair which lay softly on his forehead. His countenance glowed with unexpected delight coupled with deep emotion and boyish confusion. A pained reproachful smile formed on his colorless, but extremely sensitive lips, as he addressed Marja in Russian.

"*Viy minya ne pomnyete*"—You don't remember me.

"Oh, Maxim!" flamed Marja's recollection, as she grasped the man's hand. Maxim! For thirteen years she had not seen him. And now, Maxim stood before her; he had scarcely changed. Only the two folds around his mouth had deepened. His eyes were alight with the same tenderness, confusion and adoration.

"How did you get here, Maxim?"

"I've been at the Soviet Legation in Budapest the past few weeks."

He twined his hands behind his back, then crossed his arms on his chest again, shifting his weight from one foot to the other. He faced Marja for long seconds without being able to speak. Then he glanced at the crowd, asking, awkwardly:

"Is your husband here too?"

"Gustave? We were divorced long ago. Didn't you know?"

172

"Oh yes . . . but then you left Paris so suddenly. I thought you married again."

"And what about you? Did you marry?"

Maxim shook his head quickly, almost vehemently. Apparently he himself found the gesture too revealing, for he began some inconsequential sentence. Johy was approaching with a host's exhausted but obligatory smile. Marja quickly said:

"Take care, my name is now Schwester Hilda. We must arrange to meet . . . I'll phone you at the Legation."

That was all that happened at their afternoon meeting.

That night at Ararat Marja fell on her knees before the Villon Madonna. The picture performed a true miracle: Maxim came back.

When they met a few days later in a little tavern to have supper, they hardly spoke, just gazed into the air.

And when they did speak they only whispered, as if loath to awaken from its tranquil and beauteous dreams the Lac des Souvenirs in the Bois, on whose banks they once stood long in silence, only glancing now and then into each other's faces. Now too, they conversed just like this. And when the pause had already grown overlong, Marja asked:

"Do you still love me, Maxim?"

Maxim did not reply. He gazed, immobile, at the salt shaker, but on his face the tears streamed, completely filling the two deep folds down by his mouth. And now this face was so deeply Russian! Marja gently placed her hand on Maxim's, which lay as though lifeless on the tablecloth. The gypsy fiddler at that moment struck up the strains of a mournful Magyar song, for the gypsy secretly watched each table, and now surmised that they were a married couple, or lovers, about to bid each other eternal adieu.

Yet quite the opposite was happening.

Maxim's unexpected reappearance had resurrected Marja from a strange death. From that day she always found some excuse for missing the lengthy conferences of the underground.

She asked Zia to introduce her to the Dux Salon. She ordered a new suit. She intently studied Kristina's admirable dressing table. She returned to the make-up, not exactly of the old days in Vienna or Paris, but something between the style of Maria Darida and Countess Menti. By now, hitler, dunkirk, churchill, and even prague, were written with small letters in her mind, too. Every other day she dined with Maxim in some small restaurant.

Among the week-end guests at Ararat there were always a few members of the neutral, especially the anti-German, diplomatic corps. Maxim politely refused Marja's invitations. For a Soviet diplomat the Ararat circle was a little *too* anti-German in those days.

"Schwester Hilda! Telephone!" one of the nurses would shout twice, three times in a day.

"Who is it?" asked Marja.

"Your brother."

The war went on, and life went on, too.

In the first days of March 1941, Slobodan Tuykovich unexpectedly vanished from the Cave in the direction of Belgrade. Just previously, the Yugoslav prime minister, Cvetkovics, had sped to a Berchtesgaden audience. The world for a few instants thought that Yugoslavia, too, would fawn at the Führer's feet, wagging her tail. But no—Mihály, who had tuned in an evening broadcast, broke into Zia's room.

"The Yugoslavs!"

Wild heartbeats and blinding hope blazed from the radio bulletin. The anti-German putsch had routed Cvetkovics' government—let German Stukas come, let death and destruction rain, but Yugoslavia would not bow to orders from Berchtesgaden. That night Slobo left the Cave to reach home before the frontier closed.

Crossing the border, he made directly for his birthplace, Nyegushi, a small town some twenty miles from Cetinje, former capital of independent Montenegro. Slobo's father, Ivo Tuykovich, was a bricklayer. In the romantic economic situation of Nyegushi he was paid for repair jobs in eggs or flour, for a whole house a whole sheep. Old Ivo was a *zelena*, Slobo grew up to become a *bjela*. Zelena means green, bjela white; politically a zelena was for the former independent kingdom, while a bjela was for the new Yugoslavia. Yugo means united. After World War I the Serbs, Croats, Slovenes, Macedons, Montenegrins, all the southern Slavs were united in Yugoslavia.

174

Father and son adored each other. Slobo was twenty-one when his father gave him a mighty box on the ear in a *zelena-bjela* argument. But Slobo adored his father so much that he waited until the seventeenth slap before leaving his parental house.

Slobo had come back now: in these hours of danger there were no longer any *zelenas* and *bjelas*. He sat down on a stone bench in the empty yard of the shuttered house. The whole male population of Nyegushi had already disappeared in the mountains. Slobo had come too late to organize the resistance.

At the end of the yard there was a shanty on whose wall the rains of so many years had not yet completely washed away the chalk circles which he had used for a target when he perfected himself in archery. The stone house, its steep roof covered with rough slate had been built by his great-grandfather. It had only one big room which was the kitchen, the dining room, the bedroom for the whole family. On the stone wall there was only a small dim mirror, and next to the wall a wooden trough for washing.

Slobo, sitting alone in the yard, clearly heard from the house the sweet, soft voice of the *gusle* and saw the movement of his father's heavy hand as he led the bow-like *gundello* over the strings of the ancient violin which resembled a half watermelon with a thin, long handle. And Slobo heard his father's sonorous baritone . . . "*Ostali su ptici zdralovici*—Eagles engender young eagles—an ancient Montenegrin song dating from the long Turkish occupation. Then he clearly saw his father dashing out of the house, rifle in hand and firing a shot into the sky. An ancient Montenegrin tradition to announce to Nyegushi that a boy was born. For girls there were no shots.

His father was more than six feet tall, his shoulders a little bent, his face white, his hair deep black: a typical Montenegrin. Sundays he wore the colorful folk-costume which had become so famous from the pictures of old King Nikita: a flat cap of black silk topped with bright crimson, the embroidered Montenegrin crown in the middle; a red spencer, sky-blue trousers, thick white wool stockings, rough sandals with golden laces. His sash was of lemon-yellow silk, nine yards long, twisted tightly around his waist.

175

Ivo Tuykovich was a very handsome man. He had the most beautiful big black mustache in Nyegushi. But now as he appeared in Slobo's imagination, his dignified eagle-face was so funny, so terribly funny: the left branch of his famous mustache was cut almost to the roots.

Oh, this half-mustache had a dramatic story. Montenegrin tobacco was a state monopoly. The customs officers went from village to village to find the strictly prohibited "virgin" tobacco. They carried a pair of scissors, and quickly cut in half the cigarette, still in the mouth of the suspect, to discover if the tobacco was virgin or not; it was the only way to catch a real *zelena*. A customs officer—by accident—cut off half of Ivo Tuykovich's mustache with the official scissors. Ivo Tuykovich pulled out his pistol and shot the officer. The Cetinje supreme court acquitted him because in Montenegro, for a thousand years, the mustache has been a sanctity. A Montenegrin swears by his mustache. The mustache in Montenegro is the symbol of manhood, chivalry, courage, pride, and above all honesty—death to anyone who cuts, or even slurs the mustache of a man like Ivo Tuykovich.

Where was Ivo now? Well over sixty, he had left with the other men of Nyegushi for the mountains.

And so did Slobo—armed with a short Turkish bow of composite horn, whose power was equal to a hundred-pound English longbow. At eighteen he had killed an attacking mother-bear in the Nyegushi forest with this bow.

A few days after Slobo's disappearance from Hungary, the short-necked little Marquis de Ferreyolles, a French diplomat, whose father married Countess Suzanne Dukay at the turn of the century, arrived from Paris. He was famous for his unbelievably rapid French, in which, almost singing, he twitched the end of each sentence into the air like a small fish at the end of a long, elastic rod. But now, while the others talked about the Yugoslav and French situation, he remained mute.

"Oh yes, Adolf's boots are dancing a jig on the corpse of France," said Kristina, then turned to the silent Marquis:

"Tell me, Gaston, did you witness the entry of the German Army into Paris last year? What was it like?"

The Marquis, who was known as the most polite and talkative man in the world, did not answer. Behind his thick spectacles his eyes seemed to melt away. Then, unexpectedly, he sprang up, seized Kristina's shoulder, and shouted into her face, as red as a turkey cock:

"*Te rends-tu compte de ce que tu bafous? Vaut mieux fermer ta gueule—espèce de toquée!*"

And leaving his half-sobbing outcry of "*de toquée!*" hanging in the air, he ran away with very fast, but very short steps, on his tiny feet.

Everyone was taken aback. The French word *gueule* is the most vulgar expression for mouth, especially for Kristina's delicately cut and Biarritz-prized mouth. *Espèce de toquée* is much more than idiot.

Countess Menti beseechingly said in a toothachy voice:

"*Politisiert nicht, Kinder.*" She pronounced the word *kindeh*.

"What happened to that miniature Gallic bull?" asked Kristina.

"You insulted him," said Zia in a reproachful tone. "You said that Adolf's boots are dancing on the corpse of France."

Ursi also sprang to the Marquis' defense:

"Then it was too much to ask him to describe the scene for you. He already told me that he and his cousin Guy watched the German troops strut past from a second-floor window of the old de Ferreyolles palace on the Champs Élysées. When the Führer and his retinue marched by the little palace, Guy reached into his pocket and shot himself in the head right there."

Kristina gazed into the air for a few seconds, then said:

"Did I say the corpse of France? Well . . . a nation must be dead if one of its sons like Guy de Ferreyolles at such a moment shoots *himself* instead of Adolf."

Nobody spoke. But Kazi and Marja unanimously nodded at Kristina's words.

On April 2, in the early morning hours, the news spread that Count Pál Teleki, Prime Minister of Hungary, had shot himself in the head.

Men formed whispering groups on the street. On the faces of policemen, letter carriers, waiters, but especially on the faces of the Jews, was written the presentiment of dreadful and unknown catastrophe for Hungary. Only in the German camp did faces beam sarcastically and secretively. Extra editions appeared, carrying Teleki's short letter of farewell to his family and the Regent.

That night the Stargazers held an excited meeting in the Cave. Slobo was absent, but Freyberger was there and a few anti-German Hungarian generals. The first to speak was Grubi.

"You will remember that not long ago it was seriously proposed to crown the Prince of Aosta as King of Hungary. But since the Savoy dynasty is anti-German, the Prince of Aosta suddenly died—of some stomach disorder. According to my secret informants, the Gestapo did away with him—yet another thing world history will not have time and opportunity to prove. You also know that Ribbentrop for some days has been in Budapest, residing on Saint Margit Isle. I am convinced that last night Ribbentrop shot Teleki with his own hand."

"How do you account for the farewell letters?" asked Hamor's incredulous voice.

"My dear boy"—Grubi turned toward him in a fatherly tone —"don't you know there are German spies among the employees of the Prime Ministry? Nothing could have been easier than to get hold of Teleki's personal writing paper, his pen and ink. Advanced German techniques found it no problem to make perfect forgeries of Teleki's handwriting."

Everyone had some special information or theory, and from the tense discussion evolved this picture of Pál Teleki's last hours:

Toward six in the afternoon Teleki received the report that German troops marching against Yugoslavia wanted to use some of the Hungarian barracks in the provinces. His answer was a firm "No!"

The next witness was Hamor, who at about eight P.M. was in the midst of an interview at the Foreign Minister's office, when a telegram was handed to the Minister, who turned back and shouted through the open door toward his secretary's room: "An important telegram. Phone the Prime Minister at once!" "I doubt whether His Excellency is at his office this late," answered the secretary. "Just phone him, he is just as much of an idiot as I— working himself to death!"

"As the Foreign Minister turned around," continued Hamor, "there stood Teleki before his desk. With a comic pirouette he

178

bowed and said: 'Voilà, the idiot!' Laughingly he shook hands with us, his face turning grave only when he read the telegram, which came from London. The Foreign Office had sent the Hungarian government a stern warning that if it opened the way for German troops to attack Yugoslavia it would be considered a breach of neutrality."

Following this scene Pál Teleki went on foot to the nearby János Sanatorium, where his wife lay ill. Knowing the issue of these fateful hours, we can easily conceive what grievous cares weighed on the mind of the Hungarian Prime Minister . . . Ribbentrop, the accursed Ribbentrop, was stationed at Budapest, knowing everything, watching everything. If Hungary failed to meet the German demands, the Stukas might within hours turn Budapest to rubble, yet if she bowed to Ribbentrop, it meant war with England.

Here Freyberger, who was visiting physician at the sanatorium, took over. The telephone was in the corridor, along which Freyberger happened to pass, and heard only Teleki's angry cry: "They did!" Banging down the receiver, he took hurried leave of his wife and returned to the Prime Minister's Palace, where he lived alone with his valet.

The meaning of "They did!" was easy to surmise. It meant that despite his orders and protests, German troops had moved into the Hungarian barracks.

"The valet's deposition is important," remarked Ursi. "Teleki instructed the valet to press his uniform for the morning. If nothing else, this single fact certainly speaks against suicide."

"More than likely," said Grubi, "Teleki, on returning from the sanatorium, at once phoned Ribbentrop who may have said something like this to Teleki: 'We can't settle this over the phone —let's get together and confer at once.' Now I yield the floor to Joseph Kurdi," concluded Grubi.

"If you please, gentlemen comrades," began Joska in an officious tone, "in the early morning hours I was first to arrive at the Prime Minister's Palace—the policeman on duty at the gate that night, Imre Kurdi by name, gentlemen, is a cousin of mine. I spoke with the gateman too, who said that His Excellency had telephoned the gateman's booth saying that he was expecting two German gentlemen. Ten minutes later the two Germans arrived and walked up the steps. Half an hour later they left."

"According to the medical report, the suicide occurred within that half-hour," noted Freyberger.

"Neither the gateman nor Imre could tell me who the two German gentlemen were, but both mentioned that one of them wore an elegant raincoat, and—"

Grubi interrupted with a sweeping gesture of his hand:

"Ribbentrop without a raincoat would be inconceivable!"

Joska Kurdi looked around under the red rings of his inflamed eyelids:

"If you please, gentlemen comrades, Imre pleaded with me not to breathe a word to anyone. He has five children. Before he went off duty three men in civilian dress took him in hand, and warned him that if he talked—you know . . ."

"Sounds very plausible" remarked Mihály Ursi. "On orders from above, the police suspended all investigation. Farewell letters, suicide—the government also feels that the case must be regarded as closed."

"If you please, gentlemen comrades," Joska said modestly, "I have a man at the Margaret Isle Hotel. Works in the kitchen. Would you gentlemen comrades like us to send this Ritpen . . . Rittenbop to *gajdesz?*"

The three generals in mufti, who were among them for the first time, always turned their heads away whenever Joska used the words "gentlemen comrades" and "the Ideal." Ursi stared into space. He realized that it would be no easy task to keep the communist workers and the generals in the same camp.

The Cave now was like a strange film studio where variously placed spotlights of their mute thoughts lit up the monster of Hungary's entry into the war, faceless as yet, embryonic, head curved to knees.

"And now what?" asked a voice. "Do we enter the war?"

A general spoke up:

"War can be waged only with an army. Mechanized warfare only with machines. Luckily Hungary couldn't get into the war even if she wanted to. We have but a handful of infantry, their only arms the wooden rifles with which they drill. Artillery? A few old decrepit cannon. Ninety per cent of our supply trains consist of ox-carts."

180

Chapter 12

The Hungarian Ox-Carts Lurch into World War II.
Kazimir Kilinski's Curious Spectacles.

Wearing a horrifying human face, the black whale joyously splashes in a purple sea. Li-Pu-Ten, the great poet in the time of the Cha-ong Dynasty, whose poems Kristina translated so beautifully, could not have been thinking of the Führer. Kristina's statement that Adolf kept his heart and brain in his boots is nothing but sheer metaphor, typically Kristina.

On the other hand, it is an historical fact that the Duce, whose large photos, flanked by Julius Caesar's and Napoleon's portraits, decorated even the haberdashers' windows in Piccadilly around 1930—the Duce, who only three years ago at the Munich Conference had held the frighteningly sensitive balance of world peace on his little finger—the Duce, everybody's hope, the super-statesman of Europe, who, with the Caesarean cry *"Ora basta!"* which means: Now enough! declared war from the balcony of the Palazzo Venezia against Italy's great Latin sister, unhappy France fallen to her knees—this same Duce undoubtedly had been thinking, not with his brain, but with his stomach.

It was well known in diplomatic circles that the Duce had an ominously developing stomach ulcer.

"A man," said Ursi, in a secret conference in Peter Dukay Street, "who, during fateful negotiations, suddenly presses his two palms to his stomach and with a distorted face leans forward in sharp pain, is not fit for decisions involving the fate of millions. Before a chauffeur is permitted to take the wheel of a car in hand he has to go through a severe medical examination. His sight, his hearing, his nerve-reflexes, and so on. But a man who holds the giant wheel of government can be blind, deaf, crippled, schizoid, whatever you want. At the end of his life Calvin had been shrunk to a yellow mummy as a result of his gall bladder disease. I maintain that it was his vomited bile that changed into the seas of blood of the Wars of Religion. It is not as a natural scientist that I speak now, but I believe that social science has not advanced a single step since Plato. But I hope the day will come when not only the head of a state, but all the senators, congressmen, and everybody in the government must pass the severest medical examination."

"You have always philosophized beautifully," remarked Marja, "but do you think that these are the days for philosophy? You must act! If you think, as all of us do, that the new prime minister is a great danger for Hungary, why do you oppose Mr. Kurdi's suggestion to send him to *kadjesz*—is that the word? . . . Why do you hesitate to cut the ulcer out of the stomach of Hungary?"

Freyberger was the personal physician of the new prime minister who had an even more developed stomach ulcer than the Duce. After the death of Count Teleki, the anxiety of those few Hungarians who were not blinded by the star of Compiègne was concentrated on that stomach ulcer hidden carefully under the fashionably cut waistcoat of the new prime minister. In the tortured dreams of Ursi that stomach ulcer crawled out from under the waistcoat, and like a huge octopus, in the violet and purple colors of anger and hatred, expanded its eight long arms covered with the terrible suckers of patriotic revisionism, and enveloped first the stupid middle class, then the whole nation, and slowly but irresistibly dragged the Hungarian ox-cart into the war on the German side.

In these days it frequently happened that, when Zia had already fallen asleep, Mihály sneaked out of bed, and in pajamas paced his study from wall to wall until the early morning.

What could a man like him do? It took only a nod from the "Major" to Joska Kurdi to send His Excellency the Stomach Ulcer to *gajdesz*, and even the Regent, if it seemed necessary. And what then? An uprising of the workers and the landless peasantry? Would it mean that at the conclusion of a bloody civil war the Stargazers would move into power, and that he, Mihály Ursi, would become the first president of a new, democratic Hungary? Ridiculous! A dream, even more remote than the *Urstron* with which that lazy Ernst had gotten nowhere. In case of a successful *gajdesz* Germany would immediately invade Hungary and in a matter of hours turn it into an Austria, Czechoslovakia or Poland, and instead of the Regent, Hungary would enjoy a Reinhardt Heydrich, a Hermann Frank, eventually a Graf Johann von Dukay, as gauleiter.

Aside from all this, even the word *gajdesz* sounded terrible in his ears. During those sleepless hours he realized his own tragedy; the tragedy of all intellectuals caught between the Joska Kurdis, Slobos, Marjas, Kazis and the Führers, Duces and all the other black whales. Oh yes, as Freyberger recently remarked, history teaches us that great things can be achieved only by the cruelest means. In fateful hours there are no more impotent and cowardly words than *God, constitution, human rights* or *morality*.

He felt himself lost between *gajdesz* and Sir Thomas Harcourt's explosion theory about the universe. There were hours when he came very near to a complete nervous breakdown.

But Marja was right: something had to be done. They must mobilize everybody who had some influence on the Regent. Let somebody go for an audience, furnished with a petition bearing ten thousand names from the intellectual élite of Hungary. All the Stargazers must contact their friends, friends of their friends, so as to obtain the signature of every outstanding and non-political scientist, writer, actor, artist, and churchman—everybody to the fore!—Hungary was at her eleventh hour. Yes, something had to be done, but instead of a bloody and hopeless uprising, they must show forth the real brain, the real conscience of Hungary, through ten thousand of her finest intellectuals. And then see what would happen. Let the Regent have ten thousand such people arrested. The petition would appear in a special edition of the *Kolomp,* avoiding the *censura* with the help of the social democrat printers. A hundred thousand copies, scattered into the streets! Into the whole country before the police could ban them.

He sat at his desk until four o'clock in the morning writing the first draft of the petition, which in the following days was read to the Stargazers—arguments, cuts, inserts—but in a week the final version was ready for the collection of the ten thousand signatures. Kristina was the first to sign it.

"I fully agree with this declaration," said the professor of pomology in the Academy, "but as you know, I've never been a member of any political faction or participated in any movement like that."

"I am willing to give my signature," said the great playwright, "if you cut the second paragraph."

"Excellent!" exclaimed one of the leading actors of the National Theater. "Oh, this is so beautifully written, every line is a new hymn, it echoes in my soul with greater thunder than Hamlet's soliloquy. Oh, if I could only declaim it in front of the curtain! . . ." and with tears in his eyes he added: "I am devastated, my dear Mihály, but since my daughter is going to marry the nephew of the prime minister, you can well understand . . ."

A full month passed. The petition still bore no more than seventeen signatures, and all by second-rate hands.

What could Kristina do in her anger? She hastily finished her play, "The Eleventh Hour." Not exactly the whole play, only a short synopsis of it which reads:

The Eleventh Hour

A PLAY

by

Countess Kristina Euphemia Klementina Dukay de Duka et Hemlice *de genere* Ordony

IN THREE ACTS

ACT ONE

Charles IV, the last Hapsburg emperor, did *not* die in Madeiran exile after the first world war. He lives and reigns in the Royal Palace at Buda. A man named Florian, who during the war had played an important role in the King's secret peace plans, from his unknown grave returns to earth, but vainly begs the palace gateman to allow him before the King. Dressed in rags, he keeps shouting that he is the King's good friend, so they take him to an insane asylum. "Who are you?" asks the head doctor. "I am the Unknown Soldier." "Stop joking. Give me a proper answer. Where do you live?" "In the heart of all men of good will." They put him in a strait jacket.

Curtain.

ACT TWO

Florian succeeds in escaping from the asylum. He hides in the forest, where he begins preaching world peace and humanity to woodchoppers. Soon millions stand behind him. Now he gets to see the King.

(*Author's note:* I don't wish to influence the critics, but this scene between the peace-loving dead King and the Unknown Soldier is really tremendous, the only flaw being that it has not yet been written.)

The King, having heard Florian's idea for avoiding war, at once summons the Royal Council. Pro-German cabinet ministers and generals of German descent use cogent arguments urging that Hungary enter the second world war, too, on the German side. The King lets Florian speak.

"I also vote for war," declares Florian to everyone's astonishment. Colossal ovation.

"And now, gentlemen," continues Florian, "let us go home, write our wills and take leave of our families."

"Why? Are we committing suicide?" asks the chief of the general staff, laughing.

"No, Your Excellency," answers Florian. "Allow me to explain. His Majesty was gracious enough to approve my plan. All of us who voted for war will stand on the great balcony of the palace. As the first battalion leaves for the front—the commanding officer, drawing his sword, will shout: "Halt! . . . Right face! . . . Aim! . . . Fire! . . . and *morituri Te salutant* . . . the first battalion bound for Death will keep firing at the balcony until it has shot all of us to shreds, for we are God-fearing, honest men and cannot—can we?—go on living with the hellish weight of countless future agonies and bereavements upon our conscience. Since we have chosen war, it is fitting that we be the first to die!"

Deep silence. Then the King speaks up:

185

"I want to follow the example of the great Emperor Marcus Aurelius who said: 'An Emperor must die *standing!*' I will stand on the balcony, too, in the first row among you, baring my heart to the fire of the battalion."

After considerable stammering and rationalizing, every member of the Royal Council votes unanimously *against* war.

Curtain.

(*Author's note:* I'm not quite sure whether the beautiful words 'An Emperor must die standing,' were uttered by Marcus Aurelius or Vespasian. Please, look it up in an encyclopedia.)

ACT THREE

Florian is the new Minister of War. Hungary remains neutral, but one of the pro-German ministers somehow learns about Florian's escape from the insane asylum. Great scandal and press exposé, but when they try to put Florian in a strait jacket again he, in miraculous fashion, turns to air. Florian resumes his place beneath the huge ornate gravestone of the Unknown Soldier. Meanwhile the King also returns to his grave at Funchal, Hungary's fate once more reverting to the sober pro-Germans, and everyone is happy.

Curtain.

THE END

The magazine which had published so many of Kristina's beautiful translations of Li-Pu-Ten's inexhaustible poetry, sent back the manuscript of "The Eleventh Hour" without a word. Kristina wrote a letter to Ostie:

. . . there is still freedom of thought in your new country—my congratulations on your citizenship—and since you have good Broadway connections, I'd like you to submit my manuscript to some big producer—I'm sure the piece will be a colossal hit. I hate to talk about money but a substantial advance should come to me now in The Eleventh Hour."

186

Too bad that all the Hungarian theaters refused to produce Kristina's play, because at the end of June 1941, a week after the outbreak of the German-Soviet War, Hungarian wooden rifles and ox-carts hastily lurched into World War II.

The declaration of war against the Soviets was motivated by the fact that Soviet fliers had bombed a town in upper Hungary. Everyone knew that painted-over German machines had scattered a few light bombs on the town of Kassa, carefully avoiding rail and military installations, so as merely to blow Hungary's neutrality sky-high.

Hungarian public opinion winked at this *causa bibendi,* supposing that the Hungarian ox-carts would plod at a respectful distance between German armored units—nothing is so enticing as a war where we do not bleed, yet share the laurels of victory. When, early in the war, the Soviet Union attacked Finland and Poland, Ursi made strenuous efforts to forestall a break between Stargazers and communist workers. Now they had all turned ardently pro-Soviet, and considered Hungary's war declaration a tremendous catastrophe.

The train taking the Budapest Soviet Legation back to Moscow was to leave next morning. At seven that evening Marja waited in the little tavern where she had first dined with Maxim last fall. Maxim was an hour and a half late. He arrived wan and exhausted, his necktie askew—since dawn they had been packing feverishly at the Legation. Nervously he took the menu from the waiter's hands. Stuffed chicken or veal cutlet? There are questions which, even at such moments, must be resolved. The fiddler, who recognized them and remembered their first supper, launched into a gay fox trot, having ascertained that the affairs of the unknown couple were now quite in order.

Yet this time they were really saying adieu. What lay beyond the present? Would they ever see each other? Almost without words they suffered, sometimes looking swiftly and deeply into each other's eyes. Maxim put his hand on Marja's, inclining forward, and his racked face whispered:

"What if you came with me?"

"And if I asked you not to go?"

The question, in this form, did not absolutely require an

187

answer. Nor did Maxim reply. Now he, too, regarded the table-cloth as Marja did.

They had to leave. But the June night was filled with honeyed little breezes, and with the distant rustle of the sleeping capital. A car starting up somewhere sounded like the city's good-natured snore. In one of the little parks they sat down on a bench under the pretext of one last cigarette. The night was aglow with stars, whose wondrous tranquillity seemed to say that all those threatening palpitations of the world—war and declarations of war, the clash of ideologies—were dwarfed to pathetic nothingness by comparison with what filled their hearts.

"Whistle for that taxi," said Marja at about two A.M. in a tone of final farewell.

The taxi drew up before a house in Buda, where Marja stayed with friends whenever she spent a few days in Budapest. But they did not alight at once. Budapest taxi chauffeurs exhibit astonishing comprehension and timing with regard to fares hailing them from a park bench around two A.M. The chauffeur propped his elbows on the wheel and began to doze, knowing that long consultations would precede the final decision. Would the lady leave the taxi alone, or with her escort? It is the usual experience of chauffeurs in such instances, that after an hour-and-a-half-long conference, a quite different address is given.

The Soviet Legation left Budapest that same day at noon.

The state of war inevitably paralyzed freedom of thought and press. To write against war or the Germans was now treason. Since September *Kolomp* had appeared but twice weekly, its columns ever more frequently interspersed with articles entitled "The Primeval Geophysical Past of the Hungarian Plains" or "New Paths of Modern Astronomy," which passed the censor but profoundly bored the average reader. *Kolomp* subscribers dwindled, while pro-German publications—almost brazenly subsidized by German funds—appeared in mammoth issues, and could write with absolute freedom of thought about dazzling German victories.

Our data relating to the latter half of 1941 reveal little regarding the activities of Mihály Ursi and the Stargazers. Joska Kurdi and all the Communists, who in the days of the Ribbentrop-Molotov Pact had crept forth from their twenty-year retreats, again fled underground. The Cave seemed to have fulfilled its mission by providing a secret cache of arms and ammunition for several hundred men, but Ernst Tronfeld's laboratory stood untouched. Clandestine meetings at Peter Dukay Street also became few and far between. It was as though everything had lost its aim and purpose.

Ernst was in busy correspondence with his friends in England and the United States. He felt now that the Cave was nothing but a petrified prehistoric dream world, almost childish. He realized more and more clearly that he had been trapped by the beauteous but enigmatic flames of Mihály Ursi's wild fantasy when he decided to stay in Hungary.

"I think," he wrote to a professor at the University of Chicago whom he knew from Berlin, "that my knowledge is worth something and the great common cause could make more use of me at Cambridge or around you."

Regarding the hospital we have not much to report.

Marja was kept more and more busy because wounded Hungarian soldiers grew in number. Events moved differently from what Hungarian public opinion had imagined in the days of the war declaration. From the start, the German General Staff threw Hungarian troops into the most perilous line of fire. Besides, the "six weeks" had long passed, but the Germans still had not engulfed the Soviet Union.

Besides Rapczyk, the other favorite of wounded soldiers was Count Rere, whose gentle horse-face twice a day inspected the wards with all the self-importance of a professor of medicine. He was given a torn white doctor's coat, and even the gravely wounded laughed hilariously when he put his stethoscope to a patient's knee, or sometimes to the leg of a bed. He wrote prescriptions which will remain forever undecipherable.

Count Johy staged gala evenings at Septemvir Utca, and so firm was his faith in absolute German victory that in the spring of 1942, accompanied by Grubi, he appeared in the Ukraine— no need for alarm, not at the front. With spiked stick and wearing knickerbockers, he roamed the rich farmlands, expertly appraising the crumbly black humus in his palm. He was eyeing some ten thousand acres for eventual "purchase." Zealous Hungarian Nazis all seemed to have arranged for a rendezvous on the wonderfully fertile black sand of the Ukraine.

Kristina, since her marriage, had lived in the Freyberger villa in Buda. If passports were issued to villas, in the passport of Freyberger's villa would have been written: no special marks of identification. But only from outside. Inside was Kristina. The imposing pieces of Dukay furniture spoke of aristocracy fleeing toward middle-class life. With its beautifully ornate hinges and ample waist, a tremendous Maria Terézia *garderobe* in the hall gave the impression that Falstaff with his great belly had strolled by mistake into the Freyberger villa.

Of the "critical" patients only Kazi—Kazimir Kilinski, or if you prefer, Hermann Stolz—remained. He was frequently visited by mysterious arrivals from Poland. After such visits one could see Kazi's tall slender figure in the park, striding back and forth pendulum-like between two trees, shouting aloud and gesticulating to himself. From home he received terrible news of friends and relatives. His brother, Piotr, a major on the Polish General Staff, had still sent no word since the Blitzkrieg, when together with eight thousand of his fellow officers, he disappeared in the mists of the Smolensk prison camp deep in the forest of Katyn.

Hora Tenebrarum was how Pope Pius had described the Polish hell the previous fall. Ten million Poles were under German occupation, but General Frank had guaranteed that not one Pole would survive. SS soldiers slaughtered whole families to assure living space for new German settlers; walls already hemmed in the Jewish ghettos, and in some villages peasants had been locked in barns and burned alive. There was Father Wiorek, the bent-backed little old pastor . . . and Barciazewski—he had been forced to clean General Frank's car. With his tongue! He had had to lick the mud off the fenders. Oh yes, German *Gründlichkeit* was not devoid of humor, and even artistic inspiration. Executions took place under the glare of auto headlights, after which bleeding corpses were laid out in swastika patterns. Madalinski, Obaro, Janicki . . . the names brought faces and voices to life. Kazi had enough to shout and gesticulate about on his solitary and hasty walks between the two trees.

One day he told Ursi:

"I have a plan. But I need your help. I need a special kind of spectacles which I cannot make alone."

"Spectacles? You have eyes like an eagle, and you have never worn spectacles."

"I want to *look* at somebody!"

"At whom?"

"Generral Frrank!"

He locked the door, and in a whispering tone told his idea to Ursi. He had finished Trade School in Warsaw, and his mind had always been busy with fantastic inventions, but he had no tools, and *these* spectacles were too great a task for his technical knowledge.

When Kazi finished his excited and whispering lecture, Ursi stood up, and paced the room several times. Then he said:

"All right, Kazi. I'll help you."

In a few days a Stargazer engineer, employed in the Alfa Fine Tools Factory started to work overtime, sometimes up to midnight. It was not the lenses which were important in these spectacles, but the horn rims. More precisely, the bows reaching back to the ears. The elaborate blueprint showed the right arm of the spectacles enlarged fifty times. There was a hidden straight channel inside the arm . . . $zx57 \cdot 11$ . . . and $ytoo39$ . . . measurements known only to the engineer meaning the hundredths of a millimeter in most precise microscopic technology. At the back of this almost invisible tube there was a tiny but very strong spring made of special steel hardened to the utmost by columbium and alloy. The channel, hardly thicker than a hair, ended at the outer limit of the arm, in the hinge next to the lens, the hole carefully masked with a thin layer of wax. Knowing that the natural position of bows of a pair of spectacles is horizontal, aimed at the face of the person one is addressing, it is superfluous to go into further technological explanations. Kazi's spectacles formed an ingeniously contrived miniature revolver. Its bullet was a very thin needle-point, a tenth of an inch long, of botulinus crystal, the deadliest poison known. One of these tiny, almost invisible needles—the prick of which a victim hardly would notice since it was lighter than the touch of a midge's wing on the face —was composed of enough botulinus to kill a bull elephant.

On the blueprint of the spectacles, the blue and red lines

looked like the blood vessels and nerve system of some fantastic insect, which in the secret laboratory of life instinct, through millions of years of evolution had succeeded in developing tiny spines of mortal poison against its mighty enemies.

Mankind's great ideals are only empty words until they are charged with gunpowder. Words like *Freedom, Independence,* begin their biological life only when, under the terrible pressure of chaos, their gaseous state is transformed into tangible crystals, into $zx57 \cdot 11$, into $yto039$, into $Ov2ClCA6HH$, the chemical formula of botulinus—into very innocent-looking horn-rimmed spectacles.

It was the fate of Poland, the sorrow of Poland, the life-instinct of Poland, which raged with hellish force in Kazi's spectacles.

One single natural movement during a polite conversation, the mechanical resettling of the spectacles on the nose, a little pressure of the thumb and forefinger on the sensitive trigger in the arm, would noiselessly, unobservedly release the tiny botulinus needle with enough force to penetrate the skin of face or neck and into the blood stream. There would be no immediate effect. "Well, good-by, sir. I was very pleased to see you." After a half-hour, a strange headache would begin. And within two hours, certain *gajdesz.*

After two weeks the spectacles were ready and worked wonderfully in the test. Ursi took Mr. Gruber aside:

"You once said that Count Johy is a close friend of General Frank. Introduce Kazi to Johy."

Two days later Kazi and Grubi mounted the old stone staircase of the Septemvir Utca palace.

"Herr Stolz," Grubi introduced Kazi to Johy. "One of my very best friends. He comes from a fine old German family, his father was German consul in Lemberg before the first world war. Young Hermann remained in Poland as an orphan. He went to a Polish elementary school so his German is rather poor, but in the depth of his soul, of course, he has remained a true German. Sit down, Hermann. Have a cigar."

"*Herrr Grrraf,*" began Kazi, puffing the big cigar. "I should like you to consider our conversation as highly confidential."

Johy put his hand on Kazi's knee.

"Lieber Herr Stolz—I think it's unnecessary to give you my word of honor."

"Ever since Czarist and Hapsburg days," said Kazi, "the Poles have had a vivid recollection of the difference between the two occupying forces. A statue of Copernicus stands in the courtyard of the university at Cracow. But not a single statue of Polish national heroes was allowed to remain standing in the Eastern part of Poland where the Grand Duke Constantin was governor-general. After the Blitzkrieg the situation was the same. Poland was divided between the Germans and the Soviets. The western part was ruled by General Frank. A good-hearted, fine gentleman. *Sehrr, sehrr guterr Mann!"*

In his enthusiasm, Kazi even threw a kiss into the air on the tips of his fingers.

"Wirrrklikkerrr Deutscherr Herrr mit hohhen Deutscherr Kulturr! And who ruled Eastern Poland? A dirty, lousy communist commissar! A cruel beast, a monster!"

"Natürlich!" sighed Grubi, and he turned to Johy. "Hermann knows much more about the present Polish situation than anybody in the world."

"Now, thank God," Kazi went on, "our Führer's glorious Army has cleaned Eastern Poland of these godless, murdering Communists—*aberr! Aberr, Herr Grraff!* I've just come back from this former Soviet zone. There are dirty Poles over there who are planning a widespread secret organization against us! Instead of being grateful, they are in the process of organizing secret brigades to dynamite bridges, railway tracks, and sabotage everything. When I happened to learn their secret plans, my German heart bled."

Johy leaned forward and his face grew ruddy.

"Oh!"

"Hermann has a list," said Grubi, twirling his two thumbs above his big stomach, "hundreds and hundreds of names of those communist Poles who are organized in this very dangerous underground movement. He, as a good German, feels it his duty to report his information to the highest German authorities."

Johy slowly caressed his forehead as though his long white fingers wanted to probe every minute variation in the bony structure of his temples. He was excited. Finally, here was the oppor-

193

tunity to render a great service to General Frank, about whom he was anxious. He had a feeling that Frank did not like him, and that when the day came, he wouldn't support his bid to become Hungary's gauleiter.

Grubi knew exactly what was going on behind Johy's forehead under the long nervous fingers. Exchanging a deep look with Johy, he turned to Kazi:

"Herr Stolz! Are you willing to go to Warsaw and submit your list to General Frank personally?"

"Well . . ." said Kazi, but Johy quickly waved his long white fingers:

"We'll pay your expenses! Of course, we will!"

During the conversation Kazi frequently readjusted his new spectacles, which for the time being were not loaded.

Grubi knew nothing about the spectacles. He only knew that the three hundred Poles on Kazi's list were not anti-German underground men—on the contrary: they were the "dirtiest, lousiest collaborators" as Kazi put it, grinding his teeth.

Grubi knew that General Frank was a hasty man. He would immediately have these three hundred "communist rats" arrested. Grubi liked the idea and he did everything to help Kazi to obtain an audience with General Frank.

But a revolver without ammunition is less than a cigarette. The spectacles were ready, but there were no bullets. Alas, the Stargazer chemist informed Ursi that the botulinus was more precious than radium, and as far as he knew there was not a single milligram of botulinus in any of the Hungarian laboratories.

Every two months, ostensibly on a Red Cross mission, Marja would go to Prague in order to keep in close touch with the Czechoslovakian underground. At the University of Prague, there was a seventy-year-old professor of chemistry, who, with his silvery locks around his large forehead and his rather timid smile and exaggerated politeness, resembled a saint from the time of Prokop The Great.

Professor V. gave Marja two milligrams of botulinus. He explained how to make hard tiny crystal needles from the powder and even furnished Marja with the necessary chemicals. He handed the powder to Marja with the reassuring smile of an old house-doctor prescribing for his patient some mild purgative. He

194

did not ask Marja with a single word for what reason she needed it. Professor V. was a member of the Czech underground.

"I'll give you the bullet," said Marja to Kazi when she was back at Ararat, "but only if you lend me your spectacles."

Baron Neurath, first gauleiter of occupied Czechoslovakia, had soon been relieved because of his softness. He was replaced by a thirty-eight-year-old, bull-necked Prussian, named Reinhardt Heydrich.

This Reinhardt Heydrich brought the same tragedy to the patriotic Czechs that General Frank did to the Poles. The word *same* is our word. This was used neither by Marja nor Kazi. There were long and vehement arguments between them over the question of which was the greater monster, Frank or Heydrich, and which more urgently deserved a nice smiling look through the horn-rimmed spectacles.

Marja won, of course. They agreed to travel together first to Prague, where Marja could easily obtain an audience with Heydrich. And after Prague would come Warsaw.

They set out on their journey the first week of May 1942. Marja again on a Red Cross mission, and Kazi with a very warm letter of introduction from Johy to General Frank.

Chapter 13

Journey to Prague and Warsaw. The Gestapo Is Busy Too. The First Bombardment of Budapest.

Seventy-six-year-old Pontius Pilate, one-time gauleiter of Jerusalem, had retired from public office some twenty years before. After a sumptuous dinner party in his country villa in upper Italy, he reclined on his elbow on a gilded sofa and reminisced about old times to his friends.

Among other things he said: "I remember, more than forty years ago, there was some sort of resistance movement in Palestine. The loyal Jews brought a bearded fellow before me called . . . oh, Jupiter, how my memory is failing . . . what the Hades was the name of that fellow?"

He could not remember.

Though Pilate's dinner party occurred only in the imagination of Anatole France, writers' wild fancies have never been able to keep pace with reality.

It is more than probable that Pilate did not remember what had happened some four decades before in Jerusalem, so we can assume that Reinhardt Heydrich, Czechoslovakia's Pilate in 1942, would not have remembered, in his retirement decades later, the names of a few Czech fellows, with or without beards.

But the Czech people remembered. Besides, there was a great difference between Pontius Pilate and Reinhardt Heydrich. Pilate was a mild, benevolent man. Talking about the situation in Czechoslovakia and in Poland, widely discussed in world press and radio in these days, Ostie Dukay said to his father-in-law:

"The Roman occupation in Pilate's time compared to Reinhardt Heydrich's or General Frank's regime, was like a very small, primitive butcher shop compared to your modern slaughter houses in Chicago. We live in the days of mass production."

Marja and Kazi had already been staying in a modest Prague

hotel for ten days. It was not too simple, even for a former Maria Darida, now Schwester Hilda, "a German-born, devoted Nazi," to secure a personal meeting with Reinhardt Heydrich, though her offer to smuggle a new English wonder-drug through Red Cross channels in great quantity was very attractive to the German authorities in Prague.

Marja's audience with Heydrich was scheduled for 3:15 P.M., June 2. So they had to wait with patience. The days, even the hours and the minutes, crawled by with terrible slowness, but 3:15 P.M. on June 2 had been a great achievement, and Marja, too, was now wearing her new horn-rimmed spectacles which gave her pale face a more German expression. When on the terrace of a small café in Prague, Kazi leaned close to whisper something, Marja nervously pulled aside her face:

"Are you sure that these spectacles are not loaded?"

"I am positive."

"You're an absent-minded man, and you are constantly readjusting them."

"I am positive," said Kazi again. "Loading the spectacles is not a job easily forgotten. It needs the finest pincers and a powerful magnifying glass. An hour's work, at least."

It was May 27, two o'clock in the afternoon. Only five short days to the audience, when Marja with her plum-shaped large gray eyes would smile through her spectacles into His Excellency Reinhardt Heydrich's face, which bore the elegant trace of a sword cut from the *Mensura* days at the University, a long cut from the right forehead across the nose to the left chin, an indispensable embellishment for a real Prussian face.

On that afternoon Marja could not know that she would never meet Reinhardt Heydrich. Neither she nor Kazi knew what was going on at that hour. Nobody knew, not even the finest brains of the Gestapo.

That is, except for a few members of the underground, officers of the former Czech Army. At Heydrich's headquarters nobody ever knew, not even His Excellency's first secretary, when His Excellency might jump into his car and speed to Berchtesgaden or Berlin, sitting between his SS guards. His trips were purposely unscheduled as a measure of precaution.

But for two weeks now, ever since his new order had come

out forcing all the Czech youths into an organization patterned on the Hitler Jugend, so as to condition the soul of the new Czech generation—the Czech underground had been whispering to each other something similar to *Ora basta!*—Now it is enough! For two weeks, members of the Czech underground had been waiting day and night for the unscheduled appearance of his big black Mercedes, which had been a birthday gift from the Führer. Innocent-looking picnic parties were camping under trees along the Prague-Berlin highway, bicycles lying in the grass. Innocent-looking peasants were working in their potato fields next to the highway.

On this Wednesday afternoon, Reinhardt Heydrich, the nape of whose neck, shaved in the Prussian style, looked like a red brick, at five minutes after three, unexpectedly as usual, jumped into his car which immediately took the Prague-Berlin highway at top speed.

At 3:50, twenty-eight miles east of Pilsen, near the town of Rotkitzen, two men suddenly leaped out of the roadside ditch. As one of them threw an object, Heydrich's chauffeur, always gripped by a panic-fear of death, swerved the big Mercedes into the opposite ditch to avoid being hit. But the bomb struck the careening automobile and blew it over onto its side. The other man immediately ran up and pumped some ten bullets from an automatic pistol into the wrecked car, now lying in the ditch. Then the two men raced off on bicycles.

The chauffeur and one SS guard were immediately killed. Reinhardt Heydrich received two bullets, one in his kidney, one in his back.

Within an hour in the nearby small town of Rotkitzen, an innocent family of seven members was executed by the Gestapo, without investigation, without any questioning. But it was only the beginning.

In the evening hours, ten special Gestapo planes landed at the Prague airport. The great Heinrich, the greatest Heinrich of all Heinrichs, Heinrich Himmler hurried to the hospital room of Reinhardt Heydrich, his right hand and best friend. Yes, the great Heinrich arrived, and took the whole affair personally in hand.

The radio broadcast only a few insignificant words about

the attempt, triumphantly announcing that Heydrich's condition was not serious.

"Too bad," said Kazi to Marja, "that they anticipated you. Now this monster will survive, but I'm afraid your audience will be cancelled."

Kazi planned to leave for Warsaw the next morning, to present Count Johy's very warm letter of introduction to General Frank. But neither he nor Marja could leave. Prague was already in a state of siege; train service to and from the city had been discontinued.

The Gestapo, headed personally by Heinrich Himmler, was very busy. These darkest pages of Czech history do not belong to our story, we only briefly mention that ten million crowns reward was offered by Himmler for information leading to the seizure of the culprits, dead or alive. The greatest German surgeons surrounded Reinhardt Heydrich's bed in the hospital, among them the personal physician of the Führer. The radio had lied about Heydrich's condition, which was hopeless from the very first moment. He died within a week. In the evening hours, after his pompous military funeral, SS troops marched into the small mining village of Lidice, and in honor and memory of their chief, exterminated all the male population of the village, regardless of age, then razed Lidice to the ground. But it was not the end. In the following weeks no fewer than two thousand Czechs were killed in one single concentration camp alone.

Marja left Prague for Budapest at the end of June. The same day Kazi left for Warsaw, in his pocket the very warm letter of introduction to General Frank. But even a letter from all the ancient Teuton gods would not have been enough to get an audience with Frank. After the Heydrich assassination, the dark-haired, short SS general, who had guaranteed that no Pole would survive his regime, and who was responsible for the massacre of thousands of Poles, became very cautious about his precious life. The SS guards were doubled around his headquarters. Not only his antechamber but all the corridors were filled with secret service men. No audience for anyone. General Frank did not go anywhere, not even to the toilet. According to reliable historical sources, he used a stool-chair in his office behind locked doors.

199

It was very warm in Warsaw even for a Hermann Stolz furnished with an enthusiastic letter of introduction from Graf Johann von Dukay. Kazi left Warsaw in the middle of August.

The Gestapo was much more successful in eliminating important persons.

Young István Horthy, since February Vice-Regent of Hungary, had worked in the United States in a Ford factory as an engineer before the war. Ribbentrop, among other things, did not like the American past of a man who was now the actual Regent of Hungary in place of his aging father.

On August 20, at eleven o'clock in the morning, the young and pretty Madame Horthy was standing on the steps of their special plane, ready to fly back to Hungary after her husband had visited the Hungarian troops on the Ukrainian battle-front. István Horthy, with warm handshakes, was saying good-by to the German authorities at the airport, when an excited German officer dashed up to the group and reported that three Ratas were approaching the airport and there were no German fighter pilots at hand. *Rata*, which means duck, was the name of a certain type of Soviet bomber.

The panic-stricken German officer turned to young Horthy, who was an excellent pilot.

"Oh! Your Serenity is just leaving . . . ?"

Madame Horthy grabbed the arm of her husband.

"No, István, don't go . . ."

But, for the thirty-six-year-old Horthy, Vice-Regent of Hungary, it would have been an eternal source of shame not to display the traditional Hungarian bravery before the Germans in such a perilous moment. Commands were shouted . . . the Germans were in a hurry to help him into a special German fighter plane. István Horthy took off alone in the plane and went out against the Ratas with two other German interceptors that had turned up.

Within minutes his plane crashed in flames.

An accident.

Only two things appeared inexplicable to those Hungarians who witnessed the tragedy. After the plane hit the earth, German soldiers were ordered to rush to the plane, and bury the wreckage in soil "in order to smother the flames." They buried the possibility, too, of any further investigation of what had been the cause of the crash, what was inside the plane. And another curious thing: the Ratas did not arrive after all. They were nowhere to be seen.

And so did the young Vice-Regent die in an "accident," after the Prince of Aosta's "stomach disorder" and Pál Teleki's "suicide." At the funeral, friendly Germany was represented by Ribbentrop. With a profound bow he kissed the hand of the bereaved mother, and never had the *Bitt' schön* issued so sweetly from his face of ice, as when, with exaggerated politeness, he paused to usher even lesser Hungarian officials before him at every door.

But the old Regent was still blind when he looked into the soul of his great German friends.

Today we know perfectly well that in August, 1942, the tide of World War II had already turned completely in favor of the Allies. But the thronged open terraces of cafés along the Danube, resounding to gypsy music, were then not yet aware of this. On September 5, around midnight, over fully illuminated Budapest, Russian bombers unexpectedly appeared.

We shall let Zia's diary speak of this night:

Around eleven o'clock, after Kristina's sumptuous dinner, a bridge party formed on the terrace of Freyberger's villa. A radio from the neighboring villa was broadcasting Italian bulletins of victory, but already with a certain reserve—you could often catch the word *probabilmente*. It was a delightfully mild and fragrant September night. A branch of one of the plane trees hung over the terrace and at times a yellow leaf from on high would flutter down to the bridge table. Kristina, whose luck had run out, slipped one of these leaves among her cards and said: "Thank heavens, at last a good card!"

"The early bird gets the worm," said Jani Hamor in the tone of card players who never listen to what they are saying. We were in fine spirits. Down at the foot of the hill, the city glittered in a flood of light. I best enjoy gypsy music on such a tranquil evening, when it sounds mysteriously from afar. In the second year of the war, Budapest had completely forgotten about the discovery of the airplane: not for an instant did it occur to her that she might be bombed. By and large she acted like someone who had no intention of dying and was convinced that the lack of such intent in itself was all that was needed to stay alive.

"One spade!" said Freyberger.

It was five minutes before midnight.

"Two clubs," said Kristina, pronouncing it more like "kwubs."

Suddenly all of us looked up at the dark sky, seeming to hear some approaching, deep, unfamiliar whistle.

"Two hearts," Hamor still had time to say, and the next instant everything went black. A fierce rush of air struck me in the chest and the sharp blast was so horrible that I felt as if an immense cleaver had sundered my body in two. Kristina began screaming hysterically—I did, too, I think, but don't remember clearly. Men's voices shouted, there was a sound of running steps, on the terrace a big umbrella flung high by the concussion fell back point first and silenced the screaming Kristina. It struck her exactly on the forehead. In these frenzied moments I had the feeling that harmless pieces of furniture had turned into deadly weapons. Kristina collapsed in a faint, someone running in the dark had stepped on her hand, breaking two of her fingers. In the dining room a few bulbs in the chandelier still glowed. The chandelier, rocked by the blast, still swung wildly, like an infuriated caged monkey on a trapeze—its glass decorations tinkled as if with mocking lunatic laughter as it swung and swung, wildly swung. On the city too, darkness had descended, the air filled with giant boomings near and far, as if, from the mysteriously humming black sky, great crates had been dropped, seemingly filled with fragile things, roofs of houses, tiles and twisted splinters of bridges. "Everyone to the shelter!" shouted Mihály from somewhere in the darkness. Now the anti-aircraft guns were roaring; in fiery garlands against the dark sky appeared the cone-shaped shells. This too was so dreadful, something I had never yet seen: cannonballs in flight. The footman appeared with a candle on the terrace—only then did we discover the bleeding and unconscious Kristina. Mihály caught her up in his strong arms and swiftly carried her down the steps. The cellar did not know that this night it would have guests in evening clothes, on which Kristina always insisted. A smell of rotting potatoes filled the cellar. We laid Kristina on some empty sacks on the ground, Freyberger was already kneeling near her with his doctor's kit and bandages. Kristina opened her eyes, not knowing where she was, and spoke in delirium: "Is the king alive? Is he safe?" Then at the sound of a great detonation nearby, she relapsed into her faint. As newer and newer explosions shook the whole city, even the walls of cellars seemed to grow flexible. I thought of Zizi, who had stayed home alone with the maid; half-crazed I rushed for the door, but Mihály barred my way, he took hold of me and forcibly sat me back on a wooden chopping-block. I prayed aloud, in a wailing lament, I think. Others too, but I don't know who, because there were also strangers in the cellar. I recognized the cook—the others may have been charwomen. Modesty stripped off all veils when I, the "Countess," and the cook with the varicose-veined legs, over a tin pail, in everyone's view, squatted and obeyed the command of our bladders. The sounds of metabolism on the side of a tin pail mingled with the wailed words of prayer to the Holy Virgin: both forced from body and soul by the ecstatic fear of death. The footman finally located the air-defense tools: a shovel and a pick for breaking down walls. He set the tools against the cobwebby wall with much the same gesture as if he were handling a sandwich platter and a champagne cooler. So new were the tools that they might have been bought that very day in some toy shop. Everyone looked in their direction. Our gaze was especially riveted on the shovel which, in a whisper clearly audible above the thunderous din, seemed to say: "Prepare to dig your graves!"

Suddenly everyone buried his face in his hands, because the sirens began blaring wildly. We didn't know that this meant the end. Someone opened the cellar door: "It's over! They've gone!" Now, through the open door, the "All Clear" of the sirens sounded like the trumpets of the

Resurrection. Death, which the imagination of every man holds imprisoned in some obscure future, in the past hour had snapped his chains and rushed so close to his jailers that his gorilla-arms had shaken the brick walls—but already the sirens sounded, sounded, and Death, gnashing his teeth, retreated to his chains.

I rushed to the phone . . . Zizi, Mama . . . there's nothing wrong, everyone is alive. At such times the word "everyone" refers only to ourselves. In Budapest not everyone was still alive.

Someone shouted down into the cellar: "Rescue team! The Z. Villa got a direct hit!" Already cars had surrounded the ruins, spraying them with the beams of their headlights. The villa was not afire but smoked in ghostly fashion, the smoke descending on them from above, as though the catastrophe had occurred somewhere in the dark sky. Thick dust descended after the explosion and the myriad tiny stars of this dust cloud danced in the glare of the headlights. As it stood there on the hilltop, cloven in two by a single gigantic ax-stroke, the great villa was like some fantastic modern stage decor from Korngold's opera, *Die tote Stadt!* Into the second-story bedrooms, opened walls and all, the beams of auto headlights penetrated, falling upon the silk coverlets of two carefully made beds which seemed the picture of tranquillity, but one huge wardrobe leaned tottering on the brink, and poised hesitatingly as though contemplating a suicidal plunge. On the ground floor lived a bank director; out to dinner somewhere, he and his wife could not yet be aware of what had happened, but by the time we got there and made our way to their rooms through the rubble of walls and twisted staircases, two of their children, three- and five-year-old little girls, were already laid out on the dining room table, plaster dust on their nightdresses and dead little faces. "Rescue teams" were multiplying, they made the rounds and rummaged through every room, but curiosity seemed greater than the urge to help. "How many dead?" asked a tall thin gentleman. "Three," said someone. "Three? Only three?" he turned on his heel and left, disgruntled. The governess asleep in the room nearest the bomb-burst had been compressed to the size of a child by the concussion. I didn't go to look. Someone explained that the blast zigzagged like a slashing sword or the strokes of a great bludgeon. In the salon it had ripped an iron girder from the wall, crumpling it like paper, but a yard away in the glass cabinet the fragile cups of the china collection remained intact in their places. It was all so weird and devilish. Why this frightful havoc, why had the great villa tumbled into ruin when the bomb hadn't even pierced the roof, but fell ten yards away in the garden? People gathered round an artillery expert who explained that at the point of detonation a powerful vacuum arises and the terrific force of this vacuum "tore down" the great villa. By now the crowd was so thick that it was hardly possible to move. Mihály roared at a young man sporting an elegant gray hat: "Where are you taking that typewriter?" He twisted the portable machine from his hands and struck him full in the chest. The elegant gray hat quickly vanished in the dark.

The explosion had completely denuded the branches of the great trees. High up between two thicker boughs a dark velvet chair had settled itself and, with its legs toward the sky, looked like some strange and prodigious bird's nest. From the branches of another tree hung a child's narrow fur collar like some giant hairy caterpillar. In the crown of one tree, a frock coat drooped its swallow tails like a black flag and flashed its silk lining under the glare of the lights. But there were other exhibits on the trees too: a blue dressing gown, a broom with a broken handle, half a pair of women's silver sandals, a Teddy bear, head downward, probably belonging to one of the little girls, a white kitchen chair with broken legs, an oval mosaic window along with its frame—all this was as if the birds of some unfamiliar underworld, bald-necked vultures, had overrun the trees in expectation of the moment when they might alight upon the dead carcass of the world. A picture of the Holy Virgin with the infant Jesus on her arm, flown from its frame, had

205

landed on a bush and in an almost horizontal position the Holy Mother seemed as if reclining on her back in deathly exhaustion, gazing questioningly toward the heavens.

Mihály, in a voice trembling with rage, outshouted the clamorous throng pressing into the rooms: "Police! Aren't the police here yet? Everybody here wants to rob! They have already stolen the silk nightdress off one of the dead little girls!"

On the last night of August 1939, I ended my chaotic diary with the words: "It has begun. Merciful God, have pity on us: it has begun."

I could now finish this diary Kristina-style with the words of Shakespeare: "Our revels now are ended." *Really ended.* Something has begun, but we don't yet know exactly what.

Chapter 14

Hungary Wants to Jump Out of the War. Secret Mission in Istanbul.

Nowhere was there a light, nowhere a human soul aside from a few silent and motionless German sentinels standing near the tracks at the bomb-gutted Belgrade station. The moonbeams from the tips of the German bayonets flashed like weird candle flames. In this tomblike silence the ruins of the Belgrade railway station looked like the strange bier of the Middle East.

A few travelers appeared from somewhere among the ruins, carrying valises, waiting for the Sofia train. One battered suitcase contained a stock of neckties; that man over there looked like a Bulgarian truck-farmer. From the side pocket of another prospective passenger peeped a copy of the Rumanian paper *Averul,* and still another wore the toga of a Greek Orthodox priest. Three women, too, were of the company, two of them young and the other one elderly. The man who appeared to be a truck-farmer was Mihály Ursi, the salesman was Ernst Tronfeld, the Red Cross nurse was Marja, and next to her Zia. The reader of the *Averul* and the Orthodox priest were standing separately.

Nobody spoke; they were waiting patiently for the train. Then, far to the south a ghostly splutter of small-arms fire could be heard from the hills, as though it were no longer men, but the Yugoslav mountains, forests, caves, winds and gales that were warring—unyielding partisans fighting in the name of a veiled and powerful god. And it was as if a single name expressed all this in Mihály Ursi's mind: Slobodan Tuykovich.

Through their underground channels Ursi had sent a letter to Slobo two weeks before that they were going to Istanbul, by way of Yugoslavia, and would board the train at 10:45 P.M, April 9, 1943, at the Belgrade station. Had the message reached

Slobo? It hardly seemed possible that they could meet. The northern part of Yugoslavia was strongly in German hands.

Finally the rickety train clanked in. The conductor opened only one compartment for the seven passengers. It meant that Ursi, Zia, Marja and Ernst could not talk in the presence of the Greek Orthodox priest and the *Averul* man. One could not know for certain whether they were men of the Gestapo or of the English Secret Service. The broken windows of the train were boarded over, and owing to the blackout only a tiny blue lamp glowed above the door of the compartment. A dubious stain darkened one of the seats, where a man perhaps had been murdered or some bomb victim had bled to death. In this ghostly blue light they traveled in ghostly silence, no one saying a word. The bearded Orthodox priest and the *Averul* man shut their eyes as though intending to sleep, but then an eyelid would rise furtively to scan the faces of fellow passengers; they could be spies of the sort who with feline swiftness and fanaticism make use of revolvers or knives whipped from under their coats. One thing was certain: anonymous hands rather frequently shoved corpses from the windows of this train. The Belgrade-Sofia-Istanbul line was the route of spies, for the role played by Zurich in the first world war now had been assumed by Istanbul and the new Turkish capital, Ankara, where the cook at the American Embassy was a German spy and the porter at the German Embassy a Soviet secret agent; but both of them being counterspies, nothing changed in world history, except that they pocketed the money from both sides. The major-domo at the French Embassy was a counter-counterspy, a role much more difficult for laymen to understand than the formula of relativity or entropy.

This eastward shift in the spy center from Zurich to Istanbul was made necessary by reasons paralleling those that in the fourth century A.D. impelled Constantine The Great to shift the capital of the failing Roman Empire to Byzantium, later named after him Constantinople, today Istanbul. Asia then for Emperor Constantine was becoming important, just as Soviet Russia now after the great Stalingrad victory.

The train was slow; it stopped at every small station. Ursi always looked out, still hoping that Slobo would appear, perhaps in the uniform of a German officer. But Slobo was nowhere.

They traveled on in silence, except that the Greek Orthodox priest, his fingers crossed in prayer over his stomach, sometimes started to snore, then making a loud snarl like a dog when it catches a fly in the air, awoke; his big round beard looked around apologetically, then closed its eyes again.

After midnight the *Averul* man left the train, so Zia and Marja dared to whisper to each other. The priest was snoring again.

An hour later the elderly lady next to Ernst stood up and disappeared in the direction of the washroom. Then something peculiar happened. The Orthodox snoring suddenly stopped, the priest turned to Zia and said to her in dreadful Hungarian:

"*Kezicsakala, grafni*—I kiss your hand, Countess."

He was Slobo. It had not only been the poor bluish light in the compartment which had disguised him, but—instead of his habitual sparse Gonzaga beard from the time when he had been Signor Scipio di Caruccio, art dealer from Rome—his beard was now very typically Orthodox, thick and round, covering almost his whole face and reaching to the middle of his chest. It was not a shiny black any longer, it was graying. Two hard Partisan years helped the gray dye on it.

"My God!" exclaimed Ursi," why didn't you speak? We've been alone for an hour now!"

"Who is the elderly lady who went to the toilet?" whispered Slobo's big beard.

"She is my mother," said Ernst Tronfeld.

"Oh, I didn't know that. I was afraid she was a German general in female dress."

They began to talk. They had hardly an hour left, because Slobo had to leave the train in Nish, not far from the Bulgarian frontier. Ursi briefly explained why they were going to Istanbul. In the first months of 1943, the Hungarian government asked itself more and more frequently: where were the left-wingers, the liberals, the pro-Anglo-Americans, who yesterday were still accounted traitors fit for the noose? Who had friendly or family connections with England, America or the Soviet Union? Where was Count Sigray, where were the Szechenyis with their Vanderbilt relations? Where were men like Ostie Dukay and what were they doing? Hurry, hurry, everyone on deck! Mihály and Zia were being awaited in Istanbul by Ostie; Marja by her fiancé, Maxim Narokov, the Soviet diplomat; and Ernst Tronfeld by an old friend of his, a professor of nuclear physics from England.

"What special business have you been in since you left us?" asked Marja.

The conversation went on in German.

"Vielleicht du weisst," said Slobo "that when I left my parental house, I made my living in cabarets as an archer. I still can handle the bow very well."

"You don't mean that you are fighting against the German panzer divisions with bow and arrow?" laughed Marja's large plum-shaped gray eyes under the Red Cross cap.

"Why not?" Slobo lifted his Orthodox beard, almost insulted. "Listen, my dear: didn't you read about the English sportsman who killed a bull elephant with an arrow? A razor-sharp arrow causes much greater hemorrhage than a Cordike bullet. I've heard there are specially trained archers in the English Commandos. The arrow has a tremendous advantage. If you are hiding in a thick bush, an arrow doesn't make any smoke, not even the smell of it. And it is noiseless. Absolutely noiseless, my dear Schwester Hilda."

"I see . . ." said Marja, remembering Kazi's spectacles.

"Strange," remarked Ernst. "Strange," he said again. "The fantastically large scale of weapons, from arrows and bayonets, to TNT and perhaps very soon to uranium-bombs, gas-chambers, and sterilization—this war seems to be a final universal demonstration of the greatest human science."

Mrs. Tronfeld, the timid elderly lady, came back from the washroom.

"Good evening, General!" Slobo greeted her. They laughed.

The train slowed down cautiously as it reached the temporarily repaired tracks. A passenger train lay in the deep ditch, showing its belly to the moonshine, like a huge and fantastic dead insect of civilization. Nothing stirs the imagination more than the silent carcass of a turned-over passenger train a few days after the catastrophe.

"I hope," whispered Zia, "our train won't be blown up."

"Not *this* train, and not *tonight*," said Slobo with the polite smile he used toward ladies. His reassuring remark did not need any explanation.

"How is Rapczyk?" asked Slobo after a few seconds silence. "I am very grateful to him. Last month I used his Polish technique but, of course, in a Yugoslav version. Our hidden lines were only a half-mile from the German headquarters. One dark night I ventured to their stables and stole two horses. I led them noiselessly to our lines. For three days I gave them plenty of well-salted oats, but no water at all. On the fourth day I strapped to each of them sixty kilograms of dynamite, then freed them. They galloped back to the water troughs in their stable in a frenzy, and within five minutes the whole German headquarters went up in the air. The poor creatures! I mean the horses. One was a nice roan mare, the other a piebald colt."

In the silence which followed Slobo's words, Zia chuckled. A short, loud laugh rang out of her throat, almost a cry.

"What are you laughing at?" asked Mihály in a bad humored tone.

"Excuse me . . . I listened to Slobo . . . his priest cassock . . . his apostolic beard, the golden cross on his chest, and he said in a benign voice: 'sixty kilograms of dynamite.' Oh, my God, what a strange world we live in!"

"Oh, yes, everything is so strange," said Ernst's mother, her thoughts far away. Then Ursi spoke up, in Hungarian, rather to himself:

"*Különös, különös nyáréjszaka volt . . .*"

It was the first line of Ady's poem, and he said it in the cadence in which sounded the mysterious drumming in heaven: "It was a strange, strange summer night . . ." And he added: "Quite a nice, long night. It began in 1914 and we still don't know when the dawn will come."

"Don't start your boring philosophy!" said Slobo. "Let's get to business. We have only a half hour left to Nish."

And he started to talk in detail about the secret contact channels between the Stargazers and the Yugoslav Partisans in case Hungary, jumping out of the war, should break a leg.

Zia was not listening to them. She was remembering Tintoretto's words, when the great Renaissance master once said to one of his pupils: "Have you ever noticed how heavenly beautiful are the faces and hands of every man and woman in the streets of Venezia—in twilight?"

It was a bluish twilight in the compartment. Zia looked at Marja's hands, and again noted that Marja had beautiful hands. Not too small, but white, soft, warm hands which now lay in Marja's lap like two sleepy kittens, pressed close. Such hands in the lap of a woman always stir the sexual imagination of a man. It was not the first time that Zia's thoughts had been touched by the remote and sharp pain of jealousy.

At Nish, Slobo left the train. His tall, benign priestly figure disappeared among the few passengers at the station.

At two o'clock in the morning they changed trains for Sofia at the Bulgarian frontier and the next afternoon arrived in Istanbul where Ostie was waiting for them at the station.

"Where is Zizi? Didn't you bring Zizi with you?" These were Ostie's first words, once they were past the tumultuous emotions of reunion. Zia for a long while sobbed mutely on Ostie's shoulder.

It was almost four years since they had last seen each other— at their father's funeral. Ostie had put on some weight, and now he was in the uniform of a lieutenant-colonel of the American Air Force. He had become an American citizen the previous year and was with the OSS. When they sat down, Ursi opened the conversation:

"I fear that soon American bombers may appear in force over Septemvir Utca."

"I'm afraid of that myself," said Ostie, pensively scratching the nape of his neck. "The time has come for us to establish regular contact. I'd like to introduce our short-wave radio expert to you."

He strode to the other room and returned with a young American soldier, who sprang to attention before Ursi. With an embarrassed smile, the soldier gazed at him, his lips quivering a little from emotion.

"Don't you recognize him?" asked Ostie.

"I don't know him, and have never seen him," said Mihály. "What is your name?" he asked the young soldier in English.

He replied in Hungarian.

"I'm Andrew Szanto. From Brooklyn."

Ursi fell on his neck. Andrew! How could he have recognized him? Andrew had been only twelve in 1930 when Ursi saw him last.

For the afternoon they arranged that Zia, Ernst and his mother should see the sights of the town, while Ostie, Andrew, Marja and Ursi sat in consultation. Ostie naturally was aware of Marja's role as an important member of the underground movement, but to Zia or Kristina she was still only Schwester Hilda.

This was the gist of Ostie's talk:

"I do not wish to mention names, but I have had an opportunity to speak in very high circles about the Magyar question. The Hungarian government is naïve to think that with one or two secret emissaries, such as you, it can atone for all its stupid and evil deeds. Rudolf Hess, landing in England, thought Churchill would rush to embrace him. Churchill didn't even deign to speak to him. Concisely put, the Allied view is this: we want not words, but deeds."

With regard to deeds, Ursi had this to say:

"In Hungary, the Church, the working class, and the peasantry are anti-German. To my mind, primary responsibility for the present disastrous situation rests with the middle class which, strongly infused with German blood, behaves even more disgracefully than the aristocracy. They find it very convenient to accept the 'regained' territories from the hands of the Germans, and even more convenient the idea of expropriating all that Jewish industry has accumulated while they listened to the gypsy play. There are few exceptions among the aristocracy, even fewer in the middle class. Save for a scattering of fine Hungarian officers, and say our own group, at the moment of 'action' we can only count on the great mass of workers. At this point, however, I already see trouble. The Red Army is heading toward Hungary, and every man whose father wielded heavy tools and wore oily work clothes, awaits the Russians. We naturally know nothing of the Allied plans, but imagine that if invasion takes place on the Adriatic and, joining with the Yugoslav partisans, Allied troops approach through the Balkans, in Hungary at that instant anti-German revolt would flare, in which

213

even Hungarian Nazis who have lost faith in a German victory will join; and, in my opinion, after the mysterious deaths of Pál Teleki and the Vice-Regent, the Regent also will turn against the Germans. Our military experts agree that the fate of all Central and Eastern Europe will depend on whether Anglo-American or Russian troops arrive first on the scene. Do you know anything about the invasion plans?"

Ostie answered only with a perplexed gesture of his hand.

At dinner Zia asked Ostie: "What made you think we would bring Zizi with us too?"

"I felt sure," said Ostie reflectively, "that you would come with me to America, once you succeeded in getting as far as Istanbul."

"There's no sense in that now, the worst is already over," said Zia cheerfully. "Kristina sometimes has very good tips. According to a secret agreement the Allies won't bomb Hungary. Other reports say that the German General Staff is planning a putsch against Hitler and within months the war will end in compromise."

Neither Ostie nor Mihály made any comment on Zia's words. They didn't even glance at each other. But their thoughts corresponded.

Zia then related that their walk seemed to have been shadowed by furtive figures. Ostie, likewise, was of the opinion that Istanbul swarmed with Gestapo spies and that it would be wise to make their stay as brief as possible.

They were dining in a Turkish restaurant. Marja was still at the Soviet Legation. Mihály and Zia had a great argument about which was the better dish, Turkish *pilaf* or Hungarian chicken-and-rice. Ursi looked as though he were giving in, but then raised a finger and said Galileo's stubborn words: *"Eppur si muove!"*—a habitual phrase of his in arguments.

Marja came back from the Soviet Legation in a bad mood. When she had taken leave of Maxim two years before, the day the Hungarian-Soviet war was declared, Maxim had been certain he would be assigned to Istanbul. "No, Maxim is not in Istanbul, and hasn't been," was the reply she received at the Soviet Legation from Bolgorin, whom Marja already knew from Budapest. Huge portraits of Lenin and Stalin looked down from the wall as if protesting any detailed inquiries about Maxim in this room. Marja, somewhat disconcerted and ill at ease, nevertheless asked Bolgorin, who had the build of a professional wrestler, and was not only a diplomatic colleague of Maxim's, but his best friend.

"I should like to write him. Would it be possible for you to forward my letter?"

"Oh, of course."

But the slight pause preceding this "Oh, of course," greatly depreciated its value.

After dinner around eleven o'clock Zia wanted to speak with Marja about the packing. When she opened her door in the hotel, she saw Marja deeply buried in letter-writing; the desk was covered with countless, densely written sheets of paper. A half-hour later when Zia again opened the door, Marja was kneeling before the Villon Madonna.

Next morning Ursi and Ernst Tronfeld sat alone in the hotel room. After his meeting with his English colleague, Ernst told Mihály that he was going not to Oxford, as he originally had planned, but to Chicago. His friend did not give him any further explanation why his destination had changed.

"Well, Ernst," said Mihály, "I am afraid I won't see you for a long time."

They were alone, as fifteen years before in Berlin at the Holzer Restaurant, or that night in 1939 in Peter Dukay Street when Grubi had brought back Ernst from the concentration camp. They talked now, too, for an hour, but there was no heat in their talk. Mihály Ursi was not Ursa Major any longer, and Ernst not "Oh, Tronfeld . . . Tronfeld ist der einzige! . . ." Every word sounded like a farewell as they summed up the world situation.

"Hitler is an idiot," Ursi observed objectively, almost scientifically. "If he hadn't forced the Jewish issue, today every Jewish scientist would be working not for America, but for Germany."

"Hitler has a character too open and direct," said Ernst. "But Stalin is a greater statesman by far. Stalin, in his place, would have ardently clasped all Jews to his heart, so that during the embrace he might slyly extract from their pockets all their knowledge and ability. Only upon winning the war would he have exterminated them. Compared to Adolf, Uncle Joe is a

215

genius. We Jews would have snapped at the bait. To sweep the wiliest Jew off his feet, just embrace him. Did you ever see a greater German patriot than the German Jew? It was so with me, though I was not born on German soil. I, too, was embraced by the Germany of Weimar."

Ursi dropped the topic.

That day they said good-by to Ostie and Andrew Szanto, leaving Ernst and his mother in their care. That night Ursi, Zia and Marja left Istanbul, above which the half-moon lit up the graceful pinnacles of minarets, and on whose streets lay dead dogs, fiercely baring their white teeth in wrath because no one had bothered to bury them.

Zia's only worry on the way was how the contents of her luggage would get past customs—the ten cartons of American cigarettes, and especially the several pounds of chocolate which Ostie had sent Zizi.

Marja was silent, and Mihály was reading Ortega y Gasset's *Revolt of the Masses*, a book which was fitting to be acquainted with in these years. "Like it or not, human life consists in our preparations for the future," read one line in the book.

The nearer they got to the Hungarian frontier, the more Ursi felt that Hungary was in no way preparing for the future.

Chapter 15

*The Stargazers' Military Plans. Flight from German Occupation.
British and American Planes Rain Bombs on Hungary.*

Three months after the Istanbul trip, in the summer of
1943, occurred events affecting Mihály, Zia and Marja, which,
however, did not pertain to the course of world history.

Kristina and Dr. Freyberger, Zia, Zizi, and Marja already
had left the Ararat bathhouse, which had been built in the style
of a Chinese pagoda on the shores of the fishpond.

"My sunglasses!" cried Marja and turned back to seek them
in the sand where she had been basking. Ursi, who felt quite
secure in his solitude, stood naked under the shower. On glimpsing Marja, he reached in alarm for his bathing trunks, which of
course he didn't find. He gave the tap another turn so the jet
of the shower might hide him, but not even this helped much.
A naked man at such a moment finds it extremely difficult to
decide whether to show the lady his front or his rear. Instinctively
he turned sideways, the sole result being that his front and rear
showed simultaneously. Marja's glance meanwhile was hunting
for the sunglasses and she inquired about their plans for the
evening in the same tone as if the Major had been standing in
formal evening dress under the shower.

The shower was fifteen paces from the dressing room. But
these fifteen paces constituted the greatest of danger zones—
what if Zia, too, had forgotten something and came back? Ursi
negotiated these fifteen paces in the same fashion as on the
Italian battlefield in the Siege of Montello under blazing fire:
without cover.

And Zia came back. She had left in the sand neither her
sunglasses nor her cigarette holder—a vague instinctive jealousy
brought her back. She found Marja's return suspicious, just as
for quite some time she had found suspicious the behavior of

Marja and her husband. When she opened the door Mihály was just stepping back into the cabin and for Zia this spectacle thoroughly sufficed. Quickly she closed the door in front of her, neither her husband nor Marja noticing her momentary appearance. She closed the door with the feeling that she had closed the door of her marriage.

Pleading a headache, Zia did not appear for supper. She lay in her room on the bed like someone mortally wounded. Now she did not doubt for an instant that Schwester Hilda and her husband were having an affair. From the beginning an aura of mystery had enveloped this Schwester Hilda. In her figure and motions, especially in her daring bathing dress, in her whole essence there was a certain throttled tension, from which at times flashed a spirit and humor not completely in accord with the nursing profession nor with her habitual prayers. She used no rouge or powder, nor polished her nails, yet her provocative and piquant beauty seemed only to employ age and resignation as a mask. Zia had long felt that Schwester Hilda and Mihály sometimes exchanged surreptitious glances, but at first denied these apperceptions even to herself.

"Where are you off to again?" "I am going to the Café Gugger."

Mihály's nocturnal absences had become increasingly suspect and already on two occasions Zia had noted that they coincided with Hilda's day off from the hospital. Last week, racked by jealousy, Zia had sprung out of bed after midnight, dressed quickly and gone to the Café Gugger, but she found it deserted. Mihály reached home around dawn and next day said they were at Hamor's. Zia felt reassured, but, the following week end at Ararat, she once more remarked Mihály's furtive glance into Schwester Hilda's large gray eyes and in the flash of his glance thought she divined the brazenly sexual, terrifyingly beautiful look of the love-enraptured male. Then again the swimming pool—oh, yes, undeniably Schwester Hilda's boyish figure was exquisite, and exquisite were those little breasts of hers.

With such scalding thoughts lay Zia on the bed. Unable to stand it any longer, she switched on the radio to distract her thoughts. An English broadcast . . . the Aleutians . . . with

218

suicidal intrepidity the Japanese were forging ahead to the Island of Kiska . . . then German news, Rommel, Africa's desolate sands . . . the enemy, the enemy, every second word on the radio was: the enemy. Schwester Hilda's body was a greater and more perilous battlefield than the Mediterranean or the whole expanse of the Pacific Ocean. Zia felt she would perish not in the snow-mists of Kiska Island, in the burning sandy wastes of Africa or the hell of Dutch Harbor—she would perish on Schwester Hilda's body. No, no, she couldn't stand it any longer. Her first marriage, too, had ended thus, in such frightful disillusion. Filippo deceived her in exactly the same way with that cheap actress. Then she still had waited, waited long for Filippo in her Mandrian exile, nurturing within herself the brooding thought of forgiveness—but never again. No more forgiveness ever, ever, for any man on earth.

Again the moment had come: to burn all bridges behind her. Her Swiss passport was ready, she would vanish with Zizi toward America. Ostie was right—why hadn't she brought Zizi with her to Istanbul; that was when they should have left for America.

Toward evening, when they started from Ararat back to Budapest, Schwester Hilda asked if they would take her along, saying she would spend the night in town "at a friend's house." Zia's self-control worked miracles along the way, at home, too, when she and her husband had dinner alone together.

"Where are you going?"

"To the Café Gugger."

"Would you leave the car? I want to visit Kristina."

"Of course. I was going to walk anyhow."

Half an hour later, in the quiet summer night, Zia, flattening herself along house walls, followed her husband, who naturally did not proceed in the direction of the Café Gugger. Only the weak light of the moon lit the streets, so when Zia saw Mihály turn a corner, it was as if he had vanished into final nothingness—with wild heartbeats she followed in a pursuit exhausting, humiliating and disgusting, yet Zia felt that no matter how horrible the scene might be, the unmasking must take place before she effected her final resolve.

She didn't even know what street they were on. Noting the

door at which her husband rang, she waited ten minutes, or maybe only half a minute—then her gloved hand tremblingly pressed the same bell, as if she were touching her own open wound.

The first ring was answered only by protracted darkness and silence. The second time she rang longer and more forcefully. Steps sounded, but in the hall the light did not go on.

"*Wer ist da?*" sounded an unfriendly voice Zia at once recognized as Schwester Hilda's.

"Zia."

Schwester Hilda's steps vanished without an answer, and a few moments later a man's steps approached. Now the light went on too, a key turned in the lock, and in the doorway, looking nonplused and ill-humored, to Zia's immense surprise stood Hamor's long figure.

"You want to speak to Mihály?"—not even waiting for an answer, he led Zia to a large room, where around the long table were at least fifteen chairs, a few overturned, clearly revealing the instant of sudden dispersal. In the ashtrays were innumerable cigarette stubs. Mihály stood alone in the room, he barely glanced at Zia, then quickly stepped to the open window and shouted into the dark:

"Come back, there's no danger."

On the window ledge of the ground-floor apartment first appeared a red stripe, which proved to be one of General T.'s legs. On his belt the holster was not yet buttoned back, showing that he had waited revolver in hand, and in case of trouble would not have yielded his life cheaply. Back through the window clambered, one after the other, some ten or twelve men with the semblance of workmen, then a young captain, a round-headed colonel, but last of all came the great surprise: a black-booted, green-shirted old Nazi, who no longer could hoist his heavy frame so briskly through the window, one or two others laughingly assisted him. Herr Gruber! Grubi! Uncle Grubi! Before Zia everything at once grew light.

"Gentlemen," turned Ursi to those present, "I trust it is superfluous for me to say that I did not reveal the address of this apartment even to my wife."

Then he turned to Zia, who at this moment stood before

220

the table as though under police interrogation for night vagrancy.

"How did you get here?"

The eyes of all fifteen men were fixed unblinkingly on Zia, as if their fate depended on her answer. Zia was deathly pale and only the trembling of her lips replied.

"We will conclude our deliberations shortly," said Ursi, putting his arm tenderly around Zia's shoulders, as he led her to the other room.

When the door closed behind her, Zia sat down on the iron bedstead covered with a soldier's blanket, buried her face in her two hands and quietly began to weep. Long, deep beautiful tears of deliverance and happiness filled with apology toward her husband. Mihály in this room dallied not with Schwester Hilda, but with death. Now too, the whispered conversation of those men, filtering through the closed door, appeared to rise from the depths of Hades. Zia did not know she was in Peter Dukay Street, so far she had known nothing of the conspiracy, but now she felt that all they were planning was at the risk of death for each and every one of them.

Zia knew now that with regard to Schwester Hilda she had fallen victim to her own jealousy and foolish hallucinations. Of her tears of apology many fell for Grubi too, for she understood that neither she, nor Kristina, nor anyone must know of Grubi's secret and perilous role. How cleverly the rascals had staged that dismissal scene. No, no need to fear for them: they had their wits about them and were warier than the beasts of the jungle.

Zia later thought back on that night in Peter Dukay Street as the happiest hours of her life. To regain something believed irretrievably lost is always more than to gain it. In these moments Mihály for Zia seemingly had risen from the dead—risen and grown in stature. And for good measure, Grubi too had risen, and Uncle Grubi too had grown.

The secret military plans of the Stargazers' conspiracy were what they intended as "deeds" instead of words, following Ursi's talk in Istanbul with Ostie Dukay.

In the second half of 1943, as the star of Compiègne declined, so the danger grew that Hitler some fine day would be surfeited with the Hungarian government's seesaw policy.

For German forces of occupation the sole natural avenue of

approach was the Vienna-Budapest main highway, some two hundred miles long. The Stargazers' military plan contemplated mining this stretch just as the Poles had mined the approaches to Hell Peninsula, which they retained till long after the collapse of Poland. In connection with these plans Kazimir Kilinski's experience and expert knowledge meant much. The thousand reliable workmen needed were readily available from the mass of several hundred thousand socialist workers, particularly the communist group organized by Joska Kurdi. The plan called for densely interspersed machine-gun nests to receive the approaching Germans with deadly crossfire, and the secret storerooms of the Cave were already industriously garnering arms and dynamite. With the help of five generals privy to the conspiracy, a few "night maneuvers"—during which soldiers were to seal off the highway, directing the sparse night traffic to side roads— would have assured the undisturbed sowing of the mine fields.

The plan would have allowed German troops of occupation within reach of Budapest: just let them inundate the Vienna-Budapest Highway. Then simultaneously the mine fields would explode, the hidden machine-gun nests would crackle, and hand grenades burst—concurrently, from nearby Italian bases Allied planes would take to the air, so that at the crucial moment they might appear above the Vienna-Budapest Highway to shower bombs in support of Hungarian resistance. The conspiracy's secret transmitter, which was hidden in the Cave, maintained uninterrupted contact with Sgt. Andrew Szanto in Italy, as agreed at Istanbul.

They realized that the routing of the first German columns would only spur Hitler's mad fury, fresh German armored units would break through unmined stretches, the Luftwaffe would exact the same frightful retribution on Budapest as in the spring of 1941 on Belgrade; Hungary, too, would become the scene of guerrilla campaigns and perhaps murderous civil war, but it was worth every sacrifice for Hungary to regain her lost honor in the family of democratic nations.

All this sounded marvelous in the Cave—on paper. In January, General T. scratched his head more and more. Everyone feared traitors, the selection of dependable men to lay the mine field proceeded slowly.

"I am afraid," said Ursi after a secret conference in the Cave, "that Hungary has lost her soul somewhere. My wife's uncle, Peti Dukay, the historian, told me last Christmas that Hungary is simply dying. A thousand years for a small nation is quite a long life."

"Have you observed," Hamor remarked, "that Linder, Fuchs, Howard, and all the others who came up with the theory that the universe has become old and is dying and about to dissolve into its primal chaos of raging energies—that all these astronomer-philosophers were over seventy? It is not Hungary who is dying, but old Count Peti."

But Ursi's thoughts were with Slobodan Tuykovich. Last week news had come that Slobo had been wounded for the third time, and was now lying in a hospital tent, his condition extremely grave.

In February, Lieutenant Colonel S., who had undertaken to provide a vast number of mines, came up with newer and newer excuses. Ursi became progressively more nervous, the arguments in Peter Dukay Street and around the large oak table in the Cave grew endless and violent.

"Nothing but talk, talk, talk, and talk . . ." whispered Marja and Kazi to each other after each conference.

"The Major," said Kazi, "is a very fine man. He is a great man. A very great man. A very, very great—astronomer."

On March 16, a Thursday morning, a black flag appeared from the tower above the chapel at Ararat Castle and on the balcony of Septemvir Utca palace. In the seventy-third year of his life, Count Peti Dukay, member of the directorial board of the Hungarian Academy of Science, who had developed his heart ailment during vehement arguments over the question of whether or not the word *hun* was derived from the word *hiung-yang*, died of an attack in his modest country house. His coffin arrived at Ararat March 18, Saturday morning, for burial in the family vault.

The funeral, the last formal funeral at Ararat, was less ceremonious than Count Peti had been accustomed to plan for deceased Dukays. There was no crowd, no gypsy music. According to an ancient custom, when the last member of a great family dies, the stone crest of arms above the entrance of the vault is turned in a downward position, signaling that the ancient family has died out.

This was the case with the Dukay family, at least in the minds of Kristina and Zia as they escorted Uncle Peter on his last journey. Who remained of the Dukays? The half-witted Rere, the sexually abnormal and bachelor Johy, had not and would not have children. Ostie? Oh, yes, there was still hope that Gwen would give a Dukay boy to the world, but even if she did the boy would no longer be a genuine Dukay. Even Ostie was not a genuine Dukay any more. He did not use his count's title in America, he had become Mr. Ostie G. Dukay, and even his Dukay name was pronounced quite otherwise in New York than it had been in Hungary for many, many centuries.

The old and very wise historian, Count Peti, had well chosen the day for his death. He was buried in the vault on the night of March 18, one of the darkest nights in Hungary's thousand-year-old history.

At around one o'clock in the morning, Zia, who was alone with Zizi in her apartment, awoke from her dreams. Someone downstairs was rattling the kitchen window. She descended and her query was answered by Marja's whisper:

"I'm here with Kazi in a car. We've come from Peter Dukay Street with a very important message to you from Mihály. Pack quickly, only the most necessary things. We'll take you and Zizi to a very safe place in the country."

"My God—why?"

"We've received secret information that German troops are gathering at the Austrian frontier, ready to invade Hungary in the early morning hours."

"Where is Mihály?"

"He is already on the way in another car. We'll meet him there. Pack quickly, Kazi and I will help you. Hurry!"

Marja had lied when she said that Mihály was already on his way to the country. He was still in the crowded room in Peter Dukay Street, pounding the desk with his fist, shouting commands for the speediest possible mobilization of all the Stargazers—the bad news had come very unexpectedly. . . . "Where is General T.? . . . Where is Colonel S.? . . . How many trucks are at our disposal? . . . How many men can Joska

224

gather in the next few hours? . . . How many mines have been laid? . . . What! None? You told me last week . . . No! I've no time to listen now. . . . Hurry up! . . . How many machine guns do we have? . . . What! . . . Only sixteen? . . . Joska! Let the men . . . Where is Hamor? . . ."

Meanwhile feverish preparations for flight went on in Zia's apartment. "No, you don't need any umbrella now! . . . Hurry up!"

Finally they were in the car. Kazi at the wheel, next to him Marja, in the back seat Zia and the half-sleeping Zizi, who in her lap held a bird cage containing her two canaries, which not even Zia's remonstrances could make her part with.

"Take care, my dear," Marja nervously warned Zizi, whose legs were too near the Villon Madonna, carefully packed in a specially made leather bag. Kazi Kilinski did not speak during the whole trip. What must have been his thoughts? Poland at least had fought her last battle heroically in the Blitzkrieg, but into what moral slough would Hungary sink?

By now they were nearing the Cave. The car's passengers were mute, only cigarettes glowed.

"Jesus, my cards!" exclaimed Marja, more to herself than to the others.

This little solitaire deck had been Maxim's first present, back in Paris. Lost now was the tiny "devil's bible," whose fifty-two leaves the hours of solitude so often had turned. One had to treat tenderly the queen of hearts, whom Zizi at the age of three wanted to eat and had broken in two at the waist, and the jack of spades' face was disfigured by a freckle of ink. Strange dream figures, rococo kings and pages with their painted faces, mystic heralds of hope and misfortune, love and death. When we lose a world, it is in objects such as these that we feel the sharpest pain, in such a little deck of cards left behind in a desk drawer.

Last April, when the train with the boarded-up windows was taking them to Istanbul, Marja had felt herself so close to Maxim, that she could almost see his abashed smile of recognition. Had Bolgorin forwarded her letter? No reply had come from Maxim. Now the telegraph poles swishing past the car operated like the spokes of some weird unraveling machine, stripping shred after shred from her hope of ever seeing Maxim again. But her desperate thoughts turned to the Villon Madonna, and she felt certain that the picture would perform the miracle again.

As Kazi sat there in front of Zia, the faint moonlit outlines of his sports hat, head and muscular neck exerted a wondrously reassuring effect on her. She held Zizi, who, with the bird cage in her lap, yawned mightily. From time to time the canaries gave an anxious chirp. Was that merely the rush of the wind in the sky, or already the motors of English and American bombers? Might it be that before this night was over they would blow all Hungary to smithereens? She felt that around her, and in the world, the crescendo of the Great Concert was rising. Perhaps half of Europe's population of five hundred million would perish, as Kristina had once said, but it occurred to her that dying together with several hundred million others was not death, but a natural phenomenon.

There was a restive air about the night. Cars came frequently from the opposite direction, sometimes she felt as though they were being pursued by cars from behind. The Gestapo? No, at high speed they drew past, probably refugees as well.

They did not speak, so as not to disturb each other's thoughts. Only the sandwich bags rustled and a little feeble humor arose when Kazi, instead of the ham sandwich, took hold of Marja's thumb and would not let go.

The car left the highway and was rocking quite slowly over a peat meadow. It halted at the bank of a river and now for the first time Kazi spoke up, quite solemnly:

"Absolute quiet, please, and no talking!"

Only he alighted. A few minutes later he returned and the car rolled soundlessly onto a raft. In the strong current they edged downstream along a rope fastened to the trunk of a willow. Kazi again alighted, now guiding the raft with Marja's help. A few whispered directions, then the raft knocked against the far shore's steep cliff wall, whose concealed portal opened in eerie silence and closed behind them the same way, as the mountain swallowed the raft.

Zia found herself in a tremendous cave, in the middle of which an underground lake's waters sparkled blackly as the electric lights went on. She knew at once that this was the fabu-

226

lous Cave Ostie once told her of as a child, after exacting a solemn oath of secrecy.

Proceeding upward by way of the stone steps, and passing mysterious storerooms, they reached a number of cell-like chambers.

"This was Slobo Tuykovich's room," said Marja, opening one of the doors. On the unmade bed lay a guitar.

From somewhere in the grotto came the faint, sorrowful roar of a waterfall. All this was much like a dream for Zia and Zizi. It was as if the stone cover of a giant crypt had closed upon them and they were now in the other world. But from the little kitchen came a very earthly clatter of dishes.

"Who'll have a cup of hot tea?" asked Marja.

"But where is Mihály?" asked Zia anxiously.

"Don't worry, he'll be here any minute. They probably stopped in Holod at Kurdi's house," said Kazi.

Kazi lied, too. He knew that at this hour, four o'clock in the morning, something was happening along the Vienna-Budapest Highway.

Yes, Ursi, Hamor and Joska Kurdi were standing some fifty miles from Budapest on the top of a small hill overlooking the highway. Seventeen communist workers were standing behind Joska Kurdi, only seventeen out of the six hundred thousand organized Hungarian workers. But with no machine-guns, not even rifles, only shovels in their hands. They were waiting for Colonel S. who was already on his way with twenty large mines.

Five thirty, five forty-five . . . there was still time to place the mines.

Six o'clock—Ursi's eyes were fixed in the direction of Budapest from where Colonel S.'s truck had to come. But it did not come. The morning was already dawning, and when Ursi turned back to say something to Kurdi, he saw that the seventeen men had disappeared, noiselessly, just like the darkness.

"Look at it!" shouted Hamor, his long right arm pointing toward the west. In the first violet rays of the rising sun there was already visible the gray mass of the motorized German Army.

The mute wrath of helplessness choked Mihály Ursi. A kind of tearful shame as if the German tanks rumbling toward

227

Budapest had abruptly unmasked the ridiculous futility of their conspiracy. In almost superstitious fear he reflected on the senseless and irresistible power of the historic forces in whose tempest their desperate efforts to succor human rights now seemed less efficacious even than stammering prayers.

His teeth became set when the first group of gray-clad motorcyclists passed them. The flame-throwers of armored reality had seared away all flesh, blood, dreams, ideals and hopes —he had to laugh or cry—suddenly he jerked out his revolver with a mad sobbing cry . . . but Hamor quickly grabbed his wrist: "Are you crazy?" Did he want to commit suicide? No, he just wanted to greet the German motorcycles with a few bullets. He was deathly pale, he seemed on the brink of a complete nervous breakdown.

Hamor and Joska Kurdi led him to the car, and on a side road set out toward the Cave. In the car he quieted down. When they arrived at the Cave, he apologized to Zia for their delay, and with his usual greeting lifted Zizi high in the air.

"Now, I'm hungry as a wolf," he said as he sat down to his large breakfast.

At nine o'clock in the evening, the telephone rang. Grubi gave an account of events to Ursi. Hitler, some days previously, had summoned the Regent to Berchtesgaden. In Hitler's anteroom everyone was required to surrender his sword or revolver, just as one could enter the presence of the Emperor of Japan only without shoes. According to Grubi's information, the Regent repulsed the courteous admonition of the aide-de-camp; he was unwilling to relinquish his admiral's dagger. The aide-de-camp, with a derisive smile, opened the door for the old man.

When Ursi came to this point in Grubi's account, Kazi and Marja listened with bated breath, then exchanged glances of disappointment, as if they had expected the narration to continue thus: ". . . then stepping into the room, the Regent in a lightning swift lunge struck down Hitler." But that was not how the story continued, Hungary's Regent contenting himself with a symbolic expression of resistance by refusing to part with his fancy admiral's dagger that probably was so rusted into its scabbard that he couldn't have drawn it anyhow. Hitler curtly and coldly informed the Regent that since, according to his certain knowledge, the Hungarian government, at Istanbul and elsewhere, was secretly conferring with the Allies and wanted to bolt from the war, he had ordered the military occupation of Hungary. While this conversation progressed, German troops already had crossed the Hungarian frontier. At the Royal Palace in Buda a brief exchange of shots took place between palace guards and the Germans, a few yellow-cloaked halberded guards losing their lives in this "musical changing of the guard." The German ambassador had assured the Regent that his rights as head of state remained uninfringed, he could even go to the lavatory alone, but he was in fact already a prisoner. That day the Germans arrested some hundred "traitors"; liberal politicians and numberless Jews fled in despair. There was order in the city for the moment, but everyone lived in terror of the Anglo-American bombers.

This was the essence of what Grubi reported about the first day of the German occupation.

One day, some half million years ago, a group of primordial men chanced to stray from the tropical region around the Tigris and Euphrates, which the Old Testament calls the Garden of Eden. Wandering northward, one night they felt the touch of an invisible beast. This touch made them shiver—later they called it Cold. Frightened, these naked primitive men tried to flee from their new enemy, but knowing nothing about south or north, they kept on hurrying northward. The teeth of the invisible beast became more and more sharp, and one morning they could hardly believe their eyes; the entire landscape had turned white. Later they called this fantastic phenomenon Snow. Fortunately, they found a cave, crawled into it, and saved their lives. From that day on they poked their heads out of the cave only on sunny and warm days. In a short while, some few hundred thousand years, they multiplied, discovered the greatest thing in their history: Fire. But they still dwelt in the cave, which they later called hut, house, palace, and in our own days the signs they have hung over the entrances to their cave read "Hotel Danielli" or "The Waldorf-Astoria."

"Nothing has changed," said Ursi, visibly proud of the

229

modest, ascetic, but perfectly furnished rooms of the Cave. Zig-zagging steps led to the top of the mountain, where there was a vegetable garden with topsoil two feet deep.

"We must be careful," Ursi remarked, with some bitter irony, "to plant our green peppers and onions in disorder instead of in straight rows, otherwise an American aerial observer might find it very suspicious, and shower us with bombs."

And there were chickens, the Hungarian speckled variety, whose plumage mimicked the color of the rocky terrain, of course, in order to escape the bombsights of England and the United States.

Kazi, one of the designers of the Cave's interior, sharing Mihály's pride, turned to Zia:

"*Madame, Sie haben hirr olles!* Go on, ask for something —anything you want!"

Zia, in a good mood, after prolonged and exaggerated reflection, said to Kazi:

"Get me a wooden box, ten inches long, four inches high, sky-blue outside and light orange inside."

Kazi emerged from the storeroom a few minutes later with the desired box. Yes, the exact size, and, believe it or not, it was sky-blue outside and light orange inside. Kazi, the man of miracles, was marveled at by everybody, except Zia, whose fingers were still sky-blue from having painted the box that morning.

Seven-year-old Zizi screamed with laughter. As the days passed in this strange atmosphere, in this goose-footed castle, they made every effort to invent silly practical jokes; they took arms against the dread contagion of fear sometimes with forced humor.

"How do you feel this morning in our wonderful Cave?" Marja asked Zia.

"Well," said Zia, "as though I were in a telephone booth in a very heavy winter coat, both my hands full of packages."

They stored away every drop of old humor as if they were condemned to death by thirst in a lifeboat on a blazing sea.

They fastened themselves to the raging radio. They felt quite sure that the clouds of the RAF and the American Air Force would come.

They did.

On April 2, around noon, the voice of the sirens from distant towns and villages roared like a wind from the netherworld. The dog-headed gods of the Gilgames legend, who squat in a circle at the edge of the sky, started to howl.

They confined Zizi to her room before they hurried up the zigzagging stone steps to the top of the mountain.

All at once, as if the blue-gold April firmament were only built of wood, upon it began the stampede of a tremendous herd of horses, unseen for the time being, the pounding of millions and millions of hooves. It was a kind of technological thunder, only an intimation from stupendous heights, yet nerve-rackingly sinister. The giant motors of approaching bombers were thundering. For the first time in Hungarian history, American troops had appeared on Hungarian soil, or to be more exact, in the Hungarian sky.

American boys sat at oxygen-helmet height . . . there they were! . . . There too! . . . White threads appeared on the sky's blue robe, exhaust traces frozen to hoarfrost, for the moment that being all the invisibly thundering machines betrayed of themselves . . . but now! . . . There! . . . The flashing point of a pin . . . that was already a machine . . . they snatched the binoculars from each other's hands. . . . All of them shouted: look! . . . as the planes wheeled above the Danube, the sun shining under their aluminum wings, fifty, sixty . . . a hundred pinpoints flashed at once . . . look! . . . There they came, from the south too. . . . They practically filled the whole sky now . . . the sirens grew mute, like a circus band's fortissimo at the instant of a death-defying leap . . . the weird rumbling of the great motors abated too, but now you could hear those great deep boomings they had already learned to know from the nights of Russian raids, like the dropping of mammoth crates filled with fragile objects . . . Bramm! . . . Bramm! . . . Ramm! . . . Bramm! . . . more and more thickly they rained, sometimes sounding like giant hammers.

Beyond the southeastern chain of hills where poor Budapest cowered, ever darker and huger columns of smoke rose into the air . . . "Late! . . . Late! . . . You've come late!" shouted Ursi's mute, distorted face. Instead of the invading German Army, only two weeks ago . . . bramm . . . ramm . . . bramm

. . . oh, these invisible giant hammers now were pounding nails into Budapest's coffin. Even the ridges of the hills seemed to quiver at the frightful detonations . . . weeping sounds, hysterical laughter broke from Zia's throat as she thought of her mother and Kristina and everyone in Budapest . . . then again the binoculars were in Ursi's hand . . . across the circle of the lens, like rigid fish, swam the aluminum machines, swimming from the lens as if in flight, the eye had to catch them again and again. . . . Brrammm! . . . Brrrammm! . . . Lord, what can be left of Budapest?

Chapter 16

The German Occupation of Hungary.

We must devote particular attention to that portion of our story concerned with the relationship between Mihály Ursi and Joska Kurdi during the months of the German occupation.

Though disinclined to place credence in "premonitions," we find it worth noting that, in the entries of Mihály Ursi's diary from these days, the word *hangman* occurs twice.

. . . I cannot escape my consternation at the sight of how, in the immense whirl of these times, not only races, peoples and ideologies, but, within these, staunch friends and even members of the same family have become each other's hangmen. Grubi brought the news from Berlin that Professor von Johnen, in whose home I spent several pleasant evenings, had been denounced by someone for listening to the English broadcasts, and for this received a six-month prison term. After his release, returning to his villa, which was surrounded by a large garden, he cautiously closed every window, particularly on the south side, because he suspected his neighbor as the one who denounced him. He even sent his old footman from the house, only family members being in the villa when he retired to his study, turned on the radio softly, and began listening to London. A few instants later, the door crashed open and the eighteen-year-old Hans, whom the Professor adored, pale and with set teeth, approached his father: "Listen, papa! If I catch you listening to the English radio once more, I'll tell the Gestapo *again!*"

When did this horrible era of modern mankind begin? After the great peaceful epochs of Victoria and Franz Joseph, the first world war appeared like a quiescent volcano which again had become active, but the volcano's real flames were only revealed in World War II. Preliminary signs already were at hand: one of Mussolini's sons amused himself by circling low over Abyssinian villages in his plane and machine-gunning the naked native children; and during the Spanish civil war, hanging from the meat hooks of one butcher shop, was the halved body of a Catholic priest.

Should I quote from Goebbels' latest speech? "A shudder of physical revulsion comes upon me at the sight of a Jew. Even for the basest prostitute I have more respect than for a Jewess living in matrimony." After this, I am willing to believe Ernst's *"Noch einmal, Papa!"* story about the eight-year-old little girl of General von Klapper, as she watched him shooting at Jewish infants tossed high in the air.

I do not agree with the view of certain writers that the twentieth century *returned* to the moral level of the darkest Middle Ages: rather I suppose that the first half of our century exemplifies a certain recurring volcanic outbreak of bestiality, whose primal causes lie far deeper in time than the Middle Ages, and I must bear with the possibility that after another long era of peace, such an eruption will recur, no matter what advances civilization may have made in the meantime. I subscribe to Freyberger's theory, that if we place the appearance of Man at the end of the Pliocene Era, some half a million years passed until in the Tigris and Euphrates region we may speak of the first traces of the so-called civilization. Our six-thousand-year-old culture covers the depth of our brute nature's many-hundred-thousand-year-old past only like a paper-thin coating. Beneath our silk shirts, perfumes, loves and divine services we still hide a multitude of ferocious instincts of the Pliocene Man.

Our era uses the Ideal as a pretext for bestiality. In themselves, all ideals are born in the pure womb of thought, the only trouble being that in the field of religion and politics, since the days of Sennacherib, Pericles or Godfrey de Bouillon, ideals have always become hangmen.

234

Dostoievsky writes that Man is the lowest of the animals, because he can get used to anything. Within a few weeks Budapest, too, got used to the German occupation. Now Hungarian Jews wore the yellow star, but afternoons they would serenely play cards as usual in the coffee houses. Budapest had become used to frequent bombings by Anglo-American air squadrons, which tactfully avoided residential areas, only seeking out military objectives.

Under such circumstances Zia considered as exaggerated romanticism the Cave life furnished with running water, electrical illumination, all sorts of food and medicines in abundance, and where, in the daytime, by climbing the stone steps they could poke out their heads on the hilltop for a breath of fresh air, and even take a sunbath—for despite all this, the whole air of the Cave exerted a depressing effect not only on Zia and Zizi, but on Mihály too. Marja and Kazi, on the other hand, felt just as much at home in the maw of the earth as trout in a brook.

So they accepted Joska Kurdi's kind invitation to move to his house in Holod, which was hardly twenty miles from the Cave. Ursi could easily reach it even on a bicycle if he needed to make radio contact with his cousin, Andrew Szanto.

Marja and Kazi stayed in the Cave.

"We don't speak Hungarian, we would be boring for the Kurdis," was the reason Marja gave. Ursi accepted this excuse, also realizing that foreign people were easier targets of suspicion.

When they left Kazi and Marja in the Cave, Joska whispered to Ursi: "There must be some *gyanta* between them." "Gyanta" means rosin for violin bows, but in Joska's slang it meant love.

On a peasant cart, around midnight, the others reached Holod. Joska who had obtained the cart, drove the horses. He set Zia's anxieties to rest as they journeyed, telling her that at Holod they would be safer than in the Cave, since every miner was a Communist and they all had known Mihály's father and him, too, as a child.

Mrs. Kurdi, introducing herself—"I'm Erzsi"—and kissing Zia's hand, served them a hot supper. The Kurdis had surrendered their own bedroom, and slept on straw sacks in the workshop, because their tiny house afforded no other accommodations. The low-raftered room was porcelain-clean, the bedding and the monogram "S.P." on the towels laid by the iron washstand indicating that these objects had been borrowed for "Her Excellency, the Countess' and the Major's" comfort. Still another evidence of this was the divan placed crosswise before the double bed, and made up for Zizi, hardly allowing the Ursis space to move. Three scarcely nicked chamber pots of assorted sizes stood on public display near their resting places, boastfully proclaiming an advanced state of civilization, and Ursi, knowing the people of his birthplace, could picture the scene as the most dependable miners' families, apprised of their coming, brought forth the most cherished ornaments of their poverty—plates, eating utensils and even chamber pots vying for the place of honor.

All this touched Zia deeply. From the room came a rhythmic ticking, in which Ursi recognized his parental house's cuckoo-clock. He wondered at this, because he remembered that after the death of his father the clock was stolen. The affection with which Joska and Erzsi surrounded them was moving. Their faces beamed with joy, the Ursis' arrival under their roof seemed the great event of their lives. "Please, Mr. Major . . . over there if you please, Mr. Major . . . this is the good chair, Mr. Major" —Joska always used this form of address. He called Zia "Her Gracious Excellency, the Countess," and if she or the Major wanted to light a cigarette, nearly ripped off all his pockets in order to forestall them with his homemade cigarette lighter— "This is my own invention, Mr. Major, sir"—which in his great haste he never found, or if he did, it failed to work. They couldn't dissuade Erzsi either, who addressed even Zizi as "Her Excellency, the little Countess," there being no way of making her comprehend that a count's title is inherited only from a count-father. These complicated forms of address seemed all the more curious, because at the first supper, Erzsi related that while still a young girl she had joined the underground Communist Party. Her brown hair was tied back in a polka-dot kerchief, and her laughing walnut-brown eyes reminded Ursi of Joska's mother, Lovely Juli, on whose account the shepherds exacted such frightful and barbaric vengeance on the landholding seducer.

Again Mihály marveled at Zia. Men of the middle class with

236

their every word condescend from grand heights to the common people; they begin imitating their turns of thought and speech, badly of course and offensively—only among the high aristocracy are there individuals who possess the secret of regarding them as equals. With Erzsi, Zia too at once found common themes. She praised her home-sewn dress—"only the collar doesn't please me, I'll sew you another;" she showed her the little portable sewing machine, a present from Gwen, which she had brought along on this occasion too—"Did you ever see the like!"—Erzsi clapped her hands in amazement at the sight of the collapsible rubber bathtub as they unpacked. Particular wonder and comment was occasioned by Zia's toilet articles, jars and cut-glass bottles, that were mysteries for Erzsi, who continually exclaimed —women of the Hungarian peasantry always shout in a loud voice—"Of all things, come here Joska, did you ever see the like of this?"

Next day they breakfasted in the yard at the millstone table beneath the apple tree whose branches were already in blossom. What luxury hotel can provide so captivating a breakfast table? Upon the yard lay the gold-green sunflecks and long black shadows of the spring morning; swallows darted through the air, building their nests under the eaves of a little workshop tacked onto the house, and in the tiny yard the tulips and blue lilies were breaking into bloom. From the workshop came the fragrance of pine shavings, as Joska's plane shrieked gaily and boisterously, greeting in strange bird-tones the start of a new workday. Joska revealed to Zia that he was fabricating a special little chair "for Her Excellency, the little Countess." At the end of the clean-swept yard, on the shanty knocked together of waste boards, two freshly painted zeros tactfully indicated its function. Why is it that these out-houses always lean a little to one side?

Dinner was chicken-and-meat soup, beans with eggs cooked on top, mohn noodles and black coffee, which of course was brewed from dark-roasted barley. Ursi could not exist without real black coffee; Freyberger said it was medicine for him, because of his somewhat low blood pressure. Even before retiring, he customarily drank a big glass of strong coffee—it sent him to sleep like a baby. When, at the start of the war, coffee completely vanished from Hungary, and he for the first time drank barley coffee, he was seized with wild palpitations of the heart and couldn't sleep a wink till morning. Three years before, Ostie's last big consignment had arrived safely, and they had sufficient canned goods in the Cave to stock even a large grocery store. Ursi brought over a few things for the Kurdi kitchen, but very tactfully, so as not to offend the modesty of their menu, in which Joska and Erzsi had invested every effort.

During supper the conversation turned to world politics. Joska talked a great deal and showed off his knowledge. His chatter affected Ursi like the maps of the Middle Ages which pictured Africa as a rectangle and placed London in the center of France; he remembered Andrew Szanto's answer as an eight-year-old schoolboy—Andrew's father had told him about it in Brooklyn—"Where is Pittsburgh? Pittsburgh is just below the *P* in Pennsylvania."

Joska and Erzsi pronounced Mussolini's name with the *s* sounding *sh,* in accordance with Hungarian rules of pronunciation, and Churchill became "Tshoortsil."

"Tell me please, Mr. Major, sir, is this Tshoortsil a Communist?"

"No. A liberal Conservative."

"You see!" said Joska turning to Erzsi with a patronizing smile, this evidently had been a bone of contention between them.

In these days, after the great German defeats, the Red Army was already advancing over Polish and Rumanian soil toward Hungary.

"Tell me, Joska, what do you suppose will happen when the Russians come in?"

Joska pulled himself together before answering:

"If you please, Mr. Major, we have a man who slipped through the front lines, came straight from Moscow, and talked to Father Stalin. And this man tells me, sir, that the Russians will be just the opposite of that scoundrel, Hitler. The Russians, Mr. Major, sir, will bring the Ideal to every man—great freedom, great truth to every man, as the Ideal commands."

For years Ursi had observed that Joska liked to weave the word *Ideal* into every sentence.

"Tell me, Joska, when as an apprentice you attended the

communist school, what did they teach you about the Ideal?"

Joska began to scratch his brow, his huge carpenter's hand completely hiding the low forehead.

"To tell the truth, Mr. Major, sir, I don't much recollect the lessons—that was twenty-five years back."

Next day, when it was growing dark, the first visitors appeared. Hoary miners, the old friends of Ursi's late father. They laid their heavy hands on Mihály's shoulder, looked into his eyes and said: "Welcome, Mihály." These old miners were once Social Democrats, but now they too avowed themselves Communists. Those who had been Communists under Béla Kun had cemented their old Party membership cards into the wall, and awaited the Red Army. Among them were even some who spoke fluent Russian—during the first world war a million Hungarians had been prisoners of war in Russia, many of them only getting home eight to ten years later.

The village afforded complete security from the Gestapo, for the secret communist information network extended to distant villages. On dark nights, fire signals from hilltops relayed the news of danger. Zia couldn't help feeling that a dense ring of live human bodies and a fanatic hatred of the Germans were protecting them.

Nonetheless, for the time being they remained voluntary prisoners in the yard. Mihály began to grow a mustache, which completely transformed his countenance. He also put on a green apron and, to the accompaniment of Joska's explanations—too many explanations—began to learn the craft of carpentry, mainly to pass the time. The following week the eldest woman in the village died—Mihály's first independent work was her coffin.

American bombers appeared in the noon hours and the English around midnight. At such times—there being no siren in the villages—they would clang a piece of steel rail hung from a wire, but no one ran for shelter because the cellars of the little ground-floor houses wouldn't have afforded any. During air raids everyone quietly proceeded with his work, as distant bombings shook the air above the village. "Well, the firmaments of Ideals are foaming again," noted Joska from beside the lathe—he always liked to express himself in flowery phrases.

One night when they again clanged the piece of rail, they

239

went to the hilltop. The May night was all stars—clear fair weather inevitably brought English bombers, as heavy clouds do the rain.

The ball began. Sirens in distant villages sounded like a great orchestra striking up the first dreamy waltz. In the starlight it seemed as if even the hills of Pilis had donned tuxedos for the ball; in place of black cravats dark pine forests were tied round their necks. Anti-aircraft guns drummed a fanfare at the arrival of the royal guests and the arc-lamps of the celestial ballroom flamed forth; large phosphorus balls, "Tshoortsil candles" Joska called them, whose glowing whitish-green flame chased away each gaping star from this region of the sky. The great non-paying audience betrayed itself only by the tiny cold silver light of its cigarettes out in the dark, beyond the police cordon. One recalcitrant star must have received a sharp crack on the noodle from a police truncheon, because it broke into helter-skelter flight—but no, it wasn't a star after all, only the tail-light of a pursuit plane among the stars. Chased away by the light of "Tshoortsil candles," the stars gathered in the firmament's dark western sphere and it seemed as if the seven stars in the constellation Ursa Major had also vanished in the dark. The crowd, driven into a side street, grew ever denser along the Milky Way and seemed as if indignantly remonstrating: "What's this? Can't we even look?" What must the English boys have been thinking when they released their bombs over Csepel, knowing that they were destroying only little workers' dwellings? Joska was right: *The firmament of Ideals was foaming.*

This night the fans seemed larger, those bluish-silver fans which the TNT opens wide for an instant and then just as quickly closes. They must have been new or more powerful types of bombs, because the detonations reached their ears only a minute and a half later, deep and powerful even in their muffledness, but somehow grumpy. There on the spot, flash and blast were simultaneous, showing no difference in the speed of light and sound, and no mercy, except to the extent that God preserved those hit by the bomb from having to hear it too.

The densely flashing fans of light began deploying westward . . . there lay the Royal Palace of Buda and Septemvir Utca . . . Zia spasmodically gripped Mihály's arm, but he assured her that she need not disquiet herself either on her mother's or Kristina's account: the whole hill of Buda inside was nothing but an enormous grotto, an even safer shelter than the Cave, with deep long tunnels built back in Turkish times by the castle-dwellers.

In the week following, Mihály's mustache had grown so impressive that, with his green apron, they ventured for an evening stroll. Zia meanwhile, for herself and Zizi too, had sewn simple little dresses like those Erzsi wore.

Since the German occupation, the Arrow Cross Party had greatly expanded, it had an organization in every village. Its Holod representative was a little hunchbacked painter, who painted bad landscapes. So their evening strolls were not without danger. Ursi showed Zia and Zizi the house where he was born, Palm Lake, from whose shore the obese mine superintendent's tight bathing cabin had disappeared—and in the yard of Korona Tavern, the old watch-tower from the top of which he had tumbled as a seven-year-old—every memory of his childhood came alive.

One afternoon Ursi was reading alone at the millstone table beneath the apple tree, when a green-shirted hunchbacked little figure appeared before him. He clicked his heels:

"Allow me to introduce myself, Professor. I am the chairman of the local Arrow Cross Party."

It took a great effort for Ursi to dissemble his shock. Joska came from the workshop; they sat down to talk, but only of trifles. Then the little hunchback got up and again clicked his heels before Ursi:

"Professor, it would make me very happy if I could be of service to you in any way."

Joska accompanied him to the gate.

"How did he know we are here?" Ursi asked Joska, still frightened, when they were alone once more.

"It was I who told him, sir. Don't worry, Mr. Major, sir, the artist is a very decent fellow. A faithful Nazi, but a decent fellow. He distributes the ration cards properly, doesn't ask questions, reports no one, a very decent fellow. You know, Mr. Major, sir, the Ideal works differently in the country than in big towns. We like the artist very much. He is a bright man, the

241

artist is, sir, he knows too that if he opens his mouth we'll slit his throat. Don't fret yourself, Mr. Major, sir. Also don't let his title of 'chairman' frighten you. His party has only one other member, Frici, formerly the village drunkard."

Ursi had no alternative: he calmed down.

With respect to the months spent at the Kurdis', many diary notations of Zia's survive, but lack interest from the standpoint of our history, because they consist merely of sentences like these: "Today I managed to get a phone call through to Kristina. Thank God, they are all well." "For two days Zizi has had a bad case of diarrhea. I think she got it from the strawberries." "The baby swallows are being taught by their parents to fly. I watch them for hours."

Ursi went to the Cave sometimes twice a week, now alone, now with Joska, to visit the two hermits, Marja and Kazi, who were delighted with their situation.

But Joska was mistaken when he thought of *gyanta* between them. Kazi announced: "Since childhood it's been my ambition to read Tolstoy's *War and Peace*. I never had the time. Now I'm in the middle of volume two."

And all Marja's thoughts were with Maxim. She saw in the future a lovely country town somewhere in Turkestan where the climate and the civilization were mild—she saw herself working in the local hospital, and Maxim in his workshop—oh, yes, she would persuade Maxim to retire from the diplomatic service, and continue the profession he had left at the age of eighteen: wrought-iron artisan—the candelabra and those two ashtrays that he made in Paris just to pass the time were really, but really beautiful. No more Faubourg St. Germain, no more wandering around the world, no more reveling in obligatory *intrigues*. Marja dreamed of real rest at last. She was only forty-two years old; she dreamt about children, at least two, and she even called them Andrey and Natasha.

She knelt and prayed for hours before the Villon Madonna, which hung above the bed in her tiny room; now she had plenty of time in the solitude of the Cave.

Ursi's visits to the cave-dwellers also had two further motives: to fetch certain foodstuffs from the hidden storeroom, especially coffee, for the Kurdi kitchen, and to maintain short-wave radio contact with Andrew Szanto in Italy. The circumstance that existing diary entries scarcely mention this contact indicates that it possessed no particular significance.

The underground movement was quite paralyzed. Grubi sometimes showed up at the Kurdis and once brought with him Jani Hamor, who was hiding, too. For all of them the great question was the coming Allied invasion: would it be across the English Channel, in southern France or along the Adriatic? Every item of news and conjecture pointed to an invasion from the Adriatic, where, joining with Yugoslav Partisans in the Danube Valley, the Allies could slice in two the thin-spread and already weakening German forces in Europe. Zia also imagined that by September, at the very latest, Anglo-American troops would enter Hungary from the south and Ostie, too, would be with them.

Joska Kurdi was of another opinion:

"If you please, Countess, I don't think Tshoortsil will get here first. Your gracious Excellency will see, Father Stalin will bring us the Ideal."

Other reports mentioned that Johy now regarded himself lord of the estate though he was growing concerned as the Red Army approached step by step from the East. Johy placed Countess Menti and Rere in the Septemvir Utca palace, whose cellar doors led to ancient catacombs under the hill where the Royal Palace stood. Johy's generosity went so far as to invite Kristina too, naturally without her husband. Needless to say, Kristina refused the invitation. Freyberger wore a yellow star, but diligently visited his patients and carried on with his work as director of Ararat Hospital, where at present only a few German soldiers lounged about.

Despite the green apron and the mustache, Grubi dissuaded Ursi from venturing into Budapest. In Septemvir Utca great champagne suppers were given in honor of the German ambassador and the German generals, Johy's hospitality knowing no bounds, because he still hadn't given up his hope of becoming Hungary's gauleiter.

From the ample news sources of these months, we only touch on a few items which illuminate the economic, political and military situation then existing.

It may be considered economic news, for example, that

243

Jani Hamor ate his own shirt. Hamor dwelt in a little peasant cottage; in his flight he brought only two shirts along, both of German ersatz material, which according to instructions should be washed only in cold water. Ignorant of the secrets of modern German chemistry, his landlady boiled out one of the soiled shirts and left it on the stove in a big iron cauldron. She was not at home when, toward evening, the hungry Hamor returned. His supper was usually set out on the stove. Hamor raised the lid of the pot, tasted the grayish pap, and found it unseasoned. He salted and peppered it, added a pinch or two of paprika, reheated it and made a hearty meal of it. He became suspicious only on finding a shirt button at the bottom of his bowl.

As political news, we may mention Freyberger's experience. He was hastening to a patient of his, when an elderly German general suddenly grabbed his arm and embraced him: "Stefan! How are you, old pal?"

It was a strange sight on the streets of Budapest to see a jovial German general in SS uniform embracing a yellow-starred Jew. They had been medical students together at the University of Heidelberg, and had shared the same room for four years.

The general complained to Freyberger that he could find no hospital for his soldiers ill with venereal disease. Freyberger at once offered twenty rooms in Ararat Hospital. This spontaneous generosity later saved the lives of twenty Jewish families who had taken refuge there. They were shielded by a double ring of defenses: the beds of German venereal cases on the ground floor, and unsuspecting black-shirted SS guards in the park.

A commentary on the military situation is afforded by Zia's highly important dialogue with a German soldier, which we find thus noted in her diary:

> I sat on a bench before the small Holod station await-ing Kristina, who could not have found her way alone to the Kurdis'. The vicinity of the station was deserted, but all at once a German soldier appeared and sat down beside me on the bench. He looked into my face, and I into his. He was an older man, past forty, his lined face and heavy hands showing that in civilian life he must have been a work-

man of some sort, a smith or possibly a truck driver. I could almost see his wife and children somewhere in Pomerania. We were silent as we waited for the train.

Suddenly Frici appeared, whom Joska had described as practically the sole devoted member of the local Arrow Cross Party. Frici was an atrociously dressed, stunted figure, who carried his shop hanging from his neck. From a table-like board suspended by filthy strings he used to offer travelers a richly diversified stock of commodities: worn shoelaces, a few unripe peaches and some sort of cake horrible even to look at. On seeing the German soldier, he hurried over, stopped before him, clicked his heels and flung his arm high in the air: "Heil Hitler!"

The soldier, whom he had disturbed in his deepest thought, slowly looked up at Frici. Never have I seen a mute human glance more expressive. It pierced Frici like a great spear.

The mobile shop sidled off, and again we were alone. Once more the soldier glanced into my face, but now only briefly, and when he spoke, I felt from his tone that he had vouchsafed me his greatest confidence. This is what he said:

"A-a-haa! . . . Mm-ho . . . hoo-ya!"

It was a long, almost sobbing sigh.

I understood every word, because a human sigh is the clearest of languages. I considered it fitting to answer and I told him the following, word for word, about the present world situation:

"Ooh-oh! Mmh . . . h!"

The soldier acknowledged my response with a short nod. From his perspiring forehead he pushed his cap higher, squinted into the strong sunlight, and changed the subject. This time, in a deeper, rumbling tone he told me his opinion about somebody. He did not mention the name, but I was sure his sigh spoke about the Führer:

"Grrmm! Hrrrrh! . . . h! . . . h! . . ."

Now I was the one who nodded, and answered in weary affirmation:

"Mn . . . m! M . . ." And a few seconds later I added: "H."

For a few minutes we remained deeply silent. Then the soldier looked toward the hills, beyond which, somewhere in the far distance he surmised Germany lay. You could see by his face that he was weighing each word, and now, drawing the air from deep down in his lungs, very plaintively, he made the following pronouncement:

"Ooh-hmm . . . oh . . . ho . . . hee-ya . . . phh!"

He could not have known who I was, nor could I be sure he wasn't an *agent provocateur*. We were afraid of each other, yet already liked each other, as man to man in times of great misfortune. We fell silent, then spoke again, discussing mankind's fate in all its aspects, and for this purpose our sigh language proved inimitable.

When the train arrived, we took leave of each other only with mute glances, but were already best friends.

Also characteristic of the military situation was the scene where the German general of the Medical Corps, pointing to a big fiber suitcase, said to Freyberger:

"I'd like you to hide this suitcase and keep it for me."

When he noticed that Freyberger's face appeared to reflect a suspicion that the suitcase might contain stolen jewels, possibly a dismembered corpse, he laughingly added, "You can look into it, it's open."

The suitcase actually did contain a dismembered corpse. The German Army's giant, dismembered corpse: suspenders, shirt, tie, hat, suit, overcoat, all articles of civilian attire.

"Do you suppose," asked the German general, indicating his resplendent olive-green uniform and decorations, "that I would ever be able to escape from here in this outfit?"

As Freyberger noted, this scene took place on June 21, 1944, on exactly the fourth anniversary of Compiègne. It had been a long road indeed from the star of Compiègne to this suitcase.

Chapter 17

The October "Liberation." The Gestapo Seizes Mihály Ursi.

In these summer days of 1944 when German deserters everywhere were multiplying like white corpuscles in a disintegrating body, the Hungarian resistance was restricted to a few sabotage actions. The railway tracks between Budapest and Vienna were dynamited several times, especially in the vicinity of the Cave.

When, on that March night, Kazi and Marja fled from the Ararat Hospital, Kazi left his dog, Rapczyk, in the park. Two days later Rapczyk mysteriously appeared on the shore of the river opposite the Cave and barked tirelessly. In his barking was a kind of reproach against Kazi, at the same time an air of ironic superiority, as if he wanted to express his opinion emphatically about the useless effort to keep from him the secret of the Cave, or any other human business. Needless to say, Rapczyk had played a role in connection with the dynamited tracks. The only thing which throws a shadow on his character is the fact that after his job was done he would venture into the next town, and at the kitchen of the German headquarters, on his Bismarck-face an expression of perfect innocence, accept handouts.

Rapczyk did not like the romantic atmosphere of the Cave. He spent most of his time in the Kurdis' yard with Zia and Zizi, and carried ciphered letters to and from the Cave. He did not use the secret entrance. He swam across the river, climbed the northern slope of the mountain, inaccessible to tourists, but not to a Saint Bernard, even one with a dubious birth certificate. Reaching the top he descended the rock stairs.

But as a postman he was not very reliable because in addition he carried on his own large correspondence. Rapczyk, well over a hundred pounds, was an incurable Don Juan. As Freyberger once, during a walk in the park, scientifically explained, most of the animals write their love-letters not with ink but with the hormones of their urine. The freshness of the ink even reveals how far away the beloved lady is. Rapczyk read all the yearning letters of his girls; for the sake of simplicity he read them not with spectacles but with his nose, and answered all of them in his own brief, but effective style, lifting one of his hind legs, and using trees or milestones as stationery. His correspondence was so successful that one day he proudly introduced to Zizi his two shabby, scrawny girl-friends. Joska chased them away with a stick.

Because of the inefficiency of Rapczyk's postmanship, once or twice a week Ursi visited the hermits in the Cave, bringing always some gift: books, rumors or fresh fruits. The German occupation of Hungary was a catastrophe for Kazi because all the Hungarian eggs went to Germany, and Kazi's favorite dish was fresh eggs. It was a very difficult task even for Joska to get one or two eggs for Zia's and Zizi's breakfast.

For Kristina nothing was impossible, and once when she secretly visited Zia she brought a dozen fresh eggs. The only trouble was that when Kristina saw something white on which one can write, she could not restrain her ever-abundant thoughts. In the waiting room at Budapest she autographed one egg: "To the heroic members of the resistance, Kristina." On the other eleven eggs she wrote quotations from the great spirits of world literature. An elderly man next to her in the waiting room, watched secretly as the romantically dressed fine lady, with a large Florentine straw hat, fervently wrote on eggs. He was convinced that the poor lady would try to put the eggs into the mailbox, having some serious mental disturbance due to the heavy bombardments.

The generous Zia decided to send the precious gift to the cave-dwellers. When the eggs reached the Cave, Marja shouted rudely at Kazi:

"Are you crazy? You want to eat *these* eggs?" She locked the autographed eggs in a treasure chest.

There are people in the world who have not the slightest esteem for literature. Around midnight Kazi sneaked out of his bed, noiselessly opened the chest with a corkscrew, tiptoed to the kitchen, and ate Voltaire, Li-Pu-Ten, Kant, Gide, Tolstoy and

Ady, six eggs altogether, in the form of the most delicious Polish omelet, with chopped onions, green peppers, tomatoes and cheese.

On July 2, a curious thing befell Mihály Ursi. We note it down mainly for the benefit of those interested in problems of telepathy. On that day he again set out for the Cave, whose secret portal he always approached by boat. As a precaution, the boat was kept near the upper reaches of the river at a good distance from the Cave, moored to an ancient willow bending low over the water. A mile farther up, a railway bridge spanned the river.

It must have been around noon. Ursi hid his bicycle in a bush and started afoot toward the boat. All at once he had the feeling that a hot iron had touched the calf of his leg, but only for a split second. He thought he might have set fire to his trousers with a discarded cigarette. But no. A few steps farther, again this strange heat touched him, and now both his feet became leaden.

"I am unfamiliar with the symptoms of heart trouble or thrombosis," he wrote in his diary. "I tried to take a step, but my feet seemed rooted in the ground. Cowardice overcame me. I thought I might take sick in the boat, the oars slipping from my grasp, while the current swept me to the Danube, straight into the arms of the German river patrol. I went back to my bicycle, now suspecting some sort of nervous exhaustion, because my condition was mental rather than physical. Slowly I cycled homeward. Meanwhile my strange pain disappeared."

He wasn't halfway, when the sirens sounded and within minutes came successive waves of American bombers. Round him the whole horizon roared and crackled. The air blast pressed even the wheat fields low and a bomb burst so close to him that he hurled himself into a ditch. They were bombing the railway bridge. Joska had already told him they ought to blow up this bridge, across which the Vienna-Budapest German trains sped, but Mihály had said: "Let's leave it to the Americans." He visualized a plane swooping low and laying a bomb or two on the bridge.

That wasn't what happened. From a vast height, inside a five-mile radius, they dropped fifteen hundred large bombs, as if merely seeking to demonstrate that America's supply of bombs was inexhaustible. They hit everything except the bridge. When Ursi went back to his boat, he hardly recognized the stream. Bomb craters had completely altered the river bed; even the little woods where he picnicked last week with Zia and Zizi had vanished. After a long search he found his boat—that is, its chain! Of his boat, and of the ancient willow to which it was moored, no splinter remained. He had escaped certain death.

What was the mysterious message, or spiritual state, that halted him and compelled his return? He believed in telepathy. The human body is all atoms, each atom made up of positive and negative electricity. He could thus explain, scientifically too, that at times of tremendous spiritual tension the human nervous system acts like a transmitting station.

But what he did not believe was that one can sense things *in advance*. It could only be coincidence in the present case that his brief panic, or momentary nervous exhaustion, forced him to turn back just before the bombing.

He was mistaken.

The mystery resolved itself in peculiar fashion the following year when through the Red Cross a letter from Ostie arrived. In the summer of 1944, on New York's Fifth Avenue, the Frick Collection was closed to the public, because in one of the museum's inner chambers a committee of the U.S. Air Force was at work. As an expert on Hungary, Ostie Dukay was a member of this committee. When the Air Force on huge maps had designated the place and time of attacks, Ostie Dukay along with other European experts, would indicate the location of churches, universities, museums and historic monuments, which the Air Force desired to spare.

So after such a committee meeting on July 1, 1944, Ostie Dukay knew that next day at noon the Americans would bomb the strategic railway bridge near the Cave. He feared lest at the time of the bombing Zia, Zizi, Mihály or any other of his people might be fishing, boating or bathing in the neighborhood of the bridge. Presumably he could have sent a short-wave warning via Andrew P. Szanto, but that would have constituted the betrayal of a strict military secret.

As he himself related, during that night he couldn't shut

250

his eyes, and by six o'clock in the morning was in such a state that he was forced to take a strong sedative, something he seldom resorted to. It was in those minutes that the American bombers must have reached the bridge, because six A.M. in New York corresponds to noon in Hungary. The "transmitter," activated by Ostie's tense mental state, contacted the sensitive "receiver" of Ursi's nervous system, as he was approaching the boat.

The night after the bombing, Ursi and Joska Kurdi left home, saying they were bound for the Cave and would not return until daybreak. They did not go to the Cave. In the dark night, within a wide radius of the bridge, stood dependable miners mobilized to give whistle or light signals at the approach of danger. In their boat Ursi and Joska rowed downstream, taking great care to manipulate their oars noiselessly, because two Hungarian soldiers with fixed bayonets patrolled the bridge.

It was no easy matter to stop the boat soundlessly at the bridge pillar. The night was starless and dark. They set the dynamite in place, then, unreeling the detonating wires, drifted down with the current.

A terrific blast shook the air. Ursi buried his face in his hands at the thought of the two poor Hungarian soldiers. Joska noticed this movement of his in the dark, or possibly only read his thoughts, as he spoke: "Well, that's how it goes, Mr. Major, sir, the Ideal always demands sacrifice. From the standpoint of the Ideal a man's life is nothing!"

Maintaining the chronology of events, we come to the great day of June 6, 1944, in regard to which we find this notation in Mihály Ursi's diary:

It has happened! The radios are blaring—in the dark night, in four thousand ships, on the wings of eleven thousand Allied planes, like a tide resounding to the clouds, England's and America's technical Apocalypse flooded across the Channel, up in the sky tens of thousands of giant motors roaring the commander-in-chief's radio prayer: "Oh Lord, give us faith . . . Thy will be done, Almighty God. Amen."

It has happened. They have launched the invasion, not

251

on the Adriatic, but across the Channel. Zia weeps, prostrate on the bed: now she waits for Ostie in vain. Joska turned out to be right: Father Stalin is to bring us the Ideal.

Toward evening the little hunchbacked painter again appeared in the yard.

"Professor, I only want to remind you that I'd be happy to be of service to you in any way."

The following week the German generals' unsuccessful attempt against the Führer stirred up the greatest emotion in the Cave.

"What a ridiculous and primitive thing: a bomb!" exclaimed Kazi. "My spectacles . . ." but he did not finish his sentence after a significant look from Marja. When two years before Kazi had returned after the futile Warsaw trip, in the hospital's laboratory Marja had tried out Kazi's wonder-spectacles with a white rat. The day after the shot, the rat had become even healthier than before. They had experimented with another rat, a few days later a third, then a fourth, a fifth—all the rats simply laughed into the eyes of the wonder-spectacles.

Gazing into the air, Marja only said:

"God must want something with the world that He keeps the dictators alive."

Kazi paced the Cave's sitting room from wall to wall like a caged leopard. Not exactly like a leopard, because when he was nervous both his hands were deeply sunk in his trouser pockets, his fingers moving quickly as if he were eagerly searching at the bottom of his pockets for a poppy-seed he never found. After Marja's religiously philosophical remark he gritted his teeth:

"Maybe, by some mistake, your senile professor at the University of Prague gave you some vitamin powder instead of botulinus!"

One evening toward the end of July, Joska Kurdi introduced to the Major a figure with a workman's appearance. They sat down at the millstone table beneath the apple tree.

"Mr. Major, sir, this comrade needs dynamite. Could you please let him have a few kilograms from the Cave, Mr. Major?"

"What for?" asked Ursi.

The man's thick neck twitched slightly from time to time,

252

as if at the touch of an electric current. He was a "black conductor," as Joska called the rail dynamiters. He exchanged a weird smile with Joska and then said:

"I'm a pastryman, Mr. Major."

After two brief twitches of the neck, he added:

"At the Russwurm Pastry Shop."

Ursi knew from Grubi's reports that in the vaulted inner rooms of this little pastry shop located near the German Legation and Septemvir Utca, the German ambassador and the capital's military commandant, in the company of a few leading Germans, used to take tea, and that Johy was constantly in attendance there. By now only German officials lived in the narrow little street, SS soldiers guarded every gateway, from neighboring houses everyone not of reliable German origin had been evacuated; but not even the Gestapo could know what dwelt in the heart of one of the pastryman's helpers, who eleven years before had left Germany because of his communist convictions. This man had been a Berlin Spartacist of the variety that battled in sewers and on housetops. It was easy to picture the moment when in the private room of this shop a time-bomb would rip vaultings asunder, and then amid the rubble it would be hard to differentiate the raspberry ice cream from Johy's bloody brain splattered onto the plates.

As they talked, from the house came the sweet, calm whir of Zia's sewing machine.

Zia carried with her everywhere a few small family pictures, one showing the little red jaunting car, the seven-year-old Johy driving the white donkey, his blond locks fluttering in the breeze, while the four-year-old Zia rested her head on Johy's shoulder.

Ursi thought of the two Hungarian soldiers who had guarded the bridge. And he heard Joska's whisper in the dark: "That's how it is, Mr. Major, sir. From the standpoint of the Ideal, a man's life is nothing."

But what limits bind an Ideal? He recalled that Guy Pettiguy, who was a leader of the French underground and a master of the *garrotte*—the art of choking a man before he can utter a sound—wrote this: "Can the results of our small-scale sabotage and murder of individuals be worth the frightful consequences of retribution? As a level-headed engineer, I keep putting the question to myself: is our bloody and filthy work necessary in the interest of final victory?"

Ursi felt that in these moments not merely the fate of the Russwurm Pastry Shop, but the problem of all European underground movements had come up at the millstone table. He shook his head.

"I won't give dynamite for that."

Joska and the man with the twitching neck glanced at each other.

"Let's think the thing through," Ursi continued in a somewhat friendlier tone. "Say we destroy a few top Germans. What then? Others will spring up in their place . . . but the populace of Budapest will be decimated. Lidice! Have you already forgotten Lidice? I won't give dynamite for that."

His words were followed by a long painful silence. Only the neck of the pastryman's helper twitched a few times. Again he caught Joska's eye, then slowly rose.

"Let's go then," he said.

He left without a handclasp.

In August 1944, the tanks of the Red Army already were forging ahead over Magyar soil from the east, easily sweeping aside the "wooden guns" and "ox-carts."

From Kurdi's fence each day they watched, along the highway in the autumn rain, the caravans of people fleeing from the east. The wide-brimmed hats of the men and the brass-ornamented harness of the heavy horses showed they were Saxons of Transylvania, now streaming back toward their ancient homeland, whence, many centuries ago, they had been invited by the German consorts of Magyar kings, that they might teach nomad Magyars to build houses, mold candles and church bells, bake honey-cake, graft trees, and milk cows, because the people of Ordony drank only mare's thin milk. These Saxons had less to do with Hitler than the Germans belonging to Pennsylvania's bunds, but they would have greeted Soviet soldiers with *Guten Morgen,* because for over a thousand years they had preserved their mother tongue. They were the first *nemetskis* in the path of Soviet regiments, they had to flee the vengeance of the Ukrainian fathers roaring ahead in tanks, lest they be made to pay for infants dashed against the wall and for thousands of Ukrainian

254

villages burned to the ground, deeds with which General von Bock and his troops wrote their names into history.

Day and night, the flood of refugees streamed westward. Irons and ironing boards, shaded lamps and pots and pans, gold-framed mirrors and dirt-splattered hen-coops were crowded high on the carts—among children wrapped in quilts or blankets, among the sick and aged; on some carts a little calf gone lame sometimes waggled its big ears behind the dining room sideboard. Those among the plodders who were very weary grasped the side of the cart with one hand. A thousand-kilometer trek was behind them, and another thousand kilometers lay ahead. Ten thousand, twenty thousand such carts, without the sound of a human voice, only the creaking of wheels and the occasional plaintive lowing of a cow, whinny of a horse or bleat of a goat and the quacking of ducks. Only the throngs of the poor can undertake such massive migrations—rich men bear their fortunes in their check-books. These wandering and loaded carts made it seem as if the very church steeples and cemeteries of the little Saxon villages had been packed upon the wagons.

This migration seemed the smoke of a historical catastrophe; a millennium and a half ago, peoples must have fled before Attila's hordes in similar fashion. The difference was only that now the hordes were arriving from the east not on tiny tousled horses, but in lend-lease American jeeps.

"I wonder what Papa would say to all this if he were alive?" whispered Zia to Mihály.

On October 10, Slobodan Tuykovich, accompanied by Grubi, unexpectedly appeared in the Kurdis' yard. He was almost unrecognizable. For months he had lain in the hospital, his last wound inflicted by a hand grenade which had torn away almost half his face.

On Sunday morning, October 16, the Regent's son, by now his only child—accompanied by two bodyguards—set out for a secret rendezvous with the Yugoslav officers. But at the tele-phoned address, not Slobo and his companions, but the Gestapo waited, for someone had betrayed the negotiations.

Concealed in the bushes at Petöfi Square, lay the men of the Gestapo, who, in view of the scope of their assignment, were led by the same Skorzeny who so recklessly liberated Mussolini.

When young Horthy alighted from the car, they threw a blanket over him, shot him down beneath it, and after a brief fusillade, left the corpses of the two bodyguards sprawled on the pavement. They threw the blanket-covered wounded young Horthy into the car and disappeared with him. The news reached the Royal Palace within minutes.

The aged Regent in paternal grief gathered the last remnants of his strength: at ten o'clock the Hungarian radio resounded with the Regent's Appeal.

". . . with deep disillusion in my heart . . . I can no longer hide from the nation the German government's successive betrayals . . . They have repaid our friendship and comradely fight against Bolshevism not only with vile lies, but now with the murder of our finest sons . . . Hungarian soldiers! To arms against the Germans!"

In Budapest, at the first sentences of the Appeal, people rushed to the windows: "Liberation has come! . . . Off with the yellow star! . . . We are allies of the Allies! . . . no more bombings! . . ." Passers-by turned their heads in confusion toward those shouting from windows above the street.

Within minutes the street scene was transformed: green shirts and German uniforms disappeared, trembling hands tore off the yellow stars, and unshaven figures of the underground crept from hiding.

In the Kurdis' yard Joska and Erzsi began dancing to the sounds of the Appeal. Ursi quickly shaved off his long mustache, threw aside his green apron and, only shouting back to Zia: "I'll be back tonight!" zoomed off on his motorcycle toward Budapest.

He went straight to the detention camp to free the prisoners, among them many Stargazers captured by the Gestapo. The scene went off very much as in the fall of 1918, when the doomed deserters were freed by the revolutionary mob.

Under the effect of the Regent's Appeal, warders and prisoners, now too, were carried to the street on the shoulders of the crowd.

On his motorcycle, around three o'clock, Ursi started back to Holod. He did not know that in these moments, up in the Royal Palace, a violent machine-gun battle between the Regent's bodyguards and SS troops was over. Already in the Inner City the largest German Tiger tanks rumbled, shaking the windows; by now they had captured the radio too, which a few civilian employees defended with fountain pens, typewriters and microphones. These were the "world-conquering" German Wehrmacht's last victorious deeds of prowess. The Jews with trembling hands sewed back their yellow stars, within moments the unshaven figures of the resistance disappeared from the streets, and, from beneath the ground, German uniforms and green shirts appeared in even greater profusion. The heady joy of liberation had lasted only for brief hours.

Ursi sped along the highway toward Holod to bring Zia and Zizi back to Budapest as soon as possible. No more bombardments, no more Gestapo.

The only trouble was that while carrying the prisoners on his shoulder in the big crowd, he had lost his hat.

A speeding man, hatless, at such an hour, was obviously suspect. Another big motorcycle pounced on him like an eagle on a hare. The green-shirted policeman came so close that their arms brushed against each other.

"Good afternoon!" Ursi called calmly.

The policeman did not return the friendly greeting. His rigid eyes seemed even bluer than they were in reality. When they stopped and dismounted, his narrowed gaze turned to Ursi: "Where are you speeding to?"

He sported a Führer mustache, his accent revealed his German origin.

"To Holod. I am a carpenter."

"Show me your papers!"

"Don't hold me up, my dear friend, I'm in a hurry. . . . Listen, I'll give you fifty pengös . . . only because I'm in a hurry. Didn't you hear the Regent's Appeal on the radio?"

The policeman threw a glance at the fifty-pengö bill, already in Ursi's hand. Then he said in an icy voice:

"Your papers!"

"Look, Captain . . ."

The policeman's revolver was already out of its holster. Since the morning of March 19 when, watching the invading German troops, Hamor had grabbed the revolver from Ursi's hand, he had been unarmed.

257

"Vorwärts marsch!" shouted the policeman.

Ursi gazed into the narrow blue eyes. Only for a moment, but deeply. This face, red with the cold wind, this Führer mustache, now, was the enemy. All the German Nazis, Hitler, Himmler, Heydrich, Hess, all the H's of Hell—in that single man. He did not look like a professional policeman in his green Arrow Cross shirt with its yellow armband. He had probably been a bank clerk or a teacher with many children in civilian life, an honest, diligent little man, perhaps. But now he was panic incarnate for Ursi, the visible terror of a dreadful Ideal.

Ursa Major's friendly little smile now was nothing but guile. The muscles in his arms and thighs were tightening, he was about to leap at the green shirt, but the policeman's revolver suddenly pointed at his heart.

Ursi turned obediently in the indicated direction, pushing his motorcycle, the policeman followed two paces behind him. For a quarter of an hour they proceeded mutely until they reached the next town on the way from Budapest to Holod.

Soon Ursi stood before the desk of a colonel.

"Your name?"

"István Basha," said Ursi, and he remembered that poor Count Dupi, who had invented this name for his secret apartment in Peter Dukay Street back in Franz Joseph's time, used it for quite different purposes.

"Occupation?" the colonel asked, hiding a mighty yawn with his palm. He had been on duty the whole night but in the morning, instead of the bed warmed up by his wife, had come the Regent's Appeal, and he could not leave his desk.

"Carpenter."

"Age?"

"Forty."

"Why aren't you in the Army? A strong, healthy man like you. Your age group was called up last year."

There were a few civilians standing behind the colonel's desk, apparently secret service men. One of them leaned forward and whispered something to his chief.

The colonel turned his head with a quick movement toward "István Basha." Then leafed through the telephone book.

By now Ursi knew that the secret service man had recognized him, for the colonel was asking the operator to put through a top urgency long distance call: Budapest 5-417.

It was Johy's telephone number at the Septemvir Utca palace. The colonel gave his name as though reporting to a general.

" . . . he says his name is . . . just a minute, please . . . István Basha, but one of my men suspects him of being Your Excellency's brother-in-law."

Johy's voice faintly quacked on the receiver's diaphragm.

"Yes, sir. We will wait for you," said the colonel. He replaced the receiver and turned to Ursi, addressing him in a tone now very much awake:

"Stand over there. Face the wall!"

Ursi obeyed. The seconds passed, then the minutes, then a whole hour. Ursi looked at the empty wall on which the hand of Belshazzar quickly wrote flashing words. Death. Zia. Zizi. Death. Café Gugger. Death. Sir Thomas Harcourt. Death. The small globe on top of the bookcase. Death. The Constellation Andromeda. Death. George Bernard Shaw. Death. Sometimes he closed his eyes as though he wanted to feel that he was dead.

The door opened behind him. Ursi concluded that Johy had recognized him while crossing the room, thus avoiding a face-to-face identification, which would not have suited Johy's taste.

A soldier approached Ursi and handcuffed him.

"Come along."

When Ursi turned, Johy was facing the window. Outside the headquarters Ursi was placed in a German Army vehicle, between two SS men. The car set out for Budapest.

That same evening Grubi telephoned to Holod about the turn of events and the capture of Mihály.

"We are going to the Cave!" Joska Kurdi ordered.

Erzsi had already snatched up her things, but Zia didn't budge.

"This is no time to hesitate, Countess, Your Gracious Excellency. Are you coming or not?"

He vanished alone in the dark with Erzsi, almost running. Zia, left alone in the house with Zizi, tried to get a car for the trip to Budapest. But she couldn't even find a peasant cart.

Taking Zizi by the hand, leaving all her belongings behind,

she set out afoot in the black autumn rain on the hundred-kilometer journey. Toward midnight the "Tshoortsil candles" showed them where Budapest lay: the British were bombing the capital heavily.

For hours they wandered thus, sometimes dropping in exhaustion at the edge of a ditch, then again they would start, going, going toward Budapest, already without hope, when a milk-wagon picked them up.

Reaching home, Zia learned from Kristina that it would be vain to seek the Regent's intercession for her husband, the Germans had already kidnaped the Regent and his wife and dragged them as prisoners to Germany.

Zia put on dry clothing and by early morning appeared at Septemvir Utca. The dining salon was not yet set in order: there stood the empty champagne bottles and the traces of the night's carousing. She had to wait more than three hours before Johy came forth, green and leaden-eyed.

"Dearest Zia, you must see that I can't do a thing for your husband. Not to speak of the fact that I am bound by our Ideal. To raise my voice in the interest of a man so compromised entails the most serious danger. I can't understand Grubi, asking me the same thing. In your own interest, I advise you to start divorce proceedings at once against your husband. By the way—what's doing in town? Can I offer you a glass of cognac?"

Zia stood up and left Johy alone without a word. She slowly walked down the old stone stairs; the heavy pea-green carpet made her steps noiseless and her body weightless. As she descended she had the strange feeling that behind her the stairs and the walls of the palace disappeared step by step. On the main floor next to the end of the staircase stood the mahogany statue of a Saracen boy holding a brass tray for the visitors' cards, "Bouhou," as they had christened him when they were children. He was their lifeless but ever-grinning playmate, and she and Johy used to clean the last speck of dust from Bouhou's eyes with the tip of their handkerchief, carefully, tenderly, not to cause any pain to his wooden eyeballs. Bouhou's eyes followed Zia until she left the lobby.

She stood aimlessly at the entrance to the Septemvir Utca palace. Who could help her? Poor Kristina—she also must be in great trouble because of Freyberger. Where in Hungary was a man who could save Mihály? In the winter of 1940 from the distance of five years she clearly heard the unfriendly voice of the Regent: "Tell your husband that I will not tolerate any action against Germany!" And now his Appeal said: "To arms against the Germans!"

Her heart was full of turbulent and painful thoughts but she speeded up her steps—she must try everything, she must see the Regent. She did not realize how desperate was her plan to ask the help of the Regent who since yesterday had been a prisoner of the Gestapo, and in only a few hours was to be carried to Germany.

The pompous baroque iron gate of the Royal Palace was heavily guarded by SS troops. When Zia approached the gate, one SS man morosely waved her away from a distance of some twenty steps. No admission for anyone.

Zia turned back; then a few minutes later—like a miracle—the sirens began to scream and yelp. Since yesterday everybody knew that the most horrible Allied bombardment was to come to "help" the resistance and as a punishment for the Germans. The sirens yelped dreadfully, and everybody disappeared from the streets in a panic. And so did the SS guards.

Zia walked through the deserted gate and crossed the courtyard of the Royal Palace. The sirens screamed. She was near to collapse but when she ascended the huge and empty staircase she felt the mysteriously muscular strength of the sirens as though they were almost supporting her under her arms, politely and tenderly. She remembered where the Regent's office was in the labyrinth of the corridors; she did not meet a single human being—except a tall plain-clothes man who almost bumped into her running for shelter.

She entered the room of the aide-de-camp who used to be dressed as a Hungarian Lohengrin. The room was empty. All the windows had been smashed by the previous concussions—she knocked on the Regent's door. The knock was inaudible for three reasons: the door was cushioned with wine-red cloth, the sirens were still yelping, and the hearing of the aging Regent had not improved in the last five years.

When she opened the door, the draft swept a few sheets

261

of paper from the Regent's desk; the sheets were flying in the air like frightened gulls, and it seemed that it was they and not the sirens that were screaming. Otherwise nothing was changed in the room. The oversharpened pencils lay on the Regent's desk in the same precise array, and next to the desk stood the cherry-red leather armchair in which she had sat during her audience five years before—the same chair in which so many self-appointed prime ministers had sat with trembling hearts during the Regent's quarter-of-a-century regime—the same chair in which in the fall of 1921 had sat the last Hapsburg, poor King Charles, secretly returned from his exile and pleading for his throne, offering in vain the Golden Fleece and the title of Prince of Otranto to the Regent.

Nothing was changed in the room, except the Regent. He did not notice Zia's entry because he was packing a valise for his journey to Germany, never to return to Hungary. He did not wear his wonderfully tailored admiral's coat any longer; in his sport breeches he looked even older than he was, near to eighty; he stood next to the broken window—a human face could never be as sorrowful as a broken window.

The sirens stopped, and the sudden silence was deep and strange.

"Excuse me, Your Serenity . . ." said Zia.

The Regent turned, and with an embarrassed movement closed the valise as if he were caught in some action which was not dignifying for a regent. His narrowed eyes did not recognize the unexpected visitor.

"I am Zia Dukay . . ."

With a faint smile the Regent extended his arms toward her in a fatherly manner.

Without even sitting down, Zia began, but got only as far as: "My husband"—she burst into tears and came near to fainting. The Regent tenderly encircled her shoulder with his arm, sat her on the sofa and began comforting her:

"Don't cry, Countess . . . don't cry."

When Zia came to herself and dried her tears, she saw that the Regent, his elbows propped on the little table by the sofa, had hidden his face in his palms and by the motion of his shoulders Zia perceived that he was sobbing mutely while the

262

air was filled with the deep distant sounds of the heavy bombs, nearing and growing rapidly as though the whole sky above Budapest were drumming violently. Now it was Zia who put an arm around the shoulder of the old Regent and began comforting him with an uncontrolled cry:

"Don't cry, please . . . don't cry."

Then the door opened, and a tall German-speaking gentleman ordered Zia out of the room.

Chapter 18

The Siege of Budapest and Its Aftermath.

At Christmas 1944, the death bell tolled for Budapest. Her beautiful bridges already were mined with dynamite charges, only waiting for a German hand to press the detonator, so that as the last phenomenon of "heroic" resistance they might fly into the air, shaking heaven and earth.

Budapest was born two thousand years ago of the caprice, we might say, of an extraordinary woman, who twisted around her little finger three impetuous, ingenious and glorious, but not always sober Roman emperors. Shakespeare wrote *Antony and Cleopatra*, Bernard Shaw *Caesar and Cleopatra*, but neither The Sweet Swan of Avon nor Shaw knew what was the secret of the captivating Egyptian Goddess-Queen's phenomenal conquests.

The ladies of the old Roman aristocracy surmised that the secret lay not in the beauty and wit of that fat, duck-faced gypsy call-girl, but in the magic power of an amber ring which she always wore on her little finger. So fashionable did amber jewelry become throughout the limitless Empire, even among old, lame, deaf and poor women, that the amber merchants trampled each other in the primeval forests overspreading the territory of present-day Hungary, where the green-gold petrified resin abounded.

In the bend of the Danube where, at the foot of wondrously beautiful hills also adaptable to the building of fortifications, bubbled curative hot springs known in the aboriginal Celtic as *Ak Ink,* the first Roman settlement received the name Acquincum, whose white limestone ruins are still visible at the limits of Budapest.

After the fall of the Roman Empire, wandering Slavic tribes settled near the hot springs of Acquincum, and on either bank of the Danube were built many a *buda* and *pest*. In ancient Slavic tongues both these words mean brick-kiln. From them derives the name Budapest. Through ten centuries the Magyar settlers of these amber regions were assigned the role of waging bloody battles to defend Western Christianity from the attacks of the East. This rich national past stimulated schoolbooks to superfluous extravagance, and literature to patriotic outpourings. With the advent of the printing press and stage, innumerable bad novels and plays were written about the heroic defenders of the West, among them a prelate named János Kapisztran, who, bestriding the ramparts, with Christ's cross in his left hand and a sword in his right, fought against pagan Asia.

In the past century that part of Asia which we now call Russia appeared thrice on Magyar soil. First in 1849, when young Franz Joseph called for Czarist forces to help him crush Kossuth's fight for freedom. When General Paskievich delivered rebellious Hungary, bound hand and foot, to the Hapsburg Monarchy, Kossuth and his emigré companions sailed to America for the purpose of recruiting money, arms and expeditionary forces against the European dictators.

Some two decades after the war for freedom was suppressed, the Monarchy was threatened from the south by young Italy, from the north by a Germany forged into one. A regime in troublous times willingly pardons a former enemy. Also, Franz Joseph had great need of the famous Magyar Hussars, so the gates of musty prisons swung open and by virtue of the general amnesty, the grandfather of Zia, Count Peter Dukay, onetime companion of Kossuth in exile, could also enter into his inheritance at Ararat.

In that year of touching reconciliation, the thirty-seven-year-old sidewhiskered Franz Joseph with his beauteous consort, Queen Elizabeth—who possessed the largest chignon and worst teeth of all European empresses—toured the Magyar plain in an open carriage, and a long half-century of resplendent peace began, during which Budapest was transformed, as a caterpillar turns into a butterfly. On the right bank of the Danube the ancient turrets atop the hills of Buda preserved the landscape's oriental beauty, the little crooked picturesque streets cherished the century-old Renaissance palaces, snuggling near the Royal Palace like chicks beneath the warm wing of the mother hen, because at all periods the aristocracy felt most at ease under the protection of royal wings.

While the Hungarians after so many bloody battles began to let out their waistlines and, twirling their long mustachios, gave their heads to politics, Jewish business acumen and Swabian industry flowed out in the form of streets and boulevards. Devout Renaissance hands had built and carved and polished the ancient palaces of Buda with their stone-lace balconies, sometimes over long decades; but the "palaces" on the Pest side were born of the wild building fever we might aptly call the "Mortar Age," in which London, Berlin, and Paris also mushroomed to capitals harboring many millions. Budapest, too, threw down the gauntlet to the West. She already had a London Hotel which, among other reasons, did not resemble an English hotel because it nurtured the burliest of bedbugs. A Parisian Department Store where, from scythes and mustachio wax to Debrecen sausage and red slippers from Szeged, you could buy everything but Parisian articles. The city boasted a five-story apartment house whose ugly plaster tower seen from the left resembled a termite nest, from the right a wedding cake, and which Hungarians conceived of as a skyscraper, naming it New York Palace.

The city began to glow at the most sublime level of commercial, industrial and literary, theatrical and bordello life. The dark historic stains were washed from the bloody threshold with champagne, as over the wooden paving blocks of Andrássy Út pounded the hoofs of beautiful horses, the open carriages of the Magyar Champs Élysées speeding by with fascinatingly exquisite women under dream-world parasols, whose identity one could only conjecture, because cocottes with inimitable perfection imitated countesses, and countesses the cocottes. Budapest began to be discovered by an ever-increasing number of distinguished visitors from abroad who, misled by the name London Hotel, were dismayed at the sight of unshaven poets and dramatists still asleep, even in the noon hours, on the billiard tables of the New York Café. Already the afternoon guests began drifting in, but, at a corner table, still in full swing was a card party begun the night before by the six-foot author of the most tenderly phrased romantic novels, who, with his bare hands could wrest the sword

266

from tipsy Hussar officers in the event of any minor difference between them. All card games ended with a slap in the face, all love affairs with a duel, and all duels with friendship to the grave.

The gas lamps of the great boulevards gave way to brilliant arc-lights, the plodding horse-drawn omnibus to the careening trolley, and Budapest was the first in the world to build a subway. The Danube decked her wrist with handsome and weighty bracelets: her shores were spanned by graceful bridges; café-terraces of modern hotels delighted in the view of medieval turrets on the hills of Buda; soft gypsy music wove through the amber summer twilight, like the gold and silver strands of antique brocade from the East. On the lovely Danube Promenade exotic Balkan nabobs, Russian princes and many-childrened Dutch cheese-manufacturers hurried after the shapely legged girls from Pest. The trim ankles fled, but only in such fashion that the fattest Macedonian tobacco king could easily overtake them. Budapest had been discovered by the world. Aristocratic palaces in Buda passed the two-hundred-and-fifty-pound, goateed Prince of Wales, later Edward VII, from hand to hand; and to commemorate the great Septemvir Utca banquet, Count Dupi presented sunshades with diamond-set handles to the ladies present and gold cigarette cases to the men, some two hundred pieces in all.

Three lucky elements mingled in the Budapest of Franz Joseph: the Magyar race's Asiatic verve and love of hospitality, the German elements' thirst for knowledge and passion for building, and the Jews' business industry and diabolical humor. The dream of Charlemagne and the Byzantine Empress Irene had come true: West and East in Budapest had joyfully embraced as never before in history. In one public building an enormous fresco depicted sixteenth century turbaned Janissaries driving enchained Magyars to slavery. At the request of the Turkish minister the fresco was painted over; no one wanted to be reminded of the past, everyone forgave everyone.

Early in World War I Russia appeared for the second time on Hungarian soil, but the earthen-hued Russian troops did not reach the lowlands of the interior. The Russian colossus was stopped by the northeastern mountain chains; half raising his huge frame above the ridge of the Carpathians he just looked about, engraved the landscape in his memory and from the mountain tops practically shouted down to the plain: I'll be back!

The many hundreds of thousands of Russian prisoners were set to work on farms, and Ararat, too, was allotted its quota of these harmonica-playing fellows, who leaped high in swirling dances. The half-witted Count Rere found pleasure in harnessing himself to the tiny cinnabar-red sports car. He would make Bragiy, a Russian prisoner of war, sit in the car; Bragiy grinningly complied when ordered to give Count Rere's top hat an occasional playful flick with his whip, just for fun. Even Count Dupi laughed aloud at the sight, little suspecting that three decades later Bragiy's sons would appear in Ararat Park and the game would turn into the final tragedy of the aristocracy.

The first world war was fought in distant trenches; at Budapest not a single pane of glass was broken and after the war the Hungarian capital stood unrivaled in the Danube Valley. Vienna, the imperial city, after the fall of the Hapsburgs, became hardly more than *Die tote Stadt* on the vast stage of her opera house, while above Warsaw, Prague, Belgrade, Bucharest and Sofia rose Budapest tower-like; sparklingly tossed talents in all directions: scientists, writers, composers. Broadway producers watched Budapest *premières*, where the whispered translations of breathlessly enthusiastic theatrical agents transformed the shoddiest opuses into *Hamlets, Malades Imaginaires* and *Camilles*, and there were times when four or five Hungarian plays ran simultaneously on Broadway. A czar of Hollywood, while consuming fried chicken in a Buda tavern, looked into the face of the flower girl, daughter of an impoverished policeman, and groomed her into one of the greatest stars of the silent films. Beverly Hills was dotted with the enormous swimming pools of Budapest actors, directors and writers, and the motion picture studios were finally forced to post placards with this warning: "It's not enough to be Hungarian." The prostate operations of the Pope or the President of Mexico were performed by Hungarian surgeons; European royalty and Park Avenue millionaires sat for Magyar portrait painters; and in New York's Carnegie Hall appeared Bartók like a giant of the Mists. Dizzying careers were carved by beautiful

268

Hungarian courtesans and, even in the delicatessens of distant lands, sticks of salami tied with the national colors proclaimed Magyar glory.

By now all this had the air of primordial marshes in which dwelt the antediluvian dinosaurs of historic dreams, humor, talents, genius. In this aura of the past Mihály Ursi lived his youth, and in that knowledge we can the more easily understand his daring dreams.

Schoolbooks describe as Hungary's most frightful epoch the early thirteenth century, when Batu Khan's hordes broke in from the East. With regard to this epoch only primitive chronicles survive, so we are in no position to gauge the relative extent and horror of the two catastrophes. We may say, notwithstanding, that Hungary's blackest days began on October 16, 1944.

It was not Count Johy who filled the Regent's vacated chair as gauleiter, but an army officer assuming the title of Nation-Leader, who with a German accent and dandified stupidity dispensed his doctrine-laden pronouncements as head of state. During intermissions between air-raid warnings, operetta singers sang freshly manufactured military marches, giving the impression that the victorious Hungarian Army already threatened the walls of Moscow and Washington. Behind these gay animated marches was no longer any sort of army, only sadistic murderers, who knew there was no further defense against Russian and Allied forces joining up from the East and West.

The radio already incited openly to pogroms, and the highroads became the scene of a second exodus, armed soldiers herding Jews toward the German gas chambers. Those who, from sickness or exhaustion, dropped by the wayside, were shot dead on the spot, but so that the national economy might suffer no loss, penknives dug the gold teeth from the bleeding mouths of the dying.

North and south the Red Army had ringed in Budapest, and by late November tank battles took place even in Ararat Park. The jaws of the giant pincers had clamped on Budapest cautiously, as a cat's sharp teeth on the head of a mouse, allowing momentary caprice to decide just when the skull should be crushed.

In olden days, Chieftain Ordony and his companions, in

accordance with ancient custom, had cut their veins and dripped their blood into a common chalice to symbolize that in battle the blood sacrifice of king, chief and people was mutual. In fighting the Tartar Batu Khan, King Bela fell sword in hand, just as three centuries later Lajos II did facing the Turks. Times and customs have greatly changed since. Now Hungarian leaders were still fanatically shouting into the radio: Hold out! Hold out, Magyar compatriots!—but before the door of the radio station waited loot-laden trucks, motors running. Hold out to the end applied to everyone—infants, the aged and dying—everyone except the westward-fleeing members of the government. Johy, too, packed up the art treasures of Septemvir Utca, leaving his mother and the half-witted Rere in the cellar of the palace, and decamped for the West.

After the government's departure, press and radio became so silent that not even air raids were reported. By then it would have been superfluous anyhow, because bombs showered continually, day and night. When Marshal Tolbukin's forces had completely encircled the town, he sent emissaries to the German general "defending" the city, calling upon him to surrender Budapest in order to avoid needless bloodshed and destruction. We have noted that Hungary for a thousand years had played the role of defensive bastion for the West. Now, too, this role was assigned her, at least by the patriotic fervor of the German general who accounted as pure gain each day that postponed the Red Army's entry into Germany, and considered that, in the balance of the final campaign, Budapest with its two million inhabitants weighed less than a wooden outhouse on the German frontier.

Thus, the German general's reply to Marshal Tolbukin was understandable. He had the Russian emissaries shot. At this news the populace of Budapest descended to the cellars as into the grave.

The siege of Budapest had begun.

Tactical aspects of the siege belong to the pages of military history: we are concerned with life in the crowded cellars during these days of Dantean inferno, and so let us turn to Zia's diary.

Since the electricity is gone only a few candles glow in our cellar, deep black, violet-hued, yellow and blue candles which I had received from Gwen for my dining-room table, and which in this hall now ironically reflect the faraway light of Park Avenue. It must be around six in the morning; outside, already the snow-blanketed city is lit by the gray snow-clouds, but human life is only betrayed by the smoke of stovepipes, extending from cellar windows. The tenants of our cellar, who spent the night on chairs, or sitting on the ground, begin to awaken with great yawns and stretches and cracking of joints. As with their unkempt, stubbly faces they begin moving in the candlelight, they resemble stage figures in Gorki's *The Lower Depths*, exaggerating the garb of misery. Hamor's head is enveloped in a woman's kerchief, because he caught an earache in the cold draft; Mrs. Makkosh uses Mihály's fur jacket and sports cap as protection against the cold.

The Cardinal begins making a fire in the rusty little iron stove. Makkosh was dubbed "Cardinal" by Hamor, after his last week's barter of a hunting jacket for a pound of lard. Wrapped in a red blanket, he strides among us like Cardinal Camperra in the Vatican. The Cardinal is just feeding to the fire Zizi's velvet Teddy bear named Berili, a memento of my own childhood and considered a living creature in our family.

Half past seven. The "black coffee" is ready, which, according to Hamor, the Cardinal brews from old black hats and cigar butts. We distribute the hot drink in crystal glasses, cracked mugs or preserve jars. Poor Berili was stuffed with horse hair, but the dreadful choking fumes now charitably mitigate the smell of unwashed human bodies, and especially the stench emanating from the toilet. For the past ten days we have been without water, and use melted snow to cook with. Some thirty-five of us dwell in the cellar by now, there being two aristocrats beside myself: Uncle András and his wife, Aunt Marie, who is an Austrian countess—both of them over eighty. Their nearby palace sustained a direct hit last week. The other tenants are an

271

assortment of laborers and bourgeois, Jew and Christian, communist and Arrow Crossist. The Jews still have Christian documents, the Christians already have their Jewish birth certificates, the Communists still have Arrow Cross party cards, the Arrow Crossists already have their communist cards, all made out to false names, needless to say. Two men, sleeping through the night on a lame armchair, embraced in their dreams, and that was how they awakened, hardly able to disentangle themselves from each other's arms, but they have not yet introduced themselves, nor will they, because it is an unwritten law that no one asks the other who he is.

I myself am not acquainted with most of my co-tenants either; in the main, they happened in from the street, fleeing bombings or the "military police."

"Is this the Zia-cellar, please?" asked a stranger, seemingly a Jew, as he staggered into our cellar, pale and gasping for breath. That was how I learned that our shelter is known among neighbors as "Zia-cellar." Though far from bombproof, its legendary fame doubtless stems from the fact that each morning and evening I intone a short prayer to Saint Rita, which the others all repeat after me in chorus. Besides this I am also air-raid warden, head nurse, head cook; and I must relentlessly maintain authority not only among children who have turned into adults, but also among adults turned children. Sometimes I berate them like an army sergeant; just yesterday—earache or no—I slapped Jani Hamor roundly because during a bombing he amused himself by reaching under the coverlet and tickling one of our bedridden patients.

After breakfast everyone again takes his place. Some crouch near the beds of the sick and fall into blackest despair, and in general appear as though they were in a tiny overcrowded waiting room somewhere in the desolate icy wastes of Siberia. They are awaiting the train of Death, the locomotive roaring through the skies, spewing fire, and even now being stoked up at a nearby airfield: already hundreds of Soviet bombers are warming up their motors.

They usually arrive promptly at eight; now it is still

only seven thirty, in the tense silence everyone turns his head toward the corner where Hamor with a great clatter dumps the chessmen on the table. His partner is a mute civilian, who only mumbles and gesticulates. A medical certificate also attests to his speech defect, his papers being made out in the name of János Nagy; I am the only one who knows he is a German general of the medical corps, sent here by Freyberger. He is mute because he knows no word of Hungarian.

Ten minutes to eight.

"It's begun," says Hamor—hesitantly he holds the rook above the chessboard, debating whether to take his mute opponent's bishop, which seems a dangerous lure.

Yes, it's begun, but these are not yet the bombers. Only a few cannon clearing their throats with short puffs, like the great horns in an orchestra before the overture. A wreath of Soviet batteries surrounds Budapest, within minutes thousands upon thousands of cannon will bark, the oil-green guns after each yelp springing back, like attacking dogs.

Above the deserted and snow-covered streets flocks of pigeons and sparrows circle in alarm, the house roofs crackle, window panes fall clattering, but the apartment houses stand up to the siege, they don't crumple under the frightful cannonade.

Through the cellar's broken window a "dud" rolls in, everyone flees toward the wall, I too jump on the chair and stand there in the same posture as I do always when frightened by a mouse. The steel miter still spins rapidly on its own axis, honing itself on the cement floor with a hissing sound, then, on a sudden impulse, starts toward the dog's basket, from which Tipi, Uncle András' black dachshund, leaps in fright. The artillery shell now rolls lazily as it settles itself in the dog's basket. In shape and size it greatly resembles a dachshund, even the brass ring round its neck is like a dog's collar. Tipi inquisitively sniffs to ascertain whether it is male or female, but snatches away his nose in alarm, because the shell is still very hot. On everyone's face deathly fright: suppose it is a delayed-action shell?

273

Hamor unbinds the woman's kerchief from his head, swaddles the hot arrival in it, rocks it, prattles to it as to an infant, even pretends playfully to press its nose: *ts-ts-ts*.

Zizi laughs heartily, which encourages the others to laugh too. The heroic nursemaid braves the dangers of the street and throws the stillborn infant of steel into a vacant lot, but rushes straight back, because the bombers are here. In the hellish concert the roar of the motors sounds like the dulcet voice of many violins, then brrumm, brrump . . . the bombs beat the bass drums. Now one after the other, as we watch from the cellar window, the many-storied houses drop to their knees, the steeple of the Franciscan Church shakes its head disapprovingly before toppling.

Some anti-aircraft defense still exists here and there; one Soviet machine after losing both wings floats gracefully in the air for a surprisingly long while, then its wingless torpedo body bores into a second-floor window of the house opposite. That is how it remains, with its inquisitive nose in the room, exchanging stares with a surprised piano.

The bombs sometimes cut five-story houses in two, and these ax-strokes pierce to the roots; to the cellars. At such times the dead are left where they are, the wounded and their salvaged belongings being carried to a neighboring cellar.

In this blistering hell there are no people on the street —but yes, as we look out, two horse-drawn wagons creep past our house, then have to stop farther on, because a good-sized house suddenly tumbles across their path. The first wagon's horses rear wildly, but the gaunt horses of the second wagon are surprisingly serene. Their muzzles and ears are comically white, because they have gnawed open the bags of the wagon in front of them and voraciously guzzle the flour. The wagons are bringing flour, and the flour must get to the bakers, otherwise hundreds die of hunger.

Around eleven o'clock, with his yellow star and doctor's kit, Freyberger stops by at our cellar: the old lady lying on the sofa, who had a heart attack this morning, is his critical patient. Freyberger comes every other day, at such times also examining others who are sick. He brings reassuring news of Kristina; on several occasions he has also visited Septemvir Utca; Mama and Rere are well, their cellar is quite bombproof and Grubi is with them too.

Freyberger laughingly shakes his hat free of plaster dust, as though he had only taken cover from a summer shower. He writes the prescription and again issues out into the rain of fire.

A neighborhood pharmacy still functions, but prescriptions are valid only if countersigned by the local Arrow Cross command. The city, tossed onto the rubbish heap, is held together only by bureaucracy's tenacious tendrils, as a huge cracked pot with thin wire.

Freyberger leaves the slip of paper in my hands, though doubtless one or another of the men would volunteer to take the urgent prescription to the pharmacy. It was not my heroism, but a matter of cellar psychology, that such requests must be avoided, even if only because one's conscience receives an everlasting wound if the individual fails to return.

Four blocks away, I find the Arrow Cross command post, in a thoroughly bombproof shelter of course. The colonel peruses the prescription quite a while.

"Is this Dr. Freyberger a Jew?"

"I don't know. We are Christians."

The colonel tears up the prescription and snarls:

"You should know that we don't sign any Jewish doctor's prescriptions."

I reach home in a rain of bombs, but amazingly unafraid. I feel absolutely certain that God is watching over us, that Zizi and Mihály also will survive these times. No news of Mihály, all I know is that along with other political prisoners, he too was taken westward. At least there is no bombing there.

Twelve noon. The cannonade is stilled, and the bombing too. But in the silence one misses the midday peal of church bells, which the Pope some four hundred years ago decreed throughout the world to commemorate our Turk-vanquishing Hunyadi's victories. Lunchtime lasts but half

275

an hour. Soviet planes gulp their gasoline sandwiches and rush right back to their desks, the snow-clouded sky, where they are writing our doom.

Toward four in the afternoon, when darkness is fast falling, the sky quiets down again. But these are the hours when the "military police" go raiding: young hoodlums sporting green armbands over ragged mufti, the straps of heavy rifles dragging at their narrow shoulders. Formidable figures these, intoxicated with the death-dealing authority given into their hands.

In our district each cellar sets a guard to watch the street. At a whistle Hamor and six other men jump up and, crawling on their bellies, vanish through a cleft in the cellar wall. In front of the hole the others quickly shove the sofa on which lies the old lady with heart trouble.

But not everywhere is the approach of military police received by whistle signals. Last week, in the third house from us, a violent revolver battle took place on the dark staircase, because not everyone is ready to yield his life for nothing.

This time our cellar escapes the raid, the human rats again creep forth, first Hamor's bekerchiefed head appears in the dark hole, and at this the children always squeal with laughter. Hamor takes his place at the chessboard as if he has merely been called to the telephone. "My move?" he asks, though only last night he noted on a slip of paper the causes of death awaiting him, as his remaining chattels, seven in all. Shell, bomb, desertion, spotted typhus (he too swarms with lice now), resistance movement, famine, and seventh, his disregard for the grave-digging summons which, under pain of death, ordered every able-bodied man to report each evening at seven before Arrow Cross headquarters to inter that day's bombing victims. Hamor, whose long figure would be recognized at once, wants to spare his associates the labor of digging his grave. "I am always think-of others," he said.

Six in the evening, supper time. Beans cooked with sunflower oil keep the spark of life in us. Uncle András with his wife has occupied the head of the table from the very first evening, in view of the fact that one of his ancestors, Otto Morva, in 1093 espoused King Bela I's daughter, whom historical sources diversely call Eufenia, Buzilla and Odola. But these matters still have not lost their significance: the old butler each evening ceremoniously sets the table for them with crested silver and Meissen porcelain. Aunt Marie opens her enormous crocodile leather reticule and counts out tiny pearls on the tablecloth with the air of a jewel merchant. The old butler cooks the numbered pearls in lightly salted water and serves them on a silver platter. The pearls of course are rice, but supper consists only of a walnut-sized portion. Since five new tenants have arrived in the past few days, and many eat standing, the princely couple and their long mealtime ceremony incite an air of mute rebellion.

"Uncle András," I remark diplomatically, "by now all this ceremony, I think, is superfluous."

Uncle András has some sort of liver trouble. His dark yellow visage looks up at me in sudden irritation.

"Would you have us sit on the ground and eat with our hands, like dogs?"

Hamor replies in my stead, with polite objectivity.

"Your High Excellency, may I be permitted to observe that dogs have no hands."

Great laughter arises, but Uncle András shouts rudely at me, not at Hamor:

"Don't poke your nose into our affairs!"

A man dressed like a workman steps to the table, officiously takes from before them the Meissen crockery and dashes it against the wall piece by piece. Uncle András and Aunt Marie, mutely maintaining their dignity, rise and disappear into their bedroom—the small vegetable cellar. Deep silence follows their departure; I can't help thinking of the tale told me by my old French governess, whose grandfather was a footman in Marquis Raverney's castle. *Perdreaux truffés*, partridge with truffles, was the dinner, when unexpectedly the Great Revolution burst into the room, some ripped the cloth from the table, sent the dishes crashing, fired the lace curtains with the candles . . .

piercing screams . . . I feel that in our cellar too, the Great Revolution has appeared.

Hamor, hatchet and big kitchen knife in hand, calls out to a man:

"Come on, let's go zebra hunting."

This sounds bizarre. The explanation is that the cellar dwellers, like vultures, each night descend on equine carcasses frozen rock-solid, working with saws and hatchets in the dark. Hamor last night lugged home an entire haunch of horse meat, which here in the candle light to his immense surprise proved to be a leg of zebra. It made a wonderful roast. We sent a taste to tenants of the neighboring cellar, who responded by sending us ostrich-cock stew. The bombed-out inmates of the zoo have scattered throughout the city.

Ten o'clock. The candles go out. The night is calm. Only an occasional shell whines through the air, a rather reassuring sound, and once in a while a few bombs thump, but we have grown so used to that, we don't even awaken.

In such fashion the night passes. Then in the morning the same thing begins all over again.

Not exactly the same. Every morning is more and more horrifying. There are hours when I am not quite sure about my sanity.

There are passages in Zia's diary which clearly show her mental disturbance. These lines are written in the style she used in that fateful night when the war broke out. These passages sometimes sound like philosophical or religious meditations, sometimes like deep prayers, sometimes like wild curses. Needless to say these passages were full of Mihály, about whom she knew nothing.

In the first days of January the eastern suburbs were the scene of tank battles, while the Russian infantry advanced below ground, breaking through the cellar walls of adjoining tenements. The cellar dwellers greeted with a roar of triumph the ice-hued fur cap of the Soviet soldier emerging from the wall; he could hardly disengage himself from their embrace. Waving his revolver before him like a flashlight he smilingly asked:

278

Nemetsky? . . . and the response resounded in a joyous chorus: *Nyet Nemetsky!* . . . No Germans here!

Naturally, liberation did not everywhere occur in such friendly fashion. There were still SS nests in some houses and the German military communiqué, had there been any, would have read: "In the bathroom we carried out elastic maneuvers with a view to deceiving the enemy, but the southern sector of the kitchen is still firmly held by the Third Army."

The Inner City remained under heavy bombardment, but in the outer boulevards came and went in all directions the sleighs and large Soviet trucks, which were directed by big-bosomed Soviet soldier girls with little colored flags in their hands. Their faces were apple-red from the cold, their blond hair curling from beneath military caps, and so briskly did they execute the motions of traffic police that they seemed to be dancing to the wintry music of the jingling horse-drawn sleighs. The latter were hooded Russian troikas. Budapest, dressed in a thick white mantle of furry snow, had changed into Tobolsk. Only the smoke-blackened skeletons of gutted houses remained of the days of Franz Joseph and here and there a corpse still obstinately extended a rigid arm and clenched fist from the snow.

On January 18 the Pest side was all in Russian hands, but the Danube with its breaking ice-pack and the wrecked steel bridge-towers held them back. Concentrated artillery fire and uninterrupted bombing showered the Buda sector for another three weeks. Under the colossal ruins of the Royal Palace it would have been difficult to find the pencils which, sharpened to long points and in military array, through a quarter of a century had awaited their master on the Regent's desk, which had to be bright as a jewel, just as Franz Joseph's desk had been. The aged emperor had died sitting in his chair, with his last feeble gestures he still brushed the wine-red baize of his desk, as if yet seeking to cleanse the world of something.

Early in February the sporadic battles shifted westward and, along the upper Danube, reached the vicinity of the Cave.

It may have been four o'clock in the afternoon. Marja, Kazi, Joska Kurdi and Erzsi stood on the hilltop, whence on the nearby, wooded snowy slopes they watched the fate not only of the Cave, but of all Hungary, in fact all Eastern Europe, un-

279

folding with the classic brevity of an ancient folk-song or perhaps with the conciseness whereby the few symbols of a physics equation express the energy of the universe.

On the snow-blanketed plain a few bundles of cornstalks showed black, like the small solitary tents of an expedition on polar ice fields. The grayish winter dusk began to settle on the white terrain. Nowhere nearby was man or beast visible, but up on the hill, which wore the dense furry jacket of a tan oak forest, arose a peculiar stirring, as if the trunks of trees had turned to men, and their branches to human arms and black rifle barrels. Upon the Soviet infantry, surging forward in ice-gray, tall fur caps, the solitary cornstalk tent *pak-pak-pak-pak*—loosed a swift spray of machine-gun fire. Like mice the Soviet soldiers scampered back and once more turned into motionless tree trunks in the forests.

The cornstalk bundle, in a great arc, swept the void terrain with a final round of fire—probably the last of the ammunition, because from beneath the cornstalks crept one—just one—German soldier and, hoisting the machine-gun to his shoulder, he set off with slow deliberate steps in the opposite direction as though, with hoe and spade upon his shoulder, he was plodding homeward from work in the fields. Not looking back, taking no cover in his retreat, his slow, tired and infinitely melancholy steps expressed that it was all the same to him now. As he vanished beyond the slope it was as if, in a sphere grown timeless, he were definitively surrendering Eastern Europe.

His departure was followed by long minutes of silence, then the motionless tree trunks through some wizardry again turned into Soviet soldiers; their short boots sank all the way into the deep snow as they descended the hill and in evergrowing multitudes wheeled toward the village, which awaited them without a shot. These tiny mud-brick cottages fallen into deep apathy were no longer much concerned with whether their miserable taxes henceforth would be due Hungarian feudal lords in the form of warm beds and women, wheat and the sweat of labor, or to Turks, Germans or Russians in the form of blood and gold.

It was growing dark, but in the hush of the February twilight the forests of more distant hills also stirred, and Soviet infantry poured from all directions.

The next day at noon Joska flung wide the door of Marja's room:

"The Russians are here!"

They rushed down to the shores of the subterranean lake. The Cave's stone portal opened and the boat guided by Slobo Tuykovich glided in with three Russian officers, Grubi, and an unfamiliar civilian. When they glimpsed the tenants of the Cave, they all stood up and as the boat tipped beneath them, laughingly took hold of each other. On the strong, padded shoulders of the Russian officers the gold epaulets laughed broadly too. Marja's hand caught at her throat as though striving to choke back her sobs, then she raised her hand and shouted:

"*Da zdrastvuiet Sovietsky Soyuz! Da zdrastvuiet Krasnaya Armiya!* Long live the Soviet Union! Long live the Red Army!"

The cliff hollows threw back her voice, even from the hilltop an echo cried: *Da zdrastvuiet.*

From behind the boat, through the open portal flooded blindingly the sun-drenched radiance of the snowy landscape. In this sharp back-lighting the faces seemed black. Perhaps for this reason, or because of her great emotion, Marja in the first moments did not notice the civilian among the Russian officers.

It was Maxim Narokov. Pale and mute he stood in the boat, and the tears streaming over his thin face completely filled the two deep folds by the corners of his mouth.

Chapter 19

The Ruins and the Dead. Russians in Budapest.

Zia's Letter to Ostie

Budapest, February 20, 1945

DEAR OSTIE:

The American Legation is already in Debrecen. From Andrew Szanto I hear you have reached London and are due in Budapest within the next few weeks. Yesterday I sent you a telegram with the following text: "Kristina, Rere and Freyberger died. Mama, Zizi and I are well. No news of Mihály yet. Zia."

Now I dispatch this letter by American courier, and first of all write you of our dead.

On New Year's Eve the "military police" took Freyberger and seven others from the ghetto house. Kristina, in slippers and nightgown, followed them to the street where, running up and down in the dark, she screamed for the police—unaware, poor soul, that the police were non-existent. She kept crying for help, until finally the "military police," consisting of thieving murderous scum, silenced her with a few bullets.

They herded Freyberger and the other Jewish tenants, scantily clad, just as they had been dragged from bed, along Klotild Utca toward the bank of the Danube, whence a little later came the crackling of rifle fire. By next morning many corpses had washed against the wreckage of the bridges. The wounded clung to floating ice, and a few writhed ashore at the lower freight landing.

I spoke with the janitor, who next morning found Kristina before the house, clad only in a chemise. It was definitely she, because the janitor noticed the eleven-pointed crown monogram on the champagne-colored silk chemise. He said that her legs, naked to the thighs and frozen stiff, extended from the deep snow, the groomed toenails painted a dark mauve. I did not shiver during this macabre description; I vividly saw Kristina before my eyes—even then she looked like a human orchid among the other dead in the street. The janitor could not tell me where they took her, or where they buried her. He gave me her belongings which he found in the tiny room where she lived with István and four other unknown people in the overcrowded ghetto house. Her belongings were so much Kristina: a crocodile toilet case which she once had received from King Charles as a Christmas gift, and a large valise full of her manuscripts, and quills she herself fashioned from the wing-feathers of eagles. Now I can reveal the secret of her life which she told nobody but me. You remember that in 1928 she became a member of the La Fontaine Academy because she had translated so beautifully all the poems of Li-Pu-Ten, the great Chinese poet of the Cha-ong Dynasty. One academician wrote a long essay about Li-Pu-Ten's poetry and biography, based on Kristina's data, and in the last fifteen years all the Sunday editions of the papers published a Li-Pu-Ten poem, translated by Kristina. Last fall she confessed to me that there never had been a Li-Pu-Ten, not even a Cha-ong Dynasty. "You know," she said, "I am a great writer but whenever I wrote under my own name, they undeservedly praised or ridiculed me because, alas, I was born a countess."

Among her manuscripts I found the last three Li-Pu-Ten poems. One was titled "The Firerats," the other "The tail of a walking pheasant tenderly touches the lips of a violet in the deep forest," and the third: "From the gravestone of Li-Pu-Ten," and it read:

> I had a tiger: Ton-Soh-Tee;
> He played with me, he slept with me,
> He was my guard—oh, Ton-Soh-Tee!
> But came a beast, and ate my heart,
> My bones and hair: So-cie-ty!

Poor Kristina! I plan to erect a column in the Ararat wood with these lines carved on it above her empty grave.

Rere died a fine death. The cellars of Septemvir Utca were jammed, and Johy had taken all the food supplies with him, but the most serious lack was water, because nowhere did the water mains function. In the hail of bombs Rere carried water from an old well at the foot of the hill. As Grubi tells us, even then he would not part with his cutaway and top hat, and in his hands were the two great bronze urns that used to stand in the anteroom. Papa, you remember, looked upon them as the greatest treasures of the palace, because they descended from the days of the Huns and were of Ephthalite origin. Rere with these two great bronze urns in his hands strode with his usual, gentle idiotic grin amid the ruins, unconcerned how many bombs fell around him, because he was oblivious to danger. Now too, his pockets were weighed down by the countless keys he pilfered from everywhere. In the days preceding his death he made friends with a wounded horse standing near the wall. Each day the pool of blood around the lonely horse grew larger. Rere gave the horse water, and even his slender food ration. On the afternoon of February 4, a bomb killed them both. Next day the grave-diggers buried Rere and the horse in the deep bomb-crater.

Poor Rere, who in his lifetime afforded us so many mirthful moments, I suspect will play a joke on posterity too. If, centuries hence, they dig up this grave and some overzealous young archeologist happens upon the great Ephthalite bronze urns near the equine and human bones, he will quite justifiably relate them to an ancient grave from the time of Attila, and the keys rusted to shapelessness he will regard as Hun or Avar ornaments. So much is certain, that during a thousand years Rere alone among the Dukays had himself interred like our onetime ancestor, Ordony, who in accordance with the customs of Asiatic chieftains, descended to the grave with his favorite steed, ornate weapons, implements and barbaric adornments.

The funeral pyre was provided by the ancient shingle roof of the Septemvir Utca palace—the ruins of the palace

284

were still smoking on February 14, when I first got there. The family archives burned to cinders too; in the crackle of the flames the rusty words of goose quills spoke for the last time. As I picture it, Corot's *Woman in Purple* noticed with a shriek the flames already licking her dress, but vainly sought escape from the golden frame.

The following Saturday I journeyed to Ararat. The castle was struck by neither bomb nor shell, it is quite intact, but only from without. Oh, Ostie, if you could see the inside!

The German officers had carefully looted the rugs and the more valuable paintings, art treasures and bibliographic rarities, leaving to the incoming Soviet soldiers only the heavier pieces of furniture, and a few dead and gravely wounded.

When I arrived, two villagers with axes were chopping up for firewood the four-hundred-year-old carved oak door of the chapel. You wouldn't recognize the park. The winter has been severe, and even from the most distant hamlets people came here for firewood, cutting down the oldest oaks and chestnut trees too, carting away on hand-sleds even those tree-jewels whose slips Grandpa brought from London's Kew Gardens.

First I entered the great red salon, which Soviet soldiers had turned into a camp kitchen. They had built their fires on the lovely star-inlaid parquet floor. The white ceiling, as you can imagine, is black with soot. Among the former staff I found only an old castellan, who told me in a whisper that when the Russians came in, they also dug up that part of the cellar which he had walled in from the Germans. You can imagine the festival when they discovered this liquor cache. The people of the village were there too, dancing to harmonica music punctuated by machine-gun volleys, for our ancestors in leopard skins or knee-length hose were massacred several times over. They slashed Mama's Lenbach portrait with bayonets, while Gwen's portrait above the piano was slit to shreds by someone with a knife, but Papa's portrait, and Garibaldi's on the first floor, were left untouched, probably because Papa's hunting coat is red, and the Italian hero of liberty, too, wears his famous red shirt in the picture.

There was hustle and bustle in the camp kitchen; the Russian soldier-girl cooks, very likable and gay, set the chamber pots on the table—they are porcelain, have a handle, so naturally they took them for culinary utensils—beating eggs and kneading dough in them with a will. I didn't know whether to laugh or cry. Under the Germans we only wept, now at least sometimes we can laugh too.

The Russian command posts help in every way. Marshal Voroshilov himself saw to it that my Buda flat should receive a priority in window glass. From them I received the first food packages for Mama too. All this I owe mainly to Maxim Narokov, the Soviet Legation counselor, whose marriage with Marja is set for next month.

No news of Mihály yet. We only know that the fleeing Hungarian Arrow Crossists, retreating farther westward, took their prisoners with them. Maxim has promised to investigate, but he also says the Arrow Cross gang would rather surrender to American troops. I want to ask you to take all necessary steps at American headquarters, so I can have news of Mihály as soon as possible.

Poor Mama, too, very much awaits your coming.

Mr. Gruber's Letter to Ostie Dukay

Your Excellency!

I am likewise making use of an opportunity to write via courier through the courtesy of Sgt. Szanto. Her Excellency Countess Zia showed me her report—alas, I must report more sad news which I have not yet dared to tell the Countess. Mr. Maxim Narokov confidentially informed me that he already has learned the fate of our poor friend, Mihály Ursi. The fleeing Arrow Cross government did not drag all its prisoners to Germany, some were tried by drumhead courts martial and executed. At dawn on December 31 of last year, in the courtyard of an elementary school at Sopronköhida, they hanged Mihály Ursi. Maxim Narokov showed me the written deposition of the two eye-witnesses

286

who saw the execution from a window. Your Excellency can imagine that it will be the most difficult moment of my life when I have to tell Countess Zia.

After this, I can only write of lesser things, if indeed we can account as a lesser thing the first complete Russian occupation in Hungary's entire history. I cannot yet form a final and clear picture of these great events, but I think some details may interest Your Excellency.

What are the Russians like? That isn't an easy question, since even today in the Soviet Union more than a hundred languages are spoken, and among Soviet soldiers are Ukrainians, White Russians, Black Russians, Kirgizes, Uzbeks, Tartars, Chouvases—some the finest of men, true heroes and brilliantly cultured, others black-handed bandits, and still others gentle, but barely above brute intelligence. With my own eyes I saw two young Russian soldiers climbing steps on all fours—from the great plains the surging front had swept them directly here. Back home they were acquainted with the ladder to the loft, but had never seen a house of more than one story.

From the west the Arrow Cross radio still can be heard occasionally, and it claims that Soviet troops indiscriminately loot and burn, massacring everyone as they go. This is not true. I must say that the average Soviet soldier exhibits much warmheartedness and differs from the Germans mainly in that he doesn't murder—not systematically, that is, only exceptionally, chiefly when very drunk. Here is a case, for example. In the last two days of the siege the Russians already held the Septemvir Utca palace and the hall on the ground floor had been transformed by the Russian major into a stable for his horses. The house next door was still in German hands, in the narrow street machine-gun and hand grenade battles took place at a few yards' distance. The Russian major was a very kindly man, he immediately had food cooked for the starved tenants of the crowded cellar, his soldiers adored him. The following evening, when he went to the stable to feed the horses sugar lumps from his hand, a German soldier, who had succeeded in creeping in under cover of night and hiding in the litter, poked his revolver from the straw and shot the Russian major dead. We were in great peril, because appearances would indicate that one of the cellar tenants had let the German in and hidden him. The Soviet soldiers were already starting down the steps with their tommy-guns to shoot everyone in the cellar, when a woman who spoke Croatian threw herself on her knees before them and, wringing her hands, swore that the cellar tenants were innocent. The enraged Soviet soldiers, halted by this supplication, turned and left, and no one was harmed. I don't know what would have happened to us had they been Germans.

The Soviet soldier respects the aged, and is very fond of children; in occupied Hungarian villages I would often see a formidable-looking Russian soldier with a tommy-gun, grimy Hungarian children hanging from both his fists, and still smaller fry clutching his long earth-brown soldier's cape, as they would their mothers' skirt.

I had often heard of the Russians' gift for languages, but it's really amazing how well these Soviet soldiers learned Hungarian in just a few weeks. At this point I believe the Russian occupation represents a danger. For a thousand years the German sea couldn't engulf Hungary because, in periods of oppression, German soldiers and officials never learned a word of Hungarian. I mention only a single example from the recent past. Last summer, during the fighting, a German patrol appeared in one of the villages. Their leader, wanting to smoke, shouted at one of the peasants: *Haben Sie Zündhölzer?* Got a match? The peasant ran in fright, the German seized him by the arm: *Zündhölzer!* Matches! The peasant's son, coming to his father's defense from behind, felled the German, more out of fright than anything else—which led to dreadful slaughter, the Germans exterminating half the village.

With Russians such things don't happen, because they are amazingly clever at expressing themselves through pantomime and sign language. At the first big reception, I had the good luck of being presented to Marshal Voroshilov. He knows not a word of Hungarian, and I no word of Russian. We had a most engaging conversation, poked each other with our forefinger, wrote circles and rectangles into the air—with our hands, legs, eyebrows, the tips of our noses and our pursing lips incessantly active, we even exchanged pleasant compliments, only the word *pisatyel* forced me to turn to the interpreter: *pisatyel, pisatyel,* I couldn't guess what this *pisatyel* was until it turned out that the Marshal had taken me for a writer. *Pisatyel* means writer. The Marshal then boasted how greatly the Soviet people honored culture; just go, he said, and ask even the simplest of Soviet soldiers, and he will know all about Pushkin, Tolstoy, Gorki, and even Mayakovsky.

This information saved my life two days later. Toward evening three Russian soldiers approached me along the deserted street; a patrol, I thought, already extending my excellent Russian language credentials, but the one in the middle knocked my hand aside, seized the muffler at my throat and began choking me, the second pressed a huge carving knife to my stomach, while the fingers of the third rummaged through my pockets like wolves' teeth, and in the meantime I was turning greenish-blue from the choking. *"Pisatyel!"* I gasped on catching a breath of air, for my assailant was drunk and sometimes loosened his grip as he swayed. And when I for the second time gasped the word *pisatyel,* the Russian holding the huge carving knife to my stomach, knocked down the one who was choking me. Over this cultural question all three launched into a fist-fight, and I took to my heels.

In possession of Marshal Voroshilov's kind information, the spell of culture in a second instance saved not only my life, but that of others too. One afternoon Countess Zia came to visit her mother. Countess Menti still lives in the cellar of the wrecked palace. We were conversing quietly when from the stairway came the sound of an accordion.

I was terribly frightened. Sad to say, the Arrow Cross radio tells the truth about the raping of women. I knew that these Russians went prowling in groups of three: the accordionist drowned out the screams, the second Russian held a tommy-gun at the head of the assaulted woman,

289

while the third attended to the business in hand; then accordion and tommy-gun would fraternally change hands as they shared the booty. Three such drunken Russians showed up in our cellar, their intentions unmistakable. I confess, Your Excellency, that these were the worst moments of my life, because I knew that if they attacked lovely Countess Zia I would fight with them, like Baron Ubi, whom such a tommy-gun shot to ribbons when they raped his wife. Countess Menti would also have had to view all this. I won't continue, but Your Excellency can imagine how horribly the great and happy liberation would have ended for us.

I sprang to my feet, began embracing the three drunken Russians and kept shouting: "Hey, Pushkin! Hey, Tolstoy! Hey, Gorki! *Pisatyel, pisatyel!*"

This was somewhat as when a man suddenly squats down before huge attacking dogs in order to confuse them. The three Russians stared at me with bulging eyes as I tossed my arms and danced around them, exhausting my entire knowledge of Russian: "Hey, Gogol! Hey, Dostoevsky! Hey, Turgenev!"

They turned and slowly departed. Minutes later, from a neighboring cellar unacquainted with culture's magic spell, came a woman's terrified scream.

It may perhaps be interesting for me to mention how Russian authorities act in such matters. I made friends with a green-capped NKVD lieutenant who had several times interrogated me, and who spoke German fairly well. We were walking together on the street, when from one of the cellars came the usual screams. We both rushed there, he with revolver in hand. The helpless woman had already been trampled to the ground, ringed by three Russians—accordion, tommy-gun, and the third Russian with his pants already rolled down. The lieutenant disarmed them in a matter of seconds and stood all three against the wall, handcuffed. He summoned the house superintendent and the terrified witnesses, inquiring whether the three Russians had robbed. The reply was negative, they had only attacked the woman. Once again the lieutenant asked in a loud voice: had they robbed, because if so, he would shoot them on the spot. Again the reply, no, they hadn't robbed. The lieutenant unshackled the Russians, berated them and chased them away.

Later I asked the lieutenant how it could be that robbing a watch or a small ring merited instant death, but robbery of womanly honor merely a few angry words. The lieutenant did not reply, because these NKVD men only ask, never answer, and won't even tell you their names.

Considering this matter, I recalled hospital statistics from the first world war. Russian wounded recovered much faster than the Europeans. Autopsies revealed that the intestinal tract of the Russians generally was some twenty inches longer than that of men from the West. The Russian—speaking of the great masses—is unfamiliar with appendicitis or disorders of the heart, stomach and nerves. As Alexis Carrel writes in his interesting book, *Man the Unknown,* the American people by elevators, vacuum cleaners, innumerable cars and higher refinements of civilization have been deprived of all healthy bodily movement, the murderous pursuit of time and money undermining heart and brain. According to my physician friends the Russians, on their much lower level of civilization, have retained a great deal of their pristine animal health. Their hair is thick, their eyes keen—I haven't seen a single bald or bespectacled Russian soldier—with their teeth they can bend nails, and the primary sexual characteristics, men's genitals and women's breasts, are far more developed than in Europe, or beyond the sea. I hope Your Excellency won't take offense at this.

A primitive Russian soldier's conception of a woman's honor differs totally from ours; some of them belong to tribes from the tundras or Kirgiz plains, where the host, along with raw frozen fish or mare's milk, also offers the body of his daughter or wife to the wanderer or journeying stranger who happens into his tent.

Asia's wild sexual hunger rages in the Soviet soldiers of occupation. A woman is the first booty they seek. But one cannot generalize here either. I saw an older Russian private knock down his own drunken major and tearfully clasp the molested girl to his breast: "Don't be afraid, *barishnya*, I have a fifteen-year-old daughter too." Believe me, Your Excellency, there's nothing wrong with the Russian people. I have grown very fond of them. Never shall I forget that moment, half an hour after the Russians took our cellar, when a solitary Russian soldier strayed in. To judge by his black hands he must have been a farm worker back home. A dirty bag hung from his shoulder. He looked about at the frightened sallow faces of the cellar dwellers—reached into his bag and placed his bread ration, a whole loaf, on the corner of the table, then left. The gesture of his hand, his glance, confused and abashed, were so touching that tears sprang to my eyes. Everyone gives what he can—I rated this dried-out loaf of soldier's bread more highly than the Rockefeller Foundation, because Rockefeller was not a Ukrainian farmhand, his village was not burned, his family not exterminated by the enemy. I should also add that this "Lord's Supper" scene occurred on the first day, when the Russian command had granted besieging Ukrainian troops twenty-four hours' free looting.

The looting usually began with these words: *Chahsee, chahsee!* The *chahsee* excited them most, be it diamond wrist watch or cheap alarm clock, just so long as it was a *chahsee*. Even yet, you can see them as they block traffic on the sidewalk, squatting in a circle, bunching their heads together and showing the public only their rumps, like American football players. Breathlessly they watch as one of their lucky companions, rusty penknife in hand, dissects the mechanism of a Schaffhausen watch. Sometimes for a *chahsee* they'll kill a man, at other times they may give half a side of bacon for an old pocket-watch minus a spring. Someone told me that the sole watch factory of the Soviet Union, with its two hundred million people, was also engaged in munitions manufacture during the war. It happened at a movie theater in Szolnok, which was showing the Teheran Conference, that one scene portrayed Generalissimo Stalin's glance accidentally straying toward President Roosevelt's wrist watch, as the President's hand rested on the table. Spontaneously the whole Hungarian audience laughingly shouted: *"Chahsee! Chahsee! Chahsee!"* The performance was stopped, Russian officers present chased out the enthusiastic Hungarians with their revolvers. When I related this to Her Excellency Countess Menti, she said that Uncle Joe at Teheran stole not only Roosevelt's wrist watch but Churchill's big cigars, too. I earnestly beg Your Excellency, when you write, to be so gracious as to warn Her Excellency the Countess to refrain from such remarks. At her advanced age she no longer realizes how times have changed. In some matters she is extremely naïve. During the days of German occupation too, when the palace swarmed with Count Johy's important German guests, she continually made comments about Hitler that had me trembling, and she won't heed my advice.

In conclusion I mention only two cases related to looting and forced labor. In the country, where Russian authorities exercise less control, Soviet soldiers in some villages draw even ragged boots from the feet of poor peasants and take every last animal, even their baby rabbits. Thefts occur in Pest too, but comically, as in Jani Hamor's case. He had succeeded in saving his winter coat, in which he was promenading down the street, when a Russian with a tommy-gun yelled at him: *Idyee suda!* He peeled the fine opossum coat off Hamor and when Hamor desperately gesticulated that he would freeze in the bitter cold, *zima, zima* . . . the Russian took off his own filthy army cape, even helped Hamor put it on, then with the opossum coat on his arm quickly vanished, lest a green-capped NKVD man lay eyes on him. Hamor strolling sadly homeward in the thin tattered army cape, put his freezing hands in its pockets . . . and couldn't believe his eyes. Three diamond wrist watches! In another pocket, two large gold cigarette cases. Rings and ropes of pearls in the inner pockets. The absent-minded Russian!

The Arrow Cross radio tells the truth in stating that the Russians make every able-bodied man in Budapest do forced labor. But I approve of these measures, because after the liberation, groups in Pest met the challenge of building temporary bridges across the Danube by staging innumerable bridge parties. No one wanted to cart away even the rubble that clogged the streets. On the other hand, it is untrue that they repay forced labor only with rifle butts. Here, for example, is my case. I too was beckoned to the curb by a Russian with a tommy-gun, who asked me to help him lift a beer barrel into his jeep. I lent a hand. He reached into his stuffed pockets and gave me a ten-thousand-pengö tip. Perhaps, at some bank in Pest, he had large accounts which he had just "withdrawn." It may also be that he was ignorant of the value of Hungarian money. In any case the fact is that not even Count Dupi of blessed memory ever gave such a tip to the waiters in the Café Parisien.

All things considered, it is extremely difficult to give a unified and objective picture of the Russian occupation.

Of myself: having doffed my Arrow Cross uniform, cut it with scissors into tiny pieces and flushed it down the toilet, I joined the Social Democratic Party. To my mind only this party has a future in Hungary. With my present political connections I have been able to save much estate property. But it would be desirable nonetheless for Your Excellency to come to Budapest, the sooner the better.

The new land reform has gone into effect, in accordance with which owners of more than a thousand acres of land were left not a single acre. Ararat Estate's ten thousand acres were all distributed in five- and ten-acre parcels, and the landless peasantry already have taken over. On the other hand, the new law left former owners in possession of forests, industrial plants and apartment houses. Thus Your Excellency, after the Princes Eszterházy, is still the richest man in ravaged Hungary, though among the apartment houses only the one in Peter Dukay Street is in tolerable shape—bombs gutted the others.

I did not succeed in saving any of the art treasures. Count Johy, to the last moment, favored me with his complete confidence and in fleeing to the West asked my advice as to what he should take along. I said of every original that it was a counterfeit, of every counterfeit that it was an original, so he took only counterfeits with him. Alas, I acted foolishly, because in the conflagration of the palace everything perished, all the Courbets, Delacroix, Renoirs, Grecos, Munkácsys, Corot's *Woman in Purple* too. On the other hand, I was successful in saving the very valuable Ispahan carpet fragment, because I took it down to the cellar, folded it and used it for a pillow, for which I now crave Your Excellency's indulgence.

Anxiously awaiting Your Excellency's arrival and offering my secretarial services for the future too, respectfully kissing the hand of Her Excellency Countess Gwendolyn, I remain Your Excellency's most humble servant,

MARTON GRUBER

Chapter 20

The Brief History of Four Years.

Mr. Gruber, already seventy-two years old and with even his doughty heart feeling the strain of the past few years, gave a friend the difficult task of telling Zia the tidings of her husband's death. This friend was a doctor, so that one might be directly at hand if Zia fainted.

Zia did not faint. Though taking cognizance of the very circuitously and delicately presented news with deathly pallor, she believed nothing of what the doctor said. She didn't tell eight-year-old Zizi either.

Next day the papers devoted long columns to Mihály Ursi's memory. The Stargazers, who in place of the bomb-blasted Café Gugger had pitched camp in an undamaged room of the former German Legation, organized a committee to canvass funds for a statue of Mihály Ursi, ". . . martyr of democracy, hero of the Hungarian resistance under the name of Ursa Major. Born 1900, died 1945." A Stargazer-sculptor, whose enthusiasm was much greater than his talent, finished the clay model in twenty-four hours without sleeping.

"His waist is as long as his legs should be," whispered Hamor to Grubi.

"It resembles Goebbels much more than poor Mihály," said Grubi with a mournful face.

Among the committee members there were a few old miners and peasants, and their leader, following an ancient tradition, scattered a handful of wheat on the head of the hero. Ten days later, when the artist exhibited the model to the Mayor of Budapest and removed the wet linen covering, everybody was dumbfounded. Bushy green hair grew out of the clay head of the hero. For various reasons the fund-raising bogged down. They had to be satisfied with the town council's adoption of their suggestion:

on Mount Swabian, now Mount Freedom, in the vicinity of the National Institute of Astronomy, lovely Bear Avenue was re-christened Mihály Ursi Avenue.

At the ceremonies dedicating the new street-markers, where Hamor delivered a beautiful but, alas, overlong oration, Zia did not appear. She did not even reply to letters of condolence, but received only her most intimate friends, and listened wordlessly to expressions of sympathy, as though fearing that some new bit of information might deprive her of the blind hope wherein she had obstinately entrenched herself.

We cannot find any other explanation for Zia's strange behavior than telepathy.

On April 4, Ostie Dukay sent the following wire from Salzburg:

"According to information deemed reliable, though not yet confirmed, Mihály was picked up in Hochberg Forest near Linz last week by an American patrol."

That same evening another telegram came from Ostie:

"Mihály is alive. Letters follow."

There was no telephone communication yet between Budapest and the outside world.

The Arrow Cross judge advocate, [wrote Mihály in his first letter to Zia] read us our death sentences at seven in the evening. We proceeded to a room in the elementary school designated as the death cell. From ten to midnight the town again was heavily bombed. We sprawled there in our clothing, sleeplessly, but without speaking. I thought of Tolstoy's words: "If you would know a regime, learn to know its prisons." During more than four months of captivity I had ample time to size up these white-livered scoundrels.

When at six in the morning they summoned our first companion we didn't look at him—only heard his steps as they led him away. Twenty minutes later, I was the second to be called. Don't ask me what I saw when they brought me to the courtyard, still misty and dark. The "eye-witnesses" probably confused me with this companion of ours.

At the moment they stood me before the judge advo-

297

cate's table, Russian bombers again appeared above us and straightway all differences between judge, warder and prisoner ceased, everyone dashed for shelter in the thunder. It was frightful how everything crackled and roared around us. A blast hurled me as far as the fence. I staggered to my feet and in the cloud of smoke and dust and hailing bombs began running without knowing where. When later I reached an open field, in deathly exhaustion I lay down in the deep snow, as though it were the finest of silken beds.

I reached Linz on foot. When we meet I'll tell you at length about my days in hiding, now only this: Never shall I forget the good-heartedness of the Austrian peasants. They were deceptively surly when at night I tapped at the windows of their tiny farmhouses; they hardly spoke to me, but gave me food. They did not ask if I was Nazi or Communist, in their eyes I was only a human being who was fleeing somewhere from something. Only the deepest stratum of the people knows the ultimate meaning of forgiveness, which they've learned from life's burden. I vowed to become a vegetarian. In the ammonia-scented little barns the warmth of bovine bodies saved me from freezing. In the daytime I didn't dare budge, because no one could say what troops were in the vicinity, nor had I any inkling whether the fleeing Arrow Cross court martial was before me or behind. Only after dark did I set forth, without a goal, but ever westward.

On March 31 the sky was clear and the full moon shone almost as bright as day on the snow-covered forest. It was extremely cold in the Austrian mountains, but I was pretty warmly dressed in all sorts of rags, my tattered shoes were wrapped in old bags tied with string. With my beard of many weeks I must have been an alarming sight. So famished was I, that I could hardly drag myself further, when in the wintry silence of the forest I heard footsteps. Scarcely daring to breathe, I drew behind a bush.

In the bright moonlight I caught sight of three American soldiers. I rose and, holding both hands high, cried in English: "I am your friend!"

Never did a cry break forth from deeper in my heart

298

than that: "I am your friend!" I was unable to say more. With barely enough strength to walk, I staggered along as they held my arms on either side, supporting me till we reached the command post, and I confess that my tears flowed silently.

At the end of April 1945, on an American military plane, Ostie Dukay brought Mihály Ursi back to Budapest. They arrived in secret.

Obviously Mihály Ursi had committed a serious blunder in staying alive—at least so far as his political career was concerned—because had he fallen victim to the Nazis, it is certain that Bear Avenue still would be Mihály Ursi Avenue. Since then it has unobtrusively become Gurkin Avenue. Great political changes show extraordinary fondness and reverence for the dead. Less for the living. Heroic resistance in the living is not always a merit; in most cases it is a dangerous stigma. Those who at some time have resisted are tainted by the eternal suspicion that somewhere, for something, they again will resist, because resistance lies in their nature, like some grave flaw of character.

When in 1943, after the Istanbul trip, the military plans of the conspiracy began to assume concrete form, Mihály Ursi, in the event of success, was to have been designated president of the new democratic Hungarian republic. This idea was broached by the worker's group at the motion of Joska Kurdi, and the other members enthusiastically and unanimously concurred as a matter of course.

Now with Ursi slipping secretly back to Budapest, several months late and with the over-hasty crown of martyrdom fallen from his brow, not only were all important political posts filled, but the great throng of those left off the bandwagon pressed shoulders to every door, for what is more natural than that liberation also should mean the liberation of personal ambitions.

Yet Mihály Ursi's merits as a resistance hero did not remain unrecognized. Some weeks after his arrival, he became director of the National Institute of Astronomy, where his work, and that of his assistants, for long months consisted of pushing wheelbarrow loads of mortar around the ruins of the institute. Simultaneously he was elected director of the Hungarian Soviet Cultural Society's science division, an unsalaried post. In our hands, however, is a contemporary issue of *Pravda* portraying Marshal Voroshilov seated on an ornate sofa, on his right the Soviet scientist Parin, recipient of the Order of Lenin, and on his left, Mihály Ursi.

Ostie Dukay, who sojourned in Budapest more than three months so as to set in order the sole remaining assets of the now landless estate, the industrial plants, took a dim view of the future of private enterprise in Hungary, and it was his plan to resettle in his Connecticut home his seventy-year-old mother, Countess Menti, as well as Zia, Zizi, Mihály Ursi, plus Mr. Gruber and Monsieur Cavaignac, the former head chef. His invitation met general rejection. Zia's reply was that if God had helped them survive these horrible years, it would be disloyal to abandon the walls that had preserved them from death. Already she had tastefully renovated her flat in Buda, and Zia Photos was once more open for business. Mr. Gruber was now the manager of the fine new little restaurant called Ararat Tavern. Its license bore his name, and Monsieur Cavaignac was master chef.

The restaurant opened at Septemvir Utca, on the ground floor of the gutted Dukay palace, where four-century-old walls six-feet thick had defied bombs and fire. Sooty ruins of blasted walls lacelike in outline, resembled some colossal, grotesque coronet above the sign of the new restaurant. At the entrance, in a uniform of the Maria Terézia period, stood an old silver-haired porter who had served Ararat Castle forty years. Strikingly effective views of the tragi-romantic restaurant taken by Zia Photos had appeared in an American magazine under the title, "Journey's End." The walls of the vaulted interior were decorated with ibex horns, bear tusks and English etchings of hunting scenes. On the tables were cloths of heavy damask, precious porcelains, embossed silver, somewhat damaged, cracked, chipped and bent, after the great holocaust. Mr. Gruber would sometimes sit down at the piano, and in his reedy voice, deliver charming renditions of French, Spanish, German, English, Rumanian, Turkish and Russian folk-songs, *Yo te quiero . . . Au clair de la lune . . . Passerene vinovate . . .* and so on, enchanting his audience with his immense knowledge of languages.

There is no telling just what financial or other interest Ostie

300

Dukay may have had in the enterprise. We only know that before his departure he participated in an important conference at a corner table of Ararat Tavern with Mr. Gruber and Monsieur Cavaignac as to whether they should introduce *blini* with caviar, the dish that so entranced the Prince of Wales during his Budapest stay before the war. The capital lay in ruins, but the memory of such *blini* triumphs was still vivid in Mr. Gruber's and Monsieur Cavaignac's minds, like the petrified imprints of mastodons on lava.

Ararat Tavern must have orginated on some sort of collective basis because Marja Drda sat at the cashier's desk, while Kazimir Kilinski, sometime champion runner, rail dynamiter, dog trainer, optometrist and great-grandson of Kosciusko's general, in a worn cutaway which he received from Ostie Dukay, acted as head waiter. Slobo Tuykovich, a passionate cook, helped Monsieur Cavaignac in the kitchen, but sometimes he competed with Mr. Gruber, taking in hand his guitar and singing with his half face but in a beautiful sonorous baritone: *I ako su odletjeli zdrali* . . . The old eagles engender young eagles.

The last great table near the kitchen was hidden behind a beautiful Chinese screen, saved from the Septemvir Utca palace, reserved now for the use of the Dukay family and intimate friends. At the sound of Countess Menti's little silver bell, also miraculously saved from the ruins, the waiters would jump just as the liveried footman did in former days at Ararat Castle. The new era did not mean a great career for everybody; only half of the former footmen became secretaries of state, the other half were employed as waiters in Ararat Tavern.

After the liberation, Maxim Narokov reassumed his old post at the Soviet Legation in Budapest, and everything was readied for his and Marja's wedding.

These were beautiful days. Everyone who had survived the war was happy. Everyone felt that mankind was standing at the door of world peace and a new Golden Age. Everyone was occupied with building something out of the terrible ruins, not only spiritually but physically, too. On the hills of Buda there were deserted villas, completely gutted after the bombardments. With the help of his numerous progeny, Hamor assembled a "vacation lodge" from the stones of these abandoned villas. The toilet was at the far end of the yard and even the guests could gain access to this important chamber only by asking Hamor for the key suspended from a great ring, which opened the rusty lock with considerable difficulty. The visitors, however, were in for a great surprise. There was nothing there, the compartment had not even a back wall; in it hung merely a sign: "Please use the bushes."

The Café Gugger's old sense of humor returned. After the dark months of the siege, May was extraordinarily beautiful. Though private autos had disappeared, the *décor* of the most fashionable streets became more artistic—we should say pastoral —because rich grass grew among the ruins, and goats with huge udders pastured on the former site of the Dux Salon and the Macko Jewelry Shop.

Marja, the happy bride, changed again into Maria Darida, at least as far as her sense of humor was concerned. After a dinner party in the Ursis' newly painted apartment, Hamor turned the conversation to chess. Maxim Narokov was an excellent chess player. More than that, in 1936, at the Ostend tournament, he had won a game from Capablanca.

"Though I was a champion some twenty years ago at the University Chess Club," said Hamor to Maxim, "I have never succeeded in playing from memory. It is amazing how excellent Marja is at playing blindfolded."

"Oh," Maxim turned to Marja, "you never told me you play chess."

"Well," said Marja very modestly, "I had some talent even in school, and during the war, especially in the loneliness of the Cave, I spent a good deal of time developing my knowledge of the game."

Zia proposed a match between Hamor and Marja. They asked Maxim to referee the game. Marja sat next to the wall, with her back to the table.

Playing the white, Hamor opened the game.

"P–Q4!" shouted Maxim toward Marja's beautifully shaped back.

"Kt–KB3!" came the next move from behind her closed eyes.

Ostie, Ursi, Zia, Grubi, Kazi and Slobo stood around the table watching the game in deep silence. Maxim's breathless

302

astonishment grew move by move. "Excellent!" he whispered.

And then came Marja's seventeenth move. She sacrificed her queen, and won the game in two daring moves. Great applause.

"Fantastic!" exclaimed Maxim, looking at the notes he had taken of the game. "It was exactly the same famous match that Lasker won from Steadman for the Gastineau Cup!"

It was. Exactly. Hamor was a poor chess player and Marja couldn't play at all. She did not even know the difference between a knight and rook. They had found an old chess book, Hamor memorized the moves and Marja secretly held a slip of paper in her palm, reading the B–Kt2 and so on, having not the slightest idea what these funny signals meant.

From that day on Maxim beseeched Marja to play a game with him. Marja shook her head. "Only after our wedding."

They never played the game.

Nothing came of Maxim's contemplated marriage to Marja. Maxim's case would seem to confirm that when permission to marry is refused, one cannot divest oneself of Soviet diplomatic dress as easily as an old-world officer of the Hussars unclasped his sword, or a love-struck Catholic priest even today doffs his cassock. Some weeks after liberation, everything was readied for Maxim's and Marja's marriage. The witnesses were to have been Mihály Ursi and Bolgorin, Maxim's genial Legation colleague, who had the look of a professional wrestler. All that was missing was Moscow's permission, which would undoubtedly come. After all Marja Drda was a heroine of the Czech resistance movement.

One afternoon late in April, she parted from Maxim in the Inner City. They were to meet that night at Ararat Tavern. Maxim turned back for a moment and said: "By the way—your cigarette lighter—I refilled it." Those were his last words, last smile, and last gesture toward Marja, for he failed to keep the evening appointment. Marja waited patiently an hour, and impatiently for another. Then she telephoned Bolgorin, who said Maxim had been urgently summoned to Moscow on official business. A plane had been waiting, and he had rushed to the airport. "Didn't he phone? Well, no matter. He will be back in a couple of days."

303

Marja waited a week, three weeks—then three whole months. Maxim did not come, did not write. He only sent a message, a poignantly moving one. A message of silence such as only dead or mysteriously vanished persons send. Months later Bolgorin, too, was called from Budapest and Marja's letters to Maxim via the Soviet Legation went unanswered.

Maxim was undoubtedly overtaken by some human tragedy which imagination may picture in various ways. According to Marja, it was not in Maxim's character for him to leave the scene of life in such fashion: "By the way—your cigarette lighter—" taking his smile away with him forever. No, that was not Maxim.

Ursi and Zia thought otherwise. The Russian soul is completely unpredictable. Possibly Maxim came into contradiction with himself. Perhaps he surrendered himself to the Ideal, whose depths we cannot plumb. Perhaps he did not like Marja's deep faith. No—Zia knew that Maxim secretly was very religious, too. Perhaps he happened to learn something about Marja's colorful past. But all this was only conjecture.

Marja did not give up hope; she felt certain, oh how certain, that the Madonna would bring Maxim back to her again.

In the spring of 1945 the Hungarian Nazi leaders, who had fled westward before the siege of Budapest, happily surrendered to the American troops. One morning, some fifteen of them were ordered to board a military plane. The plane rode above a sea of clouds; the prisoners laughed and chatted; they were sure that the plane was going first to London, then to New York.

One of the guards was Sergeant Andrew Szanto. As the plane crossed the Hungarian border, through a large hole in the clouds the well-known silver plate of Lake Balaton glittered below. Sergeant Szanto knocked on the window and shouted to the chatting prisoners:

"Look down, gentlemen!"

They looked down, and their faces suddenly froze. Now they knew their destination.

On the twelfth of April, 1946, some hundred thousand people stormed the neighborhood of the Marko Street court. Not only all the windows but all the roofs of the huge court building were filled with spectators. Above the narrow courtyard one could see only a piece of the sky as though through an air-shaft. Five gallows were waiting for the big show.

Ursi, who had received a special press ticket, was deeply buried in his astronomical study. He decided not to go. "No, no! I won't go!" he had said to Zia the previous night. But a few minutes before noon he suddenly grasped his hat and hurried to Marko Street.

One could hardly move in the narrow courtyard. Ursi had never seen such a throng. The tension was horrible. He stood next to the gallows among foreign reporters, Russian officers, anonymous girl friends of cabinet ministers and other dignitaries. He watched the man in black hat and black overcoat pacing before the gallows as if he were waiting for a trolley. He had a peasant face, and he was about fifty. He pulled a rope from the pocket of his coat, and with an almost absent-minded, skillful movement tested the rope's strength. He returned the rope to his pocket, then yawned.

A man stepped from the crowd, went to the executioner, put a hand on his shoulder and greeted him with a big grin. They shook hands and exchanged a few words. Ursi recognized Joska Kurdi.

"He is an old friend of mine!" said Joska proudly when he stepped back and saw Ursi. Joska seemed to be extremely happy. Ursi had always detested crowds, and when the thousands and thousands of people, their bodies pressed together, suddenly started to shout wildly, he felt so uneasy that he wanted to leave the yard. His press ticket had been successful in admitting him, but now to get out was entirely impossible.

The shouting meant that the condemned were approaching between their guards. Next to Ursi's feet was a basement window which was crowded with faces. He stepped down onto the spectators' shoulders, then disappeared into the basement. But there he was pinned between the elbows which fought to get to the window.

He closed his eyes; he did not want to look out. The wild shouting stopped while the judge read the sentence. Ursi opened his eyes but a red-headed heavily perfumed woman blocked the view. He put a finger under one of her hanging locks, moved it a little to one side, and through the hairs—they were so close to his eyeballs that they looked like red-hot iron bars—he saw the black-booted, green-shirted "collaborator" who had been responsible for the terrible material and moral ruin of Hungary. There he stood before the judge's table, handcuffed.

When the judge turned him over to the executioner, the hysterical shouting of triumph, hatred, revenge and sadism became so wild that the red-headed woman's lock slipped off Ursi's finger, fell down like a heavy silk curtain, and Ursi did not watch as the noose was put in place.

The four years 1945-1948, comprising the period during which coalition governments in lands occupied by the Red Army —Poland, Czechoslovakia, Bulgaria, Rumania and finally Hungary—became completely communist, all of which deepened the rift between the United States and the Soviet Union—these years eventually will be important chapters of world history, but from the standpoint of our story, and especially the character development of Mihály Ursi, they are, so to speak, quite eventless.

Though he did not join the Communist Party, as the "opportunist" Hamor did, he was a firm friend of the Soviets.

He had an argument, when in November, 1945, Zia and Grubi were triumphant in the first election. The Smallholder Party, "espoused not only by those city liberals who could not differentiate oats from wheat, but also by the remnants of conservative elements and the aristocracy," as Hamor defined it, came in with a decisive majority, while the Communists received barely seventeen per cent of the vote.

"This result clearly proves," said Ursi to Grubi, "that your thesis was wrong when you said that in lands occupied by the Red Army only a sweeping communist victory is conceivable."

"Just wait!" said Zia and Grubi simultaneously.

The following year, when on a sunny spring afternoon he took a walk along the Danube bank with Zia and Zizi, watching the construction of the bridges, he remarked:

"Hungarian workers are really amazing. They have transformed gutted Budapest in one year. The work tempo in Vienna,

306

Warsaw, and even German towns, lags far behind Hungary. The Great Fallow is now galvanized by an amazing will—the people feel they are working for themselves."

On the last day of July in 1946 the new money was finally issued. Hungarian inflation, unparalleled in world history, was over at last. Ursi's pencil, though used to astronomical figures, danced with alarm in his hands as he noted the last quotation on the Hungarian paper pengö. A single dollar equaled 4,649,040,-000,000,000,000,000,000,000,000 Hungarian pengös. A few days before Zizi had picked up from the sidewalk a paper banknote someone had thrown away. One quintillion pengös. The largest banknote ever issued in the history of currency. The note, now exhibited in a New York museum, bears the portrait of a fetching little peasant girl.

"A quintillion pengös!" said Ursi. "So that is what you are worth, little maid, mother-to-be of the Hungarian people. But how much in reality, on the black market of world politics?"

Continually and in ever-growing numbers, came great Soviet scientists, writers and artists on visits to Hungary. First-rate men, wonderful heads—Ursi gained many a valuable friend among them. Some arrived in luxurious cars, their wives with sables round their necks and diamonds in their ears. They possessed imposing villas on the shores of the Black Sea or in the Caucasus.

"We can only understand an ideal," said Hamor, "after seeing how it works in practice and in everyday life. The communist principle is that everyone may exploit *himself* to the limit—but, for example, cannot establish a shoe factory employing five hundred workmen, because in that case he is not merely exploiting his own genius."

"Bravo!" nodded Ursi.

Zia, Marja, Kazi and Slobo did not make any remark. Old Grubi had left the party soon after Hamor entered the room.

From February 1947 we have an article from Ursi's pen:

. . . for by now it is indubitable that World War II was not won by England, Greece or Denmark, but only by two, yes two nations: the United States and the Soviet Union. Their victories loom like mountain peaks above

307

Europe's fatal ruins. The secret of their dazzling success lies, I believe, in the fact that both nations are the result of a tremendous leap. The United States evolved from the human electrons of Europe's outer quantum curve, when, tearing themselves from the nuclei of feudalism and religious persecution, they jumped the Atlantic. When in the era of Queen Anne, they began landing in greater numbers on the shores of New England, they started from a complete *tabula rasa* in a gigantic, uninhabited and glorious continent. They had no need to dispute, to revise old laws and constitutions, as in the great French Revolution, which led nowhere. In place of kings, aristocrats and catechisms they had only to extirpate primeval forests. The spiritual greatness and frequently childlike naïveté of the American people derives from the fact that in this *tabula rasa* they always used axes and saws in cutting down tree-trunks —never the guillotine.

History's other great *tabula rasa* was produced in 1917 at Moscow through Lenin's Revolution. The Bolsheviks had a tougher time than the voyagers on the sailing ship *Shield* bound for the new world, who from George III's British Isles brought with them the Bible, not to mention certain drugs, a few looms, small farm animals, an assortment of seeds and even a very considerable ballast of bricks.

In 1917 Russia exploded not *outward*, over ocean distances, but *inward*. Lenin and his associates had to blow up even the concrete vaulting of Czarist Russia. But they did not quibble, either, over what should be left of the past. The secret of their success, too, was that they left nothing of the past, just as the arrivals in New England two hundred years before. Naturally there are essential differences between grand dukes and giant firs. In the work of the Bolshevists even their ax-handles dripped blood, a loathsome sight—but we must think in terms of results, and the results justify them.

Among the events of 1947 we must report two deaths.
Ararat Tavern did well, becoming the favorite haunt of members of the American and British legations, and naturally

of the shadowy figures of the aristocracy. Thus, understandably, reigning political government circles regarded Ararat Tavern with a jaundiced eye, particularly since in 1947 at the August elections the Communists won by a very great majority.

"Russian trucks raced all over the country," wrote Zia to Ostie Dukay after the elections. "Arriving at the polls in some village, forty Hungarian Communists would leap from every truck, rush to the urns, vote, jump back on the trucks, which then took them at top speed toward another village. A few such speeding trucks were followed in jeeps by American reporters. They too rushed to the urns: flashbulbs, pictures, back to the jeep, after the trucks! Mr. P. showed me nineteen photographs. The same corkscrew-mustached character had cast his vote in nineteen different villages. Oh, will of the people!"

One morning in December two officials appeared on the premises to inform Mr. Gruber that Ararat Tavern was being nationalized. Mr. Gruber collapsed into a chair at the news, his face turning so livid that Monsieur Cavaignac rushed for some cognac. With a trembling hand Mr. Gruber lifted the glass to his mouth, and when he had emptied it, one of the officials, in the most natural tone requested that he pay for the liquor, for the swallowing of the cognac had occurred at a point in time when the state had already taken over the property. Technically speaking, the government official was quite right. Mr. Gruber, on the other hand, flew into such a rage at this practical application of an essential reform of society that he jumped up and grabbed his chair to defend the free enterprise system.

He could not lift the chair. He was stricken with a heart attack, and a few seconds later died on the floor of Ararat Tavern.

The day after Christmas, Countess Menti died too.

"Mama sat in the armchair while receiving Extreme Unction," wrote Zia to Ostie. "Then she remained sitting erect in the chair with an expression not unlike that with which she used to await trains in foreign waiting rooms. But now some strange other-worldly smile suffused her face. In her lap her hands, those two hands beautiful even in their dryness, were clasped in prayer.

"Zizi and I knelt down. Later, glancing behind me, I saw that Mihály was kneeling too. But an even greater and more wondrous thing happened in that long mute silence lasting I know not how long. Through the open doorway entered several of the neighbors, and I think some passers-by too, without the slightest sound, as though sensing that now some very great thing was in progress. And as I glanced back, there knelt two Russian soldiers by the door. Oh, Ostie, if you could have seen these two primitive Russian peasants, their wide eyes and moved countenances, as they beheld the wonder of death.

"Mama just sat in the chair and smiled, even after she was no longer able to stay erect, and slowly leaned back in the chair. But her gaze was crystal clear as she met my eyes. And she spoke, but her voice already was very faint. These were her last words: 'Tell Ostie . . . and tell Johy too, that I prayed for them. And now I shall pray for you. For all of you . . .'

"Her glance took in the strangers kneeling in the room, and this wondrously mild glance also lighted on the two Russian soldiers. Then she mutely prayed, long and deeply, her eyes shut; she never opened them again. This was how Mama died at nine minutes past four in the afternoon.

"I had never told her the news of how Johy, the year before last, had committed suicide somewhere in Austria.

"We are alone, Ostie. By now, only the two of us bear the Dukay name. Uncle Peti and Uncle Zsigmond—all in the grave. Why, oh why haven't you children? Perhaps it still isn't too late.

"Not even the walls of the Dukay mausoleum in Ararat survived the tank battle. We buried Mama in the little Buda cemetery, next to Mr. Gruber and Berili, my old French governess. Aristocratic titles for quite some time have been strictly prohibited, so on her simple little gravestone is marked only this:

KLEMENTINA SCHÄYENHEIM-ELKBURG
WIDOW OF ISTVÁN DUKAY
1873-1947"

Chapter 21

Mihály Ursi's Farewell to His Wife and Daughter.

On the night of February 10, 1949, Zia burrowed her head into the dark blue silk cushions of the divan, her outstretched right arm clutching the back of the divan, her left hand dropping lifelessly toward the rug. Her gesture resembled that of a drowning man whose strength is so far spent that he can only grip the side of the boat with one hand and has already allowed his head to sink beneath the waves. The waves now were represented by the crumpled blue silk cushions, from under which only a few tresses of her ash-blond hair showed. And from beneath the cushions could be heard her weary little crying, faint and exhausted as the anguished buzz of a bee caught in a spider's web.

Mihály stood motionless before the bookcase, hands clasped behind him, his glance not on Zia but focused in the distance. In the fold which recent years had carved deeper in the middle of his strong chin, and in the two sharp lines cutting perpendicularly into the soft skin of his face, in his lips firmly but almost tearfully compressed, in his clouded brow, in the tumult of his brown hair already touched with gray, Zia's weeping was as exactly mirrored as in the waxen grooves of a sound recorder.

This scene between them had begun after supper at around eight, and it was now nearing three in the morning. The room, too, showed traces of the great altercation. One small rug had slipped askew and lay in a great fold on the floor like a large furrowed brow, while two light chairs were in quite unaccustomed positions, one aimlessly turned toward the wall, where someone's excited progress had shoved it. An ashtray had fallen on the rug and no one had picked it up. Ashes and countless cigarette stubs were scattered on the floor, scarcely smoked cigarettes, their backs broken by the trembling nervous motion of the same hand, rouge on their twisted lips. In a vacant armchair, rolled into a tiny ball and damply wilting, sorrowed Zia's little handkerchief. On a leather chair lay the evening paper, wrinkles pressed into it by someone who had sat there; another indication that the tornado of heated debate had tossed them from chair to chair.

On top of the bookcase stood a small globe. For the seventh hour Mihály over and over again took the eight steps between the bookcase and the wall opposite; a moment before, he must have leaned his tired shoulder against the bookcase, his movement jolting the globe, because its brass crescent holder still trembled as sensitively as a plucked string. For long seconds the brass crescent's imperceptible trembling was the only movement in the room, but this minute and sensitive vibration seemed somehow to hint that this long February night of 1949 witnessed no senseless wrangle between spouses, but something of vital import to the whole globe there above the bookcase.

Mihály was forty-nine years old, and Zia had reached her thirty-eighth birthday two months before. Never during their thirteen years of marriage had there occurred the kind of conjugal quarrel which emanates from the husband's dropping cigarette ashes on the rug or the wife's saying over the phone some paltry, idiotic nothing. For them there had been no minor infection of the family peace, which after a brief hour and a half of altercation assumes the symptoms of dangerous blood poisoning. This sort of thing is nothing but exhausted nerves, wherein the chain reaction of fancied slights or long-forgotten memories evokes such uncontrollable moments that toward dawn the wife threateningly locks the door of the bathroom behind her. No, it was nothing of this sort that was troubling Mihály Ursi and Zia Dukay.

In this always-peaceful room the great problem of their lives had appeared after supper unexpectedly; now for the first time stomping heavily, slamming doors, shouting loud words— that problem which till now had only dared to appear on cat's feet during sleepless nights along shadowed corridors, but otherwise hid motionless in the cellar, in the old trunks of the attic, or deep in closets, holding its very breath. In the secret nooks of their souls it had always been present, but never appeared in the open. This tamed and invisible problem on that night for the first time resolved to rear up on two legs with threatening growls and appear before them baring teeth and claws. Now it lurked there somewhere by the door and watched its victims: Zia on the divan and Mihály before the bookcase, his gaze focused in the distance.

There are domestic problems which are present in a bed, in the kitchen, in a medicine bottle, a trinket or a pack of cards. The gravest are those standing beside a door, and connected with a certain departure. Their problem, as it stood there now, waiting at the door, heavy winter cap in hand, wore in the black cavern of its mouth only three great yellow teeth with which it grinned incessantly, but this grin only made its freckled face more glum and spectral. The problem had taken on the aspect of the big-nosed driver who bore strong and not quite pleasant smells in his clothing, in his mouth, in fact even in his glance, and whom they awaited this morning at six o'clock, so that he might take them in a legation truck to Vienna.

Ostie had arrived in Vienna five days ago from New York. He couldn't proceed to Budapest because by then, owing to certain diplomatic tensions, the State Department had voided passports of American citizens for travel in Hungary. Since Christmas Mihály and Zia had known Ostie was coming. It was quite understandable that Zia wanted to see Ostie, the sole surviving member of her family, and Mihály too, after four years, also looked forward to reunion. Since the spring of 1945 the situation between the United States and the Soviet Union had greatly altered, and there would be much to talk about.

Everything began so smoothly. There was no trouble in preparing the Vienna journey. Hamor, who after the entry of the Russians immediately joined the Communist Party, had been deputy foreign minister since last year, and through him they succeeded in procuring the very rare and exceptional permit allowing them to travel to Vienna on a legation truck with the object of buying astronomical instruments and minor parts for the bolometer and reflecting telescope, which were unobtainable in either Budapest or in Moscow. The permit was for Zia too, who since Zia Photos was doing poorly, worked with her husband at the National Institute of Astronomy. Although Zia pleaded with Hamor, the travel permit did not include twelve-year-old Zizi, for that would have meant the whole family. Hamor requested Ursi's word that within a few days they would return with that same truck, but he regarded as an even greater pledge than Ursi's word the presence in Budapest of his only child.

Two days before, the three-toothed ever-grinning driver of the truck had come to discuss details of the trip and the exact time of departure. Between Zia and the communist driver occurred a long and private conference in which Ursi did not wish to participate. As a result of the conference the chauffeur was to receive a twelve-carat diamond ring in advance, and a thousand dollars from Ostie on their arrival in Vienna, if he took no notice that in the back of the truck, covered by blankets among the luggage, Zizi was also traveling with them.

This child-smuggling had a more far-reaching aim than simply for Zizi to see Ostie again. In their correspondence the idea often cropped up that Ostie might take Zizi to America with him for a few years. At first Zia wouldn't hear of the plan, but this last year she had capitulated. Zizi was a tall, slender little girl who had inherited her mother's improbably slim waist, thin bones and large green eyes flecked with tiny golden specks. In her twelfth year she was some thirteen pounds below normal weight, and her elongated wan little face showed traces of undernourishment. For a year and a half now, Ostie's generosity had come up against a stringent decree: a Hungarian family could receive monthly gifts from American relatives only in restricted amounts. If more arrived, it was confiscated and distributed to worthier recipients.

But Zia had another reason for wanting Zizi to go to America. With Gwen she thought Zizi's education would be in the best of hands, because the situation in Budapest made it quite impossible for Zizi to learn English and French. In this respect Zia remained a Dukay: she could not picture her daughter without a command of languages. If sometimes absent-mindedly she addressed her in French or English, Zizi would answer only with a frightened and troubled glance of her green eyes. At such times Zia would feel as though half a lung were missing from the little girl's flat chest, or as if something were wrong with her tongue. Evenings, returning home from work, wearied and late, Zia had neither strength nor time to give Zizi language lessons. In elementary schools, the new curriculum emphasized a single foreign tongue—Russian, which had never before been taught in Hungarian schools.

Ursi did not object to Zizi's American trip; for one thing, he too was secretly worried over Zizi's weight. For another, he stood firmly by his conviction that the perilous tension between East and West would cease in a few years at the latest. At the same time, with the "shepherd's wile" inherited from his grandfather, he reasoned that he had promised Hamor only that he and Zia would return, but this pledge said nothing of Zizi. Anyhow, a twelve-year-old child could scarcely be of concern to high government circles.

Regarding developments in world politics Zia did not share her husband's optimism. And though in the last few years she had avoided all political controversy with him there were things about which she felt quite differently. If, walking evenings along the Bastion, they would encounter the onetime friend of her father, eighty-year-old Prince András, the famed nabob of Franz Joseph days, like a fantastic ghost from the past, reduced to rags, limping by them leaning on his cane, not even recognizing Zia with his half-blind eyes, such a meeting would strike quite different chords in Zia than in Mihály, though their opinions regarding the old man pretty much coincided.

When in 1933 they had met by accident in Mandria, their meeting had been on the same intellectual and social plane. In the tiny room of the Pension Zanzottera not only their outlook on the world, but the first true love of both their lives and the ardor of their young bodies also met. And later, too, during their thirteen years of married life, they remained on this intermediate plane. Never was the warmth of their joined lives disturbed by the fact that Ursi had come there by forging his way upward from an abysmal proletarian lot, while Zia through bitter disillusionment had descended from the ethereal summit of aristocracy. The common ground on which they met and on which they established themselves proved firm even during the grievous trials of the war years. But when the Communists seized complete power in Hungary, it became ever more apparent that their meeting ground had been merely a state of equilibrium brought into being through the love and respect each felt for the other. In the dramatic tension of the last years their contrasting birth, childhood and rearing had tipped their seesaw balance into social heights and depths.

And now on this February night, at the pre-dawn hour of three, that six o'clock deadline was not far when, briefly and cautiously, with a guilty conscience, the bell would sound in the hall announcing that the Vienna-bound legation truck was waiting. Their problem, personified by the live apparition of the communist driver, was conjured up by Zia's irrevocable decision, of which she wanted to inform her husband only when all three of them were safely in Vienna. Through sleepless nights she had reached the decision that she too would go with Zizi to America and would persuade Mihály to join them in flight. Ostie had long since informed Mihály that it would take but a word to secure him a chair at some great American university.

Zia, now just as in the spring of 1940, when they only got as far as Calais, concealed her plan of flight because she knew that the matter wouldn't go smoothly and felt herself too weak for such a major battle. Only in Vienna would she broach her plan, where Ostie would stand by her, the strong Ostie whose person and opinions Mihály had always respected. Mihály liked to confront people, sometimes even Zia, with a *fait accompli*. Now for once, when they got to Vienna, she would confront *him* with a *fait accompli!*

Zia had gone through this a hundred times, and tested the snare in her conscience as though it were some actual trap with jaws of steel.

For weeks now she had secretly been preparing for the great journey, at times asking St. Rita's opinion in the chapel at Buda, long kneeling in silent prayer. In secret she packed a large trunk containing Zizi's things.

It is never a simple matter to pack for a long journey. But it was particularly difficult for Zia. First because it was in her nature always to overpack. Kristina had said of her that she couldn't even part with small rags, which was not true. Ostie's wife, Gwen, when visiting at Ararat, sometimes watched Zia's interminable packing as though it were some mysterious and ancient Magyar custom quite unknown in the United States. With

Gwen, packing was a matter of minutes; often she would travel to Mexico City, Honolulu and even Europe, with only a slender valise. In former days, Rere always helped Zia with her extensive packing, and in utmost gravity would meditate with his great half-witted horse's-head, wondering what could still be squeezed into the luggage, and in the end it would be his bull-like strength that coped with the straps of dangerously swollen pigskin bags which six footmen couldn't manage. After one such packing, when Zia opened one of her bags in Venice at the Hotel Danielli, to her surprise she found three raw potatoes, an empty paint can from the rubbish heap and eleven tiny live turtles among her silken underthings. These indispensable objects had been secreted in the bag by Rere in an unguarded moment out of sheer considerateness. While packing, Zia again wept a tear for Rere.

In the Ararat days Zia could always indulge her flair for packing to her heart's content: she could take along as much luggage as she pleased. Now, however, she had to pack a whole nation into a single trunk. She had a premonition that she would never see Hungary again. It was no light task to pack up the ancestral past of the Dukay family descended of the Ordony clan, but the packing of the castle at Ararat and the palace in Septemvir Utca posed especially complex problems.

In these weeks, while Mihály nightly elaborated his study relating to the light phenomena of the super-galaxies, Zia in the next room similarly immersed herself in the immeasurable glimmering distances of her own and the Dukay family's past, working on her packing list as on some insoluble puzzle.

Objects such as these were on her secret list: Countess Menti's little ivory-bound prayer book; a huge wall-cross of gold which she received at her First Communion from her uncle Bishop Zsigmond, learning only from her first husband, Prince Filippo Ozzolini, that it was merely gilt; the monocle belonging to her father, Count Dupi, which a Czech glass factory made to order from pale-rose glass for certain purposes of selective perception; also a walking stick of Count Dupi's, whose buckskin sheath concealed a handle which Filippo's expert eye had appraised as sixteen carat solid gold; a torn bedraggled top hat in which Rere invariably kept green walnuts even when wearing it, so that on doffing his hat with an immense flourish to someone in the park, the nuts would roll out of the top hat in a hundred directions, this curious behavior of the hat always astonishing Rere more than anyone; also Rere's great signet ring which he wore on his right thumb; nearly a thousand manuscript pages of Kristina's novel entitled *The Ordony Chieftain* which still were only part of the introduction; a photograph of Crown Prince Otto, showing him in Tyrolean dress when he was ten years old, and dedicated in a childish scrawl to Kristina; an old worm-eaten round wooden case hanging on a silken cord, in it, broken into many pieces, the beeswax seal of Emperor Ferdinand II, who in 1632 had granted Mihály Dukay the rank of Count and confirmed him in the ancient possessions of his family—the original document was destroyed when an English bomb set the Septemvir Utca palace ablaze, but this seal, falling from its burnt cord, rolled from destruction as if in flight, and Zia later found it among the ruins; a fist-sized marble fragment, from the second-story staircase of the Septemvir Utca palace, which had been constructed by the sixteenth century Italian Renaissance master builders whom Queen Beatrice brought with her from Naples to the Court at Buda; a very old wrought-iron door handle dating from 1414, when Sigismund, King of Hungary and Poland, permitted Demeter Dukay to build on the site of today's Ararat a fortified castle: *unum castellum lapideum seu fortalitium aedificare*—the iron door handle for more than five hundred years had served to open the chapel gate at Ararat Castle, and Mr. Gruber had rescued it.

We can understand Zia's view that such things could not be left out of the trunk, though this iron door handle in itself weighed more than fifteen pounds. Also on the list was a canvas bag, in it a pound of soil from the three-thousand-acre farmlands of the village of Duka, the last of the Dukay lands received at the founding of the country, and which, as the so-called Terézia Manor received by way of inheritance and dowry, Zia distributed among landless peasants. Smaller linen sacks contained flower seeds: sage, snapdragon, larkspur, cornflower, euphorbia, bridal wreath, mainly seeds of wildflowers from Klementina Meadow, in fact even wild chestnuts and acorns, because Zia thought that when she settled in Ostie's Connecticut home on the seashore, she would surround herself with these flowers as with the live wreath of a dead Hungary. Probably Zizi would marry an American, but little bronze tablets on stone markers would remind even her great-grandchildren that the wild chestnuts and oaks were born in Ararat Park.

The greatest problem was presented by the huge photo albums which occupied a whole stand in Zia's room. As a girl of fifteen Zia had begun learning the art of photography from Monsieur Mongés in Paris almost twenty-five years previously. And during this quarter-century Zia had accumulated innumerable photographs, from a very artistically perceived, drenched little sparrow preening itself, to Mussolini, when the Duce in the Palazzo Venezia for a second assumed a Napoleonic pose before Zia's camera. And who can list the happenings of twenty-five years in Europe and Hungary: family circle, bustling corridors of Parliament, wondrously shaped fleecy clouds, enchanting beauties of things great and small, numerous or tragic instants purloined from fleeting time and the swirling universe, and now sealed in albums? The sorting of such a tremendous mass of photographic material, the stirring of our memories, is the keenest self-torture. In the midst of her work, Zia ofttimes would rush hurriedly to the bathroom, close the door behind her, press her face into her palms and, wounded by one or another photograph, would cry herself out. Then she would return and proceed with her work.

In these days, sometimes around dawn, Mihály's sleepy and grumpy voice would sound from the dark bedroom:

"Why don't you get to bed?"

"I'm sorting Zizi's things," Zia would answer, and go on selecting photographs. Finally pictures like these went into the trunk: some fifty variously-dated photographs of her father, Count Dupi, among them the two final ones, taken three days before his death. One showed Mr. Johnson, the slightly built English stablemaster, exerting all his efforts to lift the aged Count Dupi into the saddle, a picture also interesting because this was the first time Count Dupi had brooked such personal assistance. The second picture likewise depicts this last ride, a distant rear view as Count Dupi, astride his magnificent dapple-gray mare named Emmy, disappears beneath the foliage tent of Ararat Park three days before the outbreak of World War II. In this picture he seems to be vanishing on one of the steeds of the Apocalypse in a direction whence he will never return. She sorted out some thirty photographs of her mother. One showed Countess Menti in the great red salon, in the summer of 1936, a few seconds before Ostie's American bride entered her presence for the first time. Countess Menti stood before her own life-size portrait, a work of Lenbach's depicting her as a young woman toward the end of the last century. At that moment she stood as in the Lenbach painting: her lowered hands clasped before her, holding her little fan of ivory lace, erect, her head somewhat raised, but still with the amazing humility of pride and that even more amazing glacial condescension, so that from the height of the house of Schäyenheim-Elkburg she might receive the boisterous American relatives already approaching up the corridor. In another picture, Countess Menti at a village festival stuffed the index fingers of her two gloved hands into her ears, assuming an expression of comic fright because she knew that a moment later the mortar would go off. Alas, no photo remained of the moments when sitting in the cellar during the siege of Budapest, her two hands, even amid the heaviest rain of bombs, remained in her lap without a muscle of her face twitching. A third picture depicted the deceased Countess Menti, sitting in an armchair, her head tilted slightly awry, on her lips the clearly perceptible and beautiful other-worldly smile of the Catholic believer. Some twenty photographs preserved Kristina's memory. One showed her skimming through the air with matchless grace, as she dove into the pool near the Chinese pagoda. In another she leaned one arm against the trunk of an ancient oak in the park, meditating on the most exquisitely inspired moment in the sixth act of the never-finished play entitled "Storm within the Storm." All of Zia's photographs bore her own titles. Rere was preserved for all time in forty photographs. The proportion betrays that Rere occupied a greater part of Zia's heart than Kristina. One photograph showed Rere in his inevitable bedraggled top hat and cutaway, but barefooted and with his trousers rolled up to his knees, in one hand a long-handled broom, in the other a lady's hat, weighed down by grave cares, visibly pondering important projects as he hurried along a path in the park toward some goal quite unknown.

It is worth noting that among the collected photographs, neither Zia's brother, Count Johy, nor her first husband, Filippo Ozzolini, figured. "To kill someone, the simplest and surest way is to forget him," said the noble and profound Marquis R. to his son in a fragment of one of Kristina's unfinished plays. There were many photos showing only places and objects without persons, lacking titles too, which made them the more mysterious and significant: a gateway, a birch bridge across the brook, a solitary cliff on the Mandrian seashore, an even more solitary man's hat on a rack in the hall, the low broad divan in the Pension Zanzottera, things to which crucial and profoundly intimate memories linked Zia. Then there were pictures which had no secrets to conceal: the Eiffel Tower so cleverly retouched as to resemble a giraffe cropping at a very high branch, the obelisk on the Place de la Concorde, or the Palazzo Volpi in Venice. One picture portrayed the Septemvir Utca palace on the first day of liberation following the siege; the palace's antiquely beautiful shingle roof, resembling the wing of a brooding hen, had already burnt to ashes, but the sooty walls were still smoking heavily, and in the light breeze the banners of smoke sent undecipherable Morse signals to the clear blue of the cold February sky. Under this picture Zia wrote: *"La mort sans phrase"*—Death without comment—doubtless recollecting the words of Abbé Sieyès, when he voted the death sentence demanded against Louis XVI. Then Budapest's pride, the Chain Bridge, blown up by the Germans "defending" Buda, laving its great chains like shattered bleeding hands in the waves of the Danube—with this title: ". . . *alle Leiden—die Unendlichen!"* which were Goethe's words.

And beside her own photographs were still those countless old family pictures in the wild-cherry-colored velvet album with the silver clasps. Daguerreotypes the color of withered leaves, whereon the pencil of the photographer "By appointment to the Emperor and the Royal Court" subsequently made mouse-eyes of blurred eyeballs; pictures the size of a visiting card, in which twenty-year-old men concealed romantically handsome faces behind huge mustachios and full beards; women of whom one could not know whether they were sixteen or already grandmothers, governesses or royal princesses, who had erected upon their heads ten-pound coiffures of arm-thick triple-braided tresses a foot and a half high—the sixties thus bearing witness to the fabulous accomplishments of the nineteenth century in the production of human hair. Then children, dressed generally as grownups and scared to death of the camera's weird owl's eye, and infants so ingeniously photographed that their faces could not be differentiated from their posteriors.

From this silver-clasped old album only the pictures of the four grandparents went into the trunk: Peter Dukay in gala Hungarian dress, wearing around his neck the Golden Fleece as the King's personal minister, his wife the Baroness Adrienne Zoskay, last of the great Zoskay clan, who, after the birth of her first child, Count Dupi, deferred to the fashion of the day and died in childbed fever, but entrusted her lineaments and short neck for safekeeping to her grandson Ostie as heirlooms of the now finally extinct Zoskays. And the two grandparents on her mother's side: Prince Ferdinand Schäyenheim-Elkburg and his wife the Austrian countess Amelia Schönberg-Taxis-Tolavicini, of whom Zia still had vivid childhood recollections, as with her black ebony cane Grandma Lia pattered at the age of ninety in the park of Ararat, always snatching her head away in horror at the sight of her top-hatted and barefoot idiot grandson, Count Rere. Ancestors vanishing in the haze of more distant centuries were represented by a single aquarelle medallion predating photography. No bigger than a walnut, this miniature portrayed the Royal Princess Elizabeth, Marie Antoinette's niece, whom the royal chief steward, Prince Rudolph Schäyenheim-Elkburg, married in 1806, and through whom in Zia too a sixtieth part of Hapsburg blood "clanked," as Count Dupi used to say, whereof her daughter Zizi, *née* Elizabeth Ursi—who these days was dangerously underweight and in whose apple-green eyes were minute flecks of gold, as on the flanks of tarn-trout—by now only inherited a one hundred and twentieth part.

An outdoor photo from 1906 shows Countess Menti at the Longchamps Races, sporting an ostrich-feather hat the size of a millstone, which conversed with the giant top hat of the side-whiskered Fallières, President of the Republic. Some two hundred persons, meticulously ranged according to rank, constituted a group picture taken on the great marble staircase leading to the Dukay palace garden on Bosendorferstrasse in Vienna. The occasion was the memorable garden party at which the fifteen-year-old Kristina recited with resounding success her first literary effort, a poem entitled "The Goose-Girl," which also appeared in the weekly, *Aristocratic World*; the ten-crown honorarium, the first earnings of her life, was a source of infinite pride to Kristina who knew nothing of the fact that Count Dupi had paid a renowned Austrian poet a thousand crowns to "spruce up" the verses a little, and that another thousand crowns had gone to the editor of the journal to cover printing expenses. This garden party was also memorable because after the musical program, during the very silly parlor game named *Apfelstrudel*, devised early in the past century by mamas of the high aristocracy possessing marriageable daughters, Kristina's forfeit in conformance with the decreed penalty—a kiss—was redeemed by young Crown Prince Charles, the heir presumptive, who fourteen years later, as Charles IV, died in his Madeiran exile as the last Hapsburg emperor. Zia, as she now—almost forty years later in the first year Hungarian Communists exercised complete power—reflectively held in her hand this group picture; clearly heard what was absent from the picture—the imploring cries of the photographer "by appointment to the Emperor and the Royal Court": "Don't move. Please!" And she saw the master photographer as he threw over his head the big black cloth, then with an angry motion snatched it off again and, obsequious deference mingling with wrath verging on apoplexy, shouted: "Please, please, Your Excellency the Minister of War: I beg you not to move! You too, General, there on the right! Please, gentlemen! Be so gracious as to follow the example of His Highness. Careful! Now one, two, three . . ."

Unfortunately, thought Zia to herself, the Minister of War and the generals did not take to heart the master photographer's words, they moved too much, and three years later the first world war broke out and this is where we landed.

His Highness, the presumptive Crown Prince, at the center of the group picture, did not move. In his lieutenant's uniform his young face was clearly visible, even to the engaging and somewhat sulky pout of his Hapsburg lips, like those of a three-year-old who has just drunk a big glass of milk. The fifteen-year-old Kristina standing there next to him, moved, of course, doubtless in the fever of her youthful beauty and success. Only a grayish-white cloud revealed her place, the same intangible and wondrous human cloud which she remained to the moment of her death. Oh, Kristina, Kristina. A few tears remained for her memory too.

When Zia finally finished sorting this enormous array of pictures which, from the walnut-sized little medallion to the burning of the Septemvir Utca palace, embraced nearly a century and a half, she propped her elbows on the middle of the table and took her tired head in her hands. This, only this remained of Europe, Hungary and her whole life. The iron door handle, the broken wax seal of Emperor Leopold II, and these random mementos, the selected photographs, flower seeds, acorns, all, all had found their way into the trunk, uneasy in those cramped quarters and almost fused into one. So much, and no more, would she be able to bring with her to Ostie's home in Connecticut.

After two weeks' packing, but especially after the night's selection of photographs, Zia felt as though she had been sitting for two weeks in the radioactive lithium-charged waters of the Rudas Baths: the past permeated and suffused her every nerve. The last afternoon, she went marketing, though there was nothing she needed to buy. At Dulik's Grocery she purchased two pounds of black pepper. She liked this condiment, although Freyberger had once warned her, when he examined her, "The fewer spices the better!" She used it only twice a week, just a pinch. Now she purchased the two pounds not for fear that black pepper might be unobtainable in the United States, but calculating that this two pounds would suffice her for twenty years, and imagining that later in America with this two pounds of pepper, as with some magic potion, she might prolong in her veins by twenty years the life of Hungary. While in the shop, she looked down at the bag of onions which stood there before the counter. Suddenly she turned away and stepped quickly to the window, as if she had seen someone on the street, but only because her eyes filled with tears at the thought that never again would she see this bag of onions or Mr. Dulik's soiled white apron.

In this mood she sat down to supper. Soon after the meal, she put Zizi to bed, after praying with her for a long while. Then, seated in an armchair in the study, she watched as Mihály began to pack a small hand valise, only for a few days, for he and Zia would be back shortly. In those minutes everything overturned in Zia: the carefully prepared trap set up somewhere on the Prinz Eugenstrasse sprang of itself prematurely, like the jaws of a real trap, whose sensitive and secret spring her conscience accidentally had touched. As she regarded Mihály, who in the course of packing occasionally stopped to consider whether he wasn't forgetting something—usually he forgot his razor, for some strange reason only the handle. As he reflected, pressing the nail of his little finger on the narrow silver band at the base of his right eyetooth —his accustomed gesture when in deep thought, or when meditating on the light phenomena of the Super Nova, for after all the handle of a razor or an unknown solar system at times occupies the same space in our thoughts—Zia looked long at Mihály's brow, on which thoughts could appear visibly as on no other. She watched him carefully fold his "good," but by now also worn-looking, tie as if it were some valuable museum-piece, the sole exemplar in the world. She watched the motions of his hands— "the most exquisitely formed man's hands I have ever seen," as Kristina once remarked—hands which spoke of strength, loyalty, tenderness and constantly awakened sexual awareness. All at once Zia found it impossible, just at the last moment, on a Vienna street, to inform him of her final resolve. No, no, she must tell Mihály everything now—she pressed her palms to her throat—before the journey, now, she must have it all out with him. He was not one whom she could delude, this man, from whom in thirteen years of love and marriage, she had received not only Zizi and the greatest presents of life, but, even in lesser matters, the illumination and guidance of sublime thoughts.

Mihály, holding the razor handle for which he had had to return to the bathroom this time too, suddenly turned his head in the midst of packing and looked at Zia. Zia, her face buried in her hands, wept silently.

That was how the great nocturnal battle began. The first response, for which Zia was prepared, the mute and deliberate sign of the brow: No! Then for hours: No, no, no! And meanwhile the hands, sometimes interrupting the packing, with quietly expressive gestures but using rock-founded arguments, as from great granite blocks built this No! into a tower of stone.

325

Seven hours of undisturbed talk, dispute—such lengthy discussion can embrace many things. There were lighter moments, too. Around ten o'clock, when Mihály, packing only with mechanical movements, and unaware that he was gesticulating with his already folded necktie, laid out the whole contents of his valise, as if he had just arrived from somewhere, then, in a pause between sentences or while taking a choked breath, would put something back—around ten o'clock he thus cut into Zia's words:

"You're right! Absolutely right, but only from your own standpoint. I quite understand your regarding the rechristening Peter Dukay Street to Bogulyubov Street as a personal insult, but try to remember . . . please let me finish my sentence . . . try to remember that Peter Dukay after all betrayed his fine past when, at the end of his life, he became personal minister to the King, while Kossuth . . ."

" '. . . in Turin ate the bitter bread of exile!' I have heard it a thousand times."

"To my mind," continued Mihály calmly, "the Soviet scientist Bogulyubov, with his notable achievements in seed bacteriology and the vernalization of plants, even in Budapest merits a side street more than Peter Dukay's Golden Fleece which . . ."

"So you think Hungary was much worse off under the Monarchy than now under communist rule?"

"Not for a minute. What was good in the last decades of the Monarchy was not due to the personal merit of Franz Joseph, but to the great European era of peace. By the turn of the century the spirit of Vienna followed the fatal Pan-German policies of Kaiser Wilhelm. That spirit dragged us into both world wars. The present ruins of Hungary were planned at the Ballplatz in Vienna and in the Royal Palace of Buda."

"This conclusion always sounds to me like the singular opinion of the Café Gugger."

"I'm sorry, but I still feel greater respect for the Café Gugger than for the Council of Five at Versailles. The shabby-trousered young Stargazers of the Café Gugger could have saved not only Hungary, not only the Danube Basin and Europe, but the whole world."

And as he again, who knows how many times now, carefully folded his necktie, with a long-drawn sigh he added:

326

"But alas, politicians direct the fate of the world."

"Oh, yes," Zia leaned back her tired head on the armchair, "the Café Gugger could have saved everything. It had profound inspirations: 'Please don't take away the lemon!' and others."

Ursi laughed aloud. This was the only laughter all night long. Their serious debate, to be sure, had taken a ridiculous and inane turn. This remark referred to Hamor's inscription in the lavatory of the Café Gugger, of which Zia had heard so often.

Thus the debate proceeded, sometimes with mild irony, sometimes grasping at humor, but all this only served to divert each other's attention from the consciousness of deadly danger as they swayed, as though on a tightrope above prodigious depths.

There were moments when Zia felt she would win out, that at the last minute Mihály wouldn't be able to tear himself from her. And whenever this hope slipped from her grasp, in her despair she lost even her self-control and improvised such hysterical scenes that Mihály Ursi tried to stop her mouth with his palm: "For the love of God, you'll wake Zizi!" Indeed it would have been horrible had Zizi witnessed a scene such as this, which had never before occurred between her parents.

Around midnight, when Zia, trembling all over, fell on the divan, Mihály sat down next to her, took her cold little hand between his palms, reassuringly pressed it along his face, and said:

"Try to understand. There are several reasons why I must return from Vienna. In the first place I gave my word to Hamor, and if . . ."

"Oh, yes," said Zia softly, half to herself, in her exhaustion looking rigidly into space. "I know you gave your word to Hamor. When you married me you swore never to leave me. Who is more important to you? Hamor or I?"

"All right, let's forget Hamor. I take back Hamor. It is not to him I want to return but . . ."

He did not conclude his sentence. Then he said:

"You see, you have silenced me. There are words on my tongue which I cannot utter now. Because I too feel they would sound like an editorial's empty phrases."

"Just say them, don't hesitate to say them. We are used to telling each other everything."

327

"I'll try then. Perhaps you're right—there are phrases that sound disgustingly empty, yet which hold more sincerity than a first declaration of love. It is not Hamor I want to come back to, but Hungary. Can you imagine me in a tuxedo, red carnation in my buttonhole, at some elegant night spot in New York, while here at home—"

"I know, I know. . . . Don't go on! You think Ostie is a traitor too! He left Hungary, Ararat, when war broke out. He left the land which for a thousand years gave the Dukays everything; he went to become an American citizen, president of Agricultural Chemical. Traitor, traitor, traitor! And now, in your eyes, I am also a traitor!"

"You're talking nonsense. If you keep twisting my words . . . why should I continue?"

He rose, left Zia on the divan, and again began pacing the eight steps between the bookcase and the opposite wall, now at each turn seeming to have made the journey between Moscow and New York, with tired slow steps, but still in comparatively short seconds. At least Zia had the feeling that the bookcase meant Moscow, and the wall opposite, where the door to the hall was, New York, and when Mihály in the course of his silent walk turned back from the bookcase and proceeded in this direction, hope gleamed within her that all was not yet lost.

Zia began to wring her clasped hands, and her tired little face, cruelly distorted from weeping, beseechingly whispered:

"Come with us, Mihály! For the love of God, I implore you, come with us!"

The silent walk again ended before the bookcase. Mihály Ursi's hands, entwined behind him, the plainly visible tension of the muscles, affected Zia as if the man had been fettered with the shackles of his own mania. After long seconds, Mihály with a ravaged countenance, rudely, yet in anguish, cried:

"Won't you understand, that I . . . that I *must stay here!*"

With immense force his voice carved out these three words: *must stay here.* Zia slowly turned her head toward him with a gaze as if now for the first time during that whole night she were looking into his face. The peculiar stress of these three words: *must stay here!*—it was like some curtain drawn aside, behind which Zia glimpsed a horrible secret. These last months she had

328

been disquieted, though not unduly, by visits of Marja, Slobo, Kazi and a number of other, unfamiliar figures. True, in her presence they only played chess or bridge, talked of inconsequential matters in a jovial vein, but then they would stay on long after she had retired, sometimes till dawn. Zia now seemed to have sensed something behind these gatherings. Clasping her hands to her throat, she whispered in horror:

"Are you taking part in some conspiracy again?"

Ursi's brow signaled two short no's. Then aloud, too, he said: "No."

There are short human words, particularly at such moments, which demand no sort of explanation or proof. That was just how Mihály's short and unaccentuated "no" sounded too. A half an hour before, in the heat of argument, when her despair found no other explanation for the obstinate rejection of her plan for flight, she had asked: "Have you joined the Communist Party?" The smilingly tossed "no" had not sounded convincing, and without pressing the matter she even began to list extenuating circumstances: the ration cards, fear that he might lose his position . . . As Zia now, with wildly beating heart and rigid eyes, stared at him there before the bookcase, he all at once became foreign to her, as if a wild and barbaric thought had assumed corporeal form, on its brow the black sign of doom . . . No, no! Be it this kind or that, every ideal is but barbarism if it leads to the embrace of the executioner. . . . Let me be only a pampered woman, I accept this accusation, let me be a traitor blemished by decadent aristocratic birth, but no, no thank you, I don't want to wake up in some dungeon with Zizi, I don't want to see communist secret police come some night for Mihály and me, taking us as they took Sibi, his wife and sixteen-year-old boy last month . . . no, not for any ideal has a father, a husband any right, any right at all, to expose his wife and child to such danger.

When she got that far, all at once her whirling thoughts swept in another direction. Impossible! It was utterly impossible that Mihály should participate in such a conspiracy. How often and how soberly, how brilliantly he had elucidated the other day, right in the presence of Marja, Slobo and Kazi, when a similar Polish attempt was mentioned, what absolute madness it would be to think of any internal conspiracy or armed revolt, when

Soviet divisions could appear on the scene within hours. So sober, so calm was he in these matters, so obstinately did he cling to his fixed idea that within a few years all tensions would lessen.

Then why did he want to stay? After all, an American university chair had always been his ambition. What was behind his brow as he stood there now before the bookcase? What unknown elements and forces of his childhood, of his birth, over which perhaps he himself had no control?

"I don't understand you. I don't understand you," whispered Zia's tired voice, rather more to herself. Her gaze was fixed somewhere in the air like some damp rag hung out to dry, from which no thoughts could wash the mysterious stain. "What keeps you here? I cannot think of anything else . . . you've fallen in love with someone. There's a woman in your life, of whom I do not know. She keeps you here. Do you have a liaison?"

The silence which replied from the bookcase could be the only worthy answer to these words. This Zia herself felt. The woman doctor who not long ago had inquired about Zia's sexual life had acknowledged the numerical data supplied by Zia with an ecstatic "tss!" and two pinched fingers raised high. In truth, beyond this surprising performance on the part of a man of forty-nine, for another woman, even if only physically, there would have been nothing left. But apart from all this, there was Mihály's constant tenderness, which was not the good husband's attentive politeness, but some unquenchable inner fire which actually had to be concealed, lest the glance penetrating beneath clothing, the glance momentarily fired by desire, become apparent during the most serious conversation in the company of others. Even during supper, cautiously, lest Zizi notice, Mihály moved his hand closer over the tablecloth, just so far that their hands could touch, but from such a furtive little movement their whole bodies would ignite at once. No, for this man, neither physically nor spiritually was there room for another woman.

About two hours after midnight, Mihály was again shouting from the bookcase:

"That I deny! That I ab-so-lute-ly deny! Your assumption is the greatest of stupidities when you say that if I serve this communist government, I too am a Communist. This is the greatest of errors. In a literary or philosophic work, or in the themes of

330

art, a communist trend can easily be incorporated. Not so easily in music. Stalin's hand is very long, but does not reach to the clouds of Magellan. Astronomy has nothing to do with Communism! All right, let's not start arguing all over again: you say that in directing the National Institute of Astronomy I serve the Communists, even if indirectly. I say no! Don't forget that when I—"

Zia's eyes suddenly regained their apple-green flame and the tiny gold flecks in her pupils seemed to throw sparks, as always when she became highly roused:

"You accept your salary from them! From a government that steals the money to pay you! Yes, steals it! You know very well that now I am not speaking of estates and ecclesiastic domains—but of little men whose only sin is that they were bourgeois, men whom the government has robbed of their homes and businesses secured through industry and ability and long years of struggle, whom the government has robbed only because they were not Communists. Look at this divan, this armchair. These we got from the Furniture Center through some such requisitions, after our things were destroyed. Who can tell whose they were? Perhaps by now they are deported or have starved to death. . . . Ostie is a traitor! I am a traitor too! And what are you? Aren't you a traitor when you sit in this chair? Must we live among such furnishings? I want you to see, I can't stand it any more, every morning I go down to Dulik's to do my marketing with stolen money, sometimes I can't swallow the morsel in my mouth, I am so sick of it that at times I almost feel as if I were eating corpses!"

"Zia!"

Zia pressed her hands to her forehead and kept shouting:

"No, no! . . . This I cannot understand! Someone who has a chance to teach at Harvard or the University of Chicago . . . if you say that astronomy is so far from everything . . . why can't you 'serve your people' there?"

"Don't be sarcastic."

"All your arguments sound as childish to me as school recitations!"

Her face was distorted by derision and scorn as she mockingly quoted the words of the national anthem:

"Who *cares for* and buries you! Here must you live, and die!"

One of Ursi's eyebrows twitched with quiet irony:

"A man who cannot draw strength from himself, but only from litanies and anthems, is far more dangerous than one who after reading a handbook thinks he can drive a car or a plane. Is that the sort of man you find me? Why do we dispute about such nonsense? I repeat and now for the hundredth time I repeat: I *must! stay! here!*"

Zia rose and with her two palms smoothed her slender waist with a movement as in bygone days at a Paris salon when she was still a countess and every inch a Dukay:

"And I, now for the last time, say: I *won't! stay! here!*"

"I can quite understand you. I respect your decision. I give you back your freedom. In fact, if you find it more practical—"

"No, no, no! . . . Don't say it!" Zia began shrieking unexpectedly, as if her resolute words of a moment ago had been only the result of uttermost exertion beyond which lay nothing but spiritual collapse.

Tripping on the little rug as she backed toward the wall, she held her two hands defensively in front of her, her eyeballs staring from her death-white face, and uncontrollably she kept screaming as if in her husband's hand the unsaid word were already a kitchen knife at the instant of some ghastly family massacre:

"No, no! . . . No! . . . Don't say it! . . . Don't say it! . . ."

Ursi hurried to her, in his face lines of deep dread and infinite pity: tenderly, but still forcibly, he stopped Zia's screaming mouth with his palm and, pressing her face to his, whispered: "For God's sake, you'll wake Zizi!"

He embraced her and wanted to help her toward the divan, but Zia was already so weak that her knees gave way. He took the light feminine body into his arms and so carried it to the divan; seating the half-swooning Zia in his lap, he put her lifeless arms around his neck, again pressed her face to his, and whispered:

"Why are we torturing each other? We love each other. We do love each other, don't we?"

332

Zia's closed eyes twice signaled yes, with scarcely perceptible movements. Into her lifeless arms strength surged back as she hugged tightly, and ever more wildly, her husband's neck; and then her head slipped lower and she rested on Mihály's breast with that beautiful languid gesture with which after deep sexual gratification the woman thanks the man for her rapture. The movement of Zia's head now expressed the memory not of a single hour, but of thirteen years.

Ursi still held her in his arms, as into Zia's ash-blond and lily-of-the-valley-scented hair he whispered:

"Listen to me, Zia. Why must we think of parting forever? Believe me, trust my intuition. One year, two years, perhaps three . . . something will happen, something unexpected, and affairs will take a turn for the better . . . the world cannot perish . . . all right, you go to America, too . . . it will be better for Zizi, anyhow, if you are near her . . . we'll correspond. And you will see, one fine morning from the hall of Ostie's house in Connecticut I shall call out to you: 'Good morning, Mrs. Ursi!' Will that satisfy you? Will you accept this solution?"

From beneath the ash-blond tangle of hair came a little gasp. One couldn't quite tell whether it was a cry of laughter or tears.

Then after long mute seconds her head moved, she extended her right arm and from the ample sleeve of her dressing gown shook out her wrist to note the time. It was the same movement as at their first meeting in the Pension Zanzottera when, with regard to the urgent passport photos, Mihály Ursi had asked when they would be ready. Zia then, under the guise of consulting her watch, swept back the long sleeve of her silken dressing gown to reveal her white wrist, like some artistic masterpiece with whose marvels she sought to stun her visitor—a movement yielding to the deepest, and perhaps only subconscious, instincts, which also tried to say, with the finest and most hidden shade of womanly coquetry and natural sexual hunger, that the other portions of her body were equally beautiful.

Her present motion was addressed only to Time. Her glance filled with horror: the watch hands showed ten past five. Then her voice sounded, coolly and soberly.

333

"I must wake Zizi."

She disappeared behind the door. Mihály remained seated there on the divan, elbows resting on his knees, his head in his hands. It was a terrifying feeling, as from his knees and lap the warm weight of Zia's body abruptly disappeared.

That was how long, long minutes passed in utter immobility and silence. Only now and then would a door close or the running tap be heard from the bathroom. Minute little rustlings of life than which nothing can say farewell more afflictingly.

When Ursi raised his glance, Zia and Zizi already stood before him fully dressed, ready for the trip. Zia spoke first:

"Forgive me, there wasn't time to make breakfast. I'll take sandwiches with me for the road."

Ursi got up, but remained silent. Zizi's little white face in the creased lines of early rising seemed even smaller than in reality. Her gaze reflected the terror of a child's soul, always instinctively and impalpably sensing crucial matters that pass between its parents. Her sleepy little voice was like a broken reed:

"Isn't Papi coming with us?"

Zia adjusted one of the little girl's blond locks curling from under her dark-green traveling cap.

"Papi won't come with us now. He'll follow later. Say goodby to your father."

At this moment the hall bell sounded. A brief, cautious little ring, expressing a bad conscience. Zia went to answer it: at the door stood the communist driver, already respectfully holding his winter cap in his hand, the three great yellow teeth in the black cavity of his mouth flashing a friendly smile of complicity in no way reminiscent of what is generally referred to as the precarious tension between East and West.

While Zia opened the door, Ursi took Zizi silently into his arms, clasped her to his breast for a long time, then kissed her, enclosing Zizi's little white face in his two great palms and for seconds looking deep into her eyes which now quite plainly showed the tiny gold flecks.

Zia returned. Ursi started toward the wardrobe for his hat so he could accompany them to the truck. Zia's gloved hand detained him. With half-closed eyes she said:

"No, don't come. Don't come with us to the street, I'd rather you didn't . . ."

She had to rise a little on her toes to kiss her husband's lips —a thing which Mihály endured rigidly, unmoving, with an expression as if some dark and unknown Inquisition's torture were tearing his flesh and bones. And he appeared barely conscious. His eyeballs, too, seemed filled with tears and blood when Zia looked deep into his eyes. With her gloved hand she made the sign of a tiny cross on Mihály's forehead and quickly went out.

Perhaps Ursi did not even see Zia and Zizi disappear through the door of the hall. For a long time he stood there, as though turned to stone. Then he stretched out his hand and put out the light. Such confused, senseless and absent-minded motions are sometimes the most expressive of all. This motion perhaps subconsciously now expressed that all brightness around him had been extinguished. Yet the room did not remain completely dark. Through an opening in the curtain streamed the bluish light of the February morning. He stepped to the window, drew aside the curtain and looked down into the street.

The driver was occupied in loading the luggage onto the truck. His movements indicated that he was having a hard tussle with the weight of the largest trunk, in which were the iron door-handle of the chapel at Ararat, Emperor Leopold's wax seal, the marble fragment from the Septemvir Utca palace, the countless photographs, the seeds and other objects. Last of all he stowed Zizi back there among the bundles, rolled up in a blanket; aside from the seeds, she was, so to speak, the only live piece of luggage.

All this occurred in the bluish semi-darkness of the wintry dawn, with hazy contours, as if only in a dream, because dreams never come by lamplight or sunlight, but always in the strange bluish half-light of dusk or dawn.

Near the truck stood Zia with her back toward the window, from which Mihály regarded them. But then Zia slowly turned, and by the movement of her head it was apparent that her glance was scanning the windows of the upper stories. She could not have seen Mihály in the darkened room, her unsure glance could

335

not even find the windows of her own apartment, because one always leaves home in haste, and hurriedly returns, without noting the location of the windows even after living in the same apartment house for decades. This was why their eyes in these moments no longer could meet.

Ursi pressed his forehead to the cold windowpane as Zia got into the truck, taking the seat next to the chauffeur.

The car set off, turned at the corner, and vanished.

Chapter 22

Alone.

The *Queen Mary* was already in mid-Atlantic, which now was an even wider gap between East and West than before the days of Columbus. Zizi, who was a poor sailor, remained in the cabin, but Zia and Ostie had been circling the deck promenade for two hours. As Ostie counted the steps—every passenger counts them—one circle took 273 steps. Quite an enormous space for someone imprisoned in a cell like one of those in the Cave, where in the Dark Ages unfortunate Tartar and Turkish prisoners were not even able to stand erect, but if someone is surrounded by the blue and gold infinity of the ocean, even a *Queen Mary* seems like a rock cell.

Ostie had never been a passionate walker. Back in the years of the silent films, Kristina used to call him Bustie, instead of Ostie, in reminder of a gag in a Buster Keaton film, in which Keaton, as a most dignified English lord steps into his car before his palace; two butlers very carefully arrange the plaid over his knees, then the huge Rolls-Royce starts the hopeless maneuver of turning around in the very narrow street, and finally succeeds and stops before another palace just on the opposite side of the street, less than six steps away from where His Lordship has ascended.

And now Bustie-Ostie had circled the deck for more than two hours. They were the only passengers on deck in the very strong and whining wind, which with a million tiny teeth combed back their hair and gave an electric massage to their skulls. Leaning forward they could only advance as if they were struggling, as they had done against the strongest currents of the River Ipoly, chest deep in the water, in their childhood. They could not even talk; whenever Ostie opened his mouth, the wind snatched every word from his lips like a hungry seal the fishes from the keeper's hand.

In such weather this endless walk was not a great joy to Ostie, but he was very anxious for Zia. Since they had left Vienna, Zia had hardly eaten, hardly slept, and talked not at all. Sometimes she did not even answer Ostie's or Zizi's questions, and just gazed into the air. Her eyes lost their color, her pale face became visibly smaller. Ostie, on various and cunning pretenses, did not leave her alone for a moment. He regarded Zia's state of nerves very seriously; he was even afraid that in a distraught moment she might throw herself over the rail into the ocean.

Since the truck had turned the corner of their street in Budapest that early morning, Zia's mind over and over ground out one, but only one, word: why, why, why? Why did Mihály leave her? Again and again his words shouted in the heat of their argument came back to her: "Won't you understand that I . . . that I *must stay here?*"

Now, in the middle of the ocean, where distance and the strong wind cooled down the heat of that night and freed Zia from Mihály's ever persuading and convincing physical presence, this: I *must stay here,* however much he denied it, could mean nothing else but that he had sworn a secret and terrible oath to the devil. He must be involved in some insane conspiracy against the communist regime. She remembered her dreadful night of jealousy six years before when she had burst in among the surprised anti-German conspirators in Peter Dukay Street. This conspiracy was much more dangerous. According to the code of such conspiracies Mihály could not under any circumstances talk to her about it. Oh, yes, that was the only answer to the great WHY. Like some congestion of blood, into her consciousness rushed all that she knew of this man, of his fanatical respect for human rights and freedom, for the constitution and independence of small nations. . . . Could it be accidental that this Czech Marja, this Pole Kazi and this Yugoslav Slobo, just these three persons, came to him so often these days? . . . They too were just such visionaries affiancing themselves with death at the great orgies of fanaticism.

Zia's intuition was right.

Yugoslavia's break with the Kremlin rumbled below the

surface like the earthquake which does not destroy towns, does not even shatter windows, but makes the people sit up in their beds, put on the lights, and with sleep-dazed faces ask each other: "What was it?" "The thunder of Freedom" would have been too beautiful and metaphoric a phrase for a proper answer to such a sleepy question, though these were the words closest to reality.

Slobodan Tuykovich, who frequently traveled back and forth from Budapest to Belgrade, one day in January 1949, informed Ursi that the plan was already in blueprint for Hungary to follow Yugoslavia's example. Then, Czechoslovakia and Poland!

But this conspiracy differed in many ways from the Stargazers' method against the Germans. There were no conferences, there were no visible men, not even names, except Slobo, Marja and Kazi. But no other Stargazers, though it seemed very probable that the old comrades were involved in the plan, too, without knowing about each other.

Ursi occasionally met Jani Hamor, but they never talked about politics by now. Their old friendship had cooled gradually now that Hamor was a Party member and held a high government position.

This underground movement was buried in a much deeper layer of secrecy.

In Li-Pu-Ten's tale the huge black hippo wore a human face. In the Yellow Sea lives a crab, called by the Japanese *huyei*, because its shell perfectly resembles the face of an old Huyei warrior. In Budapest, on the top of Gellért Mountain, not far from the monumental winged statue recently raised by grateful Magyars to the liberating Red Army, under the dense bushes, ten steps left of the serpentine road, lay a head-sized stone which wore a frightful human face. There were many smaller or bigger stones around the bushes, but this stone had the lineaments of a Hungarian Medusa—at least in Ursi's imagination.

During a walk Slobo whispered to Ursi:

"This stone will be our mailbox. You won't forget? Ten steps left from the silver pine on the roadside. You'd better take a snapshot of it."

From that day Ursi took a walk every morning on the road

339

before going to the office. Under the stone in a tiny rusted steel tube there was always a piece of paper for him. Sometimes only short messages, almost ideological slogans; but mostly detailed instructions, signed by *MK*. Ursi did not even know what these two letters meant, he only guessed that the *M* must mean Magyar.

The detailed instructions were important. He was charged with propaganda. The tiny rusted steel tube asked him many times to write the text for secret pamphlets addressed to the common soldiers of the Army of People's Democracy, which by then had grown in a short time from nothing to four well-equipped, motorized divisions. These soldiers in great part were the sons of forty- to fifty-year-old workers, who all were now members of the Communist Party, though in their hearts they kept alive their old social democrat faith. It meant that they secretly hated the Communists just as the Communists openly hated the Social Democrats. From the time of the futile efforts against the Germans, Ursi had preserved the list of those workers who had been organized into the Stargazers' movement.

The tiny steel tube did not give any details yet about the *MK*'s positive plans, but as Slobo hinted, the conspiracy was on a grand scale, involving the head of the communist military police, and even two so-called "Titoist" members of the government. The negative plans were more clear. No uprising against the Soviet Union, for that would have been a bigger blunder than against Hitler's occupying panzer divisions. No attempts on the Muscovite members of the government, no new Lidices or Katyns, no *gajdesz* at all.

Then what? Under the stone for the time being there was no answer to that huge question mark. But the Medusa-faced stone for Mihály Ursi was the real face of Hungary, the severed head, the baleful grin on her lips, the dire curse on her dark blue and dangling tongue, the serpents writhing in her hair, the dreadful bleeding neck cut off by the Perseus-sword of the Kremlin, still in the extreme agonies of death, as Leonardo's brush or Daujon's chisel might have brought her to life.

This was the situation on that February night when Ursi desperately shouted to Zia: "Won't you understand that I . . . I *must stay here!*" For the *why*, of course, he had to remain as

340

mute as the stone which lay ten steps left under the bushes from the crippled silver pine, not far from the tower-tall, winged statue.

A few days after the departure of Zia and Zizi, Ostie wrote the following letter from Paris to Ursi:

Hotel Crillon, February 14, 1949

DEAR MIHÁLY:

I know that Zia has already written you several times from the Vienna-Paris Express. I trust that our secret post operates smoothly and that this letter, too, will reach your hands. Zia said she gave you a thorough account of everything, yet now I think there may be certain details which Zia may not have noticed, or about which she was silent intentionally. Some of this, I think, will interest you.

As we agreed, I was waiting for them in Vienna, where I arrived a week before Zia's arrival. To tell the truth, I wasn't at all optimistic about her plan to bribe the communist chauffeur. So I got in touch with your cousin, Andrew Szanto, who is stationed now in Vienna at the USA Provost Marshal's Office where most of the Hungarian refugees end up. I studied all the other possibilities, and I think it worth while letting you know the results, not only because a contemporary astronomer-columnist-social-scientist-historian like you ought to know how transportation in LIBERATED Europe functions in these days of wondrous aircraft, but for practical reason, too, in case you might want to bid Uncle Joe a hearty good-by in the near future. Andrew introduced me to a Hungarian textile man freshly arrived, who acquainted me with precise details of the latest technique. Now, open those big ears of yours and learn something.

First of all: the professional smuggler. He is usually an Austrian smallholder, who knows every tree, every stone, every anthill on his farm next to the Hungarian frontier, which, so that one might not absent-mindedly overlook it, consists of two barbed-wire fences, separated by a fertile mine-field. Different species of mines grow in abundance here: for example, plate-mines, which don't explode under

341

the weight of a hare or a fox, or a five-year-old child. If nothing else this clearly demonstrates the highly humanitarian principles of your government. Of course, under the weight of a twelve-year-old girl, like Zizi, it is another story. Then there are the so-called Stradivarius-mines—take care, don't stumble on their tight strings hidden in the grass. Knowing that you love wildflowers, I must warn you not to try to pick any; remember Ophelia's words—"There's fennel for you, and columbines: there's rue for you . . . we may call it herb-o-grace o'Sundays: O, you must wear your rue with a difference"—for they are often disguised mines.

On a moonless night Herr Smuggler climbs over the first barbed-wire fence. He never cuts it. He does not want to cause the Hungarian Treasury any loss. At the same time a cut fence next to his field would destroy his business. Landing between the two fences in the mine-field, he lies on his stomach in the darkness and starts to swim. Yes, rather to swim than to crawl because these days the fields are liquid mud from the heavy spring rains. His swimming is not for an Olympic prize. He swims very slowly, with his extended hands very carefully feeling for the mines. His probing fingers are as wonderfully sensitive as those of a famous gynecologist in a womb. Having swum through the mine-field, he climbs over the second wire fence. Now he is in Hungary. But he does not stand up. No! out of reverence for the thousand-year-old Hungarian soil, he enters, not on his shoes, but his shoulders. He rolls his body—in order not to leave any suspicious footprints around his land —to his neighbor's territory. It does not help too much because his neighbor is a professional smuggler, too, and plays the same trick on him. Finally standing up, he starts east— in reverse. If you would have such a brain as clever Herr Smuggler, you would immediately understand why he walks backwards. This way his last footprint is lost in the universe, it leads nowhere. In one of his pockets there is a home-made primitive false document, and in the other a heavily loaded revolver in case he gets into some ideological argument with the Hungarian guards. It never happens.

The guards know very well what is in his sagging pocket, and when the huge floodlights happen to catch him climbing the wire fence, they turn their heads away. The Moscow radio is right: the satellite people are truly pacifist. They don't like shooting.

Herr Smuggler meets his contraband at a certain milestone in the darkness. The contraband is heavily loaded with dollar bills, but no valise! No smuggler accepts anyone with the smallest package. It would be too obvious. Now he guides his clients back the same way. Naturally, everybody must walk backwards. These footprints, leading from West to East, are wonderful propaganda for the Communists, proving that the people of Austria are fleeing from the hellish English and American zones to the heaven of the People's Democracy in Hungary. Nearing the frontier, everyone must lie down in the mud and roll himself to the first wire fence. They climb over the fence, then swim through the mine-field. Herr Smuggler leads the group; after him swims the lady, then the children, and last the brave husband as a rear-guard. After having climbed the second fence, you can now land with your feet. You are already in New York—almost. Very simple for a young and strong fellow like you. Not exactly as simple for some well-to-do textile man's wife who weighs upward of two hundred pounds. Be calm and careful during your swimming. Last week a slightly nervous Hungarian lady lost both her legs. For this comparatively short journey you pay about twice as much as for a round trip on a luxurious ship from the Mediterranean to the South Sea Islands.

Fortunately, it was not necessary to choose this solution for Zia and Zizi. When at the appointed hour I was anxiously waiting for them in Vienna at the end of Prinz Eugenstrasse, the truck arrived promptly. Keeping the sentimental aspect of our "Reunion in Vienna" as brief as possible, I put Zia and Zizi in my car and then I said to the communist driver: "Let's unload that luggage, I'll give you a hand."

The driver—if I remember rightly, he had only two teeth—grinned at me without moving, only rubbing together the tips of his thumb and forefinger. Apparently this secret

343

international sign language, even behind the Iron Curtain, means: Let's have the cash first! I couldn't take this business precaution in bad part, because how could my tovarish know which of us was the greater scoundrel, he or I? When I gave him the envelope, he turned toward the truck with his back to me, spread his legs wide and looked down. Don't get the wrong idea—he wasn't doing anything indecent on the street; he was just counting the fifty-dollar bills with what I might describe as a certain shyness. He stuck the envelope beneath his dirty shirt, and grinning with his two, or maybe three teeth, he turned toward me and to my vast surprise said in English: "Okay, baby!"

Under the effect of the "Okay, baby!" it occurred to me that perhaps you may be right: the tension between East and West is not so perilous.

While the tovarisch and I transferred the baggage to my car, Zia, on a hand valise resting in her lap, scribbled a note in pencil. She lowered the window and beckoned to the driver:

"Would you be so good as to give these few lines to my husband?"

Our tovarish, thick winter cap in his hand, and the two great yellow teeth in his mouth, grinned a fawning apology:

"For God's sake! Did Your Excellency think that I was going back?"

Sound idea, I thought. With a twelve-carat diamond ring and a thousand dollars one can start a tidy new life in the western zone of Austria, particularly if one is so absent-minded as to bring a truck along, too.

But at once it flashed through my mind that this might cause you a lot of trouble with the Hungarian authorities. They will learn of Zia's flight, and, of course, they will think that Zia has stolen the truck, kidnaping the tovarish. It greatly worries Zia, too. So don't hesitate to repudiate your traitorous wife and child, the accursed spawn of capitalist aristocrats, should the Hungarian chief of police call you to account. If you see fit, start divorce proceedings

344

against Zia, too—it is only a formality, anyhow. But I hope our fears are groundless, and that your friend, Hamor, will smooth the matter over.

As far as the formal divorce suit was concerned, Ostie's suggestion came too late. When the Ministry of Foreign Affairs reported that the truck was two days overdue, a detective brought Ursi to police headquarters. He was politely treated, and after the questioning, released. He went directly to the Ministry to explain the situation to Hamor, but the secretary came back from behind the cushioned door saying that "the tovarish deputy foreign minister is very sorry but he is busy." In every secretary's vocabulary the word *busy* tenderly but very definitely means that the boss does not want to see the visitor. Ursi smiled back as every visitor does at such a humiliating moment, and walking home, he felt himself more than humiliated.

He had lost his best friend. He had lost the dreams of his youth. The shabby sofa in Hamor's room, on which he had slept for almost two years, now seemed to him like a coffin. Walking home, he passed the Café Gugger which had been converted into a People's Kitchen. He did not look through the window as he usually did; he had the strange feeling that on that corner table of the Stargazers he would see the bleeding, frightful Medusa-head. But he did not blame Hamor. He had four children. When in 1945 he entered the Communist Party, he said: "First I am a father. Then a Hungarian citizen. Then a European, and then a citizen of the world."

On April 1, Ursi, instead of his paycheck, received a curt notice that he had been relieved of his duties as head of the National Institute of Astronomy. This was not a great surprise for him. He did not see in it any connection with Zia's departure, nor with the stone under the bushes, not far from the huge winged statue on the top of Gellért Mountain. A great purge was on its way, involving many government employees.

In the middle of April a cabinet minister was arrested; then within hours the head of the military police, and several generals.

Were all these arrested people behind the mysterious *MK*? What was the *MK*? What was its final aim? Though Ursi con-

345

tinued his usual morning walks on the serpentine road, the Medusa-stone remained impassive. The usual instructions for pamphlets, the usual slogans, but nothing else.

The only man who could have thrown some light into this darkness was Slobo, but Slobo had not shown up since January. After Yugoslavia's break with the Kremlin, the Hungarian-Yugoslav frontier was guarded more severely than the barbed-wire fences across from Herr Smuggler's potato field. Without a doubt, Slobo was the greatest exponent of barbed-wire globe-trotting, but even—as the Hungarians say—a jug goes to the well only until it breaks. Ursi did not even know whether Slobo was still alive.

Mihály Ursi was left entirely alone except for Kazi, whom he knew was involved in the MK. But Kazi, who did not speak Hungarian, could not as a foreigner form any opinion about the growing purge. Finally they agreed that it was nothing but the usual periodical cleansing of the Communist Party, like the Moscow trials of Marshal Tukhatchevsky and others in 1937.

Kazi kept his job in the Fine Tools Factory. But he frequently peddled between Budapest and Warsaw and Prague, as a courier for the Polish movement. Most probably he too had a stone somewhere for his mailbox, but he never talked about it to Ursi, as Ursi never mentioned his own stone to him following the strict instructions of the tiny rusted steel tube.

Kazi, so devotedly pro-Soviet a few years before, had become violently anti-Communist.

In 1944, in the days of the raging radio battle between Goebbels and the OWI, Kazimir Kilinski was convinced that it was the Germans who had killed his brother, Piotr, along with eight thousand other Polish officers. By now, from his own underground sources he was convinced that the massacre was perpetrated by the Russians, though in their vehement arguments in that greatest "whodunit" of world history, Ursi held on to his own conviction that the Germans did it.

Marja, still in her Red Cross uniform, worked and lived in the Saint Rita Hospital. She did not have any close friends, except Mihály, Kazi and Slobo, but she did not participate in their secret talks. Though she was a patriotic Czech, when Jan Masaryk committed suicide in March 1948, just as Count Pál Teleki had, and Kazi told her that he definitely knew through secret channels that Masaryk had been thrown from a third-story window, already beaten to death by communist agents, Marja said evasively: "We cannot be sure about such rumors." She did not seem to be reliable enough for any anti-Soviet movement.

At the end of April, through their secret post, Ostie's second letter arrived from New York.

When we arrived in New York, Gwen awaited Zia and Zizi with an elaborate program: museums, picture galleries, stores, theaters, the terrifying height of the Empire State Building's tower, the terrifying depth of cocktail parties—in a word, everything with which new arrivals are tortured.

Zia canceled all itineraries because she felt very tired. And she altered her plan of residing with me in Connecticut. She said she would open Zia Photos in New York—that she wanted to work. I shall be happy to finance that project with an eye to good business. As a chronic capitalist, I shall do all in my power to exploit Zia.

I was not satisfied, though, with the state of her health. Don't be alarmed. This is, rather, a matter of moods. She hardly ate, her face grew small, her eyes larger. Sometimes she wouldn't say a word for hours, just stared into space. I had a neurologist examine her. He advised absolute rest. After all she went through, this reaction was only natural. On the doctor's recommendation, I have placed Zia and Zizi in a convalescent home, situated a few miles from Manhattan, atop a beautiful hill.

At first Gwen and I visited them every afternoon, but Zia asked that we come less often. I could understand that our visits stirred her memories. She asked me for a dog, if possible a dachshund. She named the puppy Elmer Turn-Kruegenthal-Wittelsbach on the grounds that a long dog merits a long name. In this little gleam of her old humor, I perceived a sign of improvement, but I still was not satisfied.

One Sunday, I found her quite overwrought.

"Have you seen Mr. Bryan?" she asked excitedly.

347

"Who is Mr. Bryan?"

. "A new patient. It's incredible! Never, never in my life have I seen such a resemblance. Absolutely fantastic! His resemblance to Mihály is uncanny!"

She seized my hand, led me to the lobby, whispering with a shudder: "Fantastic! Incredible!"

She drew aside slightly the curtain in the lobby:

"There! By the window! In the wheelchair. . . . Did you ever see anything like it?"

Mr. Bryan sat near the window and with a vacant face gazed into the garden. He was a man about your age; his hair, too, was brown. He also had a nose and ears, like you, but otherwise did not resemble you in the slightest. In the United States, I should imagine there are at least ten million men resembling you as much.

Zia whispered again:

"Look at that forehead! The mouth . . . those hands! Well? What do you say?"

I realized that this "fantastic" resemblance was the creation of my poor Zia's tortured fancy. What could I have said to her?

"You're right! It's really fantastic! He is the image of Mihály. Even the nose. Have you spoken with him?"

"No. Mr. Bryan scares away even the nurses. He survived an auto accident, and suffered a nervous breakdown."

I had dinner with Zia and Zizi in the convalescent home. In another corner of the dining room alone at a separate table sat Mr. Bryan in his wheelchair. During dinner, I entertained Zia with gossip and with the latest jokes. Zizi, whose little face by now was rosy and round, giggled a great deal, but Zia did not pay attention to my words. Her nervous glance kept flitting toward Mr. Bryan's table. She watched his every move. As I was telling my best joke, just before the point, she beckoned to one of the waitresses:

"Sarah, please ask Mr. Bryan if he would like some more butter."

Sarah cautiously approached Mr. Bryan's wheelchair. Her soft whisper was repulsed by a rude "Na-aw!" Sarah

348

fluttered back in alarm to our table. "Oh, he's dangerous! He bites!"

After dinner, a nurse who offered to push the wheelchair was routed by a similar "Na-aw!" Mr. Bryan by himself maneuvered the wheelchair among the tables.

The next week I again had dinner at the convalescent home. Zizi, in the meantime, had gained another few pounds and I perceived a happy change in Zia. At last I could tell last week's interrupted story about the absent-minded professor in Ithaca. Zia laughed heartily at it. Gone was the tenseness with which last week she had kept her eye continually on Mr. Bryan's table. Now she no longer bothered with him.

But when Mr. Bryan finished his dinner, something quite astounding happened. Zia sprang up, skipped over to him—you know those engaging light skips of hers—took Mr. Bryan's face in her hands, looked smilingly into his eyes, brushed back a lock of hair from his forehead, and when he addressed her, Zia laughingly pressed her face for a moment to his, and your "double," too, for a long time warmed in his two hands the hand of your lawful spouse— I have never in my life witnessed so scandalous a love scene in public. Zia rolled Mr. Bryan's wheelchair from the dining room—I followed them along the corridor—before the room they bid adieus with eyes, eyebrows, and with smiles almost swimming in tears.

"What's this?" I asked Zia.

She gave an embarrassed laugh. "It's a very weird story," she said. "Last week again Mr. Bryan was sitting by the window, just looking, looking into the garden. I asked him if he didn't want something to read. For a long time he did not take his eyes off me. 'Stand there in the light of the window!' he shouted at me in a commanding tone. I stood there and waited to see what would happen. 'Turn your face a bit to the left,' he said in a strange, trembling voice. He kept looking at me with widening eyes. 'Oh, my God!' he whispered. 'Never in my life have I seen such a resemblance! Good God . . . just as if I saw my wife before me!' 'Your wife, Mr. Bryan?' 'She's dead. In my car. I was

349

driving . . .' I pressed my face to his, and our tears mingled. It is since then that we are such good friends. He gave me his wife's photo, too. Come, I'll show it to you. And do you know what the most curious part of it is? Here, look. His wife doesn't resemble me in the least. Does she? Not one bit!"

Now you can see that you need have no compunctions about initiating divorce proceedings against your faithless wife.

Last week a most interesting letter arrived from Rio de Janeiro. You'll never guess from whom. Johy! For my part I never believed the suicide story, which I suppose he himself spread, taking fright at the Nürnberg trials, and especially at the news that Americans were shipping leading Hungarian Nazis back to Hungary. Johy writes that he would like to settle in New York and asks me for an affidavit that he never was a member of any fascist party. Johy, like the Nazis in general and, alas, some American authorities too these days, suffers from serious lapses of memory.

Zia, whom Johy so shamefully abandoned when she asked him to help release you, after reading Johy's letter looked toward the window and then, more to the window than to me, said: "Let's forgive Johy." The window did not answer. Nor did I. Though I am not unfamiliar with the virtue of forgiveness, nevertheless there are, shall I say, technical obstacles to his settling in America. I am not willing to sign an obviously false affidavit.

I shall send him some money because in his letter he complains that the art treasures brought from Septemvir Utca, "which, my dear Ostie, I sought to save exclusively for you" proved counterfeit one and all, and he warns me against the person of one Dr. Marton Gruber, not knowing that poor Grubi is dead.

One night in the middle of May, Ursi was alone in his apartment writing an astronomical essay, not so much for scientific purposes, but to chase away the torturing thoughts of his loneliness. "What Galileo proclaimed in his legendary *Eppur si muove!*—is now confirmed by Professor Alfred Wegener of Graz through the evidence of geophysics, primeval geology and . . ."

The bell rang. Ursi's first thought was: the police. He instinctively looked around for what to hide, what to save, but in that tense second he realized that he had nothing left to hide or save. He calmly went to open the door. It was Slobo. His arms were full of bags from the grocery, two bottles of wine weighed down the side pockets of his coat.

"I brought something to eat. I happened to learn that this is your cook's day off," he grinned. "How are you, Mihály?"

Ursi's first question was whether the present purge, the continuing arrests of people in high positions, were in any way connected with the MK.

Slobo shook his head. He seemed to be in a very good mood.

"No. It is possible that they were mixed up in some sort of business, but if they had any plan, it had nothing to do with the MK. You Hungarians have too many organizations. As far as I know, before the war there were more than seventeen thousand legal and registered social organizations in Hungary, to say nothing of the secret ones like your Stargazers. Too many organizations, and too little action. The MK grew out of one of these legally illegal, or if you want: illegally legal organizations—it means that Teleki knew about it, supported it, and denied it. The MK's aim, back before the war, was to check and counteract the German infiltration into Hungarian life under different patriotic titles. I don't wonder that you knew nothing of the MK —its efforts were futile, its methods stupid, just like—excuse me —the Stargazers. The entire MK soon became idle, then dissolved and was forgotten. Last year it came to life again. It had one hard seed. One word. *Independence*. I ought to be very proud when the world press calls such movements in the satellite countries Titoist. But the Yugoslav past and present are entirely different from Hungary's, Poland's, or Czechoslovakia's. We were not occupied by the Red Army. We have outlets on the Mediterranean. Let's call the MK a simple independence movement. To pull your neck out from under the Kremlin's yoke—that's all. *Prosit!*"

Slobo lifted his glass, but Ursi didn't drink.

Then Slobo described the plan in detail. September 15 was fixed as S-Day. His every second word was new to Ursi and Slobo

351

had to explain constantly. The annual autumn maneuvers of the Hungarian Army, of course, under the guidance of Soviet experts, and, of course, near the Yugoslav frontier, was scheduled from September 5 to September 15.

"We know exactly," continued Slobo, "who are the anti-Communists among your officers and who are the tough, unapproachable Communists. At 2:00 A.M., September 15, when the whole Army will be concentrated no more than fifteen miles from the Yugoslav frontier in preparation for a mock blitz against Yugoslavia—we know the plans of the maneuvers in exact detail —well, at 2:00 A.M. an alarm command will come through for a real attack against Yugoslavia. The communist officers and their Soviet experts will be sleeping very deeply at this hour because they will, of course, have consumed a quantity of nice sleeping powders along with their shashlik and vodka. Our men won't sleep at all. Telephone and radio commands . . . speeding motorcycle couriers . . . infantry . . . artillery . . . aircraft . . . within seconds the whole Army will be on its feet . . . then the blitz! We know there will be those whom the sleeping potions won't have knocked out, but we have taken every precaution for such cases. Fifteen miles—the whole alerted and motorized Army in its stormy attack will reach the Yugoslav frontier within half an hour. There won't be any shooting. Not a single guard . . . they will find the gates wide open. When the whole Army has penetrated Yugoslavia—let's say some fifty miles, the Yugoslav Army will move up to the border and make a ring—the Hungarian divisions will be swallowed up. Of course, it won't be as simple as I tell it to you now, but it will work. It's the only solution for Hungary, whose soldiers don't like the prospect of fighting for the Kremlin. But, my dear Mihály, you must forget the word heroism. Yes, it is a treacherous, cowardly plan, but there is no other way of combating those filthy Muscovites who wear the masks of democracy and liberty. Imagine the effect of S-Day on all the satellite peoples!"

It was three o'clock in the morning and they still talked, whispering behind the locked door. It would have been suspicious to put on the light at this late hour; they sat in the fantastic twilight of the moonlit summer night. As Slobo talked his head

352

kept nodding and he managed to keep his eyes open only with difficulty.

"Now, my dear UM," said Slobo, "your task will be very important. You know better than any of us the mind and language of the young Hungarian conscripts. You have a wonderful pen for the necessary pamphlets. Of course, not a single word about S-Day. Only the slow and careful preparation of their minds. As a matter of fact, as a Yugoslav mountain wolf I don't believe too much in propaganda, not even the Voice of America. Propaganda, my dear Mihály, is nothing more than patting the hands, let's say the knees, of a girl—it does not mean a child. But still, we have time till . . . S-Day . . . and if . . . you . . ."

Slobo didn't finish the sentence. His head bent over his chest, he fell asleep. He had drunk the two bottles by himself. He was so exhausted his eagle-face seemed to be a death-mask. God knows for how many days he hadn't slept.

The early dawn had painted the windowpanes with light blue. Ursi was alone with Slobo who, sitting in his chair, slept as comfortably as though in the finest French bed. They were alone except for Zia, who, in a photograph, stood on a cliff in Mandria and looked far over the sea.

Next evening Slobo disappeared again, but from that day the tiny rusted tube under the stone was waiting with more and more stringent orders for Ursi's short slogans and pamphlets for the mobilized Hungarian soldiers.

On July 20, Marja, in her rather poor French, wrote a letter to Zia:

Chère Madame la Comtesse!

Now, through a friend of mine traveling to Vienna, I have an opportunity to send you this letter. I am afraid Mihály's letters omit mentioning much that I feel myself duty bound to tell you, Countess. I assume he may not even have written that after he lost his job, he did not get his pension.

To decrease the rent and lighten the burden of housekeeping, Kazi has moved to Mihály's house. During the past months, Mihály tried to earn something by giving

353

English and German lessons, but only one pupil showed up. And at Slobo's advice, he gave up that one, because the little and very ingratiating lady—Slobo, in such matters, has an unerring nose—was a secret agent.

There is nothing wrong with Mihály's health, but the lines of his face have lengthened and we see his smile ever more seldom. It was a great disappointment for him that the Dutch pipe collector, with whom he was in correspondence, backed out of the deal. Mihály finds it difficult to comprehend why a Dutchman should be unwilling to pay a high price for a hundred-year-old broken *chibouk* owned by General Damjanics, whom the Hapsburgs sent to the gallows. In short, Mihály's pipe collection is unsalable.

One cannot help Mihály without insulting him to the quick. Last week Kazi, when he returned from Warsaw, brought a whole ham as a present for Mihály, but he threw Kazi and his ham out. "Idiot! Do you think I am starving?" Yet he loves Kazi even more than Slobo. On this one point his pride and sensitivity are more than senseless; I might almost call it a neurosis. Last month he sold his fur coat. He has given up cigarettes, "on doctor's orders."

I hope you won't be angry, dear Countess, for my writing all this. I think I've hit on a crafty plan. At the close of one of your letters to Mihály couldn't you just casually mention that you have an eccentric rich American friend, a fanatic pipe collector continually on the lookout for unique specimens?

Write me, dear Countess, as to whether you approve this pipe plan and are willing to take part in the conspiracy. In my experience if someone is in serious financial straits, he is apt to be more credulous of good news, but we must be careful all the same, because if Mihály smells a rat, the deal will fall through.

It's a special problem how to get the dollars to him. And if the dollars are here, how we can sell them on the black market, which grows more and more dangerous. Luckily we have Slobo here.

Last week Mihály gave me a little photo depicting you in Mandria, standing on a cliff and looking far over the sea. As a passionate photographer, even an expert I might say, I find the photo truly beautiful. Mihály commissioned me to have it enlarged. I went up to Zia Photos, which a comrade naturally had already taken over, equipment and all, but she let me use the enlarger—in fact, when I told her what it was about, she obligingly began to help. No getting around it—there is a point of solidarity deep in women's souls which cannot be eradicated by any ideological differences.

Several times it happened that I accidentally opened the door on Mihály. He was always sitting in the armchair facing your almost life-size picture on the wall of his study.

Dearest Countess, not only Mihály, but all of us keep thinking of you. I pray often to my Madonna for you, for Zizi, for Mihály, but most of my prayers—I'm sure you will understand—are for my Maxim. I am certain he will come back one day.

My English is very poor, would you be kind enough to give my heartfelt thanks to Countess Gwennie for the beautiful cocktail party dress and hat she sent me. My best regards to Count Ostie, hug and kiss Zizi for me, won't you?

Wishing you all the best,

Old SCHWESTER HILDA

In the last week of August, Ursi walked twice a day, in the morning and evening hours, to marvel at the beauty of the huge winged statue on Gellért Mountain's top. Under the Medusa-faced stone, the tiny tube became more and more talkative. September 15, S-Day, was only two weeks away. Twice a day, Ursi placed in that mailbox the typed scripts of the pamphlets for the soldiers. These slogans and short pamphlets—like the nightshade seeds dropped from the sack of the witch in the old tale—clearly showed the path of the last five years which had led him to complete disillusionment. He did not hate the Soviet Union; Communism was much closer to him than any other political system —he felt a sorrow for it, almost a fatherly sorrow: the child had grown up and would not behave—the giant child of the Hindu

355

Gilgames legend who had been born to make order in the world. Communism was grown up, Ursi thought, just like Urstron, oh yes, Urstron, the dream of their youth in Berlin, written on the back of the Holzer's menu, a weapon which could not attack, only defend and command . . . what an amazing tool for world peace! But Ernst went to Chicago, and Urstron became something else. Marxism went to Moscow, and became something else, too.

He remembered how, in 1932, when he was enthusiastically pro-Soviet, he had angrily flung away Freud's book after reading these lines: "The Soviet-Union is on the way to resembling dangerously what she is fighting against." Now he realized that Freud had been right.

He had the first disillusion about the fate of liberated Hungary in the fall of 1945 when in the coalition government the conservative smallholders held the majority, but in the office of a communist minister there were two direct telephones: one to the Soviet Legation, the other to Moscow. They rang every few minutes, and the talk was always in fluent Russian. But when he had to visit the anti-communist ministers, their conversation was never interrupted by any English telephone, for two reasons: on the desk of the smallholder ministers there were no direct telephones either to the American Legation or to Washington, and these ministers did not speak a word of English.

One of his pamphlets explained the use of these direct telephones. Moscow only wanted to ask our independent communist ministers many times a day: "How is your dear grandmother today?"

Another pamphlet listed the new street names in Budapest: Red Army Road, Lenin Circle, Moscow Square, Voroshilov Avenue, Pushkin Street, Mayakovski Street, Makarenko Street, Gorki Street, Gusev Street, Gogol Street, Bogulyubov Street, to say nothing of Stalin—every Hungarian town had its Stalin Avenue now, the new kindergarten was named after Stalin, the new steam mill, the new artesian well, the school for midwives, the stud farm—all of Hungary had become Stalin; the new textile plant in Poland, Prague's new foundry, the Rumanian oil refinery, the Bulgarian irrigation works—Stalin's name had overgrown everything like a thick weed. The pamphlet ended: "One day you will see new signs along the Milky Way: Stalin Way." This pamphlet appealed to the rough sense of humor of the peasant soldiers: "You can buy in every grocery Stalin-cheese, Stalin-ham, and even Stalin-sausage, prepared with special Russian spices."

For a man like Mihály Ursi, nothing was more hideous than the deification of a living man which reminded him of the worst days of the Führer. One of his pamphlets ridiculed the "Applause Decree" of a local community, which ruled that at public gatherings, when Stalin's name was mentioned, everybody must *jump* from his seat and fervently clap *thirty* times. At the prime minister's name it would suffice to rise *quickly* and clap *twenty* times in all. "When cabinet ministers' names are mentioned, you need merely half-raise your posterior from the seat and clap ten times, not too wildly."

As the days passed, and September 15 slowly—oh, how slowly!—approached, these pamphlets became longer and more and more ardent, but still did not mention the fateful S-Day.

In the afternoon of September 2, in Ursi's apartment, the bell rang again. It couldn't be Kazi, he was abroad, Ursi expected him the following week. To be alone, and suddenly hear a doorbell ring, was not a good feeling for anybody in those days when the purge, trials, and executions raged furiously in Hungary.

It was Joska Kurdi, whom Ursi had not seen for two years. There was a basket in Joska's left hand, filled with beautiful apples from the tree in his garden under which five years ago Zia and Zizi used to sit.

"I happened to come to Budapest," said Joska. "I brought these apples for the Countess and Zizi. Oh . . . they are abroad? I did not know that!"

The word *abroad,* as Ursi pronounced it, obviously was intended to say: Don't ask any more questions.

Under Joska's right arm there was an old cuckoo-clock.

"When your father died," said Joska, "and his belongings were auctioned off, my mother bought this clock, she used to call it Ursi-clock. I thought you would like some souvenir from your parental home. It still works very well!"

"Thank you, Joska. Sit down. How is Erzsi?"

To sit down for Joska took long and empty seconds. He did

357

not answer immediately. While he wiped the sweat from his forehead with his very dirty handkerchief, he fixed his small black eyeballs, framed in the red circles of his chronically inflamed eyelids, to one leg of the table, and said evasively:

"My wife lives with her mother now."

His intonation was exactly the same as when Ursi had said "abroad."

They avoided speaking of politics. Ursi did not ask Joska Kurdi what he was doing now, why he had come to Budapest, nor did Joska ask any questions.

"It's a damn hot day."

"It is."

The silence was awkward. Ursi felt that Joska had come for some special reason. Finally Joska pulled a small piece of paper from his waistcoat pocket.

"This message came from the Soviet Union for Marja, but I don't know where she is," he said. "My friend told me the message is important."

The small, dirty worn paper looked as though it had made a long and secret journey. A few words were written on it in Russian, but Ursi understood them. "For Marja Drda. Maxim Narokov is dead. Before he died he told me to let you know."

Nothing else. No signature. Did Maxim die in sickness, in an accident, in prison, or some other way? Joska did not know anything. He stood up.

"Well, good-by, Major. I will bring you some grapes after the vintage."

Faint, embarrassed smiles, a mute handshake, and Joska Kurdi left.

Ursi felt that it would be very difficult to give the message to Marja, about whose nervous state he had been very anxious in recent months. He decided not to tell her the bad news immediately—first he would tell her he had heard a rumor that Maxim was seriously ill. And he would arrange for a doctor to be present.

He arrived at the hospital late in the night and picked up a doctor whom he knew. Marja was not in her room which was dimly illuminated by the vigil light of the Madonna above her

358

bed. They found her on duty on the second floor; she was alone at the nurse's desk, reading a book.

Something peculiar happened in Ursi's tensed nerves when Marja lifted her smiling eyes to him and said: "Oh, what a pleasant surprise!" He forgot all the carefully prepared sentences, took Marja's hand and told her simply: "Maxim is dead."

He gave her the piece of paper. Marja read the message, then slowly and very carefully folded the paper, and put it in her pocket. She seemed to be calm, strangely calm. She stood up and started with slow steps down the corridor, which in these late night hours was deserted. Ursi and the doctor followed close behind her. Marja did not speak a word, but as she descended the stairs she hummed the faint melody of an old Russian song.

She made her way to the empty kitchen, pulled out a drawer, and after some hesitation selected a large knife. Then she turned toward her room. Ursi and the doctor followed her closely, ready to grasp her wrist. They watched her breathlessly.

In her room, she climbed onto the bed and in a kneeling position before the Villon Madonna, with slow and almost dreamy strokes she cut the image into pieces. Then she threw away the knife, sat down in an armchair, folded her arms, and gazed into space. After a few seconds she spoke as if nothing had happened:

"Have a cigarette, Mihály."

But her hand trembled, when she opened the box.

Two days later she went to Mihály and Kazi.

"I am at your disposal," she said. "For anything."

From that day she worked as feverishly as she had during the war against the Nazis. Her Red Cross uniform enabled her to act as secret courier for the Czechoslovakian movement.

In the first week of September neither Kazi nor Marja arrived on the scheduled days. September 7, 8, 9, 10, Ursi paced alone in his study from wall to wall for hours.

The cuckoo-clock, which had disputed the accuracy of the rust-cogged silver watch of the old-fashioned mine doctor, claiming that Mihály Ursi was born not in the nineteenth but in the twentieth century, hung on the wall of his study, opposite Zia's enlarged photo, ticking gaily, the cuckoo joyously nodding its head and shouting every quarter of an hour: September 15, September 15, September 15!

S-Day was approaching with unknown size and force, mutely and mysteriously, but already terrifyingly heating the atmosphere like an invisible comet coming with terrific speed from the Andromedes.

On the morning of September 10 the tiny rusted tube was empty. No instructions, no message from under the Medusa-headed stone. The tube was empty at the evening hour, too, that day. Then came September 11, 12, 13, 14, and the Medusa-head with the baleful grin on its lips, with the dire curse on its dark, dangling tongue, with the writhing serpents around its forehead, remained stubbornly mute. Frightfully mute. What had happened? Why had Marja and Kazi not arrived? Where was Slobo?

The fourteenth of September was a sleepless night for Ursi. He paced his study from wall to wall, then at midnight the cuckoo shouted twelve times: S-Day, S-Day, S-Day! . . .

Then came 2:00 A.M. and the cuckoo shouted twice: Alarm! Alarm! There was the thundering storm of buzzing telephones and short-wave radios, shouted commands in field tents, the dazed faces of awakened soldiers grabbing for weapons, the motors of half-tracks already murmuring threateningly, waiting like tigers for the leap, while with tails vertically high in the air, all the blades of the airplanes' propellers roared and the great *blitz attack* against Yugoslavia was on its way with full force.

Through the open windows nothing was heard but the sweet silence of a tired September night. The tension in Ursi's nerves was the same as during the night of March 18, 1944, when the German troops were already marching on the Vienna-Budapest highway to occupy Hungary, but Ursi was now alone, entirely and dreadfully alone, except for Rapczyk who slept in the kitchen under the table.

He spent the whole of S-Day in his apartment, utterly exhausted, in a strange half-sleep, listening to the radio news.

There was nothing on the radio. In the late afternoon he went down to buy the newspapers. There was nothing in them, either. The street looked unusually calm.

Next morning, the sixteenth of September, he found two

short and vague official remarks about the maneuvers. Nothing more than two lines.

He walked up to Gellért Mountain. There was no message for him under the stone. He realized now that the whole movement had collapsed. *"C'est fini!"* he said to himself, because people sometimes express the inexpressible in a foreign language which they do not speak perfectly.

His solitary walk took him to the tower-tall winged statue. "Raised by grateful Magyars to the liberating Red Army," as the dedication read.

The monument was colossal and imposing, though all such winged statues are feeble imitations of Paeonius' *Nike,* he thought.

In his pocket he found a little stub of black chalk he had used in the laboratory. He looked around—he was alone on the hilltop with the great statue—and did a very childish thing. On the base of the colossal statue he wrote: *To the memory of a little nation.*

That night, sitting alone in his study, he clearly heard Zia's voice from the Mandrian cliff overlooking the sea: "Where are you, Mihály? I am waiting for you."

There were no tears behind his closed eyelids, but hot tears flowed in his thoughts as he decided to leave Hungary. As soon as possible, leaving everything behind him, except the five thousand dollars which he received through a secret channel for his pipe collection. But no valise—Herr Smuggler does not accept any passenger with the smallest package. He would meet Herr Smuggler at a certain milestone, then the long walk in the darkness with backward steps, then the climb over the first barbed-wire fence, then the swim through the mine-field, then the climb over the second fence . . . and he would be in a chair at Chicago University as a visiting professor of astronomy. And he remembered a wedding he had seen in Washington in 1931, and he seemed to see another bride coming out of the church—strange custom, he had never seen it in Hungary—the bride was showered with rice. And it was Zizi, and Zia wept quietly on his shoulder.

It was about an hour after midnight, when the doorbell

rang. His first glance flashed to the window . . . the third floor
. . . and if it was the police . . . there would be detectives in
the street, too. Who was it? Marja, Kazi or Slobo?

He went to open the door with a sinking heart. He did not
switch on the light. Who was it?

Four plain-clothes men forced their way through the half-
opened door. One of them flicked on the light.

"Will you come with us?" said a tall, muscular man who
seemed to be their leader.

"Who are you?" asked Ursi in a calm voice.

There was the usual movement, flashing some insignia from
behind the lapel of his coat.

"What do you want with me?"

"Don't ask so many questions."

They looked deep into each other's eyes, for only a second,
and then Ursi stepped quickly back behind the cherry-wood sideboard in the hall, pulled out his revolver, and began firing.

A shower of revolver bullets was the answer. After firing all
his six bullets, Ursi dropped his empty gun to the floor and—
both his arms lifted in the air—stepped out from behind the sideboard, an old piece of furniture saved by Zia from Ararat Castle
after the siege.

No one had been hurt in the wild shooting. Ursi was taken
away by two men. The two others remained in the apartment and
immediately started the house-search.

Chapter 23

The Trial.

The mysterious cause of the delay of Marja's and Kazi's scheduled arrival from Warsaw and Prague was very simple. Marja was arrested in the train on her way to Budapest on September 8. Kazi on September 10. Slobodan Tuykovich, as the Budapest papers reported it, was captured in a Hungarian village near the Yugoslav frontier on September 11.

Twenty-six Hungarians were indicted in the plot, among them fifteen former Stargazers, and to everybody's surprise János Hamor, deputy foreign minister, too. These twenty-six men were the unknown and invisible hands who had written the messages and instructions under the Medusa-faced stone for Ursi.

Hamor was taken into custody at his summer quarters, but pleading urgent human need, asked the detectives to excuse him for a few moments. The secret policemen escorted him to the shanty at the end of the yard and waited patiently. Hamor meanwhile, heeding his own sign inscribed: "Please Use the Bushes," vanished in the shrubbery. Most probably he constructed the shanty, with its missing rear wall, not solely to play jokes on his guests. Data at our disposal does not indicate whether Hamor has been rearrested since.

The trial began November 28, 1949, and ended the same day in the evening hours.

Mihály Ursi was the chief defendant. The first indictment against him was that during the German occupation, in the summer of 1944, he collaborated with the Nazis, when a helper of the Russwurm Pastry Shop, in Josef Kurdi's yard, asked him for dynamite. This helper was a witness for the prosecution, and the likewise questioned Joska Kurdi confirmed his deposition that Mihály Ursi refused him the dynamite and thus prevented the destruction of a key German center.

According to the indictment, the plans of armed insurrection aimed at the overthrow of the People's Democracy were served by the weapons found in the so-called Dukay Cave, as well as by the secret physics laboratory, the explanation of the accused that this laboratory had not been in operation since Ernst Tronfeld left it in 1943—an unacceptable defense, because not even the accused could deny that he was in continual contact with Count Ostie Dukay and Ernst Tronfeld, now residing in the U.S.A. This unquestionably demonstrated that this ring of conspirators was under the control of an alien power.

At noon the presiding judge ordered a half-hour recess, and the defendants were led out to the overcrowded corridors, where their sobbing wives, relatives and friends tried to throng around them if only to exchange a mute glance.

The tension and the excitement was so great that a woman began to scream and another fainted. Shouts for a doctor . . . momentary tumult . . . Slobo was standing next to the winding iron staircase, and when the guard returned his gaze—distracted for a split second—to his prisoner, Slobodan Tuykovich was gone. The guard leaped after him, but his rifle, to say nothing of his old legs, were a great handicap on the narrow, steep winding stairs.

"Stop him! . . . Lock the gates!" he shouted, but he could not even see the damned Yugoslav who had descended the stairs as if he had wings. The police loudspeakers closed the neighboring streets, and the recess took more than two hours. How he managed to escape with such a distinctive mark as his grenade-torn face, is a mystery.

The trial opened again around three o'clock in the afternoon, and the prosecutor began his long and dynamic speech. Among other things he said:

"Microscopic examination has incontrovertibly established that the libelous inscription on the Mount Gellért statue was written with the identical black chalk found in the pocket of the Accused. I demand of the Accused: what has he done with his sense of justice, daring now to deny that it was not the aristocracy, not the Cardinal's clerical legions, not the historic Hungarian middle class, not the social-democrat workers or peasant millions, and not the Stargazers who rescued this nation from

Nazi hell, but, solely, the tens of thousands of heroic Soviet soldiers who sacrificed their blood and lives, yes, Dr. Ursi, their lives, battling from village to village, from cellar to cellar, for Hungarian liberation."

The audience in the courtroom applauded these words of the prosecutor lustily and long; in vain did the presiding judge threaten to clear the room.

The prosecutor now turned to face Mihály Ursi squarely, and raised his voice still higher:

"And I demand of the Accused: what has he done with his manly conscience, when, at the skirts of his countess wife, he forgot his origin and childhood, forgot the shocking misery of the Holod miners, forgot his own father murderously exploited by capitalist greed! This man was sent forth on his earthly road endowed with great ability from the most grievously suffering stratum of the people, but never during my long career at the bar have I met with so vile an example of spiritual baseness and class treason!"

At these words Mihály Ursi, thus far mute and motionless, arose and cried passionately:

"Mr. Prosecutor, you forget—"

"Sit down!" rapped the gavel of the presiding judge.

With warders' hands on his shoulders, Mihály Ursi, silenced, sank back into his chair.

One of the observers, a friend of his, who wants to remain anonymous, informs us that—". . . he was cleanly shaved and neatly dressed in a double breasted charcoal-blue suit. He sat as I have seen him so many times in the Café Gugger: clasping his right knee with intertwined fingers, but now it seemed not a movement of relaxation. It made the impression of a terrific effort to control himself, almost as if he were riding a stampeding horse and pulling back the bridle with all his strength. Even his neck muscles were tense. While on the gray faces of most of the other defendants the signs of total annihilation were clearly discernible, from the moment of the sharp "Sit down!" Mihály's face was almost black with the impotent wrath of the insulted and the injured. He did not move an eyelash even during the reading of the sentence."

The sentence was read at six o'clock in the evening.

Mihály Ursi, Janos Hamor, Slobodan Tuykovich, Kazimir Kilinski and Marja Drda—two of them: Hamor and Tuykovich in absentia—were sentenced to death. The other defendants received sentences of from five years to life imprisonment.

The defendants' faces remained immobile. During the prosecutor's long speech Kazi's right eyebrow sported a tiny, carefully twirled half-mustache, the result of his absent-minded mannerism. Marja wore a small black velvet off-the-face hat with an ornamental pearl pin and a heavy dark red silk suit with black braiding which she had received last summer from Ostie's wife. This vogue from New York cocktail parties was the only spot of color in the gray row of defendants. On her face, so unaccustomed to sorrow and in her large gray eyes, wide-set above her short Slavic nose, was a kind of expression—her head tilted a little aside—as if she were saying: "How strange."

With regard to the Ursi trial, our latest Budapest report relates that inasmuch as the Dukay Cave mentioned in the indictment was "the secret den of a reactionary fascist movement endangering the existence of the People's Democracy," the Cave had been thoroughly searched on several occasions.

As we already noted, even in bygone centuries of Tartar and Turkish peril, the desire for liberty had entrenched itself in the deep hollows of this Cave, and also in the summer of 1944 sought refuge there from the Gestapo.

And now, according to the indictment "the accused had gathered at intervals in the Dukay Cave to hatch their satanic plans."

In the course of the investigation it seemed unfeasible to search the inaccessible recesses with absolute thoroughness—though presumably, in black stalactite hollows, weapons, secret radios, ghosts of forbidden thoughts still lurked—perhaps even living men who had walled themselves in.

Consequently, after the November trial, authorities evacuated the vicinity of the Cave and, under the careful supervision of Russian demolition experts, blew up the Cave throughout its whole depth.

Chapter 24

The Last Words.

In 1950, on January 4, an emigrant Hungarian paper in Germany published the following item:

> A well-informed source reports that in Budapest yesterday, the death sentences passed in November against Dr. Mihály Ursi, former state astronomer, and two of his confederates, were carried out. All three were hanged.

Most of the news from behind the Iron Curtain is unreliable or exaggerated.

Count Ostie Dukay made every effort to find out the truth. Not even the "well-informed" source of the small emigrant paper claimed that the executions were public.

Ostie asked Mihály Ursi's cousin, Andrew P. Szanto, for information. Sergeant Szanto served in the U.S. Provost Marshal's Office in Vienna, and as a New York paper reported, he had had a dramatic encounter with a Hungarian refugee, a very important witness in this case, named Josef Kurdi.

Sergeant Szanto in his letter to Ostie Dukay described his encounter with Josef Kurdi.

It may have been around three in the afternoon on January 16, when a Hungarian refugee appeared in his office in Vienna. It was Josef Kurdi. He wore a crumpled overcoat; his peasant-like face was easily remembered because the edges of his eyelids were hairless and inflamed. His hands were still covered with blood from struggling through barbed-wire barricades. He said he had not eaten for two days. After giving him a bottle of milk, Sergeant Szanto jotted down his personal data. Age forty-nine, divorced, no children, occupation: carpenter.

"Religion?"

367

"I, Mr. Szanto, sir, profess the Roman Catholic faith, I was born a Roman Catholic too."

Sergeant Szanto thought it peculiar that he should use so many extra words, but Josef Kurdi lifted his big forefinger and said:

"Because, Mr. Szanto, sir, the Lord when He saw the sisters of Lazarus weeping at the grave, wept and cried: 'Lazarus, come forth!' And he came forth, bound hand and foot with grave-clothes, and the man had been dead four days!'"

Szanto stared at him and changed the subject:

"Tell me, Mr. Kurdi, did you know Mihály Ursi?"

He habitually asked this of every Hungarian.

"Of course," Kurdi said quickly, "of course, of course I knew him. Ursa Major! That was what we called him, that was his alias when I worked with him against the Germans. He liked me very much, sir. He used to say all the time: 'Take an example from Joska Kurdi! Joska is my most reliable man. I'd put my life in his hands'—he used to say. I could tell you a lot about him."

Seemingly nervous, he quickly changed the subject.

"I came, Mr. Szanto sir, to ask you to help me get to America."

"Just why do you want to go to America?"

"My brother is a farmer in New Jersey."

"Were you ever a member of the Communist Party?"

"Yes sir, Mr. Szanto, sir, I was an eighteen-year-old apprentice when I joined the Young Communists during the First Commune back in 1919 under Béla Kun. During the white regime, too, I remained a loyal Communist, though only underground of course."

This frankness shocked the sergeant. He decided that a man who wanted to get to the United States and admitted to such things was either very stupid or completely insane.

"Mr. Kurdi, you said very emphatically that you were a Roman Catholic."

For a few seconds the refugee stared at the window, then said:

"Mr. Szanto, sir, every man's life is divided into two parts. One is his childhood, the other is when he grows up. I grew up too, but these last few years, more and more, the prayers my mother taught me kept coming back to me."

"Why did you leave Hungary?"

He raised his two big hands into the air, then dropped them on his knees.

"I couldn't stand it any more! I just couldn't stand it."

"Why not? You were an old loyal Communist, and a worker too. No harm could have come to you."

Now he intertwined his big clawlike fingers over one of his knees as though wanting to wring his hands. Even his hard wooden face twitched, and under the taut skin of his temple a blue vein pulsed.

"Please understand me, Mr. Szanto sir, I just couldn't stand it any more!"

Sergeant Szanto felt that something extraordinary must have befallen this man.

"Why did you divorce your wife?"

"I didn't divorce her, sir. It was she who left me."

"Why?"

He produced a dirty handkerchief out of his pocket, and pressed it to one of his inflamed eyelids.

"When this . . ."

Only his handkerchief wrote the unspoken words in the air. Again he looked toward the window; his black gaze in those crimson rings full of some strange fright. Long seconds later he said:

"Mr. Stalin, sir—excuse me, I mean Mr. Szanto, sir—you know, back in the communist school I was taught that the Idea came first, before everything—family, wife, life, death—what the Party said had to be done no matter what! I loved my wife dearly, but I had to choose between her and Party discipline."

"Was your wife anti-Communist?"

"Not at all, sir! She's still a loyal Communist."

"Then what was the trouble between you?"

Again he stared at the window, there was only silence for long seconds. With his big fingers he flicked the cigarette ashes from his knee, took a big breath and said:

"Mr. Szanto, sir, I won't beat around the bush any longer. I don't care. Go ahead and arrest me. I don't care any more what

369

happens to me. My life isn't worth a pin, anyhow. I'll tell you the truth, sir. During the past two years I was state's executioner in Hungary."

Sergeant Szanto could speak only moments later, and he hardly recognized his own voice:

"Did you hang Mihály Ursi too?"

"Yes, sir."

He glanced behind him to see if anyone was there, then leaned closer and said with a strange smile:

"Mr. Szanto, sir, I hanged Stalin too."

Sergeant Szanto closes his long letter with the following words:

I stared into his face, for by now I knew for sure I was wasting my time on a nut. "Have another cigarette, Mr. Kurdi, I'll be right back," I said to him.

I reported to my commanding officer, we telephoned for an ambulance and had him taken to a booby hatch.

After Ostie Dukay received this letter he took the next plane from New York to Vienna, and after his arrival he visited Josef Kurdi in the hospital. When he stepped into Joska's private room accompanied by a doctor, Kurdi was sitting on the edge of the bed, reading a little prayer book. He seemed much calmer than when Sergeant Szanto first interviewed him a few days before. Now, with every nerve tense he and the doctor watched Joska Kurdi's face and listened to his words to see if he was really insane, because it would decide whether or not Mihály Ursi was still alive somewhere. They began indirectly—speaking of the weather, asking him whether he was satisfied with the food, and whether he had any requests. Then Ostie said, just by the way:

"Tell me, Mr. Kurdi, what was your last official act?"

"The Ursi case, sir."

"You said that Stalin was the last . . . did the sergeant understand you correctly?"

"Stalin? Stalin is alive, sir. Nothing wrong with him. Did I say that? Maybe so. I was very much upset then, sir."

And he seemed on the verge of tears as he uttered these words. Reassuringly the doctor said to him:

"That is very understandable after all that happened. We aren't tiring you with our questions, are we?"

"No, not at all, sir. Go right ahead. By now nothing matters much any more."

He put aside the prayer book, but first with his hard thumbnail he made a cross at the word where he had stopped.

"I'd like more exact details about January 3," said Ostie.

In a calm voice Joska Kurdi began:

"Well . . . this one went off just like the others. It was Tuesday morning. They began at six. Only official persons were present. Maybe you know the courtyard of the Marko Utca prison? Above the narrow yard you can see only a piece of the sky as though through an air shaft. It was pretty dark, barely dawn. An ugly, sleety rain was falling and over the judge's head a clerk held an umbrella. The three condemned prisoners stood there before the table. In front was the Major . . . I mean Professor Ursi, beside him Kilinski, then Marja, the Czech woman. The judge had Marja stand back because the night before they had commuted her sentence to life imprisonment. I didn't look at them. I couldn't. I kept my eyes on the black umbrella which was rather torn; I watched as the sleety rain poured down through a half-span hole onto the neck of the judge while he was gabbling the long sentences."

Joska paused for a few seconds, looking at the floor with an expression on his face as if he would have seen on the floor the most important thing during the whole scene: the half-span hole in the umbrella. Then he continued, still calmly:

"First the warder brought me Kazi. I mean Kilinski. When the rope was around his neck—excuse me, I don't want to insult anybody, but the Americans do a very nasty job of it. All right, the rope of their noose is some ten feet long, and when the condemned man falls through the trap from a ten-foot height the weight of his own body jerks the knot under his left ear so violently that it breaks the neck, and the job is done. All right, but what if the knot wasn't put in the exact way under his ear?"

Every craftsman likes to go into the details of his art, but

371

by now Ostie Dukay and the doctor fidgeted listening to Joska Kurdi's expert critique.

"I read in the newspapers, sir," Joska went on, "that after the Nürnberg trial poor Rittep—Rippentrob was hanging for twenty-seven minutes on the rope—still alive! Imagine that! We Hungarians do it in a more humanitarian way. I have two assistants, and when the condemned man steps onto the trap, they put a noose around his legs; at the same second I place the upper noose around his neck; then they pull on the rope of the leg-noose as hard as they can; this stretches the spine so taut that when I take the head between my palms, a slight, quick twist is enough, and the neck is broken. There is no risk, no pain in our job. And another thing, sir! I always have a large, white kerchief ready in my pocket, and I immediately cover their faces. They did not do it in Nürnberg. I have seen photos of the uncovered blue and distorted faces. Excuse me, sir, but my American colleagues did not do a proper job. And when . . ."

"Did Kilinski say anything?" the doctor interrupted nervously.

"Yes. Before the rope was around his neck, he shouted something."

"What did he shout?"

"He shouted in his mother tongue. I don't know either Polish or Serbian. Later the interpreters said that he shouted: 'Long live free Poland.' These idea-criminals always shout such things."

"What did Mihály Ursi shout?"

Joska Kurdi slowly shook his head, and, almost inaudibly, said:

"He didn't shout anything."

"Didn't he say anything when he recognized you?"

"He didn't recognize me, sir. Thank God, he didn't recognize me."

"How could that be? You were good friends."

"It wasn't only because the morning was gloomy, and rain was falling, but at such times, sir, they don't see any more. I know from experience, sir—they don't see what's around them, you can tell by their eyes. He didn't recognize me, thank God he didn't recognize me. Because I was afraid, so afraid that he would look into my face and recognize me, I even pulled my hat down over my eyes, and while they read the sentence I stood so the gallows would hide me."

All at once his tears began to flow.

"He didn't recognize me . . . God be thanked . . . God Almighty be thanked, he didn't recognize me. He saved my life once, when we were children, when I was fighting with the Crows and the Turkeys captured me, and wanted to execute me, he was the Major of the Turkeys, and had mercy on me."

And Joska Kurdi cried aloud.

The doctor stroked Kurdi's head, and Ostie Dukay also tried to comfort him, but his voice shook: "Come, come, Mr. Kurdi . . . take hold of yourself."

He quieted down. A little while later he raised his head and looked around as if he didn't know where he was. Then he sat up, looking wearily into space with his chronically inflamed eyelids. Ostie Dukay and the doctor did not ask any more questions, but then Kurdi continued by himself:

"The Major spoke some foreign words at the end—but not to me. Just quietly and only into the air. He even smiled a little."

"Do you remember the words?"

"I told you, sir, he spoke some foreign words."

"Maybe the names of his wife and daughter. Zia, Zizi . . ."

"No, not those! There weren't that many Z's!"

"Don't you remember the sound of the words? Try to think."

"He said only a couple of words, maybe three. It sounded something like . . . *ebru* . . . *ebur* . . ."

"*Eppur si muove?*"

"Would you please say that again."

"*Ep-pur si mu ove!*"

"That's it! That's how it sounded, sir."

Ostie did not ask Joska Kurdi any more questions; he signaled to the doctor, and they took leave of him. When he was alone with the doctor, he said:

"Doctor, I'm afraid this man isn't crazy. He's telling the truth."

The doctor shrugged his shoulders.

"I still don't know. Probably he saw such an execution, perhaps more than one. Very frequently an egocentric imagines him-

373

self in a role which he only witnessed or read about. One of our patients says he's Faust. In my ward we have two Mussolinis, three Hitlers, two Stalins and one Toscanini."

"But doctor, this Kurdi is an ignorant, uneducated man. How could he have known Galileo's words, even the sound of them?"

The doctor smiled:

"Dr. Ursi was an astronomer. Can't you imagine that this 'Eppur si muove' was an habitual phrase of his? And that this man's ear had sometime during his long friendship with Ursi caught the words, if only their sound?"

The doctor's words, scientifically objective, and spoken not to reassure Ostie, made him hope again.

While Ostie was still in Vienna he was informed that the official Budapest press hadn't written a word about the executions and that the Hungarian government a few days before had abolished the death penalty. When other newly arrived refugees told him that the condemned men most probably were secretly transported to Russia, Ostie flew back to America.

Chapter 25

Six months have passed since Sergeant Szanto's letter. No news has come from Hungary.

But yesterday we received a letter from Salzburg, informing us that another important witness in this case had succeeded in fleeing from Budapest. He was a court clerk who witnessed the executions. We no longer have any doubts concerning the fate of Mihály Ursi. This newly escaped man described the scene that ugly, rainy January dawn exactly as Joska Kurdi did.

It was he who held the umbrella above the head of the judge who gabbled the death sentences—it was a strange, strange dawn —the dense drops of the heavy, sleety rain drummed, drummed, and drummed mysteriously like a black angel on the torn umbrella with its half-span hole.